MARRIED TO A STRANGER

An unputdownable psychological thriller
with a breathtaking twist

PATRICIA MACDONALD

Revised edition 2022
Joffe Books, London
www.joffebooks.com

First published in Great Britain and the USA in 2006
by Atria Books

This paperback edition was first published
in Great Britain in 2022

Cover art by Nick Castle

ISBN: 978-1-80405-664-6

To my friend Mary Jane Salk, who is glamorous and witty, wise and good

CHAPTER 1

The wizened girl turned her head and stared at Emma Hollis with large, blank eyes. "Leave me alone. I'm too tired to talk anymore."

Emma gazed worriedly at the frail teenager sitting opposite her. Tasha Clayman had been admitted to the Wrightsman Youth Crisis Center the day before. Emma could see every one of the sixteen-year-old's bony ribs beneath her thin sweater. Her cheeks were hollow, her blond pony-tail dry and lank. An image of Ivy Devlin rose into Emma's thoughts, and Emma had to force down a feeling of panic. You did everything you could for Ivy, she reminded herself. It was too late for her. It wasn't your fault. But it was hard to convince herself. Nightmares about Ivy, her large, sunken eyes full of rueful accusation, still woke Emma in the middle of the night.

"Tasha?" Emma asked gently. "Let me ask you this. Can you tell me what would it take to make you want to live?"

"I didn't say I didn't want to live," the girl protested in a monotone voice so weak it was hard to hear. "I just have to watch my food intake because I'm too fat."

Emma hesitated, choosing her response carefully. At twenty-six she had a Ph.D. in psychology, but this position at the crisis center was her first full-time job as a clinical psychologist. Working with patients was much more daunting than doing research in the university library and treating clients under the constant supervision of an experienced professional. Sometimes she felt as if she hadn't recovered her equilibrium after Ivy succumbed to her anorexia six months ago. Burke Heisler, the psychiatrist who ran the center, had supported the decisions she'd made about Ivy's treatment. Even after Ivy Devlin's death, he had refused to allow Emma to second-guess herself. You are not to blame, he had assured her. You did all you could to help her.

He's right, she thought. This girl needs you, and you are capable of helping her.

"Tasha, we both know that starvation can lead to death. And death is a way to escape from whatever it is that's hurting you. Something is hurting you, putting you in so much pain."

A tear rolled down the girl's sunken cheek. She did not bother to wipe it away.

"Talking about it is a way of escaping too," Emma persisted. "A better way. Once you can say it out loud, we can look for solutions."

The girl looked at Emma with haunted eyes. "I hate myself. How do I escape from myself?" she asked. "I'm fat. I'm a failure. I have no boyfriend because no one can ever love me. My grades aren't good enough. I'm not pretty. I'm a complete disappointment to my parents . . ."

Emma thought about Tasha's parents. They were educated, attractive, and well-to-do. And Tasha was their only child. In her brief conversation with them yesterday, Wade Clayman had told her that he and his wife were people with means, who had given their daughter everything. They did not see themselves as part of Tasha's problem.

Their opinion was simply that, Emma reminded herself. Your job is to save this girl's life. "Okay," said Emma, taking a deep breath, "tell me about your parents."

* * *

After the session, Emma headed down the cheerfully painted hallway leading to the office of Dr. Heisler. She had a few minutes before she had to see her next client. Emma entered the open door to the director's reception area. His secretary, Geraldine Clemens, looked up at her over her half-glasses.

"Is he in? Can I see him for a minute?" Emma asked.

"I'll check," she said. Geraldine picked up the phone and buzzed her boss.

"Hello, Dr. Hollis," said a voice behind her.

Emma turned and saw Kieran Foster, one of the members of her Thursday morning therapy group for drug abusers. She had started the group almost a year ago, shortly after she'd arrived at the Wrightsman Youth Center. There had been three teens in the group when she began, but now there were usually eight, sometimes more, which she counted as a success. Kieran was sitting in the reception area. It was nearly impossible to look at Kieran without flinching. The troubled seventeen-year-old, dressed all in black, had a tuft of magenta hair at the top of his head, and a tattoo of an eye in the middle of his forehead. Emma thought that the tattoo artist responsible for that atrocity ought to be arrested.

"Kieran," she said. "Hi. We missed you at group yesterday."

"I was busy," Kieran muttered. Abandoned by his alcoholic mother, Kieran was an outpatient who lived with a half sister and her extremely wealthy husband. His guardians provided him with all the cars, electronics, and spending money he could ever want, and then went about their lives as if he weren't there. Kieran had a long history of drug abuse and had dropped out of high school. His only real interest was in playing his electric guitar and writing atonal songs with lyrics focused on death and decay. He had been a member of Emma's group for about nine months, although he rarely contributed to the discussion.

"Is something wrong?" Emma asked.

"No," he said, looking down at the floor. He rarely made eye contact with her or with anyone else. "Dr. Heisler asked my sister to come in."

3

Uh-oh, Emma thought. What now? She knew that Burke must have had to threaten the woman to get her in here to talk about Kieran. She showed absolutely no interest in her troubled, younger brother. "Well, I hope you'll join us next Thursday," said Emma, smiling at him. "I always like to see you there."

"Dr. Heisler says he'll squeeze you in," said Geraldine, setting down the receiver and looking up at Emma. "Go on in."

Emma opened the door and looked in. "Hey," she said.

Burke Heisler looked up at her and smiled. He was young to hold such a responsible position—only in his mid-thirties. His blond hair was cut short and combed back, and he had a broad, rugged-looking face that would have looked more appropriate on a boxer. His gray-eyed gaze was keen. Emma had first met Burke Heisler when she was a college freshman and he was a graduate teaching assistant who taught her freshman psych course.

She had had a mad crush on him at the time, although he never paid her any more attention than he did the other hundred students in the class. She told herself it was because he wanted to avoid any teacher-student impropriety, but then he ended up courting, and ultimately marrying, Emma's beautiful roommate, Natalie White. A year ago, when Natalie invited Emma to visit them at their home in Clarenceville, New Jersey, Burke seemed pleased to learn that she had pursued her doctorate in psychology and that they shared the same specialty. Before the weekend was over, he had offered Emma a job at the Wrightsman Youth Center, part of the huge complex that was Lambert University.

Burke gestured for her to come in and sit down. "Finding it a little hard to concentrate today?" he asked.

Emma blushed, wondering if it showed on her face. She was trying to remain as professional as possible, but it was difficult. Tomorrow was her wedding day. "That's an understatement," she admitted.

"Well, it's only natural. Hey, now that you're here, what do you want for a wedding gift? I was thinking of something practical, like a food processor."

"If you'll come over and show me how to use it," Emma said with a smile. Burke was known for his culinary skills. His wealthy father had owned a casino in Atlantic City, and Burke had spent several summers working in the kitchens.

"Done," he said, pretending to make a note. "Buy Cuisinart and demonstrate." He set down his pen and gazed at her. "So, what's up?"

"Well, I'm a little worried," said Emma, "about being away all weekend."

Heisler frowned. "Why?"

"There's a new patient . . . Tasha Clayman."

"The anorectic," he said.

"I can't help it . . . after what happened," she said.

Burke nodded. "I understand. Ivy Devlin. Look, I don't want you to worry about this. I'll have Sarita keep close tabs on Tasha." Sarita Ruiz was a youth counselor who tended to her teenaged charges with skill and kindness. "If Tasha shows any signs of dehydration or kidney failure, Sarita will recognize it, and we'll get her into the hospital right away. You just enjoy your big day, you hear me?" he said, smiling. "Although I don't understand why you two are only taking a weekend for the honeymoon. You could have had the week off if you wanted it."

"This is fine for right now," Emma said. "My mother is giving us a trip to Europe as a wedding present, but that will take time to plan. And this has all . . . come together rather quickly, so right now we can only spare a weekend. Besides, David has an important interview in New York next week with some big-shot producer who is coming in from L.A. So we're just going down to the Pine Barrens for a couple of days." Emma was referring to the million-plus acres of sandy, boggy, pine-covered wilderness called the Pineland National Reserve, which was located right in the center of New Jersey. It was a nature lover's paradise, crisscrossed by rivers and sparsely populated by a reclusive, xenophobic group of people widely known as Pineys, ever since the publication of John McPhee's 1968 book *The Pine Barrens*. "We're going

5

canoeing and hiking—David and I both love that sort of thing."

"You staying in that fishing cabin his aunt and uncle own?"

"That's the place," she said.

"His uncle used to take us there when we were boys," said Burke. Burke and Emma's husband-to-be, David Webster, had been best friends since boyhood. "We were always afraid the Jersey Devil would get us," Burke remembered, referring to the reputedly immortal demon-child said to have been born to a colonial housewife named Leeds, who, many claimed, still haunted the Pinelands.

"I'm not into folklore and monsters," said Emma. "As far as I can tell, most monsters are human."

"I couldn't agree more," said Burke. "I've put away those childish things myself, except on dark and stormy nights, of course."

"Anyway, it'll be great just to get away together."

"Those days when you're first married, it hardly matters where you are," said Burke with a sigh. "Being together is all that counts." For a moment, his gaze fell on the framed photo of a beautiful, pale-skinned woman with silky red hair, looking pensively out over a Venetian canal. Three months ago, Burke came home from a business trip to find Natalie missing. The police found her car parked on a bridge over the Smoking River, her purse and keys still on the front seat. Her body did not surface for a month, but the note she'd left behind had clearly stated her intentions.

Emma's brilliant, accomplished former roommate, a published poet, had been bipolar and often had refused to take her medication, claiming that it dulled her perceptions and her ability to write. Emma remembered many bouts of Natalie's manic highs and depressive lows from when they were college roommates. When Emma arrived in Clarenceville, Natalie had been exuberant. She had just published her latest book of poems to great critical acclaim. Six months later the book won the prestigious Solomon Medal, which seemed to increase both her joy and her renown. She was interviewed for local and national publications, and because she was both articulate and beautiful, she became a popular TV guest on public television and book-oriented talk shows. Inexplicably, despite her success, Natalie's spirits began to plummet. She grew disconsolate but refused to take her medication. Emma feared that Natalie was tumbling into a severe, depressive cycle. But when Emma tried to talk to her about it, and urged her to seek counseling, Natalie reacted angrily, insisting she was fine. Emma knew better. Still, despite the warning signs, Natalie's suicide came as a terrible shock to her husband and to Emma as well.

"I hope being in this wedding won't be too painful for you," said Emma. "I know you're still recovering."

Burke sighed. "She's going to be very much on my mind tomorrow."

"Mine too," said Emma.

Burke shook his head, but there was pain in his eyes. "But I'll be proud to stand up for David. I'm happy for you. For both of you. I feel like Natalie and I were the matchmakers for you two."

"You were," she said. "You introduced us." Burke had invited Emma to a dinner party at their house to celebrate Natalie's receipt of the Solomon Medal. Burke's friend, David Webster, a freelance writer from New York City, was invited also. The gathering was festive, and Natalie was witty and luminous. Emma would always remember that night because it was the last happy evening Emma could remember spending with her old friend. But Emma would never forget that evening for other reasons also. The sparks between her and David flew instantaneously.

Emma's memory of that fateful night was interrupted by the sound of her pager beeping. She checked it. "Speak of the devil," she said.

"The groom?" Burke asked.

Emma nodded and glanced at her watch. She only had a few minutes till her group was due to start. But the thought of seeing David Webster, waiting for her in the lobby, filled her with the same giddy excitement that she'd felt the first time she'd set eyes on him six months ago. "Thanks, Burke," she said, standing up.

"Don't worry about a thing," he said. "See you tomorrow."

As she passed through the reception area, Emma heard Geraldine saying to Kieran, "That was your sister. She has to cancel. I'm sorry, Kieran."

Emma sighed and shook her head. Sometimes it seemed hopeless to try to help kids like Kieran, when they faced such massive indifference at home. But sometimes, in spite of the odds, she actually could help, and that made her job feel very worthwhile. Emma pushed the doors open and scanned the lobby. David was leaning against the front desk, making conversation with the new receptionist. Emma drew in a breath at the sight of him, as she often did. He was, to her eyes, the most attractive man she had ever known. One of the handsomest she had ever seen, in fact.

"David," she said.

When he heard her voice, he turned to look at her, his eyes widening. "Hey, baby." He was Burke's age, thirty-three, but despite the gray that flecked his long, dark brown hair and the lines around his fine, hazel eyes, he looked much younger than his old friend. He had a strong jaw and perfect, white teeth, which he flashed in a dimpled, boyish smile that made Emma's heart turn over. Today he was dressed, as usual, in jeans and a leather jacket—an urban cowboy style that suited his maverick image. He admitted to having a stubborn resistance to all authority and told her that he had become a freelance writer because he could never stand the constraints of a regular job with a boss.

Before they'd met, David had lived abroad and traveled far and wide doing articles for a variety of magazines. His steadiest source of assignments was *Slicker*, a glossy men's magazine in the *Esquire* mold, but with a younger slant. When he'd attended the fateful dinner party at Burke and Natalie's, David had been living alone, subletting a New

York City rent-controlled apartment. He never talked about old girlfriends, but Emma knew that he was just being chivalrous. Women always looked twice at him. Right at this very moment, the new receptionist was devouring him with her eyes. Even other men seemed to light up in his presence.

Emma ran to him, hugged him, and kissed his soft, insistent lips. She felt the flush that raced through her whenever they touched. We're getting married tomorrow, she thought, and marveled anew at her luck and her happiness. "Hey," she whispered. "What brings you here?"

"I'm here to make you change your mind," he said.

"About what?" she asked, drawing back from him.

"About staying at Stephanie's tonight. This is corny. It's old-fashioned."

Stephanie Piper, a middle school teacher who had been Emma's roommate in Clarenceville since she'd first moved here, was going to be her maid of honor at the wedding tomorrow. Only a month ago, Emma and David had faced up to the practicalities of their impending marriage, and in deference to Emma's job, they had rented a house here in Clarenceville and moved in together. Luckily, despite the stresses of adjustments and wedding plans, their new home had proved to be almost as delicious a hideaway as his bachelor apartment. But tonight, Emma was returning to her old digs for one last "girls' night" before the wedding. "I don't care," Emma said. "I am old-fashioned. I don't want to see you until I'm walking down the aisle. Go have a bachelor party or something."

"With who?" he said. "I don't know anyone here anymore." She knew it was true. He hadn't lived in Clarenceville since high school. When she and David met at Burke and Natalie Heisler's house, he was in town from New York City to visit his mother, Helen, who had advanced heart disease. As Emma had left the dinner party that night, she'd thought she might never see the mysterious writer again, but as soon as she got home, her phone was ringing. David was calling from the Clarenceville train station asking her to come back to New York with him that very night. After a moment's hesitation, she had thrown caution to the wind and met him on the platform.

The rest was a whirlwind romance. Their six-month courtship had been confined to weekends and carried out at a distance. Because Emma shared her apartment in Clarenceville with Stephanie, they'd spent much of their time together in David's place in New York. In fact, much of that time had been spent in the sparsely furnished bedroom of that apartment, ignoring the outside world altogether. They would take an occasional walk in Central Park or attend a movie or a play. But once they returned to David's apartment, they would repair immediately to the bedroom, their lovemaking an insatiable addiction interrupted by late-night dinners of Chinese food eaten out of cartons, long conversations and helpless laughter, and games of nude Scrabble in bed, that generally ended with the board shoved aside, tiles scattered across the bed, and wooden letter holders clattering to the bedroom floor as they were distracted once again by desire. Through their entire courtship, she'd felt as if love made the rules. But tonight was different. This night was about traditions and transitions.

"So go out with Burke," Emma suggested.

David grimaced. "I'm not sure he's in the mood for a bachelors' night. I mean, it's asking a lot of him just to be in the wedding."

Emma sighed, knowing he was referring to Natalie's death. "I know. You're right. Well, maybe you could run up to the City. I'll bet you could enjoy yourself at the Short Stop." The Short Stop was David's neighborhood bar, where he had taken her a few times to have a drink and shoot the breeze with other writers and artistic types. "Just make sure you're back here by ten tomorrow, mister."

He grinned at her. "Nothing could keep me away," he said.

"Dr. Hollis," said the receptionist.

Emma tore herself away from his gaze and tried to look businesslike. "Yes?"

"This came for you." She held out a plain, white envelope with EMMA HOLLIS printed on it in large letters.

"You're busy. I'll let you go," David said.

"No, wait," Emma said, clutching his arm.

David suddenly looked wary. "Is that one of those letters?"

Emma reached for the envelope as if it were volatile and tore it open with a slight tremble in her fingers. "I don't know. It looks like the others." She pulled out a sheet of paper. Her pulse was racing. "YOU COULD NOT UNDERSTAND THE DEPTH OF MY LOVE OR YOU WOULD NOT BE MAKING PLANS TO HURT AND SHAME ME."

Emma nodded and tried to make her voice light. "I'm afraid so."

"Let me see that," said David, snatching the letter from her fingers.

Emma turned to the receptionist. Her heart was pounding, but she kept her voice calm. "Where did this come from?" she asked.

"I found it on the desk when I started my shift," the receptionist said. "Is something wrong?"

"Goddammit," said David, through gritted teeth.

"No. No. It's all right," said Emma to the receptionist.

David looked at her gravely. "This is not all right, Emma."

"I know," said Emma. First there had been a rose, left under the windshield wiper of her car. She remembered feeling . . . surprised and slightly flattered at the time. She assumed at first that it was from David, until she asked him about it. And then the notes began to arrive. "This is the fourth one."

"Baby, we need to call the cops," he said.

All the notes were on the same plain paper, printed on a computer. Whenever one of them arrived, Emma's heart sank, and she spent the next few days reading hidden meanings into ordinary conversations, trying to imagine, as she talked to people she saw every day, if any of them were the ones studying her, dreaming of her. After a while, she would relax and begin to think that it was over, that the writer had found someone else to focus on. And then the next one came. Emma retrieved the latest letter from David, folded it, and stuffed it into her pocket. "The police can't do anything about them. They aren't threats."

"What do we do? Wait until this guy does something crazy?" David said angrily.

"It probably is one of my patients. They get these crushes that spin out of control. Believe me, it creeps me out too. I feel like he's watching me, whoever he is."

"We can't just let it go and do nothing," David insisted.

"Most of the time, these . . . crushes don't amount to anything," she said.

"And other times . . ."

"And other times you get John Hinckley," Emma admitted. "I know, David. But I'm trying to keep a cool head about it, because the police are not going to do anything about it. Ask Burke if you don't believe me. He has experience with this stuff. Sending a love note is not a crime. Even if the writer is obsessed."

"He's hounding you . . ." David said, clenching his fist.

"I know," she said. "I know. Believe me, I am hoping this will wind down on its own. I hate it too, but I'm afraid it comes with the territory." She ran her hand down the side of his clenched jaw. "Don't let this ruin things. Please, David. I know it makes you angry. You have to take it with a grain of salt. I won't deny that it makes me . . . uncomfortable. Because it does. But it's par for the course in a place like this. We've got a lot of troubled kids here with a boatload of problems. Whoever this kid is, he's probably young and lonely, and not able to communicate."

"I'm not sure it is one of these kids. What if it's some . . . lunatic?"

"Lunatics tend to be a little bit . . . showier," said Emma wryly. "He probably would be strapping himself naked to the hood of my car."

"Do you really believe that? Professionally speaking, I mean."

"Yes, definitely," she said. "So, come on. Try and forget about this for now."

He took a deep breath. "Some pencil-necked geek probably has his closet walls plastered with your pictures," David fumed. "Every time I think about that . . ."

"Jealous?" she said, squeezing his hand, trying to lighten the mood.

He sighed, and one corner of his mouth turned up. "I'm the only pencil-necked geek who's allowed to do that."

"You aren't pencil-necked," she said.

He made a growling sound and pulled her to him, squeezing her. She began to laugh. "Look, I really do need to get back to work," she said.

"You won't change your mind about tonight?" he said in a husky voice into her ear. "You're going to leave me all alone in that big bed of ours?"

"Well, you better be all alone," she teased. When Burke had first introduced them, he'd described David as his "playboy" best friend. And when she first got involved with David, Emma had truly expected it to be no more than an exciting fling. Now things had changed, and she hated thinking about his playboy past. But she wasn't really worried. Their love went way beyond sexual attraction, even though their sexual chemistry was something rare and wonderful. She knew that irresistible attraction would eventually fade, as their lives went on together. Everyone told her so. But right now, it was impossible to imagine that she could ever see that smile, those eyes, and not feel stirred by desire. She gave him one more lingering kiss and pulled away from him.

"Tomorrow, babe," he said. "You and me."

"I know," she said, beaming.

"My wife."

Emma's heart swelled at the sound of the words. "My husband," she whispered.

CHAPTER 2

The General Crossen Inn was a colonial-era building with a mustard-colored clapboard facade, crisp white trim, and brick chimneys at either end. It was located at the end of a quiet street with houses hidden from the road and was surrounded by acres of gardens and trees on three sides. Emma's mother, who lived in Chicago, had rented the whole eight-bedroom inn for the night, even though Emma had told her repeatedly that the hastily arranged wedding was going to be tiny.

As she pulled up in front of the inn, Emma saw that Stephanie's car was already parked there, as well as the florist's van and the caterer's truck. Last night she and Stephanie had had a great "girls' night" together, eating junk food, giving each other pedicures, and dancing to their favorite tunes. They had parted this morning when Stephanie had insisted on going to the hairdresser, in honor of her role as Emma's attendant in the ceremony. Emma had decided to stick with the natural look.

Emma parked beside Stephanie's car and carefully removed the fat garment bag that she had hung from a hook in the backseat. The obscenely expensive wedding dress, which her mother had insisted on buying for her, was inside the bag, swaddled in tissue. Emma would have been content with a dress off the rack from Bloomingdale's, but Kay had pleaded with her to let her fly into New York and take her to designer showrooms, and Emma had reluctantly agreed. Her last-minute wedding was not what Kay had always pictured for her only child. Emma thought that at least she could give in on the dress. Now, to be honest with herself, she was glad she had. She could hardly wait to put the dress on and see how she looked. Emma crossed the porch and opened the door to the inn. At the far end of the room, a young guy with glasses and a crew cut was setting up the chairs and music stands for the jazz trio that was going to play. Stephanie, dressed in jeans, her blond hair coiffed in an upswept, ringleted style, was studying the placement of the floral arrangements in the timber-beamed room where the ceremony would be held.

Stephanie turned around at the sound of the door opening and exhaled in relief.

"There you are. It's about time. You'd think it was my wedding. The caterer is asking for instructions. I'm dealing with the florist. I thought these people knew what to do. Isn't that why you hire them?"

"Don't worry. My mom will be here any minute to whip everything into shape. I spoke to her on her cell phone a few minutes ago. She doesn't want to miss a moment of this. Hey, I like your hair."

"Oh please. I look like something out of *Gidget Goes to the Prom*."

"It's very elegant," said Emma loyally.

"And yours makes you look like a sex goddess."

Emma glanced at her hair in the mirror above the flower-bedecked mantel. It fell below her shoulders, honey colored and wavy. "David likes it loose. What do you think?"

"You look gorgeous. You're glowing. But then . . ."

"Pregnant women do," said Emma wryly.

Stephanie nodded and looked down at Emma's waist. "I hope that wedding dress has some wiggle room."

"Come on," Emma protested. "I'm only two months along."

"Good thing you didn't plan the wedding for Valentine's Day," said Stephanie.

"I'm working as fast as I can," said Emma.

The truth was that when, four months into their commuter romance, Emma found herself unexpectedly pregnant she secretly, sadly, expected it to be the end of her relationship with David. He had lived out of duffel bags in temporary quarters all of his adult life. Part of her was certain that, despite the intensity of their romance, it was just another fling for him, and that this news would send him fleeing. To her shock, he'd responded with an abrupt proposal of marriage. He wanted her and he wanted their baby. He could not be dissuaded. When she pressed him, asking him if he was sure this was what he wanted, he told her that she was his miracle.

"How can you be so calm?" said Stephanie. "Don't you have jitters? All brides have jitters."

"Well, I did throw up this morning after you left, but these days I often start the day that way. Morning sickness. Not jitters. What can I say? He's the one. You know?"

"How would I know?" Stephanie said ruefully. When Emma first came to town and moved into the apartment, Stephanie had just kicked out Ken Treeman, the aptly named landscaper she had hoped to marry, until she found out he'd been cheating on her.

Emma was trying to think of an encouraging reply when she heard a familiar voice behind her. "Didn't you two leave anything for me to do?"

Emma turned to see a fit-looking, platinum-haired woman in a turquoise bouclé suit standing in the doorway, beaming at her.

"Mom," Emma cried, rushing to embrace her mother. "You look great."

"Well, thank you. I was afraid I'd get all rumpled on the trip." Emma's mother and stepfather had flown in from Chicago and driven down from the Philadelphia airport this morning. Tonight, Kay and Rory were spending the night at the inn. Emma had wanted them to come the night before, but there had been no rehearsal dinner planned, and Rory insisted he had to attend a meeting with the family attorney in Chicago that absolutely could not be postponed. Emma did not believe him. She believed that Rory was avoiding her, with good reason.

"Rory bringing the bags in?"

"No . . ." said Kay. "He dropped me off. He said he had to make one more brief stop. Something about business. I don't know. He was very mysterious about it."

Emma tried to keep her face expressionless. All her life Emma had adored her father and idealized her parents' marriage. In her eyes Mitch and Kay Hollis had the kind of love that people wrote songs about, and Emma's childhood in their rambling mansion on the shore of Lake Michigan had been blissfully happy as a result. When her father died during Emma's first year of graduate school, she was devastated for herself but even more for her mother. She couldn't imagine how her mother would be able to survive without Mitch Hollis. Ten months later, at her health club, Kay met Rory, a divorced investment banker. Before Emma knew it, her mother was remarried.

Kay and Rory sold the suburban mansion and moved to a fabulous penthouse on the Chicago Loop. Emma had rushed out to Chicago to rescue a trailerful of mismatched bric-a-brac and mementoes from her childhood home that her mother planned to jettison during the move. At the moment, Emma's trove of white elephant objects resided in a storage unit by the Smoking River in Clarenceville. One of these days, when she got organized, Emma planned to empty that storage unit and distribute her mementoes around her and David's new house, which had room to hold them.

As for Kay, she seemed to slide seamlessly into her new city lifestyle and gratefully handed over the family's financial reins to Rory, who now managed Emma's trust fund as well as the fortune from her grandfather's shipping business, which Kay had inherited. Rory McLean was fifteen years younger than Emma's mother, and Kay was thrilled to have a second chance at happiness. Though Emma did not understand how her mother could marry again so quickly, Emma had tried her best to be happy for her mother's sake until one evening, two months ago, when she was out for dinner with David and saw her stepfather seated at a cozy table in a New York Italian restaurant called Chiara's with his arm around another woman, laughing and whispering in her ear.

Emma froze in horror at the sight. By the time she'd decided to get up and confront him, Rory and his date had exited the restaurant. Emma was furious and wounded for her mother's sake. Torn about what to do, she and David discussed it. David warned her against breaking her mother's heart until she knew the whole story. Emma called her mother anyway, and Kay had cheerfully recounted that Rory was in New York on a business trip. Emma hesitated and then told her mother that she had seen Rory in Chiara's, but that he'd left before she'd had a chance to talk to him.

"Wait until I tell him," Kay had bubbled. "He'll be so sorry he missed you."

Sorry indeed, Emma thought. Once Rory heard that she had seen him in Chiara's, he would be squirming and would certainly realize that he'd better explain himself. Emma was anticipating the moment with grim satisfaction.

"This inn is a lovely spot for a wedding," said Kay, looking around the room.

"It's not anything too fancy, but it's such a small wedding," said Emma.

"Well, they seem to have things well in hand. I suppose that table back there is for the gifts people will be bringing," Kay said, pointing to a table that already had several white and silver wrapped boxes on it. "Honestly, what ever happened to the custom of sending them to the house?"

"Oh, Mom, don't get all Emily Post about this. It's fine."

"I know, I know," said Kay. "Don't mind me. Everything will be perfect. It's going to be a beautiful wedding. Now let's get you dressed."

"Your mother's right," said Stephanie. "Don't you know that the most important thing about a wedding is how the bride looks?"

Emma beamed. "Of course."

"You two run up there and get started," said Kay. "I want to talk to the caterer for one minute and then I'll be right up to join you."

"Thanks, Mom," said Emma, hugging her again.

"Let's go, bride," said Stephanie. "We have to see if we can still squeeze you into that gown."

* * *

Emma studied herself in the full-length mirror. "Well, what do you think?"

"Wow," said Stephanie wistfully, gazing into the mirror. "That dress is fantastic."

Gazing at the formfitting, strapless Duchesse satin gown, Emily had to admit that it was spectacular. The color of the fabric was the shade of Devonshire cream. The dress clung to her in a perfect line, and there was no telltale tightness around the middle. Her cleavage was slightly more pronounced than usual, but that was attractive. "It is pretty," she said.

She turned and looked at Stephanie, who had come with her to help her pick a wedding dress, and then had chosen her own lovely, olive green gown the same day. "So's yours."

Stephanie stood up and twirled around. "I know. I love it. I'm glad your mother took charge of this dress business."

There was a tap at the door, and Kay stuck her head in. "Can I come in?"

"Of course," said Emma.

"Oh sweetie," Kay breathed. "You are magnificent."

"Thanks, Mom. The dress is gorgeous. How's everything going downstairs?"

"Everything's perfect. The flowers are beautiful and the fire is going in the fireplace. That little jazz group is setting up. The waiters are assembled. There are buckets of Veuve

Clicquot, and there is a divine scent wafting in from the kitchen."

Emma smiled. "Great."

"And you look incredibly beautiful. There's just one more thing. Close your eyes."

"What?"

"Just close them. And lift your hair."

Emma did as she was told. She felt her mother fastening something around her neck. "Wow!" she heard Stephanie exclaim.

Emma opened her eyes. A diamond choker blazed against the warm tones of her skin. "Oh, Mom."

"It was your grandmother's," said Kay. "It looks perfect on you."

Emma smiled at her reflection in the mirror and took a deep breath of satisfaction.

"There are earrings to match," said Kay. "Here. And Stephanie, you look lovely too. You two really do look like you could be sisters."

"I feel like her sister today," said Stephanie.

Even as Emma looked tenderly at Stephanie, she could not help thinking about her dear friends who would not be here today. Foremost on her mind was Natalie, whose absence, of course, was tragic. Natalie had been erratic and often difficult in the months preceding her suicide, but Emma would always remember her the way she was when she first knew her. A scholarship student with a brilliant mind, she was a mimic and a daredevil whose antics made life thrilling and funny. Once, when Natalie had not studied for an exam, she stole into the classroom early and wrote "Professor Smith has postponed today's test" on the blackboard. All the arriving students read the notice and left. In those early years, Emma hadn't realized that Natalie's reckless charm was a harbinger of mental illness.

Emma's thoughts turned from her dear, lost Natalie to her childhood friend Jessica, who lived in New York. Jessie's and Emma's mothers had been friends from girlhood, and they had been thrilled that their daughters had forged an equally strong friendship. Emma had always assumed that Jessie would be her maid of honor on her wedding day, but it turned out that Jessie, and her husband, Chris, would not be attending the wedding at all. Jessie was six months into a very difficult pregnancy, and the doctor had put her on bed rest.

The impromptu nature of this wedding had made it impossible for a number of people close to Emma's heart to attend. But Emma thought that she had always been lucky in her friendships, and even though Stephanie was a recent friend, they were already as close as if they had known each other for years. "Thanks for being here for me, Steph," she said.

"Don't cry. You'll wreck your makeup," said Stephanie.

There was a knock on the open door. Rory, wearing an expensive suit and tortoiseshell schoolboy glasses, his graying auburn hair slicked back off his freckled forehead, asked, "Is this ladies only, or can I come in for a minute?"

Emma turned back to the mirror and began to put on her earrings.

"Done with your business?" said Kay, walking over to her husband and kissing him on the cheek. "Oh, you're perspiring, honey."

"I've been rushing. Emma, you are a vision," said Rory.

"Thank you," said Emma.

"Where were you, anyway? What business could possibly be so important?" Kay asked.

"Well, that's what I came up to talk to our girl about." Rory looked at Stephanie. "Young lady, would you excuse us for a minute?"

Stephanie stood up awkwardly. "Me. Sure. I'll just . . ." She lifted the hem of her olive green gown off the carpet and edged toward the open door.

Emma felt alarmed. Surely Rory couldn't be choosing to explain his secret tryst right now, just minutes before her wedding. She watched as Stephanie swept out the door into the hallway beyond. "What's this all about?" Emma asked indignantly.

Rory cleared his throat and reached into the inside pocket of his jacket. "This wedding has come about so suddenly that we haven't really had a chance to discuss this. I was just over at your new home, talking to your husband-to-be."

Emma stared at him. "Talking to David?" She had an unpleasant image of Rory trying to give David fatherly advice about their wedding night. "What did you have to talk to David about?"

"Well, this is why we couldn't come down last night. I was meeting with our attorney to hammer out the last details." He reached into the inner pocket of his jacket and pulled out an envelope. From this he extracted a few folded sheets of paper that were stapled together. "This document is a prenuptial agreement, and I strongly advise you, as I advised him, to sign it before the wedding goes forward."

Emma stared at him. It was so far from the excuses and apologies she had expected from Rory that she was momentarily stunned into silence.

"I must say that your husband-to-be was very polite. He said that if it was what you wanted . . ."

"You can't be serious!" Emma cried.

"Completely serious," Rory assured her. "There's nothing more serious than large sums of money."

"How dare you?" Emma demanded. "I can't believe you did this. Mother, did you know he was doing this?"

Kay McLean looked flustered. "Rory, honestly."

"Now, Kay, there's a lot of money involved here. As the manager of your trust fund, it is my duty to advise you on this matter. This is not meant to cast any sort of aspersion on David. It's a formality. I know it's last-minute, but we didn't know about the wedding until—"

"Get out of here. This is insulting. Get out of here!" Emma cried.

"Rory," said Kay. "You better go. Just put that thing away and go. My daughter is a grown woman. If she doesn't want to do this . . ."

"There's a lot of money at stake, Kay," said Rory.

"My money, not yours," Emma cried.

Rory tucked the document back inside his jacket pocket, a grave expression on his face. "This is not something to be emotional about. We need to be realistic. In this day and age, the divorce rate being what it is—"

"Rory, go!" said Kay, forcefully steering her husband out of the room.

"Emma, I'm sorry if I upset you. I'm only trying to do what's best for you . . ."

Emma was shaking and refused to meet his gaze. She could hardly believe it. Instead of being guilty and ashamed of himself, Rory had marched in here and insulted her. She wanted to turn on him and blurt out all that she knew. But she couldn't. Rory stepped into the hallway and Kay closed the door firmly behind him.

"Oh, Em," said Kay. "I'm sorry. I had no idea he was going to spring that on you. His timing can really be atrocious."

"I think this is about a little more than bad timing," Emma fumed.

"Don't be angry. He's only thinking about your welfare."

"My welfare," Emma scoffed. "David must be freaking out . . ."

"I'm sure he understands," said Kay soothingly. "He knows that your family only wants to do what's best for you. Please, darling, don't let this spoil your day."

"Oh my God, I need to call him and explain." She began to rummage in her bag for her cell phone. With shaking fingers, she sat down on the bed and punched in the number at their house. It rang several times, and there was no answer. Then she tried David's cell phone. Still no answer. "Damn," she said.

"Maybe he's downstairs already. Take it easy, Em," said Kay. "It will be all right."

"He's probably furious," Emma said.

"I doubt it. He knows it wasn't your idea. If he loves you, he'll understand."

"If?" Emma cried.

Kay took her daughter's hands in hers. "Of course he loves you. I know that."

"What if he's not on his way? What if he's so mad he decides not to show up?"

"He'll show up. Have a little faith," said Kay.

Emma, still shaking, took a deep breath. It was all she could do not to expose Rory's secret. She reminded herself of how cruel that would be to her mother, who didn't deserve to have this day ruined. Emma peered at her mother. "Look, Mom, I'm not trying to act like a stubborn child. I realize it's a lot of money. David and I have talked about it. He understands the situation. He just feels as if it's not really his concern. He's just not someone who thinks all that much about money. He says it's my money to do with as I see fit. Let me ask you something. I don't mean to be rude, but after what Rory just did . . . Do you have a prenup?"

Kay shook her head. "I'm like you. I'm a romantic. I believe in getting married without hedging your bets. Trust and hope. You need those things in a marriage."

Emma nodded agreement, but there was a sickening feeling in her gut, and in her mind's eye, an image of Rory McLean seated in a darkened alcove nuzzling another woman.

"And I can see that you are happy," Kay continued. "And very much in love."

"I am," Emma insisted.

Kay put her arms around her daughter and rested her cheek softly against Emma's face. "Stay that way."

CHAPTER 3

Emma's heart was thudding as she descended the narrow, carpeted staircase to the lobby of the inn behind her mother and Stephanie. At the foot of the stairs, Stephanie picked up their bouquets from the hall table and handed the bride's bouquet up to Emma. Emma peeked into the timber-ceilinged room. All of the guests fit into a few short rows of straight-backed chairs that faced the flower-bedecked mantelpiece and blazing hearth.

Standing in front of the fireplace, in his robes, was Judge Harold Williamson, who was going to perform the ceremony. David had insisted on a civil ceremony. He had no use for organized religion. David wasn't godless, as he carefully explained to Emma, but he was definitely anti-organized religion. In her heart of hearts, Emma would have preferred a church wedding, but she deferred to his strong feelings. A wedding was a wedding. Next to Judge Williamson was Burke Heisler, wearing an impeccable gray suit that looked attractive with his blond hair and matched his gray eyes. Those gray eyes were now trained anxiously on the entrance to the room through which one could see the front door of the inn. Clearly, he was looking for David Webster. The space reserved for the groom was empty.

"Where is he?" Emma whispered.

"Let me duck out and see if his car is in the parking lot," said Stephanie.

"Thanks," said Emma. Her bouquet of white roses and lily of the valley trembled in her hand.

"Don't worry," Kay whispered soothingly, rubbing Emma's back. "He'll be here."

Somewhere behind her, she heard Rory clear his throat.

David has changed his mind, Emma thought. Oh my God! She closed her eyes, wishing she could make herself disappear. I should have known, she thought. He's always been a free spirit, a guy with no strings attached. He didn't want a house and a wife and a baby. I always knew that. What made me think he could change overnight? Why did I agree to this wedding? And he's probably furious about the prenup, she thought. He thinks it was my idea, that I sent Rory over to blindside him. He doesn't want any part of me or my family. But still, it's so cruel. Oh, David, how can you leave me here like this? This is one of those nightmares that you think can't possibly be real.

"Here he is," said Kay.

Emma opened her eyes and looked at her mother, faint with relief. "David, where?"

"Right there," said Kay, pointing to the man who had just entered the room and was heading toward the front.

Emma gasped when she saw him. David's dark, wavy hair had been trimmed and combed, and he was wearing a beautiful navy suit with a silk tie. He looked so handsome that her knees buckled at the sight of him. He did not look at her as he hurriedly walked past the fireplace and inserted himself between the judge and his best man. Burke gave him an awkward hug, and then David straightened out his jacket, crossed his hands in front of him, and glanced toward the back of the room, meeting Emma's gaze. He drew in a deep breath and his eyes widened. He mimed a wolf whistle. There was a murmur that sounded like a chuckle from the assembled guests.

Emma's face turned pink, and her anxieties melted away.

Kay took her daughter's hand in hers. "Okay, sweetie. Are you ready?"

"Yes," Emma whispered. Her heart was pounding with excitement. Kay and Emma began to walk toward the front, and Emma could feel her legs trembling beneath the satin gown. She thought for a moment of her baby, their baby, present at the wedding of his parents. Someday she and David would tell their child about their wedding day. They reached the judge, and Kay kissed Emma's cheek and whispered in her ear, "Be happy, my darling." Emma nodded, but she wasn't really listening. All she could see was her husband.

* * *

The fervent vows pledged, the rings and kisses exchanged, Emma and David tore their gaze from each other and turned to face their guests. A waiter came around with a tray of champagne, but Emma refused it, asking for a glass of sparkling cider. When he brought it to her, she and David clinked glasses, drank, and then shared one more kiss before they went to greet their guests. In the next room, silverware tinkled as guests began to visit the elegant luncheon buffet table, laden with rich pâtés, fresh seafood, and chateaubriand, which Kay McLean had arranged. The jazz combo riffed, and more hors d'oeuvres were passed as the guests began to mingle. People took seats at the small tables around the room, covered in white linen and anchored with clear bowls of white butterfly orchids and gardenias. The first person whom Emma encountered was Aurelia Martin, Kay's oldest friend, and the mother of Emma's closest friend, Jessica. Aurelia had always been like an aunt to Emma. She was seated at a table, nursing a glass of champagne. She stood up to give Emma a kiss.

"Aunt Aurelia," Emma said. "I'm so glad to see you. Where's Uncle Frank?"

Aurelia's husband was much older than she and in ill health. "Darling, he's not really well enough for an occasion like this."

"Well, give him a hug for me," said Emma. "And how's Jessie doing? She always tells me she's bored staying in bed."

"Oh, she's bored all right," said Aurelia. "But she's following doctor's orders. Anything for the baby. She hates missing your wedding though. She made me promise to give her a full report. I'll tell her how beautiful you look. And what a handsome groom you have there."

"Thank you." Emma beamed and followed Aurelia's gaze. Across the room, David was crouched down beside the chair where his mother sat. He was offering her a plate with tiny portions of food.

Helen Webster, gaunt in a pink polyester coatdress that seemed to be a size too large, was tethered, by a pair of long, clear tubes, to an oxygen tank on wheels. Her skin was white and looked bloodless. Helen's sole hope for survival was a heart transplant, but her blood type was rare, and her chances seemed slim. She was in the end stages of heart disease and her activities were extremely limited, but she watched the wedding scene with lively eyes and began to pick at the food on the plate David had brought to her.

"He seems like a very nice young man," said Aurelia.

"He is," said Emma.

"Has Jessie met him?" Aurelia asked.

"Not yet," Emma admitted. She and David had spent most of their courtship in New York City, but David had resisted her efforts to get them together with Jessie and her husband, Chris. He had insisted that he didn't want to waste any of their precious time with other people. Emma suspected that he also didn't want her friends judging him. But that was no longer an issue. "She'll meet him soon," Emma promised.

"Well, you two be happy together," Aurelia said, laying a feathery touch on Emma's hand before she resumed her seat.

"Excuse me, may I kiss the bride?"

Emma turned and saw Burke Heisler gazing warmly at her. She put her arms around his neck and could smell his elegant, lightly scented aftershave as he held her tightly for a moment. "Oh, Burke. I'm so happy."

"You look happy," he said. "And completely ravishing."

Emma made a little curtsy of gratitude.

"I was just a little worried there for a minute," Burke said. "About the groom."

"So was I," she admitted. "When I saw he wasn't here, I thought he'd changed his mind."

"I never thought that. He'd have to be insane," said Burke.

Emma blushed. "Well, thanks. And thanks for being such a good friend to us."

"I only wish Natalie were here to see it," Burke said, and she saw the pain deep in his eyes. "She would have approved."

"I like to think so," said Emma. "If only I had realized in time . . . You know, and been able to help her."

"You? Imagine how I feel," he said.

Emma squeezed his hand, not knowing what she could say to him to try to make this day easier for him. "A lot of her life was such a nightmare. I think the only real happiness she ever knew was with you."

Burke shrugged. "I won't lie to you, Emma. It was difficult to be married to her at times. But it could be great too. Those are the times I prefer to remember. Anyway, that's what marriage is all about," he said, trying, and failing, to sound upbeat. "The good times and the bad." He forced himself to smile, and Emma smiled back.

"Thanks for being here for us today. I know how hard it is," she said.

"I wouldn't be anywhere else," he said.

"I should go and say hello to my mother-in-law," Emma said apologetically.

"You go on," he said, smiling as Emma lifted the hem of her gown and started across the room toward the table where Helen sat. Sitting on the other side of Helen was a pudgy, cheerful-looking woman with short gray hair. She had high color in her sixty-year-old cheeks, probably because of the champagne. Birdie, Helen's first cousin, was a widow. A few years ago, she had moved into David's boyhood home to live rent-free and look after her ailing cousin.

David straightened up, and Emma came over and touched David on the arm. He turned to her with relief in his eyes. "Hey, baby."

Emma kissed him and then bent over and touched Helen's hand, which lay limp on the arm of the chair. Her hand was ice-cold.

"How are you feeling today, Helen?"

"Oh, I'm fine," said Helen. Her voice was faint. "I just wish Phil could have been here." Phil was David's older brother, an attorney who lived in Seattle. He had been invited but said he couldn't rearrange his schedule in time.

"Me too, Mom," said David.

Helen had struggled fiercely, working as a waitress to raise her sons after David's father, a furniture salesman and a chronic gambler, abandoned his young family. Alan Webster was a man whom David never mentioned without disgust. He told Emma that one reason he was afraid of fatherhood was because of his father's abandonment. He didn't want to be that kind of father, despised by his wife and children.

"Hey, mind if we join you, sis?" said a paunchy, white-haired man carrying a plate piled high with beef and lobster. He was followed by an extremely skinny little woman with frizzy hair and a weathered face.

"John, Tilly," said Helen. "Sit down here."

"We will. Hey, cuz," John said, pecking Birdie on the cheek as he took a seat.

"Hi, sweetie," Birdie said cheerfully, stopping a passing waitress to exchange her empty champagne glass for a full one.

"Emma," said David. "I'd like you to meet my aunt and uncle, John and Tilly Zamsky. They're the ones with the cabin," said David.

"Oh, hello," said Emma warmly, shaking their hands. She had heard many stories about the good-natured plumber and his wife, who had tried to include his fatherless nephews in his family life. "Thank you so much for lending us your place for the weekend."

John Zamsky waved a meaty hand. "You're welcome to it. I don't use the place anymore. I used to take these boys fishing there when they were little. Remember that, Davey, huh?"

"Of course. Did you recognize Burke, my best man? He came with us a few times," said David.

"Was he that little fat kid whose father owned the casino?"

David nodded. "That's Burke."

John Zamsky chuckled. "Oh hell, I wouldn't recognize any of you anymore. You guys were just pip-squeaks then. We did have some fun times there though. I just never get out that way nowadays."

"Nowadays, you can't get him out of his recliner," Tilly confided.

"How long since we been there, Till?" John Zamsky asked.

Tilly rolled her eyes. "A couple of years."

"Our kids never use it," said John. "We ought to sell it."

"Someday they might use it," Tilly protested staunchly. "Besides, you hold on to real estate. Everybody knows that. Things appreciate."

"Well, we appreciate your lending it to us," said Emma. "It should be lovely there in November."

"Oh, yes," said Tilly. "Perfect time of year."

"You kids enjoy it," said John Zamsky. "Go and have a good time."

Emma and David smiled at each other. "We will," said David.

"Look at them. They can't wait to get out of here," said John.

Tilly elbowed her husband. "John!"

Emma blushed, but David put his arm around her waist and pulled her close. "Don't expect me to deny it."

"How are you feeling, Helen?" Tilly asked sympathetically.

"I'm enjoying myself," said Helen.

"Is this too much excitement for you?" Tilly fretted.

"Ah, leave her alone. She's fine," said John Zamsky. "Hey, Davey, I like this jazz group you got. They're playing some great old songs."

David gazed into Emma's eyes. "It is time we danced," he said.

"Just don't overdo it," said Tilly to David's mother. "You don't want to collapse."

Helen's bloodless lips turned up in a weak grin and her tired eyes were alight. "Oh, stop fussing. I'm fine. I'm enjoying this. I never thought I'd see this day. This kid always said he'd never get married. We'd go in a store and he'd say, 'Look at that poor guy. His wife's leadin' him around by the ring in his nose.' I used to laugh when he said that. Remember that, Davey? You always used to say that. You said you'd never let any woman do that to you." She shook her head. "Now look at you. The ring may be on your finger, but it's a ring, all the same."

David looked at her without smiling. "I don't remember that."

Helen shook her head. "This does my heart good. If I collapse, so be it. At least I'll die happy."

CHAPTER 4

"I'm gonna have to make you quit driving," said David.

Emma opened her eyes and yawned. "Where are we?" she said.

"Almost there. Every time you get into a car these days you fall asleep. I'm not sure it's safe to let you behind the wheel anymore."

Emma smiled and sat up. "It's true. It's the pregnancy. I'm always sleepy. Although I usually can stay awake when I'm behind the wheel."

"Usually?" he said with disbelief in his deep, languid voice.

Emma laughed. "Hey, it's not your average day. I got married a few hours ago. It was a little bit exhausting."

She revisited a few of the day's events in her mind's eye. After the ceremony, the buffet lunch, the toasts, and the wedding cake, Emma had run back upstairs, removed her gorgeous dress, and squeezed into her jeans, which she could now just barely button, a long-sleeved thermal Henley shirt, and a down vest. She had pulled her shining, honey-blond hair up under a baseball cap, although a few curly tendrils fell loose around her face. She and David had escaped to their car in the obligatory shower of rice and good wishes.

Twenty minutes out of town Emma had confessed that she'd been too nervous to eat a bite at the wedding. David admitted that he had not eaten either. They got off the highway and took a scenic detour, stopping at a truckers' diner. The hostess seated them in a booth at the back, where they relaxed over a couple of hamburger platters. They got back on the road feeling full and, in Emma's case, pleasantly drowsy.

"All in all," she said, "I'd say it was a success."

"I think so," he said. "You looked incredible. I thought the other men there were going to fall over at the sight of you."

"The other men? What about you?"

He gave her a sly grin. "Oh, baby, you know about me."

Emma grinned. Then she took a deep breath and pulled down the brim of her cap. "I'm just so sorry about that business with the prenup."

David shook his head. "Don't be. Rory was looking out for you."

"Rory," Emma said disgustedly, shaking her head.

"I think he does care about you in his own weird way. Anyway, I told him I'd sign it."

"Well, I told him I wouldn't. We don't need that," said Emma firmly.

"It's your decision," said David.

"My mother agreed with me. She said we needed to start our marriage with hope and trust. I thought that was kind of nice."

"I agree with her," he said.

"Even though her own husband can't be trusted," she said.

"You didn't mention that to her today, I hope," said David.

Emma frowned. "No, of course not. She was happy today. I wasn't about to ruin it for her. Although I'm going to have to deal with this when we get back. I can't sit on this secret indefinitely. But not today. She's always dreamed of this day. And she was so thrilled. Actually, both our mothers seemed happy," Emma said.

"Well, you heard my mother," David said. "She was sure I was not the marrying kind." He was silent for a moment, and Emma saw the frown in his eyes. She wondered what was making him frown.

"I'm glad you decided to become the marrying kind," she said.

His handsome face broke into a sweet smile. "Me too. You ready for our camping trip?" he asked, abruptly changing the subject.

"It's not a camping trip," protested Emma. "There's a cabin, running water, electricity. And a fireplace. It's gonna be great."

"A pregnant woman in the wilds of New Jersey," he teased.

"Oh come on. The phrase 'wilds of New Jersey' is an oxymoron," said Emma.

"You look cute in that outfit," said David. "Just like a Piney!"

"Thanks. I guess," said Emma. Glancing in the car's sideview mirror, Emma saw herself dressed for the woods, her face burnished by the sun's weakening rays. The perceived wisdom about pregnancy was true. Or was it the glow of being a newlywed? Her skin had never looked better, and her blue-gray eyes looked softer than they ever had.

She held up her left hand and examined her wedding band. It too glowed in the light of the sinking sun.

David glanced over at her. "You like that?" he asked gently.

They were husband and wife, starting out on their life together. She felt as if she would burst with happiness. "I like it."

"Good," he said.

She gazed out the window. "It's gorgeous around here," she said.

David nodded. The November afternoon was golden, shafts of slanted light piercing the forests that surrounded the highway. "It really is remote here. You'd never believe you were an hour from Clarenceville."

"I never thought when I met you that you'd turn out to have this L.L. Bean side to you. You seemed like the kind of guy who would never leave New York."

"I'm full of surprises," he said.

She sat back in the seat and smiled, remembering. From the first day, he had surprised her. After their impulsive night of passion in his New York apartment, she had fully expected that he would be in a rush to get rid of her, wanting his privacy back immediately, and she was fully prepared to put her clothes on and head for the train back to Clarenceville. Instead, he woke her up with fresh bagels and coffee and insisted on taking her to a street fair in Little Italy, where he bought her a cameo ring. After a brief stop for a reading of sonnets in a bookstore café, and ever conscious of not wanting to overstay her welcome, Emma suggested that it was time for her to head for the train station. He had turned to her with a puzzled look in his eyes. "No, don't go," he said.

She could remember how her whole body had tingled as she'd met his gaze. How they had rushed back to his apartment and fallen back into his bed. Their love affair had been a heady, dizzy ride. But this marriage was the biggest surprise of all. From that first day they had lived for the moment, and now, suddenly, they were married with a baby on the way.

Was it all too soon, too quick? she wondered. A moment's doubt fell across her happiness like a cloud over the sun on a tropical isle. And then, just as quickly, it was gone. David was not a man bound by convention. It was what he wanted. What they both wanted. And you can still live in the moment, she thought. This is your wedding day. You are starting out on life's great adventure. Enjoy it, she thought. She began to relax and take in her surroundings again.

The deepening woods filled her with a sense of mystery and excitement. Her favorite vacations had always been camping trips. She and her father would visit national parks and go backpacking, hiking, and swimming by day, making campfires and stargazing at night, while Kay would gather up a stack of books and spend a few days at the Canyon

Ranch spa. It was something special that Emma had shared with Mitchell Hollis. Now she was going to share it with David—a love of roughing it, of being out in nature.

"Oh, look, David! There's the river," she cried. "Oh, it's gleaming. It looks so beautiful. Is that where we're going to be canoeing?"

David peered out the windshield. "Yeah, I guess so. We're almost to the cabin."

"How can you remember the way after so many years?" she said.

David hesitated. "I don't know. I guess I'm a born scout," he said.

"How many years has it been?" she asked.

David shook his head. "I can't remember. A long time."

They rode along in silence for a few minutes, each one looking around at the strange, beautiful woods they had entered. The car jounced along on the dirt and gravel for about half a mile until they came to a clearing. Set in the clearing was an actual log cabin, although not of colonial vintage. It was still faintly russet colored from the red cedar lumber that had been used to build it. The cabin had a field-stone chimney and a set of steps with wooden railings leading to the front door. A small shed and a large woodpile stood off some hundred yards from the front steps. A canoe was resting upside down on a pair of sawhorses. The gleam of the river could be glimpsed from where they parked the car.

Emma opened her door and jumped out. "Oh, David, this is precious. This is great!" she said.

"You know, for a rich kid, you are so easy to please," he said coming around to her side of the car and putting an arm around her waist.

"Promise me that we can sleep in front of the fireplace, even if it isn't in the bedroom," she said.

"It's our wedding night. We can do whatever your little heart desires," he said. "It's just you and me."

Emma took a deep breath of the pine-scented air. "Oh, this is fabulous. Talk about getting away from it all. Oh, I love it, I love it, I love it." She began to dance a little jig in the work boots she had worn for the trip. She'd thought the boots had looked ridiculous as she left the General Crossen Inn, but here, they looked perfectly appropriate.

"Well," he said, going around to the rear of the wagon and opening the trunk. "Let's go in, and I'll show you the place."

Emma walked around and tried to pull her bag out of the trunk, but David tugged it away from her. "I'll carry this stuff. You just take it easy there, pioneer girl."

Emma giggled and ran up the steps ahead of him. She turned back to her husband. "Keys?" she said.

"Uncle John always kept the key under the mat."

Emma bent over and lifted the weather-beaten welcome mat. "Sure enough," she said. She turned it in the stiff lock, pushed the door open, and stepped inside.

"Wait a minute. Stop," he cried. He set the bags down on the steps.

Emma looked back at him in alarm. "What?"

He walked up to her, lifted her in his arms as if she were no heavier than a doll, and carried her into the cabin. "Allow me, Mrs. Webster. It's our first threshold."

"That is so sweet," she said. "I forgot all about that."

"We don't want any bad karma," he said, setting her down in the room.

The cabin smelled a little musty. The great room was simply furnished with a braided rug and a wood-framed sofa and a chair that faced the large, fieldstone hearth, which smelled faintly of cooked meat. Beside the fireplace a pair of canoe paddles rested against the wall. Along the opposite wall of the great room was a countertop with a stove and refrigerator that were not new, but not ancient either. The cabinets were stained the same russet color as the outside of the cabin. A closed, gateleg table and two chairs facing each other nestled against a narrow kitchen island, which held the sink and a butcher-block countertop. "Does it look the same to you after all these years?" Emma asked.

"Yeah. Pretty much," he said. "Let me go get the bags."

Emma opened a few cupboard doors and found old jars and bottles of spices, well-used pots and pans, and some rusty cans of food.

"Good thing we bought supplies," said Emma to her husband as he followed her in, hauling the duffel bags.

"I'll put these in our bedroom," he said.

"Let me check it out with you," she said, closing the cupboards. She followed him back to where the two bedrooms were divided by a pleasantly clean and new-looking bathroom.

"Which room?" David asked.

"Doesn't matter," said Emma. "We're sleeping in front of the fire, remember?"

"Until one of us gets too creaky to stand it anymore," he said. He set the bags down in the room that had a queen-size bed. Emma went back out and opened the refrigerator. There was an open box of baking soda, a few bottles of Coke, and some jelly jars on the door. Otherwise the fridge was empty.

David looked over her shoulder. "Not very well stocked," he said apologetically.

"I don't know. I kind of like it," Emma said. "It has a little character. So many places people go now are just homogenous. You can't tell Tortola from Timbuktu. This place, you can kind of feel the presence of the family. A sense of the past."

"Well, do you want me to drag the mattress out here now?" he asked.

"No, let's wait until after supper," she said with a smile. "We might want to sit out here and read tonight. But I definitely want a fire going the whole time."

"As you wish, madame," said David. "Uncle John has an ax in that shed. I want to split a little more wood," he said. "That little stack won't last until morning. I better get to work." He made a bicep and offered it for her to admire.

Emma squeezed his arm and then tilted back the brim of her cap and kissed him. He kissed her back, playfully at first, and then harder. Her baseball cap fell to the floor as the kiss deepened, and he put his arms around her. Her body responded automatically to his, making her feel at once languid and aroused. She could feel his desire stirring too, and suddenly, nothing else seemed to matter. She reached up to unbutton his shirt.

"Whoa, wait a minute," he said. "I should get out there and start chopping before it's too dark."

"We could manage without the fire," she offered.

"Oh no," he said. "We definitely need the fire. It'll be better by the fire."

She knew he was right. They were out here in the woods, and they needed to be sensible about things. But it was the first time she could remember in their short six months that he had not been as eager as she was to fall into bed together. A little corner of her heart felt hurt by his need to be practical. "Is this the curse of married life?" she asked.

"No," he said with a shade of exasperation. "But I need to take care of you now. That means I don't want you and our baby to freeze to death tonight."

"I know," she said. "You're right. Go do your Paul Bunyan thing. But don't wear yourself out completely."

"Never," he said. "You know me better than that." He kissed her on the forehead and headed outside.

"Later," she whispered as the door slammed behind him. Then she heard the car door slam. Emma began unloading the food they had brought. I wonder if there's any ice? she thought absently, opening the door to the freezer. Inside the freezer was a can of coffee and a package of frozen lasagna, completely frosted over. Ugh, she thought. How long has this been here? She pulled out the package and wiped the frost off of the label, expecting to see an ancient sell-by date from years ago. To her surprise, the package was dated August of this year. August? she thought. How long a shelf life does this stuff have? She remembered John Zamsky saying that he hadn't used the cabin in years. Maybe one of his kids came here to visit. She debated throwing the package away, but then decided to just leave it where it was. It didn't belong to her. She filled empty ice cube trays with water and put them back in the freezer.

When she was done unloading, the fridge was not exactly full, but there was enough to keep them well fed for the weekend. She didn't want to have to go looking for a store tomorrow, so she had insisted that they bring all the basics as well as a few luxury items. David had brought beer. She couldn't drink alcohol because of the baby, but she had taken two bottles of sparkling cider from the wedding so that it would seem like champagne. Emma closed the door to the fridge. From outside she could hear the sound of cracking as David began to split the wood. She glanced out and saw him there, placing the logs on a stump and cleaving them deftly with a shiny ax.

I'd better make up the bed, she thought. Even if they did pull the mattress into the living room in front of the fire, it would be better if the sheets were already on it. Ever since she became pregnant, she had a tendency to fall asleep at a moment's notice. Out here in the fresh air, she could probably fall asleep standing up. She went into the bedroom, turned on the bedside light, and emptied their suitcases into the narrow closet. Then she went and reached for the sheets she had placed in a large shopping bag. As she began to stretch the bottom sheet around the corner of the bed, she realized that the cracking sound of the logs being split had ceased.

That was quick, she thought.

She walked around the bed, pulling on the sheet, and then she tossed open the top sheet and let it drift onto the bed. As she began to tuck it in, she felt a little twinge in her abdomen. Overdoing it, she thought. She sat down on the edge of the bed and looked out the bedroom window. A sliver of the river was visible through the pine trees. It gleamed silver like a knife. The whole world seemed to be silent, except for the odd call of a bird in the trees and a faint rustle of desiccated leaves.

I like this, she thought. I need this. She heard a creak, as if the front door had opened.

"David?" she called out.

There was no answer.

Probably the wind, she thought. Or the Jersey Devil. She thought immediately of her conversation with Burke about monsters. Over the years, the legend of the Jersey Devil, if not the devil himself, had proved durable and been blamed for much mayhem in the Pine Barrens. It added a certain mystery to these woods. But it was just a legend. Albeit a truly scary one. Don't be a dope, she told herself. Now you're scaring yourself. She took a deep breath, got up off the bed, and resumed tucking in the sheet. For a minute, she wished she had a radio to keep her company until David came back inside. Yeah. That would do a lot for the peace and quiet, she chided herself.

She finished the sheet and turned to pick up the blanket. Through the bedroom door, she thought she saw a movement in the outer room. "David?" she said.

There was no reply. She swallowed hard and took another breath. You're spooking yourself. You're just not used to silence. Emma smoothed a blanket over the sheets, put the pillows in their cases, and then picked up the bedspread.

Typical David, she thought uneasily. He probably took off exploring somewhere. Couldn't wait until tomorrow. She straightened up and patted her belly. Let's go out and call him, Aloysius, she thought, using her pet name for the baby growing inside of her. What do you say?

Turning off the bedroom lamp, she went back out into the great room. The light was on over the kitchen stove top, but everything else was in a twilight gloom, and the temperature seemed to have plummeted with the fading of the day. Still, it all looked quiet and undisturbed. She opened the front door and walked outside onto the tiny landing of the top step. There was wood, stacked by the piles of logs, but no sign of her husband anywhere. Emma thought about trying to find him, but she didn't know which direction he might have gone. From where she stood on the steps, Emma could see the shafts of golden light withdrawing from the trees and disappearing abruptly from the brown, leafy forest floor. Don't go out there, she thought. If you get lost in those woods, you'll really be in a pickle. Stop being so jumpy. He'll be back any minute.

With a sigh, she reopened the door and went back inside. The musty room suddenly felt uncomfortably dark and chilly. There were two fat, red pillar candles on flat pewter holders on the mantelpiece and a pair of squat, straight candles in ceramic holders on the little gateleg dining table. I could light those, she thought. Get the place in the mood. On the mantelpiece was an old box of wooden matches with every bit of the striking surface streaked back and forth. She pulled out a match and dragged it across the surface. It sprang to flame. She lit the red pillars and both the straight candles. The room was instantly transformed. While it was still dim, with only the wavering candlelight, it felt warmer already and cozier. I wonder if I should start the fire, Emma thought. There was one basket of wood next to the hearth and some old papers. Your mother can do this, Aloysius, she thought. She learned to make a fire when she was not much bigger than you.

Emma went over to the hearth, bent down, and began balling up the papers. She set them in the hearth with its strong smoky meat smell. At least a fire will get rid of the odor, she thought. She placed some short branches on the paper for kindling and then arranged the wood in a teepee, as her father had taught her. Okay, she thought. That looks right. Emma stood up and found the matchbox. She struck one match, but before she could bend down to light the edge of the paper the match went out.

All right, she thought. Try that again. She crouched down, holding the matchbox, and lit the match. This time she was able to set the burning match to the paper and it caught. The flame seemed to hesitate, dancing for a moment, and then it ran down the edge of the paper and began to burn, the flames leaping to ignite the kindling. All right, she thought. Wait until David gets back. He will be so proud of me.

At that very moment, as she felt the little triumph of having lit the fire, she felt the candlelight from the table beside the kitchen island disappear as if the flames had gone out. At the same time, the flames on the pillar candles on the mantel wavered and began to smoke. Emma's heart seized. Someone was moving up behind her. "David?" she said. She turned, still crouching, and looked up.

In the twilit gloom, she saw him. He was upon her. Three feet away. A figure in a bulky hooded sweatshirt. A black ski mask covered the entire face save two ragged holes outlined in red around the shadowed eyes. Emma's limbs were stone. Her heart was bursting. "Who are you? What do you want?" she cried.

He did not reply. In his gloved hand he held an ax. Its edge gleamed in the flame from her fire as he advanced on her. She put up her hands to try to shield herself, her baby. Oh my God, she thought. Oh, please! This can't be happening. God help me. As he lifted the ax, she looked around frantically. She screamed and tried to scramble away from him. It was no use. He was too close.

She saw a flash of steel descending.

CHAPTER 5

Claude Mathis had not had a good day. Last night he had bet Holly, his ex-wife, that his fourteen-year-old son, Bobby, would want to come hunting today, but when Claude showed up at dawn, in camouflage from head to toe, at the trailer where his ex lived with Bobby and her new boyfriend, Holly had come to the door in her big, old, terry cloth bathrobe and told him, with immense satisfaction, that Bobby was still asleep and was planning on going to some kind of Japanese animation festival today. Whatever that was.

Claude had driven out to the woods in his pickup, his hound, Major, patiently flopped down on the rear bed. Claude was trying not to feel angry at his kid, but he couldn't help it. Why couldn't the kid show an interest? There was a lot he needed to learn, and it was time he started learning it. Besides, it was humiliating when Holly was right about these things. "I told you so" were her favorite words. Claude had fumed about it all day, and it had probably affected his aim, because he had had a few opportunities but no luck. He had silently positioned himself within range of a pair of grazing deer, who looked up, but froze. Claude took aim, not making a sound, but when he got the shot off, he missed.

Finally, after a day of complete and utter frustration, it was time to go home. He was tramping through the woods, thinking about the bar he liked to go to, its welcoming glow visible in his mind's eye. Sausage and sauerkraut and a golden brew. He was trying to make up a story he could tell about today that wouldn't be humiliating, that the guys would find funny, when he heard the woman's scream.

Claude, trailed by Major, stopped short. It was a horrible sound that made Claude's thinning brown hair stand on end. Major knew better than to bark. They both remained dead still for a moment, and then it came again. At the same moment, Claude smelled woodsmoke, and he realized exactly where that scream was coming from. He had passed that little cabin not too far from the river. Cocking his automatic rifle, he began to lope in that direction, Major keeping pace with him.

There was still a gray light above the dark trees. Claude crashed through the brambles and toward the clearing he could see up ahead. He burst through the trees and saw the little house. There was a curl of smoke coming from the chimney, a flickering light inside the windows. And that scream raking the air. Claude bounded up the stairs and threw open the door, plunging into the cabin, which was so much darker inside than the woods.

* * *

Emma, screaming, had rolled away from the first blow, which landed with a horrible clang on an andiron. All she could think about was her baby. She had to protect the baby. She had to get away. She tried to scramble to her feet, to run, but the second blow fell, and this one hit her. The ax caught her vest and tore through it. The down filling of the vest kept the blade from landing on her with full force. But it landed all the same, slicing through her shirt, cutting her side open, bringing her down to the floor. Her blood flew through the air as she tried to lunge out of his range. Through her panic, she noticed the canoe paddle, which was propped near the fireplace. She clambered to her knees and lifted the paddle to ward off her masked assailant. The ax fell again, this time splintering her would-be shield into bits. The paddle part flew across the room. Emma was holding only the short handle. She threw it at him, scrambling across the braided rug around the edge of the sofa as she tried to escape, blood splattering in her wake. He slipped in her blood, following her, and righted himself. The sofa was no protection. She had to try and get away. The pain in her side felt like a hot poker had perforated her lungs. She wanted to curl up and wrap her arms around herself. But she couldn't just give in and let him kill her. She forced herself to her feet and launched herself toward the door, collapsing on the floor as he hit her again, a glancing blow on the back of her thigh. She let out an unearthly cry of pain.

"What the hell?"

Emma and the masked assailant looked up in the same instant and saw a man dressed in camouflage coming through the door, holding his rifle. His long, horsy face was aghast at the bloody scene in front of him. "Help me," Emma cried.

The hunter stared for a moment—a moment too long as he tried to adjust his eyes to the dimness. Spinning away from Emma, the man in the hooded sweatshirt lifted his ax and struck at the hunter. The ax came down in the front of the hunter's balding head, cleaving a bloody channel through it. His shocked gaze turned empty, and he began to crumple, the gun falling from his hands.

"Oh my God! Oh God. Oh no!" Emma shrieked in horror. The hunter was on the floor, an inert bundle of flesh and camouflage, the area around him slick with blood. Emma's assailant pulled the ax from the man's skull and turned on her again, stepping between her and the dead hunter, the rifle lying on the floor.

Now he will kill me, she thought.

She could not see his face, just the wild gleam of his eyes, encircled with red by the mask. She thought of her child who would never see this world, and what a pitiful job of protecting that child she had done. And in the instant that it took to pray for both their souls, Emma heard a horrible growl, and a brown and white setter bounded into the cabin and leapt at the man in the mask. The dog hit the assailant full force, knocking him off balance, snapping at the man's heavy gloves, and sinking his teeth into the bulky fabric of his sweatshirt.

"Good boy!" Emma screamed and scuttled across the floor to where the hunter's rifle lay, just out of reach of his lifeless hand. She'd never shot a rifle. Never even held one. She'd shot tin cans with her father's revolver. That was all. It didn't matter. It was a gun. She would use it. The assailant jammed the dog's snout with the ax handle, and the dog let go with a wail of pain. The assailant kicked him away with his heavy boot. The dog growled and shook his head, stunned. The man lifted the ax and Emma lifted the rifle. She pulled the trigger.

A deafening roar thundered in the cabin and the gun bucked in her arms. The empty shell flew from the port, and Emma heard another shell click into the chamber. The assailant staggered back, and for one moment Emma thought she had shot him. Then she saw a black, smoking hole in the wall beside the doorway where he stood. For one second they all froze. Emma on the floor with the rifle, the setter growling over the body of his dead master, and the man in the mask.

Emma did not hesitate. She had never thought she would be able to kill someone, but now she knew better. She could. She would. She held the sight up to her eye. The barrel wavered slightly and fixed on him. "Now," she whispered.

The assailant tossed the ax in her direction as the angry dog leapt at him again. The ax missed Emma and embedded itself in the pine floor. Emma fired again, but the assailant had bolted out the door, pulling it shut against the howling hound who was barking as if possessed.

Shaking where she sat, Emma clutched the rifle to her chest and crawled over to the hunter bleeding on the floor.

She tried to reach out to him, but the dog turned and snarled at her.

Help, Emma thought. Help was nearby, and yet she had been unable to access it. Help was in her pocket. She reached inside the vest, pulled out her cell phone, and dialed 911.

"Is this an emergency?" said a calm voice at the other end.

"Yes," Emma wailed. Then she began to sob so hard she could barely speak.

* * *

Chief Audie Osmund, a fifty-five-year-old native of these woods, dressed in a khaki uniform stretched taut over his wide belly, a black down vest and a black cap over his white hair, was standing beside his patrol car, talking on his radio to the New Jersey State Police, putting out an APB on the suspect. The female victim had been sedated and was weak from loss of blood, but she had given him a sketchy description of the killer. Unfortunately, it wasn't worth too much because of the mask and the probability that the killer had already discarded the clothes. The male victim, hunter Claude Mathis, was beyond all help, DOA. "Yeah," Audie was saying to the state police commander on duty. "We definitely gonna need some help on this one. These folks aren't local. The dead man was a local, but the other folks are from up Clarenceville way."

Audie was trying to sound as businesslike as possible, but the bloody scene had left him shaken. He had never come across a crime scene quite like it. The ferociousness of the attack reverberated around the clearing, like the echo of a scream, and left him feeling unequal to the level of violence. He knew that a lot of local police chiefs would be reluctant to cede any authority to the state police. But he didn't have the manpower or the technical sophistication to process the evidence on this crime.

The state police commander promised to send a detective down there tonight. "Don't let anybody mess with the crime scene," he said.

"We're guarding it," said Audie. "Thanks for the help."

Audie didn't care who found the killer. He just needed that killer found. The people around here were going to be scared out of their minds and clamoring for an arrest. Audie had grown up in the Pinelands and had known Claude Mathis slightly. Audie's youngest brother, Larry, had gone to school with him. Apparently Claude had come to the aid of this out-of-town woman, like any decent guy would try to do. And he had paid for his good deed with his life. It had been tough to look upon the violent, bloody scene without thinking about revenge, but Audie tried to keep emotion out of his job decisions. All too often, the crimes he saw had been caused by emotions run amok. It was his job, he figured, to remain calm, the eye of the storm.

There was an ambulance with its bay standing open as they readied the stretcher for the woman inside the cabin. The EMTs were in there with her now. Another black-and-white and three pickup trucks, one with a flashing light on the top, were crowded into the clearing in front of the cabin, all still idling, their headlights crisscrossing. The search of the woods had already begun. Audie could see flashlight beams bouncing among the trees.

All of a sudden Audie heard a cry. "Chief, we got him!"

The chief lumbered toward the sound of the voices at the edge of the clearing. He could hear shouting and see the bobbing flashlight beams as the men made their way back. Two men emerged, one a volunteer, the other a police sergeant named Gene Revere. They were half-dragging a third man out of the woods. He had dark hair, gray at the temples, and was wearing a canvas barn coat, heavy boots, and filthy, soaking-wet blue jeans that were torn in the right calf. He was resisting the two men who had handcuffed him, trying to get free of them.

Audie Osmund peered at the cuffed man as the three emerged from the woods.

"Where's my wife?" the suspect was pleading. "What happened here? I heard shots in the woods. Is my wife all right? Emma!"

"He said he's the husband," said Gene, a tall, muscular young father of two toddlers, who had been on his way to the Methodist Church pot roast supper when he received the emergency summons from his chief. He was wearing his civvies—a moth-eaten, old high school varsity jacket and blue jeans.

David looked helplessly at the chief. "Why is there an ambulance? Did someone shoot my wife?"

"David Webster?" asked Audie.

"I'm David Webster. Yes. Where is Emma? I need to see her."

"Your wife's been attacked," said Chief Osmund bluntly. "By a man with an ax. Where have you been, mister?"

"We found him out near the duck blind," Gene interrupted. "He says he walked out onto a rotten platform in the duck blind and fell through it. He claims it took him a while to get free."

David Webster stopped struggling and stood very still. His hazel eyes widened and sweat broke out on his forehead, above his lip. He stared at the chief. "Emma. Is she . . . ?"

Chief Osmund watched the man's reaction carefully. "She's alive," he said in an emotionless tone.

David sagged against Gene, as all the blood drained from his face.

The front door of the cabin opened, and the EMTs emerged, carrying a stretcher between them down the stairs. When they reached the ground, they unfolded the wheeled apparatus and began to rush the rolling stretcher toward the ambulance. At the open doors of the ambulance bay, an EMT was readying an IV bag and tube.

"Emma!" David cried.

Her white face was barely visible beneath an oxygen mask. The lower half of her body was raised, and she was covered to the neck with a Mylar blanket, but the stretcher mattress, where it was visible, was blotched with huge red stains. Chief Osmund nodded to his men to unlock the handcuffs that David was wearing. The sergeant unlocked the cuffs and David's arms burst free. He did not rub his wrists but staggered across the clearing, through the headlights of the running trucks, toward the rolling stretcher. He tried to reach her, but the largest of the EMTs blocked him. "You need to get out of the way, sir," he said.

"I want to go with her," he cried. "She needs to know I'm here. Emma."

"I'm sorry. There's no room," said the EMT. "She's barely conscious. She's bleeding, and she's in hypovolemic shock. We're going to need every inch of space in the bay to get her ready for the ER. Please step back and let us work on her."

David stumbled back from the ambulance, his eyes wide with disbelief. Chief Osmund and his deputy, Gene Revere, exchanged a glance as the EMTs, illuminated by the headlights from the idling trucks, loaded the stretcher into the bay of the ambulance. The siren began to wail.

"Mr. Webster," said Chief Osmund. "You're going to need to come on down to the station. You hop in my car over there and I'll give you a lift."

"NO. Emma," he cried.

"You can't see her now anyway. They're going to be busy working on her over at the hospital."

"No, I have to go to the hospital. I have to be with her," David insisted.

"You're in no shape to drive. We'll let you know if there's any news from the docs over there," said Audie.

David turned on the chief, his mouth hanging open in disbelief, as if it were the first time he had actually registered what was being said to him. "Are you crazy? I'm not going with you and leaving her there all alone in some strange hospital. Get out of my way."

Audie looked at the distraught husband, assessing his reaction and trying to keep his own temper in check. "I can see you're all tore up. But we've got our own problems here, Mr. Webster. We need to figure out what happened in that cabin. We got a murder here."

"Who was murdered?" David cried.

"A hunter, passing by. Tried to help your wife and was killed for his trouble."

"Oh my God." David shook his head and ran his hand through his hair. "Oh my God. This is my fault. I should have been here. Look, I want to help you. I really do. But can't it wait? My wife . . ." He gestured to the taillights of the disappearing ambulance.

"Like I said, we'll get this over with, and then I'll have somebody drive you on over to the hospital. Now, you go on and get into my car. The door is open."

"Wait a minute. Do I have any choice? Are you arresting me?" David cried.

"Why would I do that?" Audie asked. "I just want to talk to you. Get some answers that might help us out. Sooner we get this done, the sooner you can join your wife over there at the hospital."

David glowered and seemed about to protest again. Then, suddenly, he shook his head, turned away from the chief, and headed for the squad car.

Gene Revere sighed. "Well, we better get back to looking. We didn't realize that was the husband. I guess we got a little carried away. That nut is still out there. This is how the Pine Barrens get a bad rep. Some Piney goes berserk."

"Maybe," Audie said. He was nearing retirement age, having been on the force since he returned from Vietnam. During his tour of duty he had been trained as a recon marine, where he had learned to recognize the danger that lurked below the surface. "Anybody actually see him stuck in that duck blind platform?"

Gene frowned. "No. We just saw this guy kinda staggering along with no business being out in the woods and we figured it was the killer. So we grabbed him."

"Go on back out there to the duck blind," said Audie. "You scour that area. Get some dogs out there if need be. I want every inch of ground between here and there looked at. Check by the river too. At the water's edge. Along the banks."

"The guy probably got away by now," said Gene dejectedly.

"Maybe not," said Audie. "It'll probably be in a bag."

"What will?"

"A ski mask with red circles around the eyes, one of them hooded sweatshirts, maybe some pants and sneakers too."

"You think the killer changed out of those clothes before he got away?" Gene asked.

Audie glanced over at his patrol car. From the backseat, David Webster was staring at the open door of the cabin with haunted eyes. "Or maybe he changed out of them," said Audie grimly, "and he's still here."

CHAPTER 6

"Sweetheart," said a soft voice.

Emma struggled to open her eyes. Every part of her hurt. Even her face and eyelids felt sore. It took all her will to blink and bring her visitor into focus. She saw short, platinum blond hair, and anxious eyes.

"Mom," she whispered.

"Oh, darling, you're awake," said Kay. She bent over and kissed her daughter on the forehead.

Emma tried to nod. Her head ached. Her neck was stiff. "What time is it?"

Kay looked at her watch. "It's about midnight. They had to give you a sedative."

"David," Emma breathed. And then her eyes opened wide and she struggled to sit up. "My baby."

Kay patted her shoulder, pushing her gently back toward the pillow. "It's all right. Everything's all right. They did a sonogram. The baby is fine," said Kay, blinking back tears.

"Thank God." Emma sighed. For a moment she closed her eyes again, and the events of the awful night flooded into her mind. She knew she had lost a lot of blood. Now that she was awake, she remembered bags of blood being carried aloft by nurses, lights blinding her, people in masks and gowns, and urgent murmurs about clamps, debridement, and sutures. It had all seemed very far away at the time. As if she were watching herself from far away. But now she was back, groggy but awake. And her baby was still alive. Their baby. David. "Where's David?"

Kay's gaze traveled across the room where a man was rising from a chair. Emma followed her gaze and squinted. For a moment her heart lifted. Then she recognized her mother's husband.

"How you doin', slugger?" asked Rory, his expression hidden by the reflection off his tortoiseshell glasses.

Emma did not reply. Her lips were dry and cracked. She tried to moisten them with her tongue. Kay instantly reached for a washcloth and gently pressed it to Emma's parched lips. When Kay took the washcloth away, Emma repeated, "David?"

Rory cleared his throat and put a proprietary arm on his wife's shoulder. "David's down at the police station," Rory announced.

"He's helping the police," said Kay.

Emma tried to shift her position on the bed, but her entire left side, starting just below her armpit and reaching down her thigh, felt as if it were on fire. "Do they know who did this?" she whispered, glancing anxiously at the door.

Kay hesitated. "Not yet," she said. "They still have a lot of questions. But you're safe now, darling. No one's going to hurt you. There's a lieutenant from the state police outside who's been waiting to talk to you. Do you think you're up to it, darling?"

"I'll try," she said, her voice wobbly.

"I'll go," Rory said. Through the fog of her sedation, Emma knew there was something negative she was thinking about Rory, and then she remembered. The woman in the restaurant.

"What is it, honey? Did you remember something?" Kay asked, searching Emma's face with her gentle eyes.

Emma closed her eyes and shook her head. She thought about her father—with his soothing voice, which she could no longer summon in her memory. A tear leaked out from under her eyelids and down her face and she wished that he were here with her. How comforting it would be to lean her head against his broad chest, feel his arm encircling her.

"Mrs. Webster?"

Mrs. Webster, Emma thought, visualizing David's mother for a moment. And then she realized, she was Mrs. Webster. She looked up at the woman standing beside her bed, frowning down at her. The trim woman looked to be in her thirties and was wearing a white blouse and a fitted charcoal gray pantsuit. She was sharp featured with keen dark eyes and wore her chin-length brown hair in a simple, but fashionable layered cut.

"Yes," she whispered.

"I'm Lieutenant Joan Atkins of the state police. Chief Osmund requested the assistance of our bureau with his investigation." Joan showed Emma her I.D. and her badge, and tried not to wince at the sight of the victim. She couldn't help thinking about what Chief Osmund had told her when she arrived at the crime scene. "The victim's lost a lot of blood," Osmund said. "They had to stitch her up like a baseball." Too true, Joan thought.

"Lieutenant Atkins is here to help you, honey," said Kay.

Emma nodded. "Okay. Just don't leave me, Mom."

"Can I stay here with her while you question her?" Kay asked.

"Sure," said Joan. "I understand that you've been through a horrible ordeal, Mrs. Webster."

Kay stood at the head of Emma's bed, smoothing her hair back off her forehead, and watching her daughter with a worried frown.

The lieutenant sat down in a chair beside Emma's bed and studied her for a moment. Emma was stiff, her left side heavily bandaged, and the bandages were misted with blood. "I'm going to try to keep this brief, Emma. Can I call you Emma?" she asked.

Emma nodded slightly.

"We want to apprehend the person responsible for this terrible crime. But we need your help. Okay?"

Emma licked her cracked lips and whispered, "Okay."

Joan reached for the pad and pen in her black shoulder bag. She flipped the cover open on her pad. "Do you know who did this to you, Emma?" she asked.

Tears spilled down the sides of Emma's face and she began to tremble. "No. I told the first policeman. No. He was wearing . . ."

"I know. A mask and a hood. But was there anything . . . familiar about him?"

"Familiar?" Emma asked. Her brain felt slow and woolly. "No."

"Did you recognize him? His movements? His eyes beneath the mask?"

Emma tried to think back but felt only bewilderment. "No . . . It was so fast."

"I understand you were married this morning," said Joan gently.

Emma blinked at her, realizing that she had forgotten that. The wedding seemed like it took place a year ago. "Yes. Where is my husband?" Then her heart started to race. "Is he all right?"

"Yes, he's fine," said Joan. "Weddings can be very stressful, Emma. I know. I had one once."

Emma looked automatically at the lieutenant's neatly manicured hands. There was no wedding ring.

If Joan noticed the glance, she offered no explanation. "Did any disagreements arise between you and your husband before or after the wedding? Did you and your husband argue about anything . . . ?"

Emma shook her head. "No. Not really. No . . ."

Joan gazed at her grimly. "Has David Webster ever threatened you or attacked you physically?"

Emma's eyes widened. "David?"

"Any behavior he engaged in that might have made you suspicious of him?"

Emma struggled to sit up, to protest. "David did not hurt me. Anytime."

Joan's face remained expressionless. You didn't rise to the rank of lieutenant on the state police, despite the unspoken prejudice that still existed against women on the job, by giving yourself away. When she was working, she kept her emotions on a short leash. Her opinions as well. But her years of experience, both on and off the job, had left her with the firm conviction that there could be few things more dangerous than an angry husband. "Emma, we need to determine whether this was a random attack or whether you were a specific target. Can you think of anyone else who might have had a reason to want to hurt you? Anyone who was angry at you? Any threats you've received?"

Emma sank back against the pillow, watching Joan's lips move. She heard the words, but thinking was difficult. "No," Emma said. And then she hesitated. "No. Not threatening." Her mind was foggy. There was something. "What were we talking about . . . ?"

"Threats. Enemies," she said.

"I can't . . . no enemies."

"Can you review what happened in the cabin for me?"

Emma's eyes filled with fear. "Why?"

"It might help," Joan said. "Give us an idea of the size of the attacker. Age, build. Something more to go on."

"NO, I can't." The idea of recalling the attack filled her with dread, and her head was aching. She closed her eyes, forcing herself to see it again. That creature without a face casting a shadow over her. Looming above her, the ax gleaming. Chasing her, swinging the ax at her. The hunter. Another bit of fog burned off of her brain. The man with the dog. And the rifle. He came in and interrupted . . . The man in the mask turned on him. "Oh no," she mumbled. "Oh God! The man who tried to save me."

"No, honey," Kay crooned. "Don't think about it."

"Mrs. McLean, please," said Joan. "It's important that your daughter tell us everything she can remember."

Emma saw the hunter in her mind's eye, crumpled to the floor, the ax cleaving his skull, the blood everywhere. Emma groaned and tears sprang to her eyes. Her pounding headache tightened like a vise, and suddenly, out of nowhere, she began to retch. The spasmodic movement ignited the pain of all her wounds. She wailed as her empty stomach heaved.

"Oh, no! Her stitches," Kay exclaimed. "Call the nurse. Quick!"

Kay reached for a basin beside the bed as Joan jumped to her feet and rushed to the door of the room, nearly colliding with Rory, who was barreling in. "Rory, get some help. Get a doctor!" Kay cried. Rory wheeled and disappeared into the hallway.

A moment later a nurse appeared, as did a doctor in scrubs and a lab coat. The nurse rushed to Emma's bedside while the doctor checked her chart and ordered a tranquilizer and painkiller to be injected into her IV line.

"What happened?" the doctor demanded.

"She was remembering the attack," the lieutenant said grimly.

Kay watched her daughter helplessly, with clenched fists. "How could anyone do this to her?" she cried.

Joan felt her phone vibrating in her jacket pocket and turned away from Kay McLean, holding the phone to her ear. "Yes," she said.

It was Chief Osmund. Joan had recognized the look on the face of the middle-aged Pine Barrens chief when she appeared at the crime scene earlier in the evening and announced herself. He had felt shortchanged to be getting a woman. He had felt as if the state police commander had not taken his request for help seriously. Joan Atkins was used to that response. She always tried to ignore it. "The husband clammed up," Chief Osmund said. "His lawyer just got here. He called his brother in Seattle who's an attorney, and the brother told Webster not to volunteer anything more, that he would contact some hotshot lawyer he knew and have him come down here immediately. The attorney just walked in the door."

"I see," said Joan.

"You with the victim?" Audie asked.

"Yes," said Joan.

"We ain't got enough to hold him," Audie said. "We're gonna have to cut him loose."

"I understand," said Joan. "I'll talk to you tomorrow."

Joan replaced the phone in her pocket as Emma's retching finally subsided, and Emma fell back against the pillow, her complexion the color of clay.

"That's enough," Kay pleaded. "Please, leave her alone."

"Mrs. McLean, I won't be long. I understand your concern, but believe me, I am on your side."

"Make it quick," said the nurse to Joan. "She's gonna be out again in just a few minutes."

Joan nodded and returned to her seat by the bed.

"David." Emma was moaning. She turned her head and looked at Joan with bleary eyes. "Where's my husband?" she asked.

"He'll be along soon," Joan said soothingly. Too soon, she thought.

"When?" she whispered.

"Any minute now," she said. Any minute now, and that meant that she did not have much time left before the husband went to work on the victim, trying to convince her he had nothing to do with this. "Emma. Earlier, you seemed to hesitate when I asked if you knew someone who might be angry at you or might have threatened you. Who were you thinking of?"

Joan watched Emma's bleary eyes, calculating the small window of lucidity she had left for questions. Emma was losing the thread of consciousness.

"It's important, Emma, that you tell us whatever you can think of. If you can remember anyone who may have threatened you . . ."

Emma nodded slightly and swallowed hard. "It's not threats. I've been getting . . . messages. Anonymous."

Joan raised an eyebrow. "What kind of messages?"

61

"Like . . . love notes. But . . . a little . . . not normal."

"Do you still have them?" she asked. "How many have you received? For how long? Are you receiving them at home or at work?"

Emma closed her eyes, and Joan thought for a moment that she had fallen asleep. Then she said, "At work. Maybe . . . two months. Four of them. And a rose. I kept them."

"I'll need to see those messages," said Joan. "Do you have any idea who sent them?"

Emma shook her head. "Dunno . . . could be a patient."

A patient? Joan thought. For a moment, Joan's certainty about the husband faltered. Kay McLean had told her that her daughter was a psychologist. She worked at some kind of crisis center. Joan had once worked a case where a female patient became obsessed with her doctor and slashed the roof of his convertible when the doctor got engaged. It could be a similar thing in this case. A guy who went crazy when his shrink betrayed him by getting married. She had to explore the possibility.

"Where can I find these notes?" Joan asked.

"Ask Burke. Dr. Heisler. He's my boss," Emma said. "He knows about them."

"Thank you, Emma," said Joan as she stood up to leave. "You just concentrate on getting better."

The door to the room opened and a handsome but haggard-looking dark-haired man walked in.

"David!" Kay exclaimed.

Joan turned and eyed him. "Mr. Webster?" she said.

"Could I possibly see my wife now?" said David bitterly.

Emma's eyes opened at the sound of his voice. "David."

Joan stepped out of the man's way. She saw a worried look in Kay McLean's eyes. "I'm staying," Kay said firmly, though no one had asked her to leave.

David Webster walked gingerly over to Emma's bedside, looked down at her worriedly, and leaned over to kiss her. "Hey, baby," he whispered.

"She just got a sedative. Let her sleep," Kay warned her new son-in-law.

Emma looked up at David with eyes full of confusion. "David. Where were you? I was so afraid . . ."

David sank down in the chair beside her and lifted her hand, holding her fingers in his, and pressing his lips to them. "Shhh . . . Rest. I'm here. We'll talk later. You're safe now," he murmured. "I won't leave you."

Joan pulled open the hospital room door and then glanced back at the two of them. Emma closed her eyes and tears ran down the sides of her face. David wiped her tears gently away with his thumb. Joan frowned as she stepped out into the hallway.

CHAPTER 7

A Rustling sound nearby registered in her sleep, and Emma's eyes flew open, her heart pounding as if it would leap from her chest. She blinked at a woman wearing a shower cap and dressed in polyester pants and a tunic, carrying a tray of food. "Here we go," said the aide in a cheerful voice. "Breakfast. Better wake up, Prince Charming."

Emma turned her head on the scratchy hospital pillow, damp from tears she had shed in her sleep, and saw her husband. David was slumped in the visitor's chair, fast asleep, his head resting on his fist. He was unshaven and looked utterly exhausted. "David," she said.

David opened his eyes and jerked his head upright. In his dark eyes she saw confusion and sleepiness. But something else too. His gaze met hers and his eyes looked haunted, as if he had seen a ghost. "Breakfast is served," she said gently. She turned to the woman with the tray. "Could you put it down there?" she asked, pointing to the adjustable table on the other side of the bed.

"Okay. You be sure and eat now," said the nurse. "You need your strength. The doctor will be in shortly to see you."

Emma nodded and closed her eyes. "Okay," she said, although the familiar nausea of morning sickness was unsettling her stomach.

David shook his head and rubbed his unshaven face. Then he scraped the chair across to her bedside, stood up, leaned over the bed, and kissed her on the forehead. "Baby," he said. "How are you feeling?"

Emma took a deep breath to quell the nausea, shifted her leg, which felt as if it were on fire, and put a hand gingerly on her wounded side. "I've been better," she said. "I guess I fell asleep as soon as you got here last night."

David nodded and sat back down in the chair. "I watched you sleep for a little while. I was tempted to crawl into bed with you, but I didn't want to jostle all those stitches. I don't know when I passed out." He reached out and took her hand. "Not much of a wedding night."

Emma nodded sadly. His hand felt like the only warm thing in the whole room. "I'm glad you were here with me," she said. "I would have been afraid if I woke up alone."

"Emma, I don't know what to say. I should have been with you in that cabin. I never should have left you alone there . . ."

Tears began to leak out of Emma's eyes again. "It was terrible, David."

"I know," he said angrily. "I know it was."

"He was behind me with the ax, and I turned around . . ." Her voice faltered.

He squeezed her hand so hard that she almost yelped. "Don't," he said. "Don't think about it."

"I kept praying for you to come back."

David sighed. "I couldn't feel any more guilty. Believe me. If I could do it over . . . I went walking along the riverbank. You know, I was kind of filled up with all the events of the day. I was just thinking . . . actually I wasn't thinking. Just wandering, reveling in my good fortune. The sunset was so beautiful. I found this old duck blind my uncle John used to take us to. I climbed up on it to look at the water and I fell through where it was rotted. I could hear the gunshots. I was frantic to get out of there, but that only made it worse. By the time I got myself free the police had arrived. They were searching for your attacker, and instead, they found me."

"Did you see him?" she asked.

"Who?" David frowned at her.

"Him," she said, agitation in her voice. "The man . . . with the ax."

David hung his head. "No," he said. "I wish I had. He'd be a dead man now."

For a moment they were both silent. Then David stood up abruptly and came around to the other side of the bed.

"Be careful of the IV," she said.

He ducked around the pole and adjusted the table in front of her. "What are they giving you in that?" he asked.

"I don't know," she said. "If they told me, I don't remember. I was too out of it."

"Well, here, eat something," he said. "You need your strength."

"I'll try," she said.

He ripped the paper lid off the cup of apple juice and handed it to her. Emma took it from him and had a careful sip. Her stomach started to settle. "Were you able to help the police?" she said.

David snorted with laughter. "Help them?"

Emma, who had begun to chew on a piece of dry toast, blinked at him. She felt a sudden confusion. "They said you were at the station trying to help them."

David shook his head. "I was at the station being interrogated. Look, Emma, you have to face facts. As your husband, I'm the prime suspect."

"You?" she cried.

"The husband always is," David said. "I was at the scene. My fingerprints were on the murder weapon."

"The ax? But you were chopping wood," Emma protested.

David shook his head. "Didn't Atkins ask you about me last night?"

And then it came back to her. That lady lieutenant asking her if they'd argued. If he'd ever hurt her. Emma grimaced as she remembered the questions. They seemed so irrelevant to her that she had put them out of her mind. "She asked me if I could think of anyone who would want to hurt me. I thought about those anonymous letters. The ones I got at work . . . I told her about those."

David frowned and shook his head. "You shouldn't do that, Em."

Emma looked at him in surprise. "Do what?"

"Offer them information. My brother specifically told me not to do that."

"Phil said that? When did you talk to Phil about this?"

"I called him last night," David said.

"Oh, of course. I'm sure you needed to talk to your brother at a time like that," she said.

David hesitated, chewing the inside of his mouth. "Actually, it was a little more than that. I wanted his advice as a lawyer. Phil called a friend of his, an attorney named Yunger. The guy drove down and got me out of there. From now on, Em, all our communication with the police should go through Mr. Yunger."

Emma was silent. She set the crust of her toast back down on her plate and wiped the crumbs off her fingers, avoiding his gaze.

"What's the matter?" he asked.

"Why do we need an attorney? We have nothing to hide."

"Emma," he said, taking her hand in his again. "A man was killed. We need to protect ourselves," he said.

"From who?" she said.

"From the police."

Emma pulled her fingers away from his. She felt a little chill. "The police are trying to find the man who attacked me. Why do we need protection from them?"

He gazed at her for a long moment without replying. "The police are looking for an easy answer. I am that easy answer."

"That's stupid," she said. "We just got married. We love each other."

"You're rich. We have no prenup, remember?"

Suddenly, she felt almost guilty, as if her refusal to sign a prenup had led to this disastrous moment. "I didn't want to compromise us . . . our future. It seemed like a lack of faith . . ."

"I know that," he said. "But they don't. They see your money as a motive."

"David, no. That's ridiculous. They can't blame you."

"Emma, don't be naive. You read the paper. Innocent people get railroaded all the time. We have to avoid talking to the cops. Let the lawyer take care of it."

She stared at him steadily, although she was trembling inside. "But that seems wrong to me," she said.

David's expression was grim. "You need to be with me on this," he said.

The door to the room opened and a gray-haired man wearing a white lab coat over his shirt and tie came in. He frowned at Emma. "How are we doing here? Do you remember me? I'm Dr. Bell. I took care of you last night."

Emma blinked at the doctor. "I'm . . . I'm afraid I don't remember too much . . ."

"That's understandable. You were heavily sedated. I thought you'd like to know that you can probably go home tomorrow."

"Oh, that's great," said David. "Honey, that's great."

"Getting around is going to be difficult for a while," Dr. Bell cautioned. "The lacerations were much wider than they were deep. You had over two hundred stitches, and there will probably be some residual nerve damage. You may want plastic surgery at some point to minimize the scars. You needed three transfusions for the blood loss, which is significant, but the bigger danger we faced, actually, was that your body would shut down from shock. Luckily, the EMTs arrived in time and you resisted succumbing."

Emma shook her head. "I wasn't . . . I didn't do anything."

"We never underestimate the power of the will," said Dr. Bell.

"I appreciate all you did for me. And my baby," she said.

"That's my job," he said, but he was smiling. "As for your recovery, the good news is that no ligaments or tendons were cut. You're going to be in a lot of pain for a while. I'll give you medication for that of course."

"Is it all right to take this medication, with the pregnancy?" she asked.

"Perfectly safe," he said. "At the recommended dosage."

Emma nodded.

"With so many open wounds, we have to be alert to the possibility of infection. We have you on an antibiotic drip now," he said, pointing to the IV bag, which hung on a pole beside the bed. "Once you get home, you'll take an oral antibiotic. You have to keep your dressings clean. The nurse will show you how to change them. And you have to be careful of the sutures. No heavy lifting. No driving. Restricted activities."

"Don't worry, I won't let her do anything she shouldn't," said David.

Dr. Bell smiled. "All things considered, you were very lucky, young lady. Once the wounds heal, there should be no lasting effects."

Emma knew he was speaking clinically. As a physician. About her body. A lucky young lady. No lasting effects. She thought of the hooded man, swinging the ax above her head. She had to stifle the sob that rose to her throat.

CHAPTER 8

First thing Monday morning, Lieutenant Joan Atkins, dressed in a black suit and a striped turtleneck sweater, appeared at the Clarenceville Police Station. She introduced herself to the local chief of police and waited while the chief summoned a young detective named Trey Marbery and assigned him to work with the state police lieutenant on the investigation of the assault on Emma Webster. Joan noticed that Trey Marbery seemed to be the youngest detective in the squad and also the only one of mixed race. She understood the chief's choice. An older, white man would resist taking orders from a woman. Joan suppressed a sigh. Predictable, but tiresome all the same.

"What am I taking you away from, Detective?" she asked Marbery pleasantly.

The mocha-complected young man shrugged. "My biggest case is a hit-and-run. A retired professor from Lambert University who got killed last spring. The perp hit him head-on and left the old guy to die there like road-kill. I haven't made much headway though. It's frustrating. I could use a change of pace. I'm glad the chief assigned me to you."

"Well, I'll keep you busy," said Joan, smiling briefly. "I need someone who knows his way around this town." As she briefed Marbery, she was favorably impressed by the young man's focused attention and intelligent questions. They walked out of the station house together.

"Where are we headed first?" Marbery asked.

"The place Emma Webster works. I want to see those anonymous notes. Do you know where the Wrightsman Youth Center is?"

"Yes, ma'am," said Marbery.

"Good. You drive," said Joan.

The building that housed the Wrightsman Youth Crisis Center was a large, gray stone Colonial house that had once been the home of Noah Wrightsman, one of the richest men in Clarenceville. After his death, Wrightsman's heirs had wanted the tax write-off more than the grand old house. They'd donated it to Lambert University, which promptly turned it into the Youth Crisis Center.

Marbery parked in the gravel parking lot beside the center, and the two officers went around to the front door. Marbery pressed the bell. As they stood waiting, he observed, "I was here a few months ago."

"Really?" Joan asked. "What for?"

"Dr. Heisler's wife died. She took a header off the bridge into the river."

"Was it suspicious?"

Marbery shook his head. "Well, you always have to look at a suicide as a possible homicide. But she was a poet. Very . . . artsy and high-strung. Even though she'd just won some big literary award, she got into a depressive spiral, according to the people we interviewed. Still, she didn't wash up right away, so we were keeping the pressure on the husband. But when they found her, it was a suicide all right."

"What did the coroner say?"

"He said she actually died from the impact of the fall from the bridge."

"Sounds pretty straightforward," said Joan.

Trey nodded as a round-faced Hispanic woman answered the bell and said that Dr. Heisler was expecting them. "I'll take you to his office," she said.

Joan glanced into some of the rooms she passed in the hallways. There were teenagers watching TV or working on computers in the common rooms. The house was as silent as a library. "I expected this place to be noisy," she said to the woman who was leading them down the hallway.

Sarita Ruiz laughed. "You caught them early. A lot of them just took their medications. Give them a few hours."

They arrived at Dr. Heisler's door, and the woman indicated that they should go in. Burke Heisler was waiting for them, standing nervously in front of his desk. Joan was immediately struck by the contrast between the man's rough-hewn face and his well-cut suit. "Detective Marbery," Burke said grimly. "We meet again."

"Nice to see you again, sir," Trey said politely. "May I present Lieutenant Atkins of the state police."

"Good to meet you, Lieutenant," said Burke shaking hands. "Won't you have a seat?" Burke indicated a love seat and two chairs facing each other in front of a cold fireplace. The detectives each took a chair. "How can I help you?" he asked. "Anything I can do. Anything."

"Mrs. Webster told us that she was receiving some mysterious notes at work," said Joan. "She said she kept them here. We'd like to see them."

"My secretary can take you to her office, if you want to search it," said Burke.

Joan nodded to the younger detective. "Can you take care of that?"

Burke called Geraldine on the intercom, and Marbery left the office to meet her in the reception area.

"Dr. Webster told us that she showed the notes to you," Joan said.

Burke nodded. "She did."

"Was she concerned about them?" Joan asked.

Burke hesitated and then sat down on the love seat. "She was concerned. They made her anxious, of course."

"What about you? What did you think?"

Burke frowned. "I knew there was a possibility of erotomania."

"That's a . . . clinical term for obsession, isn't it?" asked Joan.

"Well, in its most extreme form, it's a psychosis. A person believes that the object upon whom they are passionately fixated returns their feelings. Even where there is ample evidence to the contrary. But generally speaking, the obsessed person does not remain hidden but makes himself known to the love object. Interferes in their day-to-day life, hounds them, threatening them with harm if they refuse to reciprocate their feelings."

"And this . . . delusion can lead to violence."

"Oh, absolutely," said Burke.

"So why didn't you alert the police to this situation," Joan asked, "when Mrs. Webster showed you these letters?"

Burke shook his head. "These notes didn't really fit the profile of a violent psychotic. And, as you will see, there are no threats in them. This isn't the first time I have encountered this sort of acting out in a facility populated by highly emotional adolescents. Besides, I know from experience that there is nothing the police can do about anonymous love notes."

"And there were no other incidents? Someone stalking her, Peeping Tom, anything like that?" Joan asked.

"Not that I know of," said Burke.

"Do you have any idea who sent these notes?" Joan asked. "Any of her patients have a history of this kind of . . . fixation?"

Burke shook his head. "None that I know of."

"I'll need a complete list of her patients," said Joan.

Burke nodded. "I can get that for you. Lieutenant Atkins, there is one thing I feel I have to mention to you."

"What's that?" Joan asked.

"We did have a situation here not long ago . . . Emma was treating an anorexic patient, and the girl's parents—her father specifically—took issue with Emma's . . . methods. They pulled the girl from the center, and she died shortly thereafter of her disease. The girl's father was extremely angry at Emma. He came to me, demanding that she be fired. I tried to reason with him, but when that didn't work, I had him barred from the facility."

Joan raised an eyebrow. "Mrs. Webster didn't mention this to me."

Burked sighed. "She doesn't know about it. Emma's confidence was shaken by the girl's death as it was. And, in my judgment, she had acted appropriately. I felt that the father was . . . in the wrong on this. So I ran interference. I am the director of this facility. The buck stops here, as they say."

Joan nodded and took out a pad and pen from her pocketbook. "This man's name?"

"Lyle Devlin. He's a music professor at Lambert. His daughter's name was Ivy. I need to be clear about this. I'm not accusing Mr. Devlin of anything. But he was extremely angry at Emma."

"I'll talk to him," said Joan, making a note of the name and slipping the pad back into her shoulder bag.

Marbery tapped on the door as he opened it. "Come in, Detective," said Burke.

Marbery, who was wearing disposable plastic gloves, brought a manila envelope to Joan, who, also donning gloves, opened it and pulled out the contents. Each note was short. Joan shuffled through them, reading certain phrases aloud.

"'In my dark dreams your face glows like a distant star. I try to fly to you. The pain of love is more than I can bear. How can you look through me and not see the secrets of my soul?' She seems to have inspired quite a passion in this guy," Joan observed.

"Passion can be dangerous," murmured Trey.

Joan nodded and replaced the notes in the envelope. Then she removed her gloves and tapped a pale, oval fingernail against the envelope. "Tell me, Dr. Heisler, you said that Mrs. Webster is a personal friend as well as a colleague."

"She was my wife's college roommate. As a matter of fact, I was the best man at Emma's wedding," said Burke.

"Really? So, you're friends with David Webster as well."

"We're friends from childhood. My family owned a casino, and his mother was a waitress at one of the casino restaurants. I went away to private school, but when I was home I used to hang around the restaurant kitchen, and sometimes David's mom would bring him with her to work. We became best buddies. We've remained friends all these years. Emma and David met at our home."

"Did you ever have any reason to suspect Webster's motives in marrying Emma Hollis?"

Burke recoiled from the suggestion. "No, of course not. What are you talking about?"

Joan studied the doctor's reaction. "Mrs. Webster is a wealthy woman. If she died, her husband would inherit her money."

"David?" Burke cried in disbelief. "No. That's out of the question. David doesn't care about money."

"I don't want to contradict you, Doctor, but if his mother worked as a waitress, I doubt he was raised in the lap of luxury. Maybe you don't care about money, but I suspect he probably does."

Burke shook his head. "You don't know him. He's always marched to his own drummer. No. He never had any patience with money-grubbing people or people who bragged about being rich. That's not who David is. I understand that most murder is domestic, but in this case, the answer has to lie elsewhere. Have you ruled out a random attack?"

"We haven't ruled out anything yet," said Joan.

"Well, you can forget about David," Burke insisted. "He would never hurt Emma. David is crazy about Emma."

Joan glanced at the envelope in her hand. "Is that an observation," she asked, "or a diagnosis?"

CHAPTER 9

Emma pressed her forehead against the passenger-side window of David's Jeep Cherokee as he drove. It was a gloomy November afternoon, the bare tree branches etched against the smoky, gray sky. The air had a tang that was restorative after the medicinal stuffiness of the recycled hospital air. The two hundred stitches she had received had made it impossible to move or breathe without pain the first twenty-four hours. Now, two days later, it was merely very difficult. A physical therapist had visited her room and showed her how to use a cane to minimize the pressure on her left side. "You'll get the hang of it," the therapist had said cheerfully. But when David had pulled the car up to the hospital entrance, she had nearly started to cry, wondering how she was going to manage climbing into the high front seat of the SUV. Then her husband had gone around to the trunk, opened it, and pulled out a plastic milk crate, which he placed by the open passenger door. When Emma had exclaimed with surprise over his thoughtfulness, he admitted that he kept the milk crate in the trunk for his mother, who was also unable to manage the front seat without a boost. So, with the aid of the crate, the first hurdle had been easily accomplished. But Emma knew that physical restrictions would be the least of her worries. There would be other woes, more taxing by far.

She realized, as she put a hand protectively across her abdomen, that she was lucky to be alive, lucky to have escaped, lucky that her baby was still safe inside her. She knew she should be grateful. But she was plagued by melancholy. After her initial relief that she had survived the attack, her spirits had begun to sink. A maniac, who was still on the loose, had attacked her, and a good man had lost his life trying to save her. Her honeymoon weekend in the woods had turned into a gory nightmare. She had always known that there was random violence in the world—impossible to ignore if you watched TV or read the papers. But being the victim of such a senseless attack was something else altogether. She had never really lived in fear. She always considered herself to be strong, and she thought of her strength as a shield. But now she knew better.

"Almost home," said David.

She turned to him and forced herself to smile. "I'll be glad to get back to our house," she said. "To our own bed."

"Well, you're not going to be able to make those stairs for a few days, maybe longer. You heard the doctor. I'll make up the bed for you downstairs." They had a guest room off the kitchen. David had his computer and his files in there and had claimed it for his office.

"But that's where you work. I don't want to disrupt your work space."

"It's only temporary," he said. "I don't mind."

"All right," she said doubtfully. "As long as you sleep downstairs with me."

"I'm not sure that's a good idea," he said. "I'd be afraid of hurting you. I don't want to take a chance of opening up those stitches."

The thought of sleeping alone downstairs filled her with panic. "I don't want to be by myself down there, David."

"No one's going to hurt you, honey. Whoever it was who attacked you is probably still in the Pine Barrens, looking for someone else to . . . another victim."

"I'm not saying it's rational. I'm just afraid, all right?"

"But there's nothing to be afraid of. It'll be all right—"

"It's not all right!" Emma cried. "Aren't I allowed to be afraid? Who wouldn't be after something like this?" she demanded.

"I'm sorry. Of course you are," he said. "Take it easy. You're not supposed to get upset. Maybe I can put up a cot or sleep on the sofa."

"I just can't do it by myself," she insisted.

"I get it, Em. I understand."

Emma forced herself to take a deep breath. "I'm sorry," she said. "I'm being a baby."

He reached over and put a reassuring hand on hers. "Hey, you've got a perfect right to be scared. You just lived through a nightmare. But once we get home, everything will feel better to you. We'll be there in no time. Just try to relax."

Emma nodded. "You're right. We're almost there."

"A few more blocks," he said.

Emma looked out the window at the quiet streets of Clarenceville as they drove toward their house. She pictured it in her mind's eye. Home. The house sat alone at the end of a wooded cul-de-sac, with no neighbors to block their views of the woods. It was only a rental—but she had fallen in love with the house the minute they walked into it. It was a two-story Arts and Crafts-style house, with wide mahogany woodwork that contrasted with the ecru, stuccolike walls, and the windows had angular patterns of pale stained glass. The William Morris printed fabrics and leather Mission-style antiques they'd bought suited the house perfectly. She'd even thought they might try to talk the owner into selling the house to them. But it seemed so unimportant right now.

She closed her eyes and rested her head against the head-rest. Home. She would feel better once she got home.

"Oh . . . hell," he said.

He had turned the corner onto their street. Emma sat up and opened her eyes. "What?" she asked. They had reached their secluded road and were headed for their house, which was just visible through the bare branches of the many trees that surrounded it. But instead of seeing their peaceful haven at the end of the street, they saw an assortment of haphazardly parked vehicles on either side of the road and a crowd milling at the edge of their front lawn. There were news vans blocking the driveway, and reporters with microphones and notepads assembled, waiting for them.

"What are we going to do?" she said, feeling her anxiety start to mount.

"Oh, here we go," said David bitterly.

Almost as if in answer to his words, one of the windbreaker-clad men holding a microphone in the driveway suddenly spotted their car and pointed. Every eye turned toward their car, and the reporters began to surge toward them.

David took a deep breath and continued driving slowly toward their home, not looking at the people who were swarming around the car, shouting questions at them.

Emma shrank from the passenger window, leaning against her husband and keeping her face turned away from the glass as he inched along, the reporters shouting and moving with him like a swarm of bees. The van was blocking his entry to the driveway.

"We can't get in!" said Emma.

David started to lower the window to call to the driver of the van, but a microphone was instantly shoved into the gap. "Jesus Christ." He raised the window as the reporter protested loudly about damage to his expensive equipment.

For a moment, David sat there fuming and then he pressed down on the horn. The blare of the horn was jarring, and Emma clapped her hands over her ears.

The driver of the van with a TV-station logo on the side looked startled to realize that the horn was meant for him. With an annoyed expression on his face, he finally mounted the driver's side and turned on the lights. David backed up just enough to let him get out of the way, and then he started to pull into the driveway. "Oh great, look who's here," he said. He pulled up abruptly and parked at the foot of the short walkway to the house.

Emma frowned. "Who?"

David pointed to the car already parked in their driveway. "That's Rory's rental car from the airport."

"Oh," said Emma, trying to sound surprised. But she wasn't really surprised. Her mother had rarely left her hospital room or the corridor outside of it.

David was swearing under his breath. "Of course, if we had a garage I could pull into it, but these old houses . . ."

Emma felt . . . chided. About the presence of her mother and about the old house. She didn't expect him to welcome her mother's visit, but the house was another matter. She loved the old house. She thought David did too.

"Stay right there," he said. "I'll come around and get you. They can't come onto our property, so just ignore the yelling."

Emma nodded.

David took a deep breath and opened the door of the car. Emma heard a babble of voices shouting questions at him. He slammed the door and pressed the remote to lock it. He walked around to her passenger door. She looked up at him through the window and he nodded grimly.

Emma hesitated and then began to open the door. He reached a hand in and Emma grabbed it. He opened the door a little bit more, and she slid out, feeling a searing pain in her leg and her side as she unfolded herself from the car where she had sat for an hour. She set her cane on the ground and leaned against it as David managed to get the door closed behind her.

"Emma, how are you feeling?" a woman's voice cried, using her first name in a way that felt intrusive and overly familiar.

"Don't look at them, and don't answer them," David said.

Is that more advice from Mr. Yunger? she wondered.

"Emma, do you know who the Pine Barrens killer is?" a bespectacled man holding a microphone cried out from the edge of the yard.

"What about you, Dave?" cried another man. "You have any comment about who tried to murder your wife?"

Emma glanced at David and saw that he was smoldering.

"Where were you when it happened, Dave?" another voice called out.

All of a sudden the front door to the house opened, and Rory, dressed in a green golf shirt and khakis, appeared on the doorstep. Rory wagged a finger at the assembled reporters. "All right. That's enough," he bellowed. "This woman is injured. You people gather up all your junk and get out of here."

"What do you know about this, sir? What is your relationship to the victim?" a reporter demanded, undaunted.

David steered Emma up the walk and into the house past Rory, who stood there, nearly blocking the doorway. Kay, who was waiting just inside the front door, held out her arms and carefully hugged her daughter.

"Please, Kay, let her sit down," said David.

Kay's eyes flashed at her son-in-law, but she released her daughter. David helped Emma to the sofa, easing her down onto a cushion.

"Dave, you can't let those people walk all over you," Rory said, draping his arm over Kay's shoulder.

David did not reply. "I'm going out to the car to get our bags," he told Emma.

Emma leaned back against the sofa and nodded.

"You poor kid," said Rory. "You look awful."

"I'm just sore," said Emma irritably. "It'll pass."

Kay, in a taupe Calvin Klein pantsuit, her platinum hair perfectly coiffed, sat down on the sofa beside Emma and massaged her hand between her own.

"Oh, Mom, everything hurts," said Emma. Stress and weariness had caught up with her. Tears rolled down her cheeks. They seemed to come and go without warning, like changes in the weather.

"Oh, my poor baby," said Kay.

"What are you doing here?" Emma asked. This morning, as Emma was getting ready to leave the hospital, Kay had announced to David that she wanted to stay with them and take care of her daughter. David had quickly quashed that plan. "I thought you two were going back to Chicago."

"We were," said Kay. "We are. But I wanted to make sure you were safely home. And I thought you might need help with all those flowers you got . . ."

"We gave all the flowers to other patients," said Emma. "David took care of it."

"Well, and Stephanie told me, when she came to see you at the hospital, that she was going to be bringing over a casserole for you when you got home. I wanted to make sure someone was here when she came by. And it was a good thing too. She just left a few minutes before you arrived. She sends her love."

"That was good of her," said Emma.

"Oh, and I remembered that um . . . your wedding presents were all still at the inn. So, we brought them over here for you." She pointed to the silver and gold wrapped and beribboned boxes, which were now piled in front of the cold hearth.

"Thanks, Mom. That was thoughtful," said Emma.

David came back into the house, carrying the bags. Emma gave him a wan smile and nodded encouragement as he mounted the stairs. Then she put a hand on her stomach and closed her eyes briefly.

"Those reporters act like a bunch of mad dogs," said Kay.

Emma sighed. "It's what they get paid for."

"Honey, can I get you a cup of tea?" Kay asked.

"I'm fine," Emma said.

Rory came over and perched on the edge of the armchair across from Emma. "You're not fine," said Rory in a low voice. "From what the police and the doctors told your mother, it's a miracle you're still alive."

"Actually, I'm alive because Claude Mathis came to my rescue. And got killed for his kindness." Emma shook her head. "I've been thinking about this. I want to do something for his family. His son. He has a teenage son. I want you to arrange for some financial support for the boy. Just move it from one of my investment accounts."

"There will be plenty of time for that when you're feeling better," said Rory in a placating tone.

"That family is suffering. I want you to do it right away," Emma insisted.

"You might want to give some further thought to the actual arrangements. Do you want a trust account or a small investment portfolio or—"

"Isn't this your area of expertise? Please, just take care of it," Emma cried.

"All right," said Rory. "All right. Of course. Consider it done. I'll get the papers together."

"Thank you," said Emma.

Kay rubbed her tanned, well-manicured hands together. "Emma, Rory and I have been talking this over and . . . we think it might be best if you came home with us. Come back to Chicago with us, where we can take care of you."

"This is my home. I'm fine right here, Mom," Emma said.

Kay and Rory exchanged a glance.

"What?" Emma asked indignantly. "What's the look for?"

"Nothing. I would just feel that you're safer if you were with us," Kay said.

"David will take care of me," said Emma.

"We don't know David that well," said Kay.

"He's my husband, Mother," Emma said in a sharp tone.

"Don't take that tone with your mother, now. She's only thinking of your well-being. Let me tell you something," Rory said, pointing his index finger at Emma, "from a man's perspective. A lot of men don't view pregnancy the same way that women do. They start thinking about the good old days when they were free and irresponsible. Maybe your husband had second thoughts about this marriage."

Emma's mouth dropped open. "What are you saying . . . ?"

"I'm just telling you what the police are saying," said Rory.

"How dare you?" said Emma. "You, of all people."

Rory stared at her without flinching. Kay did not seem to notice. She reached for Emma's wrist. Emma made a fist. "Come home with us, Em," Kay crooned. "Stay with us until . . . they've made an arrest. It will give me a chance to fuss over you. You're in no condition to work. It won't be for that long. We'll take good care of you. It'll be fun. Like old times."

Emma stared at her mother in disbelief. "I'm not going anywhere. This is insulting. I don't need to go anywhere. This is my house."

"We just want to protect you, Emma," Rory insisted.

"I don't need your protection."

"Sweetheart," Kay protested. "Look at yourself. You certainly do need protection. You were nearly killed."

"By some maniac in the Pinelands," Emma cried. "Not by my husband."

Kay's eyes glistened. "Oh please, honey. Let me help you."

David came down the stairs and into the living room. He glared at Kay and Rory. "We don't need your help. Pardon me for eavesdropping, but I don't appreciate being slandered in my own home. This is my house, and you two should be leaving."

"David," said Emma. "My mother didn't mean any harm."

"Do you agree with them? Do you want to go with them?" he cried. "I mean, if you think they're right, then go ahead."

Rory stood up stiffly. "Kay," he said, "I think we should be going."

"Sweetie, please," Kay pleaded.

Emma looked down at her hands in her lap and shook her head.

"At least hire a nurse who can take proper care of you."

"I can take of her," David insisted.

"That's right, Mom," said Emma. "I have David. I don't need anyone else."

Kay's eyes welled with tears, and she reached out to touch Emma, but Emma stiffened. "I'll be worrying about you night and day. Please, just call me, darling. Let me help," Kay pleaded.

"I'll be fine," Emma whispered. "Go on."

Emma did not watch them leave. She couldn't bear to see the anguish in her mother's eyes.

David followed them to the door, closed and locked it behind them. He came back into the living room. "Where are the sheets?" he asked, avoiding her worried gaze. "I'm going to make the bed down here."

"I'm sorry about that, David. My mother . . . she's . . . just . . . so afraid for me."

"Upstairs linen closet?" he asked.

"Yes," she said. "Are you mad at me?"

"No," he barked. Then his face softened. "No. You rest," he said more gently.

Emma leaned back against the sofa. David was right. Even if they were worried about her, her mother and Rory had no business coming in here and virtually accusing him. Especially Rory. The thought of his self-righteousness, considering what she knew about him, made Emma furious. She was clenching her fists so tight that her fingernails were gouging her palms. Stop ruminating about this. Think about something else, she told herself.

She turned her head and looked at the mountain of wedding gifts. There were boxes of all sizes. She knew she should be thrilled at the thoughtfulness of all the people who had given her and David these gifts, but at the moment all she felt was overwhelmed at the prospect of writing all those thank-you notes. Don't be like that, she chided herself. These are the people who care about you the most. This pile of presents is a sign of their love for you.

That thought made her feel better. It wasn't as if she had felt alone in the last couple of days. David had been in the hospital room and had answered most of her calls to keep her from getting exhausted, but she was aware of the support of the people in her life. The flowers, the cards, the brief visits. She reached for the nearest, smallest box and began to untie the ribbon. There was no card on the outside of the gift wrap, and she hoped that the sender had had the good sense to put it inside the package. She didn't want to end up with a bunch of presents with the giver's name missing. The ribbon fell away and she unfolded the distinctive gold and white paper and saw that the box came from Kellerman's, an upscale housewares and jewelry store on Main Street that had lost much of its distinguished trade to the Internet and expensive catalogs. The box wasn't large or heavy. A silver-plated egg timer she thought, with a hint of amusement. She lifted the lid, and as she did, an odd, unpleasant smell reached her nostrils. As she was pulling out the paper shavings, she realized that she was making a mistake. But it was too late. The packing was removed and she was gasping.

Nestled on a cushion of paper shavings was a silver dish in the shape of a scallop shell. Resting in the dish was the matted fur and stiffened body of a mouse, now dead, its tail curved to fit in the box, its beady eyes still open.

CHAPTER 10

The sound of a piano being expertly, but intermittently, played drifted through an open window of the white, Gothic-style Victorian cottage, which looked more like a small church than a house. A Mazda convertible sat in the driveway behind a minivan. Lieutenant Joan Atkins knocked on the arched front door and waited with Trey Marbery by her side. In a moment a large, blond woman opened the door. Her heavily mascaraed eyes were a dazzling blue and her lips were full. Her hair was arranged in an upswept, tousled style that made her look as if she had simply put a clip in it when she rolled out of bed. She was wearing a nearly sheer voile blouse that revealed an impressive décolletage, and tight blue jeans that were unflattering to her spreading figure. She looked from Joan to Trey and gave them a vague, sleepy smile. She had dimples in both cheeks.

"Morning," she said in a sweet, high voice.

"Mrs. Devlin?" Lieutenant Atkins asked.

"That's me," she said. Her voice was slightly slurred, but she did not smell of alcohol. And her eyes were unfocused, but not bloodshot. Tranquilizers or sleeping pills, Joan thought, not unkindly. A bereaved mother might well need some pharmaceuticals to get through the day.

"I'm Lieutenant Joan Atkins of the state police. This is Detective Marbery of the Clarenceville police force. We're looking for your husband."

Immediately the woman's sleepy eyes widened in alarm. "Why? What's the matter? Is Alida all right?"

"Who's Alida?"

"My daughter."

"This isn't about Alida. We have a few routine questions," Joan said. "Is your husband here?"

"Yes, he's working in his study. He's writing music."

"Before I speak to him, can you tell me, Mrs. Devlin, where your husband was Saturday night."

The woman looked confused. "What?"

"It's a simple question," said Joan.

"Saturday night? I don't remember," she said. Joan could see that she was earnestly searching her mind. "My memory," she apologized.

The piano music stopped and the dark figure of a man appeared in the corridor behind her. "Risa, who's at the door?" he demanded.

The woman frowned. "Two policemen. Well, a policeman and a policewoman."

The man walked up behind her. He was in his forties with stubbly black hair sprinkled with gray, and wire-rimmed glasses. He was wearing a black leather vest and a black turtleneck.

"They want to know where you were Saturday night," said the woman, backing up against her husband's chest.

"I hope you told them I was right here."

"I couldn't remember Saturday," she said apologetically.

"We rented that Italian movie, remember?"

She squinted. "That's right. You were here. He was," she said, nodding.

"What's this about?" Devlin asked.

Joan gazed at him. "Professor Devlin?" she said. "I'm Lieutenant Atkins of the state police. This is Detective Marbery. May we talk to you?"

Lyle Devlin pushed the glasses up on his nose. His facial expression did not change. "All right," he said. "Follow me. Excuse us, Risa."

Joan edged past the blowsy woman in the doorway. She could smell heavy, cloying perfume.

"Come on into the conservatory," said Devlin. "I'm composing on the piano."

Joan and Trey followed the man down the dim hallway to a chilly, glassed-in room with shabby wicker furniture, shelves of books and sheet music, and a large piano, which dominated the space. "No classes today?" Joan asked.

"I have some flexibility in my schedule," said Devlin with a thin smile. "The university understands that I need time for my own work. Have a seat," said Devlin, indicating a chair and a window seat. Joan sat down in the wicker chair. Trey perched on the window seat. Devlin sat facing them on the piano bench.

"Now, what can I do for you?" Devlin asked evenly. "Why in the world would you be concerned about my whereabouts last Saturday?"

"Mr. Devlin, you had a daughter named Ivy who died recently?" Joan asked.

Devlin, who had been slouched on the flat bench, straightened and stared at Joan. "Why are you asking me about Ivy?"

"I'm sorry to bring up a painful subject, but apparently you felt that Ivy's psychologist may have been partly to blame for her death. Dr. Webster."

Devlin stared at her for a moment. "I don't know any Dr. Webster," he said.

"She used to be called Dr. Hollis," Trey said. "Before her marriage."

"Oh, right," said Devlin, as if it had just dawned on him. "She was the one who was attacked in the Pine Barrens."

Joan studied Devlin. The man was acting as if this was the first time he'd made the connection. Considering all the press coverage, Joan didn't buy that. "There was an attempt on Dr. Webster's life," Joan said. "She narrowly escaped death."

"What has this got to do with Ivy?" Devlin asked.

"We have information that you were very angry at Dr. Webster after your daughter's death. Threats were made."

The man's expression became stony. "Who told you that?"

"Is it true?"

Lyle Devlin looked away from the detective. "I may have . . . vented my anger," he said at last. "I was out of my mind with grief at the time. And I acted like a man who was out of his mind."

"Why did you blame Dr. Webster?" Joan asked.

Devlin turned his head and stared out at the bare trees in the backyard. Then he looked back at Joan. "Detective, do you have any children?"

Joan pursed her lips. She did not like Lyle Devlin. It wasn't rational; it was visceral. But this question, which she had heard many times before, was one that really peeved Joan Atkins. Suspects who overestimated their own cunning, and underestimated hers, always tried to get her on their side with some variation of this question. *You and me, Detective, aren't we both . . . fill in the blank . . . parents, working people, dog lovers?* "Why did you blame her, Mr. Devlin?"

Arms crossed over his chest, Devlin sighed. Joan noted that he was wearing scuffed engineer's boots and a Mexican silver and leather bracelet. Like a student. "How can I explain this, Lieutenant? My daughter had anorexia. This is a special kind of hell for a parent. A child who refuses to eat. Can you imagine it? My wife cooked every kind of treat for her, coaxed and cajoled her. Tried everything. We brought her to the Wrightsman Youth Center out of desperation. We put our faith in Dr. Hollis. But she was, alas, only human. It's true that I did blame her, but it was simply because I needed someone to blame."

"But your daughter must have been ill for quite some time. Surely she saw other doctors besides Dr. . . . . Webster,"

Trey interjected. Joan glanced at the younger detective and then back at Devlin.

Devlin took a deep breath. "You're right. She was far from the first. But Dr. Webster was the last doctor whom Ivy saw. We took Ivy out of the center because we found Dr. Webster's methods . . . unacceptable. Shortly after Ivy came home from the center, her condition worsened. She was admitted to the hospital, but it was too late."

"I'm so sorry," said Trey sincerely.

"At the time I felt," said Devlin slowly, "that Dr. . . . Webster drove us away with her . . . intrusive and . . . unproven form of treatment. I suppose I believed that if Ivy had been . . . cared for differently, she might have . . . been able to recover."

Joan could see the anger that still lingered behind Lyle Devlin's carefully worded explanation. "So you're saying that you no longer hold Dr. Webster responsible," said Joan.

Devlin looked at her directly. "My daughter died of anorexia, Detective Atkins, and I was not able to prevent it. I blame myself for that."

Joan understood that Devlin had suffered the most grievous loss a parent could suffer. But something about the professor's mea culpa sounded . . . unconvincing to Joan's ears. Clearly, Devlin had been forced to reconsider his own behavior, to come to terms with why he had behaved as he did. He'd figured it out, and he could explain it in a most cogent fashion. But that resentment of Emma Webster was still there, not too far below the surface. Joan would bet her badge on it.

"So you maintain that you were home here Saturday night between the hours of, say, six and ten o'clock?"

Devlin glowered at her. "I don't *maintain* it," he said in an insulted tone. "I was at home with my family. My wife told you that as well."

After you told her what to say, Joan thought. In truth, his wife hadn't really seemed to remember. Joan stood up, and Trey followed suit. "All right, well, thank you for your time, sir."

Devlin rose stiffly from the piano bench and indicated that the two officers should precede him through the door. But, as Joan started to leave, Devlin suddenly touched the sleeve of Joan's jacket. "My wife takes tranquilizers to help her get through the day. Ivy's death was . . . it nearly destroyed her. Sometimes, because of the medication, she forgets things. I'm begging you, Lieutenant," he whispered, "not to bring up Ivy's death to my wife. It's an understatement to say that it is a painful subject for her."

"There's no need for that," said Joan, looking down at the hand on her sleeve.

Devlin quickly removed his hand. "Thank you," he said.

Joan could feel the professor watching her as she and Trey walked down the hallway toward the front door. Risa Devlin emerged from one of the rooms and rushed to open the front door for them.

"Is everything all right?" she asked.

Joan nodded, starting out the door. "Sorry to bother you."

"It's no bother," she assured her. "As long as everything's all right."

Trey saw the anguish in her anxious eyes and wanted to reassure her. "Just fine, ma'am," he said. Trey followed Joan out the door and fell into step with her as they crossed the road. "What a horrible fate, to have a kid die like that. Talk about feeling helpless."

Joan did not reply.

"What did you think?" Trey asked the senior officer as he aimed the remote to unlock the doors of his car.

Joan gazed back at the little chapel-like house and noted that the sound of piano chords had not resumed. "I think he's hiding something," she said.

* * *

The chime of the doorbell awoke Emma from a dream that she was being chased. She groaned as consciousness brought the awareness of her injuries back to her. She had slept little and badly during the night, but at least, while she was asleep, she did not feel physical pain. The bed quivered as David got up from the cot he had set up beside her bed. She reached out a hand to touch him, but he was already out of the room. Emma closed her eyes again, feeling the throbbing ache of her wounds in her side and her thigh. She needed to get up and take something for the pain, but it would require mustering all her will to get out of the bed. As she lay there, she couldn't help thinking of the box she had opened last night with its repulsive contents. David had nearly fallen down the stairs rushing to reach her when she'd cried out for him. Grimacing with distaste, he had taken the box, carried the dead creature outside and thrown it away in the woods behind the house. He had tossed the box and the silver dish into the outdoor garbage can. Don't think about it, he told her, when he came back into the house. Easier said than done.

David reappeared in the doorway of their makeshift bedroom. He was barefoot, wearing only his pajama pants, and frowning.

"Who was it?" Emma asked.

"Your nurse," he said. "She's waiting in the foyer."

"My nurse? What nurse?"

David glanced behind him. "The private duty nurse your mother and stepfather hired to take care of you. She's got an I.D. badge and all her paperwork, including written orders from Rory for her to show up here and only talk to you."

Emma pulled her wrapper from the end of the bed and tied it around her. "Let me speak to her."

David turned and gestured to the nurse to join them. "I'm going upstairs to throw on some clothes," he said. "Send her on her way. We don't need some stranger hanging around here, Emma. I can take care of you."

He stepped out of the doorway, and a small, fortyish woman with short, graying hair and silvery eyes took his place. She was wearing sneakers, jeans, and a gray sweatshirt, and had a backpack slung over her shoulder. "Good morning, Mrs. Webster," she said, unsmiling. "I'm Lizette Slocum."

"Nice to meet you. But I think there's been a misunderstanding," said Emma. "I mean, I didn't know you were coming."

The older woman had a cool, steady gaze. "I'm a private duty nurse. Your parents hired me to stay with you."

"Well, I'm not really sick," said Emma. "I just have to take it easy. So I don't actually need the services of a nurse."

"I also have a black belt in tae kwon do," said Lizette. "Your stepfather was very specific. He wanted someone here for your protection as well."

"Protection? My husband is here!"

"That's what he wanted," Lizette insisted.

David returned to the small room, buttoning up his shirt. "Have we straightened this out?" he asked.

"Mrs. Slocum . . ." said Emma.

"It's Lizette. Call me Lizette."

"Lizette, could you wait in the other room for a minute. I need to talk to my husband."

Lizette obediently withdrew, but before they could confer, the telephone on the desk rang. David picked it up and barked an irritable "Hello." Then his whole demeanor seemed to change as he recognized the voice of the caller.

"Nevin, how's it hanging?" David joked in the false tone of voice he always used when he spoke to Nevin McGoldrick, the editor of *Slicker*.

"The wedding. Yeah, it was fine. Everything's fine," David said. "What's up?"

Fine? Emma thought.

David hesitated a fraction of a second. "Oh damn. Right. I'm sorry. I was . . . distracted by all the . . . excitement here." Then he said, "Sure. Let me get a piece of paper." He flipped the switch on the desk lamp.

Emma stared at her husband as he rummaged on the desktop. He located a piece of paper and a pen and began to write on it. "Uh-huh. Okay. Sure. Right. Great. I'll be there. Sure. Bye."

David punched the off button and brought the phone back to where she was sitting up on the bed. He kneeled down carefully beside her so as not to jar her. "That was Nevin. Giving me the details about my interview with Bob Cheatham, that producer from L.A. Do you remember I told you about it?" he said.

"I remember. When is it?" she asked anxiously.

"Actually, it's today. He wants me to run up to New York and meet with this guy at Le Bernardin for lunch, and then I'll be right back home."

"You're going to leave me alone here?" she cried.

"No, of course not. I'll get someone to stay with you. I'll call around. Maybe Birdie can come over. Leave my mother for a little while."

"Birdie. She's a frail, old lady. What's she going to do if he comes back?" Emma cried.

"Who?"

Tears welled in Emma's eyes.

"Is that what you're worried about?" he asked. "The guy with the ski mask? Honey, he's not going to come here. Look, the greatest likelihood is that he's some nut who picked you at random. We can't be afraid to live our lives."

"You don't know that. I could be a target. What about all those notes I got? And that disgusting wedding present. It could all be the same person. Besides, you're not the one who was attacked. The one whose life is in danger."

"You don't have to remind me of that," he said quietly.

Emma looked at him balefully. "David," she said, "couldn't Nevin get someone else? Doesn't he know what happened to me?"

David ran his hand over his unruly hair. "I guess we didn't make the news in New York. You know the Big Apple. If it didn't happen there, it didn't happen."

"Why didn't you say anything to him?" she asked. "I was almost killed."

"I'll tell him about it," said David, like a child promising to do a chore. "But knowing Nevin, he won't care anyway. He's not interested in my problems. He's interested in my getting this interview. And I'm lucky he assigned it to me."

"But today? Does it have to be today?"

"Believe me, I would rather not do it today. But the guy is only going to be in New York for a day or two."

"Well, fine. You go then," she said petulantly. "And I'll tell Lizette Slocum that I need her to stay here after all. At least she knows something about self-defense. It's a good thing my mother was concerned about me."

David frowned at her. "What does that mean? That I'm not? I wouldn't have left you alone. Of course I wouldn't."

Emma ignored his protest. "I think I am going to call Lieutenant Atkins and tell her about the . . . wedding gift. I had nightmares all night about opening that box. I kept dreaming that it was sent by the man in the mask."

"I know you did. You were restless all night," he said.

Emma could see the dark circles under his eyes, and immediately she felt guilty. "David, I just . . . I feel like the police need to know about this."

"But, baby, you know what Mr. Yunger said. We can't talk to the police. I thought we agreed that we were not going to talk to them."

Emma stared at him. "I never agreed."

David looked at her ruefully and then looked away.

"I have to call them, David," she said.

"You don't get it, Emma. They're not looking at anybody else but me."

"Well, this will give them somewhere else to look," she insisted. Then she hesitated. "What's that? Do you hear water running?"

David frowned, got up off the bed, and looked out the door. Lizette had found a watering can under the sink and was filling it. "I thought I'd water your plants before they all died," she said.

David shook his head and turned back to Emma. "Lizette is watering the plants."

"They do need it," Emma said with a wry smile. She extended a hand to him, but he did not reach for it. She pulled it back. "David, the wedding present may have fingerprints or something. Something that could help the police find the man who attacked me."

"Do what you have to do," he said. "I'm going to get ready."

Stung by his rebuff, Emma started to pull herself up and ease her bandaged legs out of the bed. Every movement was torture.

"Just a minute," said David. "What are you doing?"

"I need to get my pills," she said.

"I'll get your pills for you," he said.

"I don't want to depend on you," she said stubbornly.

David stared at her for a long minute. "Thanks, Emma," he said. "That's just great."

CHAPTER 11

Audie Osmund's stiff joints told him what the dark, low-ering sky also portended. A storm was on its way. The wind whipped leaves around the desolate clearing where the Zamskys' cabin stood. The crime scene tape was still up around the perimeter of the place, but Audie batted it away like a pesky fly. He climbed the few steps and opened the cabin door, stepping inside. Audie grimaced as he looked around. The walls and floor were still stained with blood, and the smell of putrefaction hung in the air.

He kept returning to this place, walking through the crime in his mind. The killer had taken the ax, which was out on the woodpile. According to the young lady, Emma, her husband had left it there when he was chopping wood. The ax was no longer there. The forensic team from the state police had bagged it and taken it away.

The killer had climbed these stairs and come into the house. Waited, hidden, until Emma entered the main room, and made a fire, lit the candles. Audie scratched his head, thinking about the first blows that were struck. She had been on the floor, near the edge of the sofa. The splintered remains of the canoe paddle, with which she had tried to protect her-self, also had been bagged up and removed by the state police.

Audie shook his head, thinking about it. She fought back, Audie thought. She was one tough little lady. She even managed to get a hold of the dead hunter's gun and shoot at the guy. How many women would have the presence of mind to do that? he wondered.

Of course her bravery wasn't any help to Claude Mathis, whose funeral was tomorrow. Tomorrow Audie would have to face Claude's family and admit he was no closer to an arrest than he had been on the night Claude had been killed.

Audie didn't see a lot of killings in his part of the Pine Barrens. Last year a guy got drunk in a bar and shot his cousin. And two domestic disturbances ended in homicide in the last few years. Well, three, if you counted Shannon O'Brien, the pretty little Irish girl who "disappeared" one night after working her shift at a local gas station. Audie thought of that as a domestic because her boyfriend, Turk, was a known drug user with a mean temper. Turk's brother had provided him with an alibi for the night his colleen entered the ranks of the missing. Audie didn't believe it but couldn't disprove it. But no, he was sure that was not a random killing. It was true that people around here didn't like strangers very much, and sometimes, they'd wave a gun around and holler, but nothing like this. Nothing like this gruesome crime.

The floor behind him creaked. Audie let out a cry and reached for his gun.

"Don't shoot," protested a female voice.

Audie whirled around and stared at the woman in the doorway. She had washed-out skin with no makeup, short black hair, and was dressed in a shapeless, green plaid wool shirt, jeans, and muck boots. Outside the door, Audie heard the sound of a nervous whinny. He peered over her shoulder and saw a large bay horse tied to a tree.

"Excuse me," she said, "but I saw the car. Aren't you Chief Osmund?"

Audie drew himself up and frowned at her. "I'm Chief Osmund. Who are you?"

"Oh me? My name's Donna Tuttle. My son and I live in the old Fiore house about a quarter mile from here. We're actually the next house over the rise. That there is Sparky," she said, indicating the horse, who was shaking his head, trying to rid himself of the bridle. "Weather's making him nervous." The woman stepped into the cabin. Audie put up a hand to stop her, but he was too late.

"Oh my God," she cried out, clapping a hand over her mouth.

Audie sighed and looked back into the blood-spattered room. "Why don't we step outside?" he said.

The woman began to gag. Audie caught her under the elbow and helped her down the steps. "Oh my God," she said, gasping. "Those poor people."

Audie nodded grimly. "It isn't pretty."

Donna Tuttle took a deep breath and straightened up, recovering her composure. "I'm sorry about that," she said. "Usually I got a pretty strong stomach. My husband was a hunter, you know. Yeah." Her sad gaze drifted. "He always planned to retire here. Butch was a fireman up in Trenton. He got killed fightin' a fire last year when a roof collapsed on him."

"I'm very sorry," said Audie sincerely.

Donna Tuttle acknowledged his sympathy with a nod. "You know if he had retired when he was eligible, he wouldn't have even been in that building. He already had twenty-five years on the job when it happened. Of course, he started really young. We were just kids when we got married and he joined the department."

Audie nodded patiently. "Mrs. Tuttle," he said when she stopped to take a breath, "you say you're the next house over. Were you there Saturday night when this crime occurred?"

Donna Tuttle nodded eagerly. "I sure was. My boy and I were both home. One of your officers came and questioned us. A nice young man named uh . . . I forget. Roberts, maybe?"

"Revere. Gene Revere," said Audie.

"That's right," said Donna. "He didn't tell us what happened, of course. He just wanted to know if we'd seen or heard anything."

"And did ya?" Audie asked. "Anyone lurking around. Any strange noises?"

"No, I sure didn't," said Donna regretfully. "We tried to think of anything, but no. We didn't even hear the shots. The wind must have been blowing in the other direction. We heard the police arriving, of course. Can't miss all those sirens."

Audie sighed. "No, I guess not."

"But after that, of course, I paid plenty of attention to the news about it. That's why I stopped when I saw your car. I wanted to mention something. I was listening to the radio this morning and they had a recap on the local news of everything that's happened, because of that hunter's funeral tomorrow. And the reporter said something that got me thinking."

"About what?" Audie asked.

"Well, the reporter said that the couple had come here for a honeymoon weekend, that the husband hadn't visited this place since boyhood."

"That's right," said Audie.

"Well, a few months ago, I can't remember if it was late spring, early summer. I remember there was flies, so it could have been summer—"

"What about it," Audie interrupted impatiently. This woman could talk a hole through a pot.

"We ride by here all the time. Although I don't like to ride by here as much anymore because it gives me the creeps, you know?"

"So, you were saying," Audie prodded.

"Well, usually, the place is empty," she said.

"Right," said Audie.

"But this one time I was surprised because there was a guy here. Naturally I didn't want to be rude, 'cause you don't come across that many people in these woods. So I said 'Hey'

101

and he said 'Hey.' And you know, we remarked about the weather. It might have been summer, now that I think of it."

Audie pursed his lips and silently counted to ten.

"Anyway, I asked him if he bought the place. And he said no, that the place belonged to his uncle."

Audie felt a shiver of interest. "His uncle? Are you sure about that?"

"Yeah," said Donna. "So when I heard that on the radio this morning about him not being here since he was a kid, I thought hmmm . . . that's strange."

"He told us he hadn't been here in years," said Audie, excitement in his voice. "That's exactly what he said. Hadn't been here in years. That's a lie, right there."

"Of course, the uncle could have more than one nephew," Donna pointed out.

Audie's face fell. "That's right. This Webster has a brother. He's a lawyer. But he lives out west somewhere."

Donna Tuttle nodded.

"Did he introduce himself?" Audie asked.

Donna Tuttle grimaced. "He did, but I'm not much for names. I honestly don't remember what he said his name was."

Audie looked crestfallen.

"But I think it might have started with a *D*. Because, I'm Donna. So I would remember the *D*."

Audie tried to conceal his eagerness. "Would you be willing to come down to the police station and look at some pictures for me?" Audie asked.

"Sure. I can do that. Sure."

"Let me speak to this man again. See if he continues to deny being here."

"Well," said Donna. "I didn't know if I should even bother you with this, 'cause it was such a small thing, but when I saw your car going by I thought I'd follow you and tell you," said the woman brightly. "Just in case."

"Thank you, Mrs. Temple."

"Tuttle," she said.

"Mrs. Tuttle. Thank you very much for coming forward."

"Glad I could help," she said. She untied the horse, stuck the toe of her muck boot into the stirrup, and hoisted herself up on the horse's back. "I hope you get him."

"Oh we will," said Audie, and his heart felt lighter than it had in a while. "By the way, this fellow. Was he alone when you saw him?"

Donna Tuttle shrugged as she pulled the horse's reins to get him back on the trail. "I didn't see anybody, but now that you mention it, I have a feeling there was somebody with him. I don't know why. Is it important?"

"It could be," said Audie.

"Well, if he was scopin' the place out, he'd probably come alone, wouldn't he?"

Audie nodded grimly. "That's what I'd do."

* * *

After David left, Lizette did a careful, thorough job of changing Emma's bandages, all the while recounting the story of her life. She explained that she was a widow, that her young husband died in a car wreck when she was twenty-five, and she'd never remarried or had kids. She was new to the area. She lived alone, liked her independence, and was hoping someday to retire to the Florida Keys because she enjoyed fishing. At Emma's request, and under protest, she went upstairs and retrieved some clothes for her, in case Emma felt like getting dressed. "You don't need to get dressed," Lizette advised her.

Too weary to read, Emma sat up, numbly watching morning talk shows on television while Lizette worked around her, over Emma's protests, straightening up and dusting the house. The pain medication soon sent Emma back to bed for a nap. When Emma awoke, Lizette announced that it was lunchtime and prepared her soup and a sandwich. After lunch Lizette said that she was going to change the beds.

"We only slept on those sheets for one night," Emma protested. "It's not necessary."

"Let me be the judge of that," Lizette said. She disappeared into the bedroom and emerged with her arms full of sheets. "Where's your washer?"

"Down in the basement," Emma said.

"Do you have other sets of sheets?" Lizette asked suspiciously.

"In the upstairs linen closet," said Emma. "I wish you wouldn't do all this."

"I don't like to sit idly," said Lizette, inclining her head toward the basement door. "I'm not one of those aides who will sit and watch TV all day. I prefer to earn my money."

And then the energetic Lizette descended the stairs to the laundry area. Emma sighed and began to hobble around the house in her bathrobe. She leaned on her cane and looked out every window at the ominous sky, clutching in her hand a slip of paper with the phone number of the police department on it. As soon as David had walked out, she had looked up the number and written it down.

She understood that David felt under siege, unfairly targeted by the police. But he was turning it into a test of her loyalty. And ultimately, she knew she had to put her own safety first. And that of her baby. Still, several times she picked up the phone and then replaced it. She knew how betrayed he would feel if she went to the police behind his back. Of course, sometimes innocent people were railroaded. But David was taking the lawyer's advice to avoid the police too literally. Emma felt sure that the evidence on that gift box could be important.

This might help to clear your husband, she reassured herself as she limped over to the phone in the kitchen and dialed the number on the slip of paper with trembling fingers, only to learn that Lieutenant Atkins was not at the station. Emma gave the receptionist her information and then hung up the phone, sitting down on one of the kitchen chairs. Now I wait, she thought. She imagined David coming home, just as the police were showing up at the house. The look of betrayal on his face.

No, don't think about it. Your own safety comes first, and if your husband doesn't see it that way, that's his problem. Over and over her thoughts returned to the horrific wedding gift. What if the sender was, in fact, her attacker? He might have left traces of himself, fingerprints or hairs or something, in the dish or on the box that the police might be able to trace. But the longer it sat outside in the trash can, the more likely it was that the evidence would be contaminated.

She glanced out the window. The day was growing gloomier by the minute. She needed to go outside and retrieve it from the trash can, as much as she dreaded the thought. If it rained, and the lid was even partly loose, any evidence might be destroyed altogether. She pushed herself to her feet. Get dressed, she thought. It'll make you feel more . . . in control.

She ran a comb through her long, honey-blond hair and skinned it into a knot at the nape of her neck. She examined her face in the bathroom mirror. Her skin was waxy, and there were circles around her eyes. She dabbed some makeup on the dark shadows and put on some lipstick. Then she limped into the bedroom and put on the black, V-necked dress made of a light jersey in a wide, A-line style, which Lizette had brought downstairs at her request. She had bought the dress for late in her pregnancy, but she decided to wear it now because it was voluminous and didn't press on her wounds. She pulled it down gingerly over her head. All right, she thought. That will do for trash picking.

She walked to the back door and opened it, inhaling deeply of the smoky, damp November day. Lizette's voice drifted up the cellar steps. "Everything all right?"

"Yes. Fine," Emma said in a cranky tone.

She took a deep breath to prepare herself for what was coming next and descended the back steps. Slowly and deliberately, with the aid of her cane, Emma walked to the garbage can enclosure along the side of the house. As she prepared to lift the plastic lid, she inhaled, so that she would smell nothing. She lifted the lid of the trash can and looked inside.

The Kellerman's box was there on top of the bags of trash. She reached in and lifted it out. Steeling herself, she lifted the top of the box and removed it. Just as David had said, the mouse was gone. All that remained was the silver shell dish.

All right, Emma thought. Okay. Her heart was hammering. I'll bring it inside. And then, as she turned to walk back inside she had an idea. Perhaps, she thought, just perhaps, if they were armed with more information, she could convince David that it was in his best interest for both of them to speak to the police. And there was a way to obtain more information. It would not be easy, in her condition, but it was possible. And she had to do *something*. She felt caged in the house, at the mercy of her own vulnerability and Lizette's intrusive efficiency. With her sense of purpose came hopefulness and a burst of strength.

She looked longingly down the driveway at her car. Lizette's brown Toyota had blocked her in. She wasn't allowed to drive anyway, and she really wasn't supposed to leave the house today. A taxi would be a reasonable compromise.

Emma made her way back into the house and called the cab company, telling the dispatcher to have the car wait at the end of the block. Then she slipped the Kellerman's box into a paper sack and went to the hall closet for her coat. But as she tried to slip it on over her dress, it felt unbearably heavy and constricting over her flayed skin. For a minute she was stymied. Then she remembered the cape. It was a soft, blue-green alpaca cape that Rory had given to her for Christmas last year. She never wore it. It had a designer label but was not at all her style. It was still in the box it came in. She had almost given it to Goodwill when they moved into this house, but at the last minute she had felt guilty and stuffed the box in the office closet. Emma limped toward the office, now her bedroom, wondering if Lizette was still in the basement.

As she reached for the doorknob, Lizette pulled it open from inside. Emma let out a little cry.

"I was just making up your beds," Lizette said bale-fully. "I saw you outside from the cellar window. What in the world were you doing out there, rummaging in the garbage cans?"

Emma felt spied upon, imprisoned. "I threw something away by accident."

"Well then, you should let me get it for you. That's my job."

"It's not necessary," said Emma.

"You could have broken your stitches," Lizette scolded her.

"I'm fine," said Emma.

"The bed's made up, so lie down and rest," Lizette commanded. "I'm going to vacuum."

"Fine," said Emma, closing the bedroom door. Vacuuming. Good, Emma thought. The roar of the vacuum would cover up the sounds of her leaving the house. She would be able to slip out unnoticed. It was stupid, sneaking around her own house, but Lizette was intent on her agenda—to keep her patient housebound and quiet. Emma went over to the closet, looked inside, and found on the floor the battered box with the cape. She put it on over her shoulders, grateful for its lightness and warmth. She walked over to the desktop and wrote a note that read "Do not disturb." She could hear the loud whine of the vacuum cleaner from the back of the house. Perfect, she thought. I'll explain it to her when I get back.

Emma slipped out the bedroom and taped the sign to the bedroom door, closing the door behind her. The vacuum was still roaring. She quietly opened the front door of the house and let herself out. The taxi was idling up the block. Emma waved to the driver who saw her in his rearview mirror as she made her painful way down the front steps with the aid of a cane. He turned the car around, drove up to the house, got out, and opened the door for her. Emma thanked him and slid gingerly into the backseat, resisting the urge to cry out from the pain. The driver got back into the front seat.

"I want to go to Kellerman's. On Main Street," she said. "And I'll need you to wait for me while I'm inside."

CHAPTER 12

The clerk at Kellerman's, a pretty young woman wearing a sky blue turtleneck and a blond ponytail, wrinkled her nose in distaste. "What happened to the box?" she asked.

"It got thrown away by accident," said Emma, looking down at the stained box, which was sitting on top of the glass display case that served as a counter.

"In the garbage?" the clerk asked.

Emma nodded.

"It smells like it," said the clerk.

"It was a bit chaotic after the wedding," said Emma. "There's no card. Nothing. I need to know who bought me the gift so I can thank them."

"The box looks kind of old," the clerk observed doubtfully. "I mean, it could be because it got messed up in the garbage. But our boxes are much . . . brighter." She reached under the counter and placed a gleaming white box on the counter. "See?"

"You're right," said Emma. "This one is a little bit yellowed."

"Would you mind taking the lid off yourself?"

Emma shook her head and lifted the lid off the box.

The clerk reached in gingerly and lifted out the silver scallop shell dish. She studied it for a minute and then shook her head. "I don't think we carry these."

"Well, it did come from this store," said Emma.

"Maybe they bought it somewhere else and put it in a Kellerman's box," the girl suggested. "People do that, you know. They buy at Wal-Mart and then pretend it came from Kellerman's."

"This dish is silver. It did not come from Wal-Mart."

"Well, you know what I mean. Some discount place."

Emma felt suddenly weary. "You're sure you don't carry a dish like this one. Could you check with someone else? Someone in charge."

"I don't need to check with someone in charge. I unpack the stock."

"Did you ever carry a dish like this?"

The girl sighed and called out to a bald man with a bow tie and half-glasses who was dusting crystal with a feather duster on the other side of the store. "Harvey, did we ever carry a silver dish like this?" She held the scallop shell up.

The man held his duster aloft and peered over his half-glasses. Then he came toward them and set the duster down on the display case. He picked up the shell dish and examined it. "Oh yes," he said. "We carried these for years. We only stopped stocking them maybe a year ago. Where did it come from?"

"I received it as a wedding gift," said Emma. "There was no card."

The man sniffed. "I'm afraid you were . . . regifted, if you know what I mean."

Emma nodded. "All right. Thanks for your help," said Emma. She put the dish back in the box and deposited the box into her paper sack. She turned away from the counter leaning on her cane.

"Do you need some assistance there?" the clerk asked sympathetically.

"I'm fine," said Emma.

She made her way back to the front door of the store, passing display cases of jewelry and tables of linens and elegant housewares that appeared untouched. The store was quiet as a library. It took all Emma's strength to push open the front door. The taxi was waiting, the driver reading the newspaper. She slowly managed to get herself back into the cab and asked him to take her back home.

On the way home, Emma prepared her excuse. She expected that Lizette would be miffed if she had discovered her charge had left the house. You don't answer to her, she reminded herself. Stop feeling guilty. But as the cab pulled up in front of the house, and Emma paid the driver and began to get slowly out of the backseat, she noticed, to her surprise, that the brown Toyota was no longer parked behind her car in the driveway.

Emma painfully made her way to the front door and opened it, as the empty cab sped away up the street. "Lizette," she called out. "Lizette, I'm back." But there was no answer. The house was silent. All she could hear was the wind, whistling outside, whipping the trees. She closed the door behind her and locked it. Telling herself aloud that there was nothing to be afraid of, Emma started to walk through the empty house. Even though it was only late afternoon, the storm had caused the day to darken, and the house was dim and uninviting. She turned on the lights in the living room, wishing David were back. She did not like being alone in the house.

She looked around for a note or some word of explanation for why Lizette had left. There was nothing. Her backpack was nowhere to be seen. Was it possible she went looking for me? Emma thought. That would be beyond the call of duty, although Lizette had seemed to be a person who went the extra mile. The door to the office/bedroom off the kitchen was ajar. Emma walked over to it. Her heart leapt unpleasantly at what she saw there. The Do Not Disturb sign had been ripped from the door. The ragged corners of the sign were still fastened there with Scotch tape. Lizette must have torn the sign off in frustration when she realized that

Emma had sneaked out of the house. Emma's gaze swept the narrow hallway, and she saw the wadded paper on the floor. She bent slowly and awkwardly to pick it up and smoothed out the handwritten sign. She imagined the nurse tapping on the door to check on her and then finding her gone. Emma's face flamed to think of the anger her stealthy escape had obviously provoked.

Emma knew she was to blame, and she didn't want to think about it. David, she thought, when will you get back? She knew he would scold her when he heard that she had sneaked out on the nurse. At least, he would for a moment, but then she would attempt to make a funny story out of it. She tried to focus on that image of him laughing, but her heart was pounding, and part of her felt childishly angry at him for not being there with her. Lizette had departed, and now she was all alone.

Emma could feel her heart thumping and hated the sensation. It's not stupid to be scared, she told herself. It's perfectly normal. After what happened to you, anyone would be afraid to be alone. But she could not calm herself. The panicky feelings were mushrooming inside her, and nothing she could say to herself was diminishing her anxiety.

When was he coming back? How long did she have to wait here by herself? Of course he didn't know that she was alone. He thought the nurse was with her. She felt an overwhelming urge to call him and tell him. Their makeshift bedroom was dark and did not have a switch by the door. It only had a lamp on the desk and one beside the bed. Emma took a deep breath, steeled herself, and hurried across the room, jamming her shin on the cot and yelping in pain as she reached for the desk lamp and turned it on.

The small, parchment-shaded lamp threw a golden glow over the desk. By its light, she was able to turn on the lamp by the bed. The two lamps warmly illuminated the room. Emma straightened up and sighed. That's better, she thought.

She walked back over to the desk and sat down in her husband's swivel chair. Sitting there, she felt almost as if his arms were around her. She tried the number of his cell phone, but it was turned off. Of course it was. She knew he would turn it off during the interview. She thought about the restaurant where he was meeting the guy. Could they still be there at this hour? If they were, they had to be the last two people in the restaurant. What was the name of the place? It was a French name. Maybe he wrote it down.

She scanned the messy desktop, but the note he had written was not there. He must have taken it with him. Dammit, she thought. His computer was on. She pushed a key and saw that he was rewriting an interview with a baseball star about the steroid scandals that he had started before their wedding. On the wall above the desk hung a framed article he had written about spending time with a well-known Cajun chef trolling the bayous of Louisiana. The accompanying photo was a black-and-white print of a swamp that seemed to be steaming in the eerie, shadowy light.

Both articles Nevin had assigned him for *Slicker*. Nevin would know how to reach him. Maybe she should call Nevin at the office. At first she dismissed that idea. David wouldn't want Nevin involved in their personal business. He had made that clear enough. And then she thought, the hell with Nevin. I need to get in touch with my husband. She knew that David had Nevin's private line in his address book. She scanned the messy desktop but did not see it. It was probably in the desk drawer. She pulled the handle on the drawer without thinking and met resistance.

Is something stuck? she wondered. She pulled on the drawer from beneath with both hands. It did not budge. It was locked. Locked? she thought. What has he got that he needs to lock away? What did people lock away? Women locked away old love letters. Men? Be honest, she thought. Probably porn. The idea of it made her feel irritable on top of her anxiety. Surely he didn't think that she was so prudish that he had to lock that stuff up. It wasn't as if she had never seen that kind of magazine. Unless, she thought, grimacing, he was into something revolting. Animals, children, or other men. No way, she thought. That was just stupid. If there was one thing she knew for sure, it was that David's sexual appetites were healthy. She rattled the handle impatiently, but the drawer would not open. Forget the drawer. It's none of your business.

All of a sudden, the phone rang at her elbow. She jumped at the unexpected ring. Picking up the phone, she punched the button to receive the call and held the phone to her ear, her heart still pounding. "Hello," she said.

There was silence at the other end. She could hear breathing.

"Hello. Who is this?" she demanded. The caller did not speak. Emma heard a click and the call was over.

There was someone there, she thought. Why wouldn't they answer? She pressed *69 to try to retrieve the number. It was a cell phone exchange, a number that she didn't recognize. She thought of calling it back but told herself she was being stupid. Someone called a wrong number, realized it, and hung up. That's all it was.

But she no longer felt safe in the little bedroom. The ringing phone. The locked drawer. The nurse mysteriously gone. The room she was sharing with her husband in the house she loved so much suddenly felt unfriendly to her. The wind was rising, and branches from the bushes outside flailed at the windowpane, snapping at her. She wondered if all the windows in the house were locked. The prospect of getting up and going around to every window, even on the first floor, seemed like more than she was physically capable of doing. And the second floor would be impossible. I need help, she thought frantically. Her mind raced, thinking of the people she knew. Stephanie, she thought. She dialed her friend's number and got the machine. Maybe she's still at school. It took her a moment to remember the number of the school. But the secretary there said that Stephanie had left an hour ago.

Emma slammed down the phone in frustration. Part of her wanted to collapse in a sobbing heap. She tried to focus on her sensible side. You have to try to make sure the windows are locked, she thought. Anyone could come in. The thought propelled her from the chair, but it also made her start to cry. She limped out of the bedroom and into the kitchen, tears drizzling down her face. *David, why aren't you with me?* She knew it was weak and feeble of her to expect him to hover over her. But she felt weak and feeble. Emma shuffled over to the kitchen sink and started to lean up to check the lock on the window. Just as she reached for the latch, she heard a loud crack above her head. Gooseflesh broke out up and down her arms. She whirled around, her heart pounding.

Someone in the house. Upstairs. They got in. She imagined the man in the ski mask hovering on the floor above her, starting down the stairs. Emma lurched across the kitchen, grabbed the phone, and punched in 911.

"Can I help you?" asked the steady voice.

"I think there's someone in my house," Emma cried.

"Okay, calm down," said the operator. "Did you see anyone?"

"No, but a man tried to kill me and I think he might have come back," she whispered.

"Okay. Why do you think there's someone there?"

Emma was beginning to hyperventilate. "There was a loud . . . cracking sound. From upstairs. He's up there. Send the police. Please . . . I'm injured and I can't . . ."

"Okay, I will do that."

"My name is Emma Webster. I'm at 611 Spencer Drive. We're at the end of the street. The last house."

"I'm putting the call out for a patrol car right now," said the operator soothingly.

"Don't hang up on me," Emma pleaded.

"I won't," the operator said reassuringly. "The officer is not far from you. He ought to be there any minute now."

"Thank you," Emma said. "Really. Thank you."

"That's all right, ma'am. Look out your window. You should be able to see his lights any minute."

114

"Okay, I'm looking," said Emma. "I don't see anything . . ."

She clutched the phone and approached the front window to try to see outside. All of a sudden, there was a flashing light in her driveway.

"He's here," Emma cried into the phone.

"All right, ma'am. You'll be all right now."

A moment later, there was a knock at her door.

Emma picked up her cane and hobbled to the door, still clutching the phone receiver. She looked through the peephole. A young, uniformed patrolman stood on her front step. Emma unlocked the door and let him in.

"Thank you, officer. Thank you for getting here so quickly."

"That's all right, ma'am," said the policeman, who looked barely older than Emma. "You think there's someone in the house."

"Yes, upstairs," she said.

"All right, I'm going to go on up there. You wait right here. Okay?"

"Be careful," Emma said, following him into the living room.

The young man flipped the switch at the foot of the stairs and began to climb up. Emma's heart was pounding in her chest, and she leaned against the back of one of the living-room chairs.

The shrill blast of the phone in her hand made her cry out. Her heart leapt again, actually feeling painful in her chest. She pressed the button and barked into the receiver, "Who is it?"

"Emma?" said a worried voice. "It's Burke."

Emma sank back against the chair and let out a sigh. "Burke. Oh thank God."

"What's the matter? Are you okay?"

"No. I'm not. I have the police here. There's someone in the house."

"Where's David?" he demanded.

"David's not here," said Emma.

Burke was silent for a moment. "All right. I'm on my way. I'm leaving the center right now. I'll be there in no time," Burke said.

"Thank you," Emma whispered, but he had already hung up.

"Ma'am," came a voice from upstairs. "Do you normally leave the bathroom door open up here at the top of the stairs?"

Emma tried to think. "I don't know. Yes, I guess so," she said.

The officer appeared at the upstairs landing. "The bathroom window is open, and the door is shut," he said.

Emma shook her head. "I don't understand. Did you find someone? Did they come in through the window?"

The young man shook his head. "There's no one up here," said the officer. "But there is a lot of wind out there. Sometimes the wind will blow a door shut, and it makes a loud cracking sound."

Emma was silent, but her face flamed. She knew instantly, the moment the patrolman said it, that he had assessed the situation correctly. A door slamming shut. Emma had heard it before in a high wind. The window in the bathroom at the top of the stairs. Emma slumped down into the living-room chair and tried to let her heart quiet down. "I'm so sorry," she said. "I shouldn't have bothered you. I'm sorry."

Is this what my life is going to be? she wondered. Somebody who calls the police when a door blows shut? Afraid of every shadow. How do you live like that? She rested her head in her hands. It had felt so good to go to Kellerman's and try to take charge of things. But it had not amounted to anything really. And now she was more weary than ever and a bundle of raw nerves.

The patrolman came down the stairs shaking his head. "Don't worry about it," he said. "It's no problem."

"I feel so stupid," Emma said. "Wasting your time like that."

The patrolman looked at her gravely. "I mean it. Don't worry. You have good reason to be jumpy, Mrs. Webster."

Emma gazed up at him, surprised.

"It's all right, Mrs. Webster," he said kindly. "I know who you are."

Emma looked away from him, unable to meet his sympathetic gaze. A known victim, she thought. That is who you are. Then she said in a soft voice, "A friend is on the way here. Would you mind waiting with me until he arrives?"

The young patrolman did not reply but walked around her chair and sat down on the sofa.

CHAPTER 13

Rain beat against the large casement windows in Burke Heisler's kitchen, but Emma did not fear its fury. Seated with her feet up on the ottoman of a plaid club chair, a glass of sparkling water in her hand, Emma finally began to feel relaxed. When Burke had arrived at her house, the patrolman left. Burke offered to order some food and wait there with her until David came home. But Emma was overcome by a suffocating feeling of claustrophobia and the desire to be anywhere but in her own house. Burke suggested that they leave a note for David and go to his place, where he could throw some dinner together for them and Emma could rest.

"I'm sorry about all this, Burke," she said now. "I feel like the girl who cried wolf. My nerves are shot."

"Don't worry about it. I'm just glad I could help."

Burke stood facing her at his kitchen island wearing a silly butcher's apron that read Kiss The Cook. He was sipping on a glass of wine as he stirred the pasta on the stove. The fragrant sauce he had defrosted was bubbling on a nearby burner. The warmth of the kitchen, in combination with her painkillers, was making Emma feel comfortably drowsy.

"You just don't look like a cook," said Emma, smiling.

118

Burke picked up a shiny spatula and gazed into its surface. "Why? Because I have the face of a bulldog?" he asked.

"You do not," she said stoutly. "I remember when you taught my freshman psych class. I had such a crush on you."

Burke's eyebrows rose into his furrowed forehead. "You did? I'm flattered."

"Well, you were kind of a glamorous, mysterious figure to us freshmen. I always figured that you secretly liked me back, but that you didn't want to cross that teacher-student line. At least, that's what I thought until you started dating my roommate."

"I did notice you, Emma," he said. "I thought you were cute."

"Oh, don't bother saying that. Natalie was in a whole different league," said Emma. "She was so . . . magnetic."

"I actually did feel a little guilty about the student-teacher thing, but Natalie always defied the rules," said Burke. "When I tried to explain my reservations, it was like waving a red flag in front of a bull. She wanted me all the more. She wouldn't take no for an answer."

Emma felt a little prickle of indignation. "You mean, she came on to you?"

"Like a freight train," Burke said. "Why? You look surprised."

"It's just that . . . she knew that I liked you. I was always gushing about you," Emma said.

"Well, if it's any consolation, there were times over the years when I wished I had resisted her," he admitted with a sigh.

Emma saw a shade of melancholy descend on her host. She wanted to change the subject. "Look, can't I at least set the table? I feel like a lazy slug sitting here."

Burke pulled out a tray table from behind the kitchen door and set it down next to her. "No," he said. "Absolutely not. You are in no shape to do anything. I'll bring your plate to you. Set the table indeed. You probably shouldn't even be out of the house."

"Actually, I think the more I get out of the house, the better off I'll be," she said. "In fact, I'm hoping I can come back to work next week."

"It's too soon, Emma," Burke said.

"I need to, Burke. I can't sit around the house thinking about what happened to me. Besides, my patients' problems will help me get my mind off my own."

"Let's discuss it in a day or two," Burke said firmly.

He set a place for her on the tray table and then one for himself at the kitchen island facing her. He dished up the food and brought a plate to her.

"I wonder if we should wait for David," she fretted.

"I'll save him a plate," said Burke.

The smell of the food made her mouth water. "Burke, thank you again," she said as she shook out her napkin.

Burke sat down and raised his glass to her. "To your speedy recovery," he said.

Emma lifted her glass of sparkling water as well and smiled. "Thank you for rescuing me. I feel much better being here with you and getting out of the house."

"Good," he said. "*Mangia, mangia.*" For a few moments they ate in silence.

"This is great," Emma said.

Burke smiled. "Now, Emma, have you heard anything more from the police about the progress of their investigation?"

Emma shook her head. "Our attorney advised us not to talk to them. Besides, they seem to have blinders on. David says all their attention is focused on him."

Burked nodded. "I know what that's like. When Natalie . . . before they found her . . . they kept questioning me. More like harassing me. It's very upsetting, when you're grieving, to have people looking at you that way. And with David . . . well, he always had his troubles with the police. As a kid he had a bad attitude, and so whenever there was trouble in town, they'd pick him up. A couple of times my dad had to go down to the station and get him out."

"He definitely resents the police," she said.

"But, Emma, this is different. You have to talk to them. They need your input."

Emma's cheeks reddened. "That's what I think but . . . David says he's being targeted, for no other reason than that he married a woman with a trust fund."

Burke frowned. "Wads of money is a time-honored motive for murder."

Emma set down her fork and looked at him indignantly. "Burke, how can you say that? David is your best friend."

"I don't mean that I think that. Of course not. But in all fairness, I didn't get the impression that Lieutenant Atkins had her mind made up about who was responsible. I gave her the anonymous letters you had received, and she seemed very interested in those. I also—I hope you won't mind this—I also told her that they ought to talk to Lyle Devlin."

"Lyle Devlin? Ivy's father?" Emma asked.

"Well, they asked me if anyone had . . . threatened you. I didn't tell you about this when it happened, but when Ivy died Devlin came to my office and he was ranting and raving."

"About me?" Emma said.

"I didn't want you to know at the time. You were upset enough as it was."

Emma blanched. "You agreed with me about the decision I made . . ."

"I did. And I told Devlin that and sent him on his way," said Burke. "Still, I thought the police ought to know about it."

Emma nodded and tried to eat some more, but suddenly her appetite was gone. She felt tears rising to her eyes again and dabbed them away with her napkin.

"Oh, Emma, I'm sorry," Burke said.

Emma shook her head. "You didn't do anything. I think it's the pain and the exhaustion."

Burke nodded and focused on his food, avoiding her gaze. "I do understand," he said.

Emma looked at him sadly. Of course he did. There were many reminders of Natalie in this lovely, gleaming house. Piles of poetry books and sterling silver framed photos. Despite her abusive, impoverished upbringing, Natalie had had exquisite, expensive taste, and it showed in every corner of their home. And as Emma well remembered, she'd had a whimsical side as well. Emma had noticed a matching apron to the one Burke wore, still hanging in the pantry. "How are you managing, anyway?" she said.

He shrugged. "Time wounds all heels," he said.

She smiled at his joke but persisted. "I mean it, Burke. Is it getting easier?"

Burke sighed and set down his silverware. "Sometimes. Sometimes I'm very rational and self-analytical. I monitor my own grief and pronounce myself as adjusting well or dealing with it. Other times . . ." He gazed at the rain beating on the window and his expression was desolate. "Other times I . . . shake my fist at the heavens. Try to make a bargain with God. If you will only give her back to me . . . you know."

"Oh, Burke," Emma said sympathetically, but a part of her wondered how he could want a life back that had seemed so . . . difficult and . . . in some ways . . . just miserable. No one blamed Natalie for her manic depression, but her refusal to take her medication had always seemed just a little . . . selfish to Emma.

He shook his head. "I know. It's totally nuts."

"You loved her," Emma said loyally.

Burke nodded, and then a silence fell between them. Emma looked out at the driving rain. "I hope David's all right," she fretted aloud.

"Was he driving to New York?" Burke asked.

"No, he took the train."

"I'm surprised he left you alone in this condition," Burke said.

"Actually, I wasn't alone," said Emma. "My mother hired a private duty nurse to stand guard over me. But I sneaked out of the house this afternoon and I guess she got mad and left in a huff. She wasn't there when I got back."

"She didn't leave you any explanation?"

Emma shook her head. "Just picked up and left."

"That's kind of odd," Burke said.

"I know."

"Is she supposed to come back tomorrow?" he asked.

"I have no idea. She'll probably request a transfer," said Emma.

Burke looked at her with a concerned expression on his face. "So, you left the house by yourself? Wasn't that kind of dangerous? Where did you go?"

"Well, this is kind of disgusting but . . ." Emma gave him a brief recounting of the ghastly wedding present.

"Oh no," said Burke, unsmiling. "Another message from your admirer? You have got to help the police track this guy down."

"Well, I thought I might be able to track him down myself." She explained that she went to Kellerman's to try and identify the sender.

"And did you find out who sent it?" he asked.

Emma shook her head. "They don't carry this item anymore. They used to, but they don't anymore."

"Really, what was it?" Burke asked.

"Well, it was pretty actually. It was a dish in the shape of a shell. Like a scallop shell, made out of silver. The guy told me that they didn't carry that dish anymore and that I must have been 'regifted.'"

"How big was it?"

"The dish? Not too big," said Emma. "No bigger than a . . . mouse."

Burke had a strange expression on his face, and he avoided her gaze.

"Burke, what is it?"

"We received one of those too when we got married," he said.

"Really?" Emma asked.

A pounding on the door made them both start. Burke got up from his counter stool, but before he reached the front door, it opened.

"David!" Emma cried.

His hair was wet, and he had raked it carelessly off his forehead. His leather jacket was dripping. "Well, you two look cozy," he said.

"Your wife wanted to wait for you," said Burke in a teasing tone, "but I figured saving you a plate would be enough."

David waved it away. "Emma, what are you doing here? You shouldn't be out."

"It's a long story. I had to call 911 . . ."

"911?" he cried. "For what?"

"I thought there was someone in the house. It turns out it was just the wind slamming a door, but I was very freaked out. In the middle of it all, Burke called and came and got me out of there."

"Alone? What happened to Lizette?" David demanded.

"She left. As I said, it's a long story," said Emma.

"Sit down," said Burke to his old friend. "Take that wet coat off."

"No thanks," said David. "I've got the car running outside. Emma, I need to get you home. If you think you're going to that funeral tomorrow, you have to get some rest."

"What funeral?" Burke asked.

"Oh, I almost forgot. I guess you're right," said Emma, struggling to her feet. Burke lifted the alpaca cape off a hook by the kitchen door. When Emma was on her feet, he laid it gently on her shoulders. Emma clutched the cape with both hands. "The funeral is for Claude Mathis. The hunter who tried . . . to save me. And yes, I absolutely am going," she said.

David turned to Burke. "Thanks for looking out for her," he said.

"Yes, thank you very much, Burke," said Emma. "You really were a lifesaver."

Burke smiled. "Anytime," he said. He walked them to the front door and waved as they stepped out into the rain.

* * *

"How did the interview go?" Emma asked as David drove slowly down Burke's long driveway and into the rainy street.

"Fine," he said.

"Fine," she repeated reproachfully. "That's it?"

"Look, I can't talk and drive in this rain."

"Fine," she said.

They rode the rest of the way in silence, David hunched over the wheel, trying to peer through cascades of water the windshield wipers couldn't sweep away quickly enough.

When they arrived in their driveway, David told her to wait for him, that he would come around for her, but Emma opened her door and struggled out of the car putting up her umbrella. She made it a few steps up the pathway to the house before she felt his arm around her as he tried to guide her toward the door. She wanted to relax against him, but she couldn't. She felt too tense and irritated with him. When they got inside, she pulled off her cape and hung it up in the laundry room, hoping the damp edges would dry by morning. She took off the dress she had been wearing as well and hung it up, pulling on the voluminous robe she had left there when she'd changed this morning.

David came out of the bathroom, rubbing his wet head with a towel. "Can I get you your medication?" he asked.

"I can get it," she said coldly. It took all her will not to grimace as she limped into the kitchen to find her pills. She leaned against the sink to catch her breath. She had been steeling herself against the pain. David, having shed his wet clothes and put on his pajama pants, entered the kitchen, his long, wet hair combed away from his square-jawed, handsome face.

He opened the refrigerator door and took out a beer. "Do you want one?" he asked.

"No," she said. "The baby. Remember?"

"Right. Sorry," he said.

She left the kitchen and hobbled toward the little first-floor bedroom. She sank down on the bed and stared at her soggy bandages. They were seeping pink, and the idea of getting up to find clean ones and change them seemed more than she could do.

After a few dreary minutes, David appeared in the doorway, holding the box of bandages. "Can I fix you up with some of these?" he asked.

Emma sighed with relief and met his gaze briefly. "That would be good," she said.

David sat down carefully on the edge of the bed and began to peel away the old dressings. Emily felt herself relaxing at the feeling of his familiar, warm touch.

"Lizette really spruced up the place," he said.

"I know," said Emma. "She was very . . . thorough."

"So, tell me what happened," he said. "She just left? Did she say why?"

"Well, I wanted to go out for a little while . . ." Emma began.

"Go out? You weren't supposed to leave the house."

"I called a cab and I went downtown to Kellerman's to see if they might know who sent the . . . dish with the mouse in it."

"Emma. Are you crazy . . . ? You're in no condition."

"Look, I don't want to discuss it. I went. All right?"

David shook his head. After a moment he asked, "Did they tell you anything?"

"No. And when I got back, the Do Not Disturb sign had been ripped off my door and she was gone. Bag and baggage." Somehow Emma had imagined that he would chuckle when she told him the story, but his expression was grim as he carefully applied gauze and tape to her thigh. "And then when I realized I was by myself, I panicked," she said.

"And called the cops," he said.

"Not immediately. I kept waiting for you to arrive."

"I was late. I'm sorry. So, what happened?"

"Well, the storm was howling," Emma said. "Then there was the breather on the phone."

David frowned at her. "What breather?" he asked.

Emily pulled her bathrobe around her newly bandaged leg. "Somebody called, but they wouldn't speak to me."

"I'm sure it's nothing," he said. "Probably a wrong number."

She hesitated and then plunged ahead, goaded, against her better judgment, by his imperturbability. "I wanted to find you. I thought I would call Nevin. So I was looking for your phone book. Your desk drawer is locked. How come it's locked?"

David frowned. "I don't know. Why?"

"It seems . . . odd that you would lock it," she said in a challenging tone.

His eyes narrowed, and suddenly she knew she had crossed the line, and she wished she could go back. It was his desk and she was snooping in it. What business was it of hers if he locked the drawer? He was entitled to his privacy. That didn't end with marriage.

"Maybe I locked it when we moved," he said. "So the stuff wouldn't fall out."

She felt relieved at the simple, obvious explanation. "Of course. You probably forgot all about it."

David peered at her with a trace of impatience. "If it bothers you so much, I'll hunt up the key."

"No, no," she said. "It's your desk. I shouldn't have even asked."

David did not smile. "Are you accusing me of something?"

She felt stupid. Intrusive. "No, of course not. I'm sorry, David. Really."

He stared at her for a long moment. "We're not going to make it if you don't trust me."

"Of course I trust you," she said.

David picked up the messy wads of gauze on the bed-spread and stood up, gazing down at her with a chilly look in his hazel eyes. "I hope so," he said.

CHAPTER 14

The Chapel in the Pines was packed for the funeral of Claude Mathis. People from the press were not allowed inside, and Emma and David arrived early enough to slip into a pew near the back unnoticed. But a whisper rippled through the mourners as Emma took her seat, and many in the church turned to look at her. She had dressed carefully in a rust-colored knit pantsuit and a warm paisley shawl, realizing that people would, inevitably, be watching her curiously. The suit was much less comfortable than her black knit dress, but it seemed only right to take pains for the occasion. She had carefully applied her makeup, and David had washed her hair for her this morning, so that it fell in shiny waves around her pale face.

Emma paid attention to the service and tried to concentrate on the stories that were told about Claude by his friends, who seemed stunned by his sudden death. She was moved to tears several times during the service for this man whom she had never actually met. Emma tried to imagine him alive, this man who had died coming to her aid. Claude's dog, Major, was allowed into the church, and lay glumly by the feet of Claude's teenaged son, Bobby, looking more bereft than some of the human mourners.

Emma tried to find some comfort in the beauty and simplicity of the little church, its stained glass windows glowing in the autumn morning light. But despite the fact that she was safe in the crowded church, encircled by her husband's protective arm, she could not keep the images of that awful day from rising to her mind. She kept picturing that man with the ax, turning on Claude Mathis as he walked into the cabin. She could still hear the thwack as the ax struck Claude's head, stuck there. She reached for David's hand and held it tightly to ease her anxiety.

After the service, Emma stopped in the vestibule of the church and tentatively approached Claude's teenaged son and his ex-wife, who were greeting people. "Excuse me," she said. "I'm Emma Webster. I just wanted to tell you how terribly, terribly sorry I am."

Claude's ex-wife, Holly, was a brittle-looking woman wearing high heels, blue jeans, and a red vinyl jacket with a fake fur collar. She had lighted a cigarette and was turning away to blow the smoke just outside the door of the church. "I know who you are," she said dully. "I called your stepfather, like your note said. He explained to me about the money you're giving us. That was nice. God knows, we're gonna need it. Bobby, this is the woman."

The teenaged boy, dressed in a baggy black sweatshirt, his doughy face sullen, looked warily at Emma. He was holding Major on a leash. The dog was silent and patient, a forlorn look in his eyes.

"I'm very sorry about your dad," said Emma. "You should know that your father was very brave, Bobby. He died saving me, and my baby, from certain death."

The kid shrugged, but his eyes flickered, as if beneath his belligerent exterior, he appreciated what she was saying.

David shook the boy's hand as well and murmured his condolences. Then he reached down and patted Major on his head. The dog let out a low, menacing growl and then a loud, sharp bark. Everyone in the vestibule turned around to look.

"Major, shut it." Bobby yanked at the dog's collar, annoyed. "He don't like strangers," the boy explained.

David straightened up. "Sorry. Em, we better get going."

Emma stared at the dog, remembering the sight of Major lunging past her, eyes flashing, teeth bared, a blur of fur. "Major," she said, holding up a tentative hand.

The dog began to bark again, frantically, its loud, anxious barks bouncing off the walls of the chapel. The sound was terrifying, causing her to flash back to the night of the attack. She froze in place as the dog jerked madly on his leash.

"Emma, come on," David cried, pulling her by the arm. Emma felt an agonizing pain in her side as he tugged her out of the dog's range.

"Major, quit!" Bobby yelled.

"Get that damn mutt out of here," Holly shouted at her son, her voice high and shrill. "Take him outside."

Emma clung to David as the boy began to pull Major out of the church vestibule.

Crowded at the foot of the church steps were as many reporters and police officers as there were mourners. Reporters knew that the funeral of a man who had died heroically saving a pregnant young woman would make for a riveting minute on the evening news. But they scattered from the path of the snarling dog, backing away as he leapt first in one direction and then another, barely being held under control by Bobby Mathis.

"Come on," said David. "They're distracted. Maybe we can get by."

As David and Emma descended the steps, Bobby was shoving Major into the backseat of an old Electra, and the crowd of reporters, recognizing Emma from her hobbled walk and her cane, as much as her face, surged up the sidewalk toward her.

"All right, that's enough," David insisted as one photographer after another shoved a video camera in Emma's face. "Leave my wife alone." When the nearest man refused to back off, David pushed him firmly out of the way. The man immediately began to protest in a loud voice, and three police officers converged on them, including Chief Audie Osmund.

Ignoring the protests of the newspeople, Chief Osmund shielded Emma and steered her out of the crowd, with David trailing them. When they reached the edge of the crowd, they saw that Lieutenant Joan Atkins was waiting next to Audie Osmund's patrol car. She was dressed in a navy pantsuit and low pumps and wore a discreet gold choker around her neck.

"Hello, Lieutenant," Emma said.

David walked up beside Emma and took her arm. "Come on, darling," he said.

Sheriff Osmund put a beefy hand on David's shoulder. "Mr. Webster, I wonder if you would come with me for a few minutes."

"What for?" said David.

"I want to take a ride out to the cabin so you can walk me through the events of last Saturday afternoon and evening. I just want you to retrace your path for me from the cabin to the duck blind."

"My attorney has instructed me not to speak to you without him present," said David.

"Mr. Webster. You've just attended Claude Mathis's funeral. I've got his unsolved murder on my hands here," said the chief. "Don't you feel the least bit beholden to this man? He gave his own life to save your wife's."

"I'm . . . aware of that. And I'm very sorry about it. But I'm within my rights," said David stiffly.

Chief Osmund turned to Lieutenant Atkins, who was watching them with her keen gaze. "I can't force him to talk," he said.

"Let's go to the car," David said to Emma. They walked toward the Jeep Cherokee, trailed by Chief Osmund and Lieutenant Atkins. David opened the front door on the passenger side for Emma and then went around to the trunk and pulled out the milk crate. Emma climbed up on it and slid into the passenger seat. David put the crate back into the car, slammed the trunk, and walked around to open the driver's-side door.

Joan Atkins blocked his path. She smiled, though her eyes remained chilly. "You may as well go and talk to the chief, Mr. Webster. Because I need to talk to your wife."

"She doesn't want to talk to you, either," said David.

"Actually," said Joan, "I think she must, because she called me yesterday. She left me a message at the police station saying that she did."

David paled. He bent over and looked into the car at Emma. She reddened at his accusing gaze. "Is that true? That you called Lieutenant Atkins?" he said.

"I wanted to tell her about the wedding . . . gift. I told you I was going to."

"Fine. You talk to her. I'll wait for you."

Emma looked away from him for a second, trying to sort out her thoughts. He was within his rights, of course. But what about doing the right thing? She looked back at him. "David. Please," said Emma. "They're right about Claude Mathis. It's the least we can do. We don't need to hide behind an attorney."

David shook his head. "They're double teaming us, Emma," he said. "They knew you would react this way."

"Why can't we cooperate with them? It won't take long," said Emma. "Let's do it and get it over with. Please, David."

"You coming, Mr. Webster?" the chief asked. "Lieutenant Atkins can follow us in your car."

"We'll be right behind you," said Joan.

David's eyes were leaden. He tossed his car keys to Joan Atkins. Without looking back at Emma, he began to walk toward the black-and-white with the portly Chief Osmund trailing him.

Detective Atkins got into the driver's seat of the Jeep Cherokee and inserted the key in the ignition. "Your husband seems a little bit aggravated," said Joan.

"My husband is fine," Emma said.

"What's this about a wedding gift?" Joan asked. "I called you back, but no one picked up."

Emma sighed and told her about the box with the shell dish and the dead mouse.

"I'll need to collect that box from your house. Although I imagine it's pretty well contaminated by now," said Joan.

Emma did not reply. They rode along in silence, following the chief's squad car down the highway lined with tall pine trees. His right blinker began to flash, and they turned down a dirt road. With a sickening feeling in her heart, Emma began to recognize the area. Any minute now, they would be at the cabin. Emma felt her heart beating faster as they reached the clearing, and the cabin came into view. "I'm not going in that house again," she said.

"You don't have to," said Joan.

Chief Osmund stopped the car and got out. David got out on the passenger side. They began to talk, walking toward the woodpile. David pointed to the stacked logs and the stump where he had split them. Sheriff Osmund nodded. Then David gestured for the policeman to follow him. Together, they disappeared into the woods.

Emma leaned back against the seat and sighed, closing her eyes. Lieutenant Atkins drummed the tips of her fingernails on the wheel. Then she turned her head and gazed at Emma.

Emma could feel her gaze, and she opened her eyes. "What?" she said.

Joan Atkins frowned. "Emma, can I tell you something? Everyone thinks they know their mate. Believe me. Ask any woman on the street and she'll say she knows all about her spouse. What he likes. What he doesn't. Where he goes. Who he sees. All women think that. Until they find out differently."

Emma turned her head and gazed at the river.

"Emma, I used to be married. I'm saying this from personal experience. I thought I knew my husband too. If you had asked me if he would ever try to harm me, I would have said, no, absolutely not. Until one day, in a rage, he raised his hand to me."

Emma spoke softly. "That must have been . . . terrible."

Joan colored slightly. "It was. It was the beginning of the end. I'm only telling you this because I understand that you don't want to think the worst. But you need to understand the gravity of your situation. I don't know what David Webster told you about his interrogation, but he refused to take a lie detector test. Even before he called the attorney."

Emma stared out at the cabin and the clearing. The river glinted silver through the trees. The green pines rustled in the breeze. It looked so peaceful and idyllic here in the autumn sunlight. But Emma knew better. She would not willingly enter that house again. She would be afraid to get out of this car if she and David were not accompanied by armed policemen. She shook her head. But something about being here again was weirdly reassuring. She could picture the assailant, the fury with which he attacked her. It was not David. It was someone who lived here in these woods. Someone who hid out here. They were looking in the wrong place.

"Why would an innocent man refuse a lie detector test, Emma?"

Emma turned her head and met her gaze. "There could be any number of explanations, and you know it. It's a flawed tool. It's not even admissible in court. Why are you so determined to blame this on my husband? While you and Chief Osmund try to parse every word we say, there is a maniac out there who has killed and will kill again. Doesn't that mean anything to you?"

Joan Atkins looked at her squarely. "Emma, did your husband ever bring you out here before this incident occurred?"

"No," she said. "He hadn't been out here in years."

"That's what he told us too," said Joan. "But it wasn't true. He was out here just a short while ago."

Emma turned her head and glared at Joan. "No, he wasn't." She opened the passenger door of the car and climbed out. She slammed it shut behind her and leaned against the car, pulling the paisley shawl around her, crossing her arms over her chest. The trickle of breeze felt good against her skin. Joan Atkins got out of the car and came around to where she stood.

"One of these Pineys who lives back here saw him. Talked to him even."

Emma's heart was thumping in her chest. She could remember asking him, as they drove here after the wedding, when was the last time he'd visited here. And he had said years ago. Not for many years now. And then, in spite of herself, she suddenly remembered that frozen package of lasagna she had found in the cabin freezer with its August sell-by date. From the woods, Emma heard the sound of leaves crunching, branches crackling. David came strolling into view, talking to Chief Osmund, who was frowning.

"So what if he was out here," said Emma. "So what? Maybe . . . he just needed to get away for a day. And forgot to mention it."

"Or maybe he was formulating his plan."

"You don't know any such thing," she protested.

"Don't take my word for it," said Joan. "Ask him."

CHAPTER 15

Emma looked from the lieutenant's face to that of her husband.

David had fixed Joan Atkins with an implacable stare. "We've cooperated with you people more than we should have," he said. "We're leaving now."

"Go ahead," Joan said to Emma. "Ask him."

"Ask me what?" David said. He peered at Emma. "What are you supposed to ask me?"

Joan gazed at him coolly. "When was the last time you were here at your uncle's place?"

"You know damn well," said David. He shook his head. "My wife doesn't need to go over this again. She wants to cooperate with you people, but she doesn't need to relive this experience again."

"Before the day of the attack," said Joan.

David made a face. "I don't know. I was . . . what . . . ten years old. I came down here with my aunt and uncle and a friend of mine."

"That doesn't agree with our information."

"Maybe I was twelve," David said. "So sue me."

"We have a witness who saw you here recently."

Emma watched him. His eyes blazed. "What witness?"

"A reliable witness," said Chief Osmund.

"Well, that's bullshit," said David. "Come on, Emma."

"Did you forget to tell us about a more recent visit?" asked Audie.

Emma felt her stomach turning over. She put her hand out to steady herself against the car.

"All right. That's it," said David. "We are leaving. We should never have talked to you. You're making this crap up and I have had enough. And my wife has clearly had enough."

Chief Osmund and Joan Atkins looked at each other.

"Go ahead, Mr. Webster. We'll be in touch."

Without another word, David opened the passenger door on the Jeep and boosted Emma up. She looked from Chief Osmund to Lieutenant Atkins. Atkins did not look at her but handed David the keys. David slammed the door. Then he walked around to the other side, climbed in, and put the key in the ignition. The two police officers watched them make a K-turn in the clearing and raise a cloud of leaves and dust as they headed off down the dirt road.

David and Emma didn't speak until they reached the highway. Finally, without looking at her, David said, "You should never have put me in that situation."

"Don't tell me what to do," she snapped.

He did not reply. They were silent the rest of the way home. For once, Emma did not fall asleep in the car.

* * *

It was three o'clock by the time they returned to Clarenceville, and it had begun to rain. David came around to her door and offered her his hand.

"Let me help you," he said.

"I don't need any help," she said.

David sighed and let her make her own painful way out of the car and into the house. Once inside, David went directly to his office.

"What are you doing?" she said.

"Calling Yunger. He needs to know about this . . . mystery witness."

She followed him to the office door and saw him pick up his cell phone from the charger and punch in the number. Yunger was not at his office. David left him a message. "I have to speak to you. It's urgent." When he saw Emma standing in the doorway, he turned his back on her and spoke quietly.

He replaced the phone and turned to look at her. Emma was studying him with a pained gaze. "All right. What is it?" he said.

"Why did you lie to the police?"

"Lie about what?"

"About being at the cabin," she said.

David shook his head. "You're beginning to sound like a cop." He raised his hands in surrender. "All right," he said. "Don't believe me."

"You heard Detective Atkins," Emma cried. "They have a witness."

"Emma, she's making it up. She's trying to turn you against me, and it's working," cried David.

"She said it because she thinks you are lying."

David sighed and avoided her gaze. Finally he said, "Look, I am their only suspect. They are not doing anything to find the real killer. So they feed you these lies."

"All you have to do is tell the truth," she said. "If you were there before, just say so. Why is that so difficult?"

"Because I wasn't," he said. "Why do you believe them? Because they're cops? Because cops never lie? They're trying to frame me, and you're letting them."

"Now it's my fault?" she cried.

"Why is my word not good enough for you? The so-called witness was obviously mistaken. They are only seeing what they want to see."

Emma frowned.

David looked at her with narrowed eyes. "Can't you take my word for it?" he asked. "You're my wife. I love you. I need you to have faith in me. Is that so much to ask?"

Emma heard a car door slam. She craned her neck to see out the window. "That was quick. It's Yunger."

"You didn't answer me," he said.

"You better go talk to your attorney," she said.

"Thanks a lot," he said. He edged past her out the door of the office. Emma reddened and did not meet his gaze. She felt guilty about her stubbornness. What he said made sense. In a way. The witness could have been mistaken. And she owed him her trust. Emma heard the front door slam. She walked over to the desk and looked out the window. Yunger, a distinguished-looking bald man with black eyebrows holding a briefcase, and David were standing on the front walk, talking, their collars turned up against the drizzle.

She sat down heavily in the desk chair, and her gaze fell on the handle to the desk drawer. Glancing out the window to make sure they were both still outside, she tugged at the handle.

She expected resistance, but this time the drawer slid open smoothly. Since last night he'd unlocked it. She looked in at the contents. There was the usual assortment of junk one might find in a desk drawer. A stack of film cards. An address book. Paper clips and rubber bands and pencils. Nothing a person would lock away from view. At first she was relieved, and then she had a disquieting thought. If he *had* locked up something secret in there, he had now removed it. It wasn't there anymore. He had disposed of it, or put it in a new hiding place. She opened his file cabinet, wondering if she would recognize whatever secret thing he had hidden if she saw it.

And then she thought about what she was doing, and she sighed. What is the matter with you? Why must you think the worst of your husband? He loves you. You told him that you trusted him. You're letting the suspicions of the police turn you into a doubting, harping wife who snoops through his things. It was probably just as he said. He'd locked it when they moved. To keep all this worthless junk from falling out. And when she called it to his attention, he unlocked it.

She went to close the drawer. As she did her gaze fell on the key ring, which sat in the well of the desk drawer. She picked it up and looked at it. There was one key on the key ring, which had a plastic photo frame as its handle. On one side of the frame was a paper label that read Garden Shed. Inside the frame was a photo of her that David had taken. She was wearing a baseball cap and overalls and she was stacking lawn furniture in the shed. Her face was smudged with dirt, and she was smiling ruefully at him as he took her picture. Her expression seemed to say, put down the camera and help me with this. It was a cute picture, a sweet idea. He had framed the picture as a special way to remind him what the key was for. She started to smile, and then her smile faded.

The front door opened and she heard their voices in the front hall. She closed the drawer and got up.

"Have a seat," she heard David say to Yunger. "You want a beer?"

Yunger shook his head. "No. I'm going back to the office."

"I want you to meet my wife, Emma," David said. "Let me see if she's lying down. She had kind of a tough morning."

Emma walked out of the bedroom.

"Hey, honey, I was just coming to get you," said David. "This is Mr. Yunger. This is my wife, Emma."

"Hey, Emma. Call me Cal. Nice to meet you," said Yunger, extending his hand.

"You too," said Emma, shaking it.

"Listen," said Cal Yunger, "I know you've been through an awful lot. Now they're pulling phantom witnesses out of the air. I just told your husband outside. I don't think you have anything to worry about. If they were so sure about this witness, they could have brought him to the funeral to identify your husband. Obviously, they didn't do that, so my guess is that they're not sure this I.D. is going to hold up. And we know it's not going to hold up, because David wasn't there in the first place."

"Will you excuse me?" said Emma. "I'm very tired."

"Oh sure," said Yunger, looking slightly taken aback. "I'm sorry."

"Are you all right, honey?" David asked.

"I'm fine," she said. "Just tired."

Before he could reply, she went back into their temporary bedroom, closed the door, and locked it behind her.

CHAPTER 16

Emma sat down on the desk chair. For a few moments, she sat there thinking. Then she picked up the phone on the desk.

She dialed Stephanie at the middle school and got one of the secretaries in the office who said that Stephanie was out.

"Did she go home?" Emma asked.

"No. She went to Trenton for a meeting."

Emma thanked her and hung up.

Where else could she go? she thought. She thought about calling Burke but immediately dismissed that idea as inappropriate. He was David's friend and her boss. She didn't want to drag him into this. She looked at the phone, thinking of her mother, wishing she could magically transport herself to Chicago and be taken care of, like a child.

For a moment she felt guilty, remembering that her mother had tried to send someone to care for her—the nurse, Lizette—and Emma had effectively caused her to leave. But it wasn't a nurse's care she needed. She needed the care of someone she loved, someone she could trust. She thought she could even tolerate Rory's company if it meant being with her mother, but she knew it was too much of a trip to make in her condition.

All of a sudden, the phone rang. Emma picked it up. "Darling," said Kay McLean, "I know you're mad at me and I don't blame you, but I just had to call you."

Her mother's voice was like a soothing balm. "Mom, I was just thinking about you," she said. "Really. Just this minute."

Kay chuckled. "Well, we've always had a little mother-daughter telepathy, haven't we?"

Emma smiled, knowing it was true. "I guess we do."

"What's the matter?" Kay asked. "How are you feeling? Did the nurse come? I know you told me not to interfere but . . ."

"She was here," Emma said carefully.

"Was? Isn't she still there? We hired her until further notice."

Emma sighed. "She . . . left. I guess she got a little peeved because I . . . left the house without telling her."

"Emma!" her mother cried. "She was supposed to be there to take care of you. To protect you."

"I know, Mom," Emma said, not really wanting to discuss it. "And I appreciate it. Really, I do. I guess I'm just wishing I could come and be with you. Get away from here and . . . hide out for a few days."

"Really?" Kay said, a suspicious note in her voice. She covered it immediately. "Emma, that would be wonderful. Why don't you do it? Oh, nothing would make me happier than to be able to take care of you." Then she hesitated. "Honey, is anything wrong? I mean, has something else happened?"

Emma shook her head. "No. Not really. I'm just feeling . . . stressed out."

"Well, you just get on the next plane, darling. Are you up to the trip?"

"That's just it," said Emma. "I don't think I am. My luggage. The airport. The security lines. The concourse. That long walk to the gate."

"You don't have to walk. They have those trams. You know, the ones that beep to make you get out of the way," Kay said eagerly.

"I can't do it. Not yet. It's too much for me."

"Oh, Em," Kay said. "Then let me come there."

"No. Better not," Emma murmured.

"I hate being this far away from you," said Kay.

Emma nodded, but tears filled her eyes, and she couldn't speak.

"Honey, listen to me," said Kay. "If you need to get away, why don't you go up to New York and visit Jessie? You can call a car service and have them take you right to her door."

"Mom, she's on bed rest. She's in no shape for company."

"Now, Emma, listen to me. I talk to Aurelia all the time. Jessie has all kinds of help. Her mother has made sure of it. *She* listens to her mother. And there's lots of room in that apartment. She's bored to death, stuck at home. You just call her and tell her you're coming."

Emma thought of Jessie's cheerful face and the warmth she always saw in her bright eyes. "Do you think I should?" Emma asked, feeling like a child again, looking to her mother for answers.

"Yes, you absolutely should," said Kay. "Do you want me to call her and arrange it, or will you do it?"

"I don't know," said Emma.

"Please, honey. It would be good for both of you."

"Okay," said Emma. "I will. Thanks, Mom."

"Call me from Jessie's," Kay insisted, hanging up.

Before she could change her mind, Emma punched in the number of her dear old friend and asked if she could visit. Jessie started peppering Emma with questions. "Listen," said Emma, "I got your beautiful flowers in the hospital, and I know you want to know everything, but I just can't talk right now. I promise I'll tell you everything when I get there."

Jessie reacted like the true friend she was. "How soon can you be here?"

"I'll be on the next train."

"Can't wait," Jessie said. "We'll lie around together. You and me and our not-quite babies. It'll be like one of our old sleepovers."

Emma did her best to sound enthused. Then she hung up the phone and sat, staring out the front window at the drizzling sky. Part of her wanted to just stretch out on the bed and pull a blanket over her. She was so weary that she felt like weeping. But there was a knot in her stomach, and she knew she would not sleep. Get up, she thought. Get out of here. Put two or three things in a bag. She couldn't carry anything heavy. If she needed clothes, she and Jessie were about the same size. She knew her mother was probably right about calling the car service, but she couldn't wait to get out of here. She would take the train. It was an easy trip by train in those big comfortable seats. Besides, she had always loved train rides. Resting her head against the windows, watching the landscape go by. None of the anxiety she associated with airports and planes.

She went over to the closet, pulled a light, microfiber duffel bag out, and put it on the bed. Then she walked over to the closet and took a nightie and a burnt orange tunic top and stretchy black pants that she could comfortably wear over her bandages. She folded them into the bag. Then she unlocked the bedroom door and limped to the bathroom, where she took her toothbrush, a box of bandages, and her medication. Jessie would have everything else she would need.

When she walked out of the bathroom, David was standing by the bed, staring down at her open suitcase. He looked up at her. "What's this?"

"Is your lawyer gone?" she asked.

"*Our* lawyer. Yes. What is going on with you? You seem to be in a strange mood."

Emma did not reply. She walked over and put her toiletries into the duffel.

"Emma," he said.

"You lied to me," she said.

"Here we go again. How many ways can I tell you? I was not at the cabin."

"This is not about the cabin," she said. "You lied to me about your desk drawer. You said you locked it when we moved."

145

"I did," he said.

"No, you didn't." She walked over to the desk drawer and opened it, pulling out the picture frame key chain. "You see this?" she said, tossing it to him.

He turned it over, frowning. "What about it?"

"There's a picture in it of me that you took the day we moved in."

"So what?" he cried.

"So, if the drawer had been locked since we moved, how could you possibly have put that photo on the key chain?"

David stared at her. "I don't believe this. What are you doing? Building a case against me? Are you working for the cops now?"

Emma blushed, but she zipped up her bag and lifted it onto her shoulder. "That's the second time today you've compared me to a cop."

"Well, excuse me, but I feel a little bit . . . beleaguered. It's a drawer," he said. "You're walking out because of a drawer? That's my crime? I locked a drawer."

She started for the bedroom door, but he blocked her way.

"Move," she said.

He hesitated and then stepped aside. Emma walked past him.

"All right, wait," he said. "Will you listen?"

She stopped, but she did not reply or look at him.

"All right, look," he said. He sat down on the edge of the bed. "There is something I've been . . . I probably should have told you this already."

Emma stood watching him. Her legs were trembling. "What?" she said.

"I didn't want anyone to know. It's . . . embarrassing."

"What is?" she asked.

"Emma, I was seeing another woman, when we met . . ." He heaved a sigh. "Her name is . . . Connie. She's a . . . a flight attendant. She had the idea that we were . . . serious. It wasn't true, but I guess I let her think that. Anyway, when

146

I met you, I realized that I'd met the woman for me, and I dropped her. I tried to do it gently, but she was in love with me. She hounded me for a while. She wrote me a lot of letters that made no sense. In fact, they kind of reminded me of the letters you were getting. Kind of crazy."

Emma frowned at him. "How crazy?"

David ran a hand through his hair. "Well, they were . . . very . . . intense."

Emma peered at him. "And that's what was in the drawer? This woman's letters?"

David nodded. "I don't know why I kept them."

"Where are they now?" she said.

"Well, after you mentioned the drawer last night I realized how stupid it was to keep them. I mean, the police already want my head on a platter. If they saw those letters . . . between that, and their so-called witness in the Pinelands, they might jump to the wrong conclusion."

"They might think the affair was ongoing," she said.

"They seem to have no trouble thinking the worst of me," he said.

Emma nodded. "So you got rid of them."

"Last night. After you were asleep."

"And you never thought to tell the police. Or me."

"I should have. I know. But nobody wants to hear about their husband's old girlfriends. And it seemed like adding insult to injury somehow to have the cops tracking her down. I mean, it was six months ago. I broke her heart, and she wrote me some crazy letters. Didn't you ever do anything like that while you were in the throes of a broken heart? I didn't think it was fair to drag her into this."

Emma felt as if her head would explode. "My life and the life of our baby is in danger, and you want to protect this woman you used to sleep with? Did it ever occur to you that she might be the person who was trying to kill me?"

David shook his head. "Emma, it wasn't Connie. I haven't heard from her in months. She probably doesn't even know I got married. Much less where we planned to spend

147

our wedding weekend. Besides, she's a tiny little woman. She couldn't even lift an ax, never mind kill someone with it."

Emma stood up and picked up her bag. "Your priorities suck," she said.

"What does that mean? I'm not protecting her. Emma, put that bag down."

"How can I believe you?" she said. "You have too many secrets."

He looked stunned. "I have secrets? What about you? Are you saying that you don't have any?"

She stared at him. "What is that supposed to mean?"

He met her gaze defiantly. "Nothing," he said. "Forget it."

Emma set the bag back down on the bed. "No. You brought it up. Let's hear it. What are you talking about?"

"All right," he said, sticking his chin out. "I'm talking about you. And Burke."

"Me and Burke?" She looked at him in disbelief.

"You knew him in college."

"That's no secret. So I knew him in college. So what?"

"You had an affair with him, didn't you?" David demanded.

"An affair? No," she said. But Emma blushed, thinking about her confession to Burke the night before. But it was nothing. All she had done was confess to a crush. "He wasn't interested in me. He married my roommate, remember?"

"And yet he asked you to come here and work for him. After a weekend visit, he asked you to work for him."

"Because . . ." she said.

"Because what?" David demanded. "Because of your vast experience? Because there aren't any other psychologists in New Jersey?"

Emma blushed furiously. It was a simple question, but she found herself fumbling to answer it.

David looked triumphant. "I think it's because he had a crazy wife who made him miserable, and he wanted to resume his affair with you. And then I came along and got in the way."

"David, that is not true. You're just . . . imagining something that didn't happen."

"How do I know that?" he said.

"Because I'm telling you the truth," she said.

"Well, I don't believe you."

Emma gaped at him. "David."

"How do you like it?" he demanded.

For a moment Emma was stunned. And then she glared at him. "Oh. Oh, I see. This is a game meant to enlighten me."

"Games are supposed to be fun," he said bitterly.

Emma picked up her bag again. She had packed it lightly, but even so it seemed to pull the stitches that curved around her back. "Well, we're agreed on one thing. There is nothing fun about this."

"All right, stop," he said. "I was trying to make a point. Of course I believe you. I just wanted you to know how it felt. Now where are you going?"

"Thanks for the object lesson. My life is in danger, and you're playing mind games. I'm leaving, David. I'm going to see Jessie for a few days."

"Emma, you can't," he said, but before he could protest further, the phone rang again. He picked it up and barked into it. "Hello."

He listened for a moment, his jaw working. Then he held out the phone to Emma. "It's for you," he said. "You'll never guess who."

She took the phone from him as he stalked past her out of the bedroom, slamming the door behind him.

"Hello?" she said.

"Emma, it's Burke. Am I calling at a bad time?"

CHAPTER 17

Emma pushed open the door of Tasha Clayman's room at the Wrightsman Youth Center and looked inside. Tasha's mother, Nell, was sitting in a desk chair beside the bed where her daughter lay, staring up at the ceiling. Nell stroked Tasha's arm while Wade Clayman hovered in a shadowy corner of the room, gazing out the window, his eyes filled with worry. Burke had called to tell her that Tasha had begun slipping and refused to see anyone but Emma. Burke had apologized profusely for asking, but he wondered if Emma could possibly find a way to come and talk to her.

The idea of an exhausting session with the Claymans on her way to the train seemed like more than Emma could possibly manage, but now that she had arrived at the Wrightsman Center, she felt strangely happy to be back, to be needed by a patient. If nothing else, she thought, it would keep her mind off her own problems.

Wade Clayman turned and looked at the doorway. He saw Emma and greeted her with a cry of relief. His relief turned to dismay as Emma limped into the room on her cane and he saw the extent to which she had been injured.

"My God," he exclaimed. "You poor girl."

Tasha lifted her head, oversize on her skeletal frame, and stared. "Dr. Hollis. What happened to you?"

"I was the victim of a crime," said Emma, amazed that they were unaware of her situation. It seemed as if the news coverage had been unceasing. But then, having a dangerously ill child took precedence over anything else, she reminded herself. "I wasn't planning to come in yet, but I am so concerned about you, Tasha."

Tasha's bulging eyes widened, and a rare smile caused her skin to wrinkle into accordion folds. "Thanks," she said.

"I need you to work for me today," Emma cautioned.

Tasha nodded tentatively. "I'll try," she said.

Nell, who could not tear her anxious gaze from her daughter's gaunt face, let out a sound between a laugh and a sob. "Please try, Tasha," she pleaded.

Wade pulled up a chair for her, and Emma sat down.

"Let's talk about disappointment," Emma said.

* * *

Audie Osmund pulled into the clearing where the old Fiore house stood. It was a run-down farmhouse with asbestos shingles and a roof that desperately needed replacing. Two hundred yards from the house was a tin-roof lean-to, which was probably used now as the barn. Audie got out of his patrol car, climbed up the front step beside a pile of empty terra-cotta flowerpots, and knocked at the door. There were a couple of ears of Indian corn decorating the front door, although some woodpeckers had pecked off most of the corn. There was no car around. He wasn't optimistic.

As he waited, he thought about that female lieutenant from the state police. "That was a waste of time," she had said in a real tight voice after David Webster and his wife drove away together today. "Why didn't you get a positive I.D. from that witness?" she demanded, treating Audie as if he were a rookie cop. Audie knew from experience that the state police always acted superior, strolling in with their nice suits and fancy haircuts. He was ready for that. But it was harder to swallow when the state cop was a woman like Joan Atkins. She seemed to make a point of keeping her part of the investigation to herself, making sure to keep Audie out of the loop. She was a type of woman he did not care for.

Still, there was no way Audie could argue on his own behalf. It had backfired. So now Audie was out at the Fiore place, trying to make up for his oversight. No one answered his knock, and when he tried to peep through the windows, he saw that the panes were too grimy to be transparent.

They haven't done much for this place, Audie thought. It would probably be different if the husband was still alive. Audie looked around the clearing impatiently. She could be out with the horse, he thought. It was worth a try. He began to walk out toward the broken-down old lean-to, which was overgrown with a blazing red vine and up to the windowsills in dry, brushy grass. He heard a whinny as he approached.

"Mrs. Tuttle?" he called out. He could discern the horse's rear end under the lean-to. All of a sudden, the bottom half of a white face appeared out of the shed's gloom.

"Who is it?" a deep voice asked.

"Police," Audie announced. "Who are you?"

A teenaged kid wearing a gray sweatshirt and a Philadelphia Eagles cap pulled down to his eyebrows emerged from the lean-to, holding a curry comb. He looked warily at Audie.

"I live here," said the kid.

"You're Mrs. Tuttle's son?"

The boy nodded.

"What's your name, kid?"

"Sam," said the boy.

"Well, Sam, I'm looking for your mother."

"She ain't here. She had to go up to Trenton. Some insurance thing about my dad. He was a firefighter. He died in a fire."

"So I understand," said Audie. "Sorry for your loss."

"Thanks," the boy muttered. "Why do you want my mom?"

"She's helping me with a case. She came forward as a witness," Audie said. "Didn't your mom tell you?"

The boy shrugged. "I don't know."

Typical teenager, Audie thought. "Do you have a number where I can reach her?" Audie asked.

The boy frowned. "No. We had a cell phone, but we had to get rid of it. My mom said we couldn't afford it. What was she a witness for?"

"Well, a woman got attacked a while ago at the next place over. Hunter got killed. You must have heard about it," said Audie.

"I heard about it. She said she saw that?" the boy scoffed as if his mother was prone to exaggeration. "She didn't see that. The cops came here and asked us questions after it happened. She didn't see nothing. We were both home, but neither one of us saw it or heard anything."

"No. She just saw some . . . suspicious activity around the Zamsky place a while back. You see anyone over there in the last couple of months?" Audie asked hopefully.

"Me? No. I don't know nothing," said the kid.

Audie sighed. "All right, son. When do you expect her back?"

"Tomorrow, I guess. Maybe late tonight."

"Well, I'm the police chief. Chief Osmund. You have her call me," said Audie, turning away. He did not intend to call Joan Atkins and tell her that he had lost his witness. It might take a little doing, but he was going to catch up with the Tuttle woman and get that I.D. on David Webster if it was the last thing he did. In the eyes of that state police lieutenant, he was only a country cop, but that didn't mean he was ready to be made a fool of.

* * *

Emma led the Claymans through a good session and discovered that she actually felt energized by the encounter. At the end of it, Wade Clayman admitted that he regretted wasting time on late-night business meetings that he could have spent with his daughter, and Tasha had looked at him in amazement.

On her way out of the center, Emma kept her gaze lowered, so she would not have to explain her life to everyone she encountered. But she had to speak to Burke before she left. She turned the corner onto his corridor and tried not to make eye contact with the person who was coming out of his reception area as she was approaching.

"Hey," said an angry voice. "Wait a minute."

She decided to assume that the voice was not addressing her. She continued to hobble toward the door of the reception area.

"I said 'wait,'" the voice insisted. Emma stopped and looked up. She found herself face-to-face with a glowering man in a black leather vest, engineer's boots, and wire-rimmed glasses.

"Mr. Devlin," Emma said in a wary tone.

"Well, isn't this a wonderful surprise. I'll tell you what I just got finished telling him," Lyle Devlin said, gesturing back toward Burke's office door. "You have a lot of nerve, after what you did to my family, sending the police to hound me . . ."

"I didn't . . ." Emma protested.

"What's going on out here?" Geraldine called out anxiously.

"I'm going to sue you, and everybody in this place," Lyle Devlin insisted, pointing a finger at Emma's chest. "You will be sorry," he said. "You'll pay dearly for this. The worst thing I ever did was to bring my daughter to this sorry excuse for a treatment facility and let you get your hands on her."

"I'll call security," Emma said faintly.

Burke, alerted by Geraldine, opened the door of his office and looked out. When he saw Emma forced up against the doorframe by Devlin, he began to shout and rush toward the man. "Hey. I told you to get out of here."

Devlin's face was close to Emma's. "Security's not gonna help you, honey." Before Burke could reach him, Devlin turned his back on Emma and stormed toward the exit. Burke arrived at Emma's side in a moment, studying her worriedly.

"Emma, are you okay? Did he do anything to you? Come in and sit down."

Emma shook her head. "I'm all right. What set him off?"

"The police came to question him about what happened to you. About his threats against you. Now he's all bent out of shape."

"He said he's going to sue the center. I'm so sorry, Burke."

Burke shook his head. "I'm the one who's sorry. I'm sorry you had to deal with that. Don't worry about him. He's blowing smoke. When it comes right down to it, he doesn't want this whole thing to come out in the open. How did it go with Tasha Clayman?"

Emma said that the session had gone well, and she had promised to see her again the minute she got back from New York.

"You're going to New York?" Burke asked. "Is that a good idea?"

"It's just for a few days," said Emma. "I need to get away from . . . all the publicity. I have a close friend there. I can hide out at her place."

"You're not driving, I hope."

Emma shook her head. "I've got a cab waiting to take me to the train. Listen, I'm so sorry that the center got dragged into this. With . . . Devlin."

"I'll worry about Devlin," he said. "You take care of yourself. Rest and recuperate. Don't forget that we need you here. Any chance you'll be back for your group on Thursday?"

Emma sighed. "I don't know yet. I really didn't want to come in when you called this afternoon. I thought there was no way I was ready to face patients. But it felt really good to be back here. I feel stronger right now than I have since . . . it happened. I promise I won't stay away for long. By the way, speaking of my group, how is Kieran doing?" said Emma. "Has he been back since his sister bailed on your meeting?"

Burke shook his head disgustedly. "No. But what can you expect? That sister of his is a vain, stupid woman. She knows how close to the edge this kid is, but instead of trying to help, she went on a cruise. She doesn't give a damn essentially."

Emma sighed. "I'll make a special effort to engage him in the group."

Burke put his hands gently on her upper arms and kissed her cheek. "You be careful, Emma. You're very important to . . . us."

* * *

The Clarenceville train station was located adjacent to the sprawling Lambert University campus. The trip to New York City was only an hour by train, and the convenience of having the train right near the campus was an attraction for both students and faculty alike. The taxi let Emma off in front of the dull, forest green station house. She opened the door and went inside. There was one college-age kid in a parka lying on one of the benches that lined the white bead-board walls. His head was resting on his backpack, and he was sound asleep, snoring lightly. On the track side, Emma could see a couple of young teenagers, knitted caps pulled down to their eyebrows, sailing past the windows on the cement platform.

As Emma approached the ticket window, the man behind the window in a blue uniform was muttering, "Those kids! Excuse me, miss."

He let himself out of the side door to the ticket office, opened the door on the train side, and began to holler. "Hey, you kids. Take those skateboards and get out of here."

The teenagers laughed derisively, but began to roll slowly down toward the handicapped ramps flanking the stairs to the bridge over the tracks, which had attracted them to the station platform in the first place. "Get off those skateboards and carry 'em," the ticket agent yelled. Emma could not see whether or not the kids had complied.

The ticket agent came back inside, shaking his head and scowling. "They're like cockroaches. You think you got rid of them and ten minutes later, they're back." He climbed back up on his stool and peered at Emma. "Where you going?" he asked.

"New York. Penn Station."

"Round-trip?"

Emma hesitated, then nodded. "Round-trip."

The ticket agent glanced at the clock. "The next train through is an express. Doesn't stop here. The next local is at five o'clock."

"That's fine," she said. Emma paid for her ticket and thanked him. Then she went outside to wait. The platform was deserted on the northbound side. In an hour or so the commuter trains from Manhattan would be arriving on the southbound side, disgorging a phalanx of men and women in suits, talking on cell phones. But for the moment, Emma was the only traveler. There was no one else on either side. Sometimes she wondered how the railroads could keep running with so little patronage all day.

The day was growing dark, and the halogen lights on the platform were beginning to come on. Emma thought about sitting on one of the benches attached to the station house, but she was too anxious to just sit. She walked slowly down to the end of the platform, away from the station house. Standing there on the lonely platform, she began to wonder why she had even decided to go. Now that she was away from David, she missed him and began to think perhaps she had been too hasty in walking out. Obviously, their marriage had gotten off to a stressful beginning. They were coping as best they could, between the police, the reporters, and her injuries. They'd both been under a lot of strain. Surely, if it weren't for all that had happened, she would never have cared about, or even given a thought to, that locked drawer.

If she left now, was she playing into the hands of all the doom mongers? A marriage took time and trust. It was as if she was fleeing at the first sign of trouble. She shivered, glad she had on the alpaca cape instead of the shawl she had worn to the funeral. Besides, a shawl was too difficult to manage while traveling. She had abandoned the rust knit suit and her long loose hair as well, twisting her shiny blond hair up into a knot, and choosing knit pants and a turtleneck for the trip.

A bright white light appeared in the distance along with the noisy clatter of the approaching train. The shrill whistle sounded, warning that the train was an express and would not stop. Emma stiffened against the harsh scream of the whistle and stared at the white light growing larger as the train barreled down the tracks.

It's not too late, she thought. You can rip this ticket up and go back home. What do you think, Aloysius? she thought, putting a protective hand on her stomach. You'd probably vote for me to return to your daddy. Kids always vote for that, she thought wistfully. Always rooting for reconciliation.

The clatter of the approaching train was deafening. Emma took a step back from the yellow line on the plat- form, which marked the safety cutoff point when trains were approaching. As she did, she noticed a swift movement out of the corner of her eye. She looked down the platform and saw one of the teenaged skateboarders, sailing down the handi- capped ramp in his black watch cap and baggy sweats. The ticket agent's going to be furious, she thought. She shook her head, smiling. The skateboarder, zooming toward her now, began to gesture wildly. He was yelling something at her, but she could not hear him over the clatter of the express.

"What?" she said, peering at him. She could see him speeding her way. She wasn't taking any chances. She took another step back from the line and suddenly, from behind, felt a vicious thud. Hands shoved up her shoulder blades. She stumbled and screamed but was drowned out by the whistle. She saw the white light as she pitched forward into the path of the oncoming train.

CHAPTER 18

Oh God, no, she thought desperately. My baby!

Suddenly Emma was jerked back, nearly strangled by the fastened neck of her cape. Her head snapped forward. Her arms flailed, and she fell, landing on one hip with a sharp crack. The train was screaming by and she saw the lights from inside the cars careening past.

The skateboarder, in a black watch cap pulled low and a baggy sweatshirt, one sneakered foot on the board, one on the ground, bent down and regarded her warily. "You okay?" he asked.

The boy had swept behind her and yanked her cape. His young reflexes had saved her. Emma, stunned to be alive and safe, tried to speak but couldn't. She nodded.

A man in a Burberry trench coat, who had just stepped out of the station house with a middle-aged woman in a black coat, rushed up to them. "What the hell did you do to this woman?"

"I didn't do nothin' to her," the kid snarled.

The man in the trench coat crouched down and put an arm under Emma's shoulders. "Here, let me help you. Are you all right?" he asked.

"You kids and your skateboards," muttered the woman to the skateboarder. "You'll kill someone someday."

Emma was shuddering. She wanted to explain, but the fastened cape had pressed on her windpipe and only a squeak came out.

"You, young man, you stay right there. I want to talk to you," said the older man in the trench coat, pointing at the skateboarder.

The skateboarder flipped them all the finger as he resumed his swift, illegal cruise, this time leaping off the edge of the platform and into the parking lot.

"Delinquent," muttered the man. "Did he hurt you? Are you all right? What happened here?"

Emma grasped the sleeve of the man's coat. The train had passed and the station was silent again. "It wasn't him," she managed to croak. "Someone . . . pushed me from behind. Tried to push me in front of the train."

The man frowned at her. "Are you sure about that? They pushed you deliberately?"

"My baby," Emma cried. "What about my baby?"

"My God, was there a child with you?" the man cried.

Emma shook her head. "I'm pregnant," she said. Then she began to weep.

"Linda," the man said to his wife, not taking his eyes off Emma. "Get out your cell. Call 911."

* * *

Joan Atkins, alerted by the Clarenceville police, careened into the parking lot of the station. The local police were there in force, flashing red lights everywhere in the lot, black-and-whites parked at odd angles. An ambulance was there as well, the doors to the bay already open. The news media, ever alert to the police scanner, were also out in force, although they were being held outside the station itself by a uniformed policeman. Joan flashed her badge to part the crowd and hurried up the steps and into the station house.

There were at least ten cops in the tiny building. Two of them were talking to the station master in hushed tones.

Another was escorting the man in the trench coat and his wife out onto the platform. The next train was almost due, and there were reporters on the platform, clamoring for information, pelting the couple with their questions. Joan saw Trey Marbery talking on his cell phone and signaled to him. Marbery nodded grimly.

Emma was lying on a gurney while the EMTs busied themselves with her injuries. Her eyes were vacant and her face was dead white. When she looked up and saw Joan, a spark of recognition came to her eyes.

"Lieutenant Atkins," she said.

Joan took Emma's hand and squeezed it briefly, shaking her head. She looked so frail and broken that it was painful to see. "Emma. What happened?"

Emma's eyes filled with tears again. "Sorry," she said, waving a hand impatiently, as if trying to stave off a sneeze. "I'm just . . . so freaked out."

The EMTs were working swiftly to stanch the blood flow from the reopened wound in her side. One of them, a pretty girl with dark curly hair who wore a name tag that read Bobby Shields, was taking Emma's blood pressure. Joan looked up at Trey Marbery, who had finished his phone call and was approaching the gurney.

"What do we know?" Joan asked her erstwhile partner.

Trey cleared his throat. "My men questioned the couple who called 911. They came upon the scene and thought that she had collided with a skateboarder, but the young lady tells us otherwise. Apparently, somebody pushed her from behind, and the skateboarder pulled her back. Kept her from falling in front of the train."

Joan winced, imagining the close call. "Where's the skateboarder now?"

"There's a half-dozen guys out looking for him."

"Good," said Joan. She looked down at Emma. "Tell me about it. What were you doing here?"

Joan's piercing eyes were focused on Emma's face, and her calm, no-nonsense presence was comforting. "I was waiting for the New York train. Going to visit an old friend. Standing at the far end of the platform." Emma licked her chapped lips. "I saw the express train coming, and then the skateboarder. He was coming at me, really fast. He was yelling to me. Gesturing. I guess . . ." Emma let out a sob and then tried to compose herself. "He was trying to warn me. I had no idea."

"Okay," said Joan. "Take it easy."

Emma closed her eyes and then gave a shuddering sigh. She could hear Joan Atkins and the younger detective, the one with the café au lait skin, conferring out of her field of vision.

"Any other witnesses? Anyone at all?" Joan was asking.

"The platform was deserted. The skateboarder is our best bet."

"What about the station master?" Joan asked. "Or the engineer? Somebody on the southbound side maybe?"

"Nothing. The station master was inside. We were able to contact the engineer by phone, but he was moving too fast to see anything. As for the southbound side, there wasn't a soul there."

Joan came back into Emma's line of sight as she walked over to the window overlooking the parking lot. "What about those buildings there?" she said.

"That's part of the Lambert campus," said the male detective.

"Maybe somebody was looking out the window and saw something. Have you got a couple of patrolmen who could canvass those buildings?"

"I'll get them on it right away," said Marbery.

"Thanks, Detective." Joan returned to Emma's side. "Where's your husband? The police have not been able to contact him."

"I don't know," she whispered.

"Did he know you were coming here to take the train?"

Emma remembered her accusations, and David pleading with her not to leave. Emma nodded.

"Anyone else know?" said Joan sharply.

"A few people."

"Can we continue this at the hospital?" asked the EMT named Bobby. "We need to get her over there now."

"Sure," said Joan, stepping back, once again out of Emma's line of sight.

Emma closed her eyes and felt the gurney raiding beneath her. Back to the hospital, she thought, and woolly-headed though she was from the painkiller they had given her, she felt unutterably depressed at the thought.

Suddenly, there was a commotion at the door to the station house. "Hold it just a second," Emma heard Joan Atkins yelling.

Lieutenant Atkins appeared beside her stretcher, grasping the arm of a young man in a watch cap and a baggy sweatshirt.

"Don't push me, lady," the kid said. "I didn't do nothing."

"Emma," said Joan, "is this the young man you were talking about?"

Emma took a look at the skateboarder's angry features. "Yes," she said, nodding. She spoke directly to the boy. "You saved me."

"Whatever," said the kid.

"What's your name, son?" asked Joan.

"Josh," said the boy sullenly.

"Josh, that was a fine, brave thing you did."

The boy shrugged, but his tense shoulders seemed to relax a little bit.

"Now, tell me, Josh. This is really important. Did you see the person who tried to push Dr. Webster onto the tracks?"

"She's a doctor?" the kid said.

"Answer the question."

"I saw him coming up behind her," said Josh. "I could see he was getting ready to push her."

"What did he look like?" Joan asked.

Josh shrugged. "I don't know. He was wearing a ski mask. Red around the eyes."

Emma gasped. She felt as if something heavy had just landed in the middle of her chest. Bobby, who was carefully

163

attaching her ankles to the gurney, looked up at her worriedly. "Am I hurting you?" she asked.

Emma shook her head slightly. "No."

"What else?" Joan asked.

"Regular clothes. Dark pants. A hoody."

"A hooded sweatshirt?" Joan asked.

The boy nodded.

"Tall? Short?"

"Average. I don't know. It all happened so fast. I only saw him for a few seconds."

"Anything else?"

Josh shook his head.

"Okay, well, give your name and number to this officer here before you leave. We may need to talk to you again."

"Thank you, Josh," Emma whispered to the boy who was turning away.

Joan frowned at her. "You know this eliminates any possibility that the attack in the Pine Barrens was random."

Emma did not reply, but she knew.

The pretty, dark-haired EMT said, "We really have to go, Lieutenant. Now."

"Okay, we're good for the moment. Are you ready to go?" Joan asked her.

Emma nodded.

"I'll get some patrolmen to escort you out. They'll stay with you at the hospital," she said.

"Thank you," said Emma in a small voice.

Joan spoke to the sergeant, who was the ranking officer in the station house, and then a pair of officers appeared at the head of the gurney, one on either side of her. Emma lay back against the pillow and allowed herself to be moved toward the door of the train station, bumping along.

She saw someone opening the door, and then she felt herself being lifted and tilted upward so that she could be taken down the stairs. She had expected the parking lot to be dark, but it was brightly lit. Wires crisscrossed the parking lot, and some photographers had set up lights. Reporters were yelling, but Emma avoided looking at any of them. The photographers' lights were so bright in the darkness that they made the large lighted windows of the campus building opposite the narrow parking lot look dim. In a good number of the enormous windows, Emma could see people looking out curiously on the scene. She felt like a zoo animal. They were gaping at her, on her gurney, as it was lowered toward the spot where the ambulance idled. Pressed to the glass the gawkers were only visible in silhouette. In one of the windows Emma saw that there were three people looking out. One of them appeared to be propping up a large dark object that was as tall as he was, with a wide, curving base that narrowed to a long, straight neck. Emma frowned and then realized what she was looking at. A bass. The student was holding a bass fiddle.

As if to confirm Emma's visual impression, the girl beside him lifted up a violin, placed it under her chin, and moved away from the window. Her fellow musicians also tore themselves away from the chaotic scene. They had music to practice. The building, which looked out over the station, was the music building.

The music building, she thought. The station house and the long platform were clearly visible from the Lambert University music building.

The gurney was lifted, its legs folded and pushed into the ambulance. The doors were slammed shut, and the siren began to wail.

CHAPTER 19

"This will be cold," said the technician as she smeared the gel onto Emma's belly and attached the wires that led to the monitor beside her bed. A tall, bespectacled resident in a white coat entered the cubicle in the emergency room where Emma had been taken.

"All ready for you, Doctor," said the technician.

"Okay," said the young man. "I'm Dr. Weiss. I'm from ob-gyn. I think everything is fine here, Mrs. Webster. No bleeding or cramping. But just to be on the safe side we'll have a look." He switched on the monitor and began to position the scanner on her abdomen.

An upside-down fan-shaped image appeared on the screen, covered by a mass of white blotches and streaks. The doctor looked at it, nodding, and then said, "Everything looks okay. Do you hear it?"

"I hear it," said Emma. The thump of her baby's heart brought tears to her eyes. Dr. Weiss watched for another moment, and then switched off the machine. "The littlest patient is doing fine. How are you feeling?"

"Better now," she said. "I'm okay. Can I go home?"

He looked doubtfully at her newly resutured and band-aged wounds. "I think you can, as long as you have someone to look after you," he said.

Emma nodded. "Could you find out if it's all right for me to leave?" she asked.

"Sure," said Dr. Weiss. "Let me see if I can scare up the attending physician and have him sign for you to be released."

"Thank you, Doctor," Emma said.

The doctor stood up as the technician unplugged the sonogram machine and began to roll it out of the cubicle. "By the way, there is somebody outside who wants to see you," Dr. Weiss said. "Are you up to some company?"

"Who is it?" Emma said, but the doctor had already disappeared from the cubicle. Could it be David? she thought. And then she thought, no. Realistically, no. If David somehow found out she was here and tried to see her, the police who were guarding her would stop him and hustle him directly down to the police station. He was a suspect in their eyes. The prime suspect. And according to an update Emma had received from Lieutenant Atkins, the police had still not been able to find him, although they were definitely searching for him. Emma looked up as the doctor held the white curtain back, gesturing for the visitor to come in.

Stephanie, looking pretty in a navy blue knit suit and a jaunty scarf, gave the young doctor a beguiling smile as she edged past the curtain that the doctor was holding open. "God, Em, are you all right?" she asked, bending over and kissing Emma gently on the forehead. "I heard about it on the car radio as I was driving back from Trenton. I tried to call David, but there was no answer, so I rushed over here."

Emma sighed. "Somebody tried to push me in front of the express train."

Stephanie clutched her chest. "I know. Oh my God." She sat down in the molded plastic chair, which had just been vacated by Dr. Weiss. "Do they think it was the same guy as in the Pine Barrens?"

Emma nodded. "Yes. He was wearing the ski mask and the hoody but yeah . . . it was the same guy. There's no doubt now. Apparently it was not a case of being in the wrong place at the wrong time. Someone wants me . . . gone." She shuddered at actually saying the words aloud. "Detective Atkins thinks it's my husband."

Stephanie rubbed the back of Emma's hand absently, avoiding her gaze.

"You're awfully quiet," said Emma.

"I'm . . . just trying to take this all in."

"Is that what you think?" Emma asked.

"I don't think anything," Stephanie insisted.

"Yes, you do," said Emma. "Tell me what you think. Let's hear it."

Stephanie's expression was pained. "Look, I like David. He's a nice guy. And you two seem pretty happy . . ."

"We just got married, for God's sake. Why would he marry me and try to kill me on the same day?"

"I don't know. Maybe he decided it was a mistake. You're pregnant. You told me yourself that he proposed when you told him you were pregnant."

"But why marry me and then kill me and his baby? That makes no sense."

"Maybe he's got a girlfriend. Men are cheaters," said Stephanie. Emma knew that Stephanie was thinking of Ken, who had had several affairs while they were together. When Stephanie found out, she tossed his belongings out on the lawn and wouldn't let him back into the house.

"Steph, come on, we're not talking about cheating. We're talking about murder here," Emma protested. "This guy who came after me with the ax meant to kill me. He actually did kill someone."

"Emma, I'm not trying to be mean, but you have to admit, you do have a lot of money. People kill for money all the time. It's a fact. And only one person stands to profit by your death."

"He doesn't care about money," Emma insisted.

168

"Everybody cares about money," Stephanie said.

"I know what you say makes . . . sense in a certain way. It's exactly what the police are thinking. But it's so hard for me to imagine. I married this man less than a week ago. Promised to love and cherish him till death. Now people want me to believe that the man I entrusted my life to is actually trying to cause my death. My own would-be killer. Can you understand how that feels?"

Stephanie did not reply.

"I can't make myself believe it," said Emma.

"But you hardly know him, Em. It was all so quick."

"That doesn't mean it was wrong. David loves me."

"Yeah, well, if he loves you so much, why isn't he here?"

Emma's eyes filled with tears. "I don't know."

Stephanie immediately looked guilty. "Oh, Em. All right, let's say he didn't do it. If he didn't, then who would? You don't have any enemies."

Emma was silent for a moment. Then she said, "Obviously, I do."

"Anyone I know?" Stephanie asked.

"I'm serious, Steph. There may be someone . . . I had a patient at the center who died. A young girl," said Emma. "Her family, her father especially, blamed me. He even came to the center and threatened revenge after she . . . died. Security had to take him out."

"Was it a suicide?" Stephanie asked.

"Eating disorder," said Emma.

"I don't get it," Stephanie. "Why would the guy blame you? I mean, surely there were medical doctors involved in his daughter's treatment. By the time you get to the end stage of an eating disorder . . ."

Emma hesitated. "While I was treating her, I began to suspect that he might be sexually abusing her."

"Who? The father?"

Emma nodded.

"Are most anorexics sexually abused? Was that what made you think it?" Stephanie asked.

Emma shook her head. "No. Anorexia has many etiologies. And many consequences. I mean, one of them is certainly to stall or reverse sexual development, but that in itself doesn't indicate sexual abuse. And, of course, this patient was depressed, but all anorexic patients are depressed. So, no. I wasn't thinking that way. When I first met the parents I noticed that the girl's mother was very . . . fleshy, very . . . provocative, in a way. I definitely did think the anorexia might be a reaction formation to her mother—to try to be as unlike her mother as possible. That would not be unusual in a teenager. But the more I talked to the patient, the more I began to think that her condition might be the result of her avoiding having to take on her mother's role, so to speak."

"What do you mean?" Stephanie asked.

"The role of a sexual partner," said Emma grimly.

"Oh. Oh shit."

"Exactly," said Emma.

"So what did you do?"

"Well, I spoke to Burke, you know, my boss. He agreed with me that we needed to have a doctor at the hospital examine her, a gynecologist who specializes in sexual abuse cases. The physician agreed to do an exam on her. When the father found out about what we were planning, he was furious."

"So she never had the exam?"

"No, she did have it. Her mother gave us permission. The doctor couldn't find any physical evidence of penetration," Emma admitted. "The father took her out of treatment."

Stephanie frowned. "And then the girl died."

"Several weeks later."

"So, you think you were wrong about the father?"

"I may have been," said Emma. "But there are different kinds of molestation. Without the physical evidence, there was nothing more I could do."

"Did you tell all this to that woman detective?" Stephanie asked. "The one I met at the hospital when I was visiting you?"

Emma shook her head. "She knows about this guy. She went and questioned him. Now the guy is more furious than ever. He confronted me at the center today, after he got finished reading Burke the riot act. And what I started to tell you was that I noticed, as I was being carried out to the ambulance, that the music building, where Ly . . . the girl's father works, is directly across from the train station. They've got those big, arched windows, and I could see the music students in there with their instruments."

"What's that got to do with what happened to you?" Stephanie asked.

"The train platform is visible from the music building. He could have seen me waiting there and come after me."

Stephanie frowned, but then she nodded. "I guess . . . it's possible."

"But Lieutenant Atkins is fixated on David," said Emma. "I know she is only concerned about my safety. But this is a blind spot with her. She was telling me that her own husband was . . . well, let's just say she has a lot of negative feelings about marriage, it seems. So, in her eyes, it's David or no one. She's out looking for David right now."

Stephanie frowned. "Was your patient named Ivy Devlin?"

Emma looked up sharply. "Why do you say that?"

"Oh come on, Em. I teach at the middle school. There aren't many kids who die from anorexia. It was Ivy Devlin, wasn't it? Her sister is in one of my classes," said Stephanie.

Emma reddened. "Oh Lord, now I feel guilty. I shouldn't have told you all this."

"Why? You didn't say who it was. Or tell me what she said to you. Besides, Ivy's dead, and somebody's trying to kill you now. Why should you feel guilty for trying to figure it out before they succeed?"

"Still, I was wrong to even discuss it."

Stephanie ignored Emma's fretting. "Alida, that's the sister. She's undergone a real transformation lately. She used to be really shy and modest. Not anymore," said Stephanie.

"Not long after Ivy died, she started coming to school in full glittery makeup, bare midriff. Very junior sexpot."

"Uh-oh," said Emma.

"Why uh-oh?" said Stephanie.

"Nothing, never mind," said Emma. Although undeniably it worried her. Predators were known to repeat their behavior within the family. Sometimes children, long ignored, welcomed any sort of attention. Tried to please their abuser.

"Yeah, but lots of girls dress like that in seventh grade. It's the opposite of anorexia. She's flaunting her sexuality," said Stephanie.

"I know. It's the transformation and the timing of it that sets off alarm bells."

"Why?"

Emma shook her head. "I shouldn't be trying to analyze anyone at a distance. I could be completely wrong. Besides, I'm not an expert in this field. I had to do a lot of extra research and consult with colleagues just to get up to speed."

"You think he might be messing with her now? The father."

"Steph, I really cannot talk about this."

Stephanie looked at her thoughtfully. "He can't be allowed to just get away with this. As one of her teachers, I could intervene. I could talk to Alida. She might confide in me," said Stephanie.

"Please, Stephanie, don't get involved in this. I mean it. I should never have opened my mouth. I was really out of line."

"But the kid could still be suffering," Stephanie cried.

"Look, let me be blunt," said Emma. "Alida might tell her parents if you started asking questions. I will tell you this. I think Lyle Devlin could be dangerous. Promise me you won't . . ."

"Don't worry," said Stephanie.

Dr. Weiss pulled back the curtain at the front of the cubicle and looked inside. He was holding a clipboard with a form on it. He grinned at Stephanie before he spoke to

Emma. "I have your release form here. If you want to sign it, you can be on your way."

"Great," said Emma, reaching for the clipboard.

"Is there someone who can pick you up and stay with you?"

Before Emma could reply, Stephanie said, "She's coming to my house."

Emma looked at her friend gratefully. "Thanks, Steph."

"She'll have to leave in a wheelchair," said Dr. Weiss. "The orderly is bringing one right now. Do you have a license to drive one of them?" he asked Stephanie in a teasing tone.

"Actually, I'm not old enough," Stephanie purred.

Dr. Weiss reluctantly turned his attention back to Emma. "You need to speak to your attending physician before you go."

"Thanks," said Emma.

Once Dr. Weiss was gone, Stephanie helped Emma off the bed and into her dress, which was bloodstained and dirty. "We'll wash this when we get home," said Steph. "You can wear something of mine. We're about the same size."

"Thanks, Steph," said Emma. She tried to reach up to brush her hair, but her side was stinging.

"Let me," said Stephanie, brushing out Emma's heavy, honey-colored hair and then, over Emma's protests, dabbing some blusher on her pale cheeks.

"Here," said Stephanie, rummaging in Emma's purse. "Put on some lipstick. You look like a ghost."

Emma did as she was told and then looked into her compact mirror at the results. Her hair glistened. Her skin glowed with a little color on her cheeks and lips. She did not look like a woman who had barely escaped being pushed into the path of a train, she thought.

The attending physician came in and gave Emma instructions on the care of her wounds. "All right," said Stephanie, after he left. "Let's get you out of here."

Emma nodded. She was grateful to have such a caring friend, but her heart ached to think that her husband seemed to have abandoned her and was nowhere to be found. Maybe the police had caught up with him and were interrogating him right now. With a sigh, Emma gathered up her purse and the blue-green cape and started toward the door.

"Wait a minute," said Stephanie. "Into the chair."

Emma obediently eased herself into the wheelchair and allowed Stephanie to push her out the door. The young police officer who was stationed outside the cubicle in the ER jumped to his feet at the sight of them.

"Wait a minute," he said. "Hold it. Have you been officially discharged from here, Mrs. Webster?"

Stephanie handed him the release form, and he examined it.

"My friend is taking me to her house," Emma explained.

"Can you wait a moment?" he asked. "I need to call my CO for instructions."

"Sure," said Stephanie.

The police officer spoke on his two-way radio in a low voice and then turned back to them. "I'm to escort you to where you're going," he said. "Then there will be a patrol outside the house that will come around once an hour."

"Thank you, officer," said Emma.

"I'm parked out front," said Stephanie. "We'll go out the front door."

"Fine," said Emma, trying to smile. "I'll get a longer ride."

Following the signs, they wended their way out of the emergency ward, the uniformed policeman walking beside them, past the admitting, bookkeeping, and the lab areas until they reached the vestibule. As they turned the corner into the lobby area, Emma glanced at the elevators and let out a cry.

"David!" He was holding a cardboard tray of coffee cups and was waiting for the elevator.

David turned and looked in her direction. His eyes widened in alarm. The elevator doors opened, but he ignored them, dropping the tray on a nearby table and rushing toward her. He knelt down by the wheelchair and gathered her into his arms. "Baby, what are you doing here? I thought you went to New York. Are you all right?"

The cop drew out his billy club and pointed it at David. "Excuse me. Do you know this man, ma'am?" he asked Emma.

Every bit of anger she had felt vanished with the relief of seeing his face. "This is my husband," she said. "David Webster. What are you doing here? The police have been looking everywhere for you."

David rocked back on his heels. "Why? What's happened?"

Emma looked at him balefully. "I got pushed in front of a train."

"What?" he cried. "Oh my God. Oh, Emma." He grabbed her hands and squeezed them so tightly that she winced.

Emma nodded. "The same guy. In the ski mask. I was on the train platform, and he pushed me from behind. A skateboarder saved me. I tried to call you. You weren't there."

The police officer tucked his club beneath his arm, pulled out his radio, and began to speak into it.

"Jesus Christ. Are you all right? Is the baby all right?"

"They're both all right," said Stephanie coolly. "I'm taking Emma home with me."

"This is all my fault," David said. "I should never have let you leave the house that way. I shouldn't have let you out of my sight."

Emily shook her head. "You had no way of knowing. I mean, we both thought it was a random thing."

"Now we know better," he said.

"Yes," she said.

"How could anyone . . . ?" His gaze looked tortured. "Why would anyone want to hurt you?"

Emma shook her head. "I don't know. What are you doing at the hospital, David?"

He ran a hand through his unruly hair. "Oh, I've been here for hours. My mother. She took a turn for the worse. Birdie called me in a panic after you left and said that Mother couldn't breathe at all."

"Oh no." Emma looked at him worriedly. "How's she doing now?"

He sighed. "She's out of the woods now. She's stabilized. They had to do some kind of procedure. Anyway, I was about to leave," he said, gesturing toward the brown bag and tray on the table. "I just went out to get Birdie a cup of coffee."

The officer hooked his radio back into his belt and stepped between them, prodding David in the chest with his club. "Sir, can you stand up please? I've been instructed to bring you down to the police station with me. Right now."

"Officer, I think this is a misunderstanding," Emma protested. "My husband has been here at the hospital all afternoon."

"We'll sort this out at the station," the officer said. "Sir, please stand up."

"Look, I just want to be with my wife. She's been through hell."

The officer gazed at him impassively. "She's been here for hours," he said. "Maybe you should have thought of that sooner."

David glared at the officer. "I didn't know about it, all right? I thought my wife was out of town. I can't leave her now."

"You'll have to," said the young officer.

David looked at him with narrowed eyes. "Are you arresting me?"

"If necessary," said the cop. "Now let's go."

David looked at Emma with a stricken gaze, shaking his head. "I'm sorry, Em . . ." He reached out a hand to her. She hesitated. By the time she tried to take it, the officer was gripping David's arm, pulling him away.

"I said let's go, Mr. Webster."

David shook off the policeman's hand. "All right, all right. I'm coming."

The officer ignored him and continued to force him along toward the door.

"Oh my God, Steph," said Emma. "What are they doing? This is all a mistake."

"Come on," said Stephanie. "The police will take care of it. Let's get out of here."

CHAPTER 20

"I Want to go home," Emma said.

"Home?" Stephanie asked, taking her eyes off the road for a second to stare at Emma. "As in, your house?"

"Yes. I want to be there when David gets back from the police station."

"Honey, you don't know that he's even going to get back tonight."

"He was at the hospital with his mother, Steph. You heard him."

Stephanie sighed. "If you want to go home, I'll take you there."

"Will you stay with me?" Emma asked.

"Of course," said Stephanie.

When they arrived at Emma's house and got out of the car, video cameras whirred and microphones were thrust into their faces. Emma's house, glowing warmly from the lights inside, only a hundred feet away, seemed as distant as Shangri-la.

"Emma, what happened?" a reporter cried.

"Did he try it again?" asked another.

"Are you all right? What happened?"

Their questions cascaded over one another. "Leave her alone," Stephanie cried as they inched toward the front door.

Emma heard their insinuations and knew that she had to ignore them. The officer who had been following them suddenly materialized out of the crowd and held the reporters back with outstretched arms, and a nightstick in his hand.

As they entered the house, the reporters' voices were squawking behind them like crows. Stephanie closed the door and leaned against it. "God, Emma, they are brutal," she said.

"Yeah, but you were great," Emma said, shaking her head. "I thought you were going to punch one of those guys."

"I should have," said Stephanie.

They smiled at each other, and then, suddenly, they began to laugh. It wasn't exactly mirth—more like laughing to keep from crying, but it still felt like a relief.

"Mind sharing the joke?"

Emma jumped, and Stephanie cried out. Emma turned and saw her stepfather standing in the doorway to the living room. "What are you doing here? How did you get in?"

Rory's expression was placid. "Your mother gave me her key."

"So you just waltz in here without asking?" Emma cried. "How dare you just let yourself into my home?" Emma was shaking.

Rory did not reply. He turned and went back into the living room, settling himself comfortably in an armchair. Emma turned to Stephanie and shook her head in disbelief.

"I'll go make us a cup of tea," said Stephanie.

Emma had no choice but to follow Rory into the living room.

"Why are you here?" she demanded.

Rory unbuttoned his jacket and smoothed down his tie. "I was in New York on business and your mother called me from Chicago. She was terribly worried about you after you called her today. Something about the nurse leaving. And then, when you didn't show up in New York, Jessie was worried and called her," Rory explained.

"Oh no," Emma groaned. "I called Jessie to tell her I wasn't coming."

"Not until you were at the hospital," said Rory.

Emma reddened. "How do you know about that?"

"I called the police, of course. And no, I haven't told your mother yet. You'd better call her and let her know that everything is all right. It is all right, isn't it? The baby and all."

"Yes. Fine," said Emma.

"And I take it they have your husband in custody."

"You'd like that, wouldn't you, Rory?"

"Well, don't they?" he asked.

"For your information, David was at the hospital when I was attacked. With his mother. Sorry to disappoint you, but my husband did not do this."

Rory adjusted his tie and composed his hands in his lap. "I know you don't like me, Emma. But your mother adores you, and her happiness is very important to me."

"Is it really?" Emma asked. Her anger at him boiled up inside, and suddenly it seemed the ideal opportunity to confront him, to wipe that smirk off his face.

"Of course," he said.

"Is that why you date other women?" she asked.

"Please, sit down, dear," he said mildly. "You're injured. You're pregnant."

"Don't change the subject," she said. But she was feeling weak in the knees and needed to sit. She edged around the sofa and sank down onto a cushion, huddled against the arm farthest from Rory.

"What is the subject?" he said.

"I saw you in Chiara's in New York. You were nuzzling up to some woman, not my mother," she insisted.

"I'm sorry I didn't see you there. You should have spoken to me," he said.

"I didn't want to interrupt," she said.

"Not at all. I would have enjoyed introducing you to my companion. You'd like Charlotte. She's beautiful and fun. She was my first wife, actually."

"Your wife?" said Emma, surprised.

179

"First wife. Yes. I married her in college. Loved her dearly, but she left me."

"So, what now? She's changed her mind?" Emma asked.

"She left me for a woman."

Emma blanched.

"Oh, don't look so embarrassed. It was humiliating. But I survived. Now I don't really care who knows about it. I went on to have a much better marriage with your mother. And Charlotte is living with some lady veterinarian down in the Florida panhandle. She happened to be coming to New York when I was. I know you were hoping it would be something sordid that you could report to your mother . . ."

"I only mentioned I saw you . . . from a distance," she insisted.

Rory waved his hand dismissively. "Kay knows all about Charlotte. Just as I know all about Mitch Hollis. Although, admittedly theirs was a much more successful union. But, Emma, your mother and I are happy together. We are very fortunate to have found each other."

Emma blushed. His tone was only mildly chastening, but she knew that she had insulted Rory and her mother by suggesting that he was being unfaithful to her. And no wonder. Wasn't that exactly what people were doing to her and David these days? she thought. Doubting their commitment? And wasn't it maddening when it happened? "Sorry," she mumbled. "No offense."

"None taken," said Rory. Then he frowned. "So, your mother said on the phone that the nurse we hired for you left and didn't come back."

"That's right. She walked out. She got mad, and she left," said Emma.

"I called the health care agency," said Rory. "The supervisor didn't know anything about Miss Slocum's leaving."

"They didn't know?" Emma asked, a little dismayed by this news. "Were they concerned? I mean, is this par for the course, or is this the first time she's done something like that?"

"She's extremely reliable. I wouldn't have hired her otherwise. And yes, they were concerned. They were going to call her home to check on her."

"What if she's not there?"

"I'm sure they have emergency numbers and so forth."

"Maybe they should call the police," said Emma.

Rory shook his head. "I think your own experiences have you a little jumpy here. Adults are not considered missing until several days have passed," he said. "Still, it seems a little strange to me."

"It is," said Emma.

Stephanie came into the room, carrying a tray with three teacups on it. "Anyone for a pick-me-up?" she asked.

Rory shook his head and pushed himself out of the chair. "I'd love to stay and visit with you ladies, but I need to be getting back to New York. I want to conclude my business so I can get home to Emma's mother. Are you sure you're all right here, Emma? What are we doing about protecting you now?"

Emma noted the "we" but resisted the urge to object to his paternalistic tone. "Stephanie is staying until David gets back. And the police are coming by every hour. Checking on the house."

"Emma, I just don't think that's adequate. There have been two attempts on your life. The police should be stationed outside, not just driving aimlessly around. If they refuse to do that, then I think you should have a full-time bodyguard. Until the police capture whoever is doing this."

Emma sighed. "I think you're probably right. I'll look into it."

"I'd be glad to do it for you," said Rory.

"I will take care of it," she said.

"Your mother and I will check in with you tomorrow," he warned. "By the way, before I forget, I have the papers for the Mathis boy's trust." Rory reached into a calfskin folder and handed them to Emma. "If you want to sign them where it's marked, I'll take them along and set things in motion."

"Okay," said Emma, accepting the sheaf of papers and glancing at them briefly. She signed everywhere he had put an X. "Thanks for arranging this . . . Rory."

Rory snapped the cap on his pen. "Glad I could help." He tucked the pen into his vest pocket. Just then the front doorknob rattled, and all three of them looked up at it. David opened the door, walked into the front hallway, and looked around.

"David," Emma cried.

She started to rise from her seat, but he was beside her before she had stepped away from the sofa. He wrapped his arms around her and held her fiercely. Emma felt all the tension inside of her give way in his embrace. Finally, he freed her and she looked up at him.

"What happened?" she asked.

"Nothing. Yunger came over and read them the riot act and they had to let me go. As he pointed out to them, I had an alibi for the entire afternoon. I was at the hospital. I didn't even want to dignify their questions with answers but . . . that's why you have a lawyer. To keep you from acting stupid. So, anyway, here I am." He turned to Rory and Stephanie. "Hello, Rory. This is a surprise."

"I'm just leaving," said Rory.

David turned to Stephanie. "Thanks, Steph," he said. "For taking care of Emma for me."

Stephanie nodded. "No problem."

David looked at Emma. "I can take it from here," he said.

Rory put the papers back into his briefcase and turned to David. "Keep Emma and my grandchild safe," he said in a warning tone.

"I'll do my best," said David.

"So far, Dave, your best has been a little short of the mark," said Rory.

Emma felt resentment start to rise in her throat, but David smiled and shook Rory's hand. "I promise you," he said.

"Good-bye, Emma," Rory said. He patted Emma awkwardly on the shoulder.

"I guess I'll go too," said Stephanie. "Are you sure you don't want to come home with me?"

"I'm fine right here," said Emma. She and Stephanie embraced.

"I'll call you tomorrow," said Stephanie. "Get some sleep."

"I need to hang my coat up. I'll see you out," David said.

After they walked out of the room, Emma sank back down into the sofa. She felt light-headed and drained. She was still shaken from the attempt on her life, surprised by her stepfather's concern, and relieved to have her husband home again.

David came back into the room, rolling up the sleeves of his chambray work shirt. "He's not such a bad guy," he said, flopping down on the sofa beside her.

Emma nodded. "Rory? I was thinking that. Maybe I've misjudged him."

"Although I still hate that he calls me Dave," David said. Emma smiled.

"Are you sure you're okay?" he said.

Emma nodded. Then she glanced at him. "Now I am."

"Are you still angry at me? From this afternoon? I wouldn't blame you if you were. I was such a jerk. Trying to excuse my own . . . missteps, by implying that you and Burke . . . I mean, I know better."

"It's all right. That seems like a million years ago," she said.

Headlights flashed outside as a car slowed. David got up and walked over to the window, lifting the flax-colored curtain. "The police are out there."

"They said they're going to be checking on the house regularly tonight," said Emma.

"I'm glad," he said. "This nightmare just won't quit. I want you to tell me everything that happened. We need to talk about taking some serious measures for keeping you safe."

"I know. Rory said the same thing. But not now. I'm exhausted," she said.

"I know you are," he said, looking at her closely. "We better get you to bed." He walked over to the sofa.

"I wish we could sleep upstairs in our bed. The two of us," she said.

He stood gazing at her for a moment. Then he bent over and lifted her into his arms. She yelped in surprise and threw her arms around his neck. "We can," he said. He carried her to the foot of the staircase as she laid her head carefully against his chest. She could hear his heart beating. Holding her close, he began to climb.

* * *

Despite her exhaustion, Emma felt irresistibly drawn to her husband, and they cautiously managed to make love. Then she fell into a deep sleep. It was the kind of sleep that, if left undisturbed, would last until late in the morning and leave a person groggy in its wake. But sometime into the third or fourth hour of sleep, something caused her to awaken with a start. Her heart was thumping, and her armpits felt clammy with sweat. A bad dream, she thought. Must have been. She couldn't remember it now.

The heat in the bedroom, turned low for the night-time, was almost nonexistent, and she could feel the chill outside her covers. She turned over, ready to reach for David, to fold herself against him and fall asleep again, lulled by the reassurance of his animal warmth. His covers were pulled back, his side of the bed empty.

Immediately, she was wide awake, feeling a rush of panic. I'm alone, she thought. He's gone. Calm down, she thought. He probably went to the bathroom. She listened for the sound of running water, but the house was silent.

"David," she whispered. There was no answer.

Her heart was thudding now, and she felt sick to her stomach. She could feel herself spiraling into a panic. Stop it, she thought. Maybe he couldn't sleep and didn't want to disturb her. Maybe he was downstairs, watching TV with the sound muted. But none of it made her feel better. Maybe he had disappeared too, like the nurse. Vanished from the house.

She knew she could lie there in the dark wondering, or she could get up and go find out. She knew what she wanted to do. She wanted to get up. But her limbs felt leaden under the covers, and she was too frightened to budge.

You have to get up, she thought. You could be here until morning like this, staring for endless hours into the darkness, because there is no way you are going back to sleep. She perused the room mentally, thinking about arming herself somehow. Then she remembered the kitchen knife. David had gone down to the kitchen for a cold drink after they had made love. He'd brought the knife back upstairs with him and had tucked it under the mattress, just in case.

Emma stuck one arm out from under the covers and groped around with her cold hand until she located the edge of the mattress. Sticking her hand tentatively between the mattress and the box spring, she carefully felt around until her fingers touched the metal blade. Her fingers traveled down to the handle and she gripped it, wresting it from its hiding place and drawing it under the covers.

Now that she was armed, part of her just wanted to stay there, as if the bed were her fortress. But reluctantly she swung her legs out and, still clutching the knife, swooped up her robe, pulling it on, snagging one sleeve on the tip of the blade. When she had the robe belted, she searched with her feet for her slippers and, shivering, slid them on. She thought about snapping on the bedside light but then decided against it. Darkness could be an advantage. If the worst had happened, if her enemy was here in the house and had somehow subdued her husband, she was better off in darkness. She knew this house better than any stranger could. She could glide through it without the aid of light. Another person might make a misstep. Might fall.

She tiptoed across the room and out to the upstairs hallway. Easing her way down the hall, knife in hand, she looked

185

over the railing into the living room. She did not see her husband. Where are you, David? she thought. You promised not to leave me alone. For one moment she regretted that she had not stayed with Stephanie.

Stop it, she thought. You're letting your imagination run away with you. David is here, in the house. Maybe he was hungry and went back downstairs to get something in the kitchen. Or maybe he couldn't sleep and decided to do a little work in his office. Just go down there and look.

But the thought of descending those stairs, alone, in the dark, was terrifying. She stood at the top of the staircase, torn between the desire to go downstairs, or to rush back to her room, lock the door, and call Lieutenant Atkins. Joan Atkins wouldn't be angry at her. She would understand. As Emma hesitated, holding her breath like someone about to leap into a deep ravine, her eye caught a movement in the unfinished nursery across the hall.

Only a corner of the room was visible, but her eyes had adapted to the darkness. She saw something move across the patch of moonlight on the floor. Gripping the knife in her sweaty hand, she took a few steps closer to the door. As a little more of the room came into view, she saw what had caused the movement. The curved rockers on the chair had moved slightly as the barefoot man sitting in it shifted his weight. Though his back was to her, and the rocking chair was facing out the back windows, she recognized her husband right away. Wearing a T-shirt and his pajama bottoms, he was bent forward, his elbows resting on the rounded arms of the chair, the palms of his hands pressed against his eye sockets, his fingers curved up over his forehead into his scalp. He looked as if he was trying to keep his head from exploding.

Emma took a step into the room and slipped the knife into the pocket of her bathrobe. "David?" she said.

He uttered a strangled cry and dropped his hands, turning on her.

"Honey, what's the matter?" she asked. She approached the chair and sank down carefully, aware of the knife in her pocket, onto the rug beside the chair, laying her forearm across his knees. "You look terrible."

"Nothing," he said. "I couldn't sleep."

"You looked like you were in pain," she said.

He patted her arm in the soft bathrobe. "I'm fine."

"Why are you sitting in this room?"

"I didn't want to go downstairs and leave you alone up here."

Emma nodded, pretending to accept his explanation, but her mind was racing. She had not been mistaken about what she saw. He had obviously been in terrible distress, and now he was denying it, trying to reassure her. It's not so strange, she tried to tell herself. Not after the events of the last week. "So much has happened," she said. "I've been so focused on myself I haven't been thinking about you. Are you worried about your mother?"

For a moment, he looked at her blankly. Then he shrugged. "Well, sure. But unless she gets that transplant . . . this kind of thing is inevitable. She's only hanging on by a thread. She made it this time. Next time, who knows? Look, I don't want to think about my mother. Or talk about her."

"Okay," she said. "It's just that you looked so . . . despairing."

"Well, you weren't meant to see me," he said in a mild, placating tone. "You were supposed to be sleeping."

"Don't do that," she pleaded. "Don't shut me out like that. Talk to me. It scares me to see you looking so . . . hopeless. Tell me what you're thinking. We need to say what we feel. Whatever it is, just tell me."

David stared at her face, half illuminated by moonlight. In the dark room, his eyes were glittering holes in his head. "You don't want to know."

"Yes," she said, but her stomach did a sickening flip at his words. "I do."

He looked out the back windows. Then he sighed, reached out, and took her hands, kneading them absently in his. "You're such a good person," he said. "The kind of woman any man would be proud to call his wife."

The compliments alarmed her. They sounded strangely . . . impersonal. She withdrew her hands from his and sat back on her heels. "What's this all about?"

He shook his head. "Emma, you should never have married me. I know it was my idea for us to get married, but I'm not meant to be a husband. Or a parent," he said.

She felt as if he had slammed her in her heart. "Don't say that," she protested. "Why would you say that?"

She hoped he would smile or tell her it was a passing bad mood that was making him talk that way, but he turned his head back and stared at her, his expression not changing. "You asked me to tell you what I was thinking," he said.

"It's not true," she cried. "You're a wonderful husband. It's just all this . . . horrible stuff that's happened. Anybody would feel . . . overwhelmed," she said. But even to her own ears her words sounded . . . panicky. Was this depression talking? she wondered. And, if it was, how severe? She hadn't seen the signs before. But it had to be depression. And it had come on so suddenly. Or he had been masking it so well. "When did you start to feel this way?" she asked.

David shook his head and seemed to stare into the past. "Always," he said. "Having kids was too much for my father. He walked out on us when I was two. And my mother never seemed to be there. She had no choice, of course. She did the best she could, but she had to work. My brother had to take care of me a lot of the time, and he hated it. He used to play this game where he would throw lighted matches at me. Or he would take me places with him like the movies and then just . . . leave me behind," he said.

"Oh, David," she said.

"I'm not . . . fishing for sympathy. It's not that. It's just that I . . . I saw myself as a burden to people. Maybe I would treat a child the same way," he said.

She felt a terror in her heart that equaled the fear she had felt earlier in the day, teetering over the abyss of the train tracks. Maybe this threat was even worse. He was threatening, not her life, but her happiness. Her hopes, her dreams.

Stop, she thought. Depression is not the end of the world. It can be cured. Things can get better.

"David, once this mess is behind us, once they catch whoever is doing these horrible things, you're going to start to feel better. And, in the meantime, there's all kinds of medication these days that can help. I know I'm talking like a shrink, but this is my turf. I know a lot about depression. You have to trust me. You and I are going to have a wonderful life together. As for kids, lots of people with unhappy childhoods end up being excellent with their own children. They try harder. It matters more to them."

He regarded her silently.

Please God, she thought, needing faith more than expertise. Don't let him desert me. Help him to see how much I need him. "Come back to bed," she said. "Right now what you need is rest. We both do. Tomorrow things will look better."

She leaned up to embrace him and felt the point of the knife pierce through her bathrobe pocket and nick her in the thigh. She stifled a yelp. She didn't want him to know that she had the knife in her pocket. Didn't want him to know she was afraid.

CHAPTER 21

Long after David was breathing peacefully, Emma lay awake, thinking about her husband and her marriage. He seemed to have changed in the short time they had been married. Of course their experience had been nightmarish, but maybe, she thought, maybe it was her very vulnerability that was alarming him. Maybe all her injuries, her feebleness, her fears were reminding him of the difficult role that he was taking on. After all, as a father, he would be responsible for a small, vulnerable human being. The idea of having a wife who was also weak and dependent might be overwhelming to him.

There was nothing she could do about his anxieties about fatherhood, she thought. But she could try to face her own fear. Her fear was not some flight of the imagination. Her fear was real. Yes, someone was trying to kill her. Although she went over it and over it in her mind, she could not imagine who might hate her that much or want her dead. She knew that Lyle Devlin was angry at her, but was he mad enough to murder? Or could it be the person, whoever it was, who had sent her those anonymous notes? Someone who might be angry about her marriage? She tried to imagine hate like that, tried in vain to put a face to that disturbed person, but came up with a blank.

She took some consolation from the fact that the police were after this killer and surely they would catch him. In the meantime, she told herself, she was not alone. And she was not a weak person. She would prove it to David. Besides, she could not stand this sense of helplessness that was running her life. A change might salvage their brand-new marriage. If she lived through all this turmoil and lost her marriage, she would be completely miserable. She had to try. This determination, however fleeting, calmed her turbulent heart, and she was finally able to sleep.

She awoke the next morning with a sickening feeling of fear and apprehension in her heart, and before she had even opened her eyes, she remembered why. But when she finally forced herself to admit she was awake, and looked at her husband, she saw that he was propped up on one elbow, gazing at her.

"Hi," she whispered.

"Hi."

"How are you feeling?" she said.

"Better. Sorry about last night," he said.

"It's all right. I'm glad you're feeling better."

"I am. Except that I'm worried sick about you. I'm supposed to go to New York again today. Another assignment," he said. "But I'm going to cancel it. We can do it on the telephone."

"Maybe you should go. It might get your mind off . . . all this."

"No. I can't leave you here alone," he said.

"What are you going to do?" she teased him gently. "Go to work with me?"

"You can't go to work," he said.

"David, I want to," she said. "I can't just sit around here, waiting for . . . I don't know what. I need to be busy. Especially after what happened yesterday. I need to do something useful."

"You need to rest," he insisted.

Emma smiled. "Being occupied will be the best medicine."

He shook his head. "I might as well be talking to the wall." He frowned at her. "You look lost in thought. What are you thinking about?"

Emma pressed her lips together. "Something I should have thought about sooner," she said.

"What's that?"

"Now that we know that I am the actual . . . target of this . . . maniac, I have to live in a different way. I can't rely on other people to take care of me all the time. I don't want you avoiding doing your job because of me. And I can't be looking over my shoulder every minute. I'm going to get a gun," she said.

"A gun?" he cried. "That's crazy. I thought we were talking about a bodyguard."

"Well, maybe the police will provide one," Emma said.

David shook his head. "Nothing doing. I asked them about protection for you when they cut me loose last night, but the Clarenceville police chief said that there was no money in his budget for private bodyguards. Do you believe that? What do we pay taxes for? Anyway, I'm going to call a few places and inquire about bodyguards. I think it's something we have to do."

"That's fine," said Emma. "I think you should. But meanwhile, I want to carry a gun."

"I don't believe this. Do you even know how to use a gun?"

"Hey, I shot at the guy who tried to kill me in the cabin, didn't I?"

"Somehow you managed to discharge a weapon, yes," David said. "That's not the same as knowing how to shoot."

Emma made a pretend pistol out of her hand and blew on the index finger. "Well, as a matter of fact, I do," she said. "My dad taught me how to use a gun when I was a kid and we'd go camping together. We used to shoot our empty plastic bottles and cans. What's the matter? You look sick."

"Emma, I don't like it," he said.

"David, there's a man trying to kill me. I know that, for a fact. What is to prevent him from trying again?"

"Don't even say it," he insisted.

"I can't stick my head in the ground, David. I have to face facts."

David took her wrists gently in his hands and shook them. "I know that, honey. But shooting tin cans is a lot different from shooting at another person. Could you actually do that if you had to?" he asked.

Emma looked squarely into his eyes. "That's exactly what I did at the cabin."

David shook his head. "They say if you aren't an expert with a gun, it can easily be turned against you."

"I think it will all come back to me. Like riding a bicycle." It sounded like a joke, but she did not smile.

"But it takes time to get a gun," he protested. "You can't just walk in the store, plunk down your money, and walk out with a gun."

"I don't have to," she said. "I own one."

David stared at her. Then he looked around the walls of their bedroom as if he were seeing them for the first time. "You have a gun here? In this house?"

Emma shook her head. "No. You know that storage area that I keep? It's still half full of stuff from home. Stuff of my father's that my mother cleaned out when she and Rory were moving to the city."

"The gun is in there?" he said.

"I'm pretty sure it is. It's a pistol that belonged to my dad. It hasn't been fired in—I don't know how long. But a little WD-40 and I'll be in business."

"Emma, I just don't know."

Emma swung her legs slowly, painfully, over the side of the bed. "I do," she said.

"What are you doing?" he asked.

"Getting ready," she said. "I can't sit here and wait for this maniac to come and find me. I have to keep my mind occupied. I told you. I'm going to work. And then I'm going to get my gun."

* * *

David drove her to the Wrightsman Youth Center and accompanied her up to her office, helping her take off the blue-green alpaca cape. He hung it on the clothes tree in her waiting room, and although she normally kept her coat in her office closet, Emma appreciated the fact that he was being so solicitous. Beneath the cape she wore a long, camel-colored skirt in a soft, merino wool, and a matching high-necked sweater. Her shiny hair hung in a French braid with soft tendrils loose around her face. David put his arms around her and kissed her repeatedly. "You look beautiful," he said. "Now listen. Do not leave these premises alone. Not for lunch. Not for anything. Call me when you need me to come and get you. I'll pick you up and we'll head over to the . . . you know . . . storage place."

"Okay," she assured him.

"Don't let any strangers into your office." He brushed the tendrils of hair gently away from her face. "On my way out I'll ask Burke to have somebody from security follow you wherever you go today, until we can hire our own protection."

Emma was about to protest, but then she thought better of it. It was a reflex to say she was all right, that she could handle whatever might happen. The reflex of a girl, then a woman, who had always felt confident and in control of her destiny. But that just wasn't true right now, and it didn't help to pretend it was. Her life was in danger. That was the truth. "All right," she said. "Go ahead."

Emma gave David a last kiss good-bye. He turned to leave her office and let out a sudden cry.

"What is it?" she said.

She heard a deep voice say, "Is Dr. Webster here?"

David stood back, and Kieran Foster, clad in black, with his magenta-topped hair and three eyes, appeared in the doorway, wielding a guitar.

"Kieran," said Emma. "Good to see you."

David frowned and waved as the boy edged past him and seated himself in the chair next to Emma's desk. Emma blew her husband a kiss as he disappeared from view. Kieran did not seem to notice. "I wanted you to hear a song I wrote," Kieran said.

Emma smiled. She knew that Natalie, at Burke's behest, sometimes used to critique the creative writings of the center's teenaged patients. Emma had heard Natalie say once that Kieran's lyrics showed promise, and Kieran had been, by all accounts, on top of the world for a short time. But then again, Natalie was a published poet, so her opinion had a certain amount of heft. "I'm not much of a judge," said Emma, toying absently with her gold teardrop earring. "But I'd love to hear it."

* * *

The shrill bell announcing the end of fourth period rang just as Stephanie was yelling out the textbook pages for the homework. "And leave your composition books on your desk so I can grade your essays tonight."

A chorus of groans greeted the prospect of an essay grade and the news of an assignment, when they had hoped to escape without one.

There was the usual flurry of shouted insults and good-natured shoving that always accompanied the changing of classes. Stephanie walked over to a slight, blond-haired girl who was gathering up her books and placing her composition book on the corner of the desk.

"Alida?" she said. "Can I talk to you for a minute?"

Alida Devlin looked at Stephanie warily. Her lips and cheeks were painted in shades of pink that matched a gauzy shirt, which appeared to be fashionably shredded. Her push-up bra was visible through the fabric. Her blond hair was twisted into a shiny coil with a brushy end, and long, straight bangs curved down one side of her face and across her smudged, mascaraed eyes.

"I have to go to health," the girl said.

"That's all right. I'll give you a pass," said Stephanie. "Sit down for a minute."

Alida sighed and sat down at the desk she was about to vacate, a Formica, blond wood top with a seat bolted to it. Alida piled her books in front of her and took out a purple marking pen from her purse. She slumped across the desktop and began to doodle on the brown cardboard cover of one of her notebooks, avoiding Stephanie's gaze. "What'd I do?" Alida asked.

"Nothing," said Stephanie, sitting down at the desk in front of her and twisting around so she could speak to her over the back of the chair. "You didn't do anything."

"So why do I have to stay?"

Stephanie hesitated. Now that her opportunity was here, she didn't know how she was going to approach the problem. She had thought about it all night and was determined to say something, anything, that might get through to Devlin's daughter. If she was her father's victim, somebody had to try to help her. "Look," said Stephanie, "I know that you . . . that this year has been very tough for you. I know about your sister."

Stephanie could see the girl blanch, even under the layers of pink makeup.

"I don't mean to bring up a painful subject, but that's a very tough thing to have to deal with. I was wondering if you were seeing anybody. You know, a psychologist or a counselor."

Alida's heart-shaped face hardened, and she continued to doodle. "My dad says that shrinks are full of it."

"I'm surprised," said Stephanie. "Your father's a very . . . educated person. He has to know that psychologists can really help us when we have a problem."

"He said it was the shrink's fault about Ivy . . ." Her voice trailed away.

"He blamed the shrink for Ivy's death?" Stephanie exclaimed.

Alida shrank back. "I didn't say that," she said.

Stephanie realized she had overreacted. "No, of course not. It's just that when something like this happens in a family, sometimes the adults are too . . . upset to be much help to the kids. That's why it can be helpful to go outside the family."

"For what?" Alida said.

"Well, for someone to talk to," said Stephanie. "Especially if things are out of hand at home. In any way."

"What do you mean?" the girl asked, keeping her eyes focused on the scribblings of the purple pen.

Stephanie realized that she had to tread carefully. "Sometimes losing a child—parents can blame each other. It's not rational, but it happens."

Alida twisted her lips and concentrated on her doodling.

"Sometimes they turn to their children. When parents . . . depend on their children for . . . you know . . . comfort and such, it can become a . . . an unhealthy situation."

Alida stopped doodling and stared at Stephanie as if she did not understand one word of what Stephanie was suggesting. Stephanie realized that the girl was not going to confide in her. In fact, Stephanie had the distinct feeling that if she didn't stop talking, she might be jeopardizing her own job.

"Look, Alida, all I'm trying to say is, if you need an adult to talk to, you can always talk to me. About anything. I'm here and . . . I have time to talk if you want to talk. Just so you know that."

"Can I go now?" Alida said.

"Sure," said Stephanie, feeling defeated and even a little bit foolish.

"I need that pass," said Alida. "For health."

"Oh sure, of course," said Stephanie. She got up from the student's desk and walked back to her own desk. She rummaged in the papers piled on her desk and found the form for a lateness pass. "Who's the teacher?"

"Mr. Kurtis."

"Okay." Stephanie scribbled out the pass and handed it to her.

"Thanks," said Alida softly. She did not meet Stephanie's gaze but shifted her books from one hip to the other and hurried, pass in hand, out of the room.

Stephanie sighed and leaned back in her swivel chair. That went well, she thought, shaking her head. Of course, what had she expected? She couldn't state her actual speculations aloud, and the kid wasn't about to break down and tell her most intimate secrets to a virtual stranger. And it was frustrating, because she really wanted to offer the kid an escape hatch. It wasn't so much that she thought Devlin was a killer. It was still Emma's husband who was on the top of Stephanie's not-to-be-trusted list.

But she did trust Emma's instincts when it came to Devlin and his daughters. From what Stephanie had seen, Emma had a real gift for getting to the heart of other people's problems. If Emma had a suspicion that Devlin was molesting his daughter, then Stephanie was willing to bet she was right. Too bad Emma couldn't be expected to be that insightful about herself. We're all blinded by love, Stephanie thought.

Stephanie stood up and wiped the marker off the board behind her so it would be clean for her next class and looked at her watch. She had just enough time in this free period to mark a few of the essays before the next class arrived. Alida's class had left their composition books on their desks as she had asked them to. She got up and began collecting them. She walked up and down the rows, making a pile of notebooks in the crook of her arm. When she reached Alida's desk and picked up the notebook, something purple caught her eye.

On the front of the composition book was a small, purple marker drawing of a girl's face. Behind her pile of books, Alida had been doodling on it. The girl she had drawn had a ponytail that stood straight up from the top of her head, and the face was an inverted triangle with round vacant eyes and two dots for a nose. The mouth was a tiny bow. A balloon hovered cloudlike above the head, with tiny circular puffs, indicating thoughts, leading from the ponytail to the balloon.

Stephanie frowned and bent lower, looking closely at the smudged words. The letters were small and neat. Inside the balloon Alida had written, HELP ME.

CHAPTER 22

Emma listened intently to Kieran's dark ballad of teenaged angst and praised his grim images of death and destruction as sincerely as she could. She left him to keep her appointment with Tasha Clayman and her parents. Wade and Nell Clayman pleased and surprised Emma with their willingness to make the changes she had suggested. Nell had finally realized that the parade of swimsuit models through her sportswear design studio had made her teenaged daughter feel diminished and insecure. Their desperate love for their child was winning the day. Emma felt hopeful. As if to confirm her hope, she met the aide, Sarita Ruiz, entering with a lunch tray. "Yesterday, she ate a bite of her sandwich," whispered Sarita, and Emma's heart lifted. What was the old Chinese proverb? The longest journey begins with the first step. "Great," she said.

Trailed by the security guard Burke had provided, Emma returned to the cubbyhole that was her office. As she unlocked the door, the phone was ringing. She picked it up and heard Burke's voice on the other end.

"Emma," he said. "We've got a situation here. Can I see you in my office right away?"

Emma's heart skipped a beat. "Sure." She hung up the phone and turned to the security guard, who had just settled down with his tabloid newspaper. "We're being summoned," she said.

Geraldine rolled her eyes in warning as Emma entered Burke's reception area. She indicated that Emma should go on in, while the security guard settled himself on a chair.

Emma opened the door to Burke's office and walked in. Burke was sitting behind his desk. Seated in one of the chairs facing his desk was Stephanie, who waved at her as she walked in.

"Steph," she said. "What are you doing here?"

Burke answered for Stephanie. "Based on the information you provided, your friend, Miss Piper here, decided to take it upon herself to investigate the Devlin family, Emma."

Emma grimaced. "Steph, I told you not to."

"Now, wait a minute," said Stephanie. "I did not mention you, either one of you, or this place. I simply had a talk with one of my students. I told her I was concerned about her, and I offered to . . . what?" Stephanie opened her hands wide. "Be available if she needed to talk."

Emma looked at Burke's rugged face, which was now wearing a grim expression. "What's wrong with that?" she asked. "That doesn't sound so bad to me. I mean, that's something any teacher might do."

Burke picked up the composition book on his desk and handed it to Emma. "Take a look at that."

Emma frowned and then noticed the purple-outlined face with a bubble over its head. "Help me?" She felt a chill run through her. "Alida Devlin wrote that?"

Stephanie nodded.

"Did you ask her what it meant?" Emma said.

Stephanie grimaced. "I wasn't sure what I'd do if she told me. So I decided to talk to a couple of experts. What do I do now?"

* * *

Lieutenant Joan Atkins, accompanied by Detective Marbery, tapped on the door of the hospital room and stuck her head inside. There were two women in the room. A thin woman with a fringe of white bangs was lying on the hospital bed with an oxygen tube in her nose and an IV running from a suspended bag into her arm. She was so pale and bloodless that she was almost invisible against the white sheets.

Slumped in a chair beside the bed was another elderly woman, this one red-faced and healthy-looking. Both women were asleep. The woman on the bed made no sound, the rise and fall of her thin chest the only sign that she was still alive. The other woman was snoring loudly.

"Excuse me," said Joan, touching the shoulder of the woman in the chair.

Birdie started and instinctively clutched her pocketbook to her chest, as if to protect, or hide, its contents. She blinked at Joan from behind her thick glasses. Her frizzy hair was in disarray, and she smelled distinctly of alcohol. She tried valiantly to look coherent.

"Is this Mrs. Webster?" Joan asked, pointing to the sleeping woman on the bed.

Birdie shook her head as if to roust the cobwebs and nodded. "Yes. Who are you?"

"I'm Lieutenant Joan Atkins of the state police. This is Detective Marbery. You must be Mrs. Theobald."

"That's right," said Birdie. "I'm her cousin. I take care of her." Birdie sniffed and straightened up in her chair. "I'd ask you to sit but . . ."

"That's not necessary," said Joan. "I wanted to ask you about yesterday afternoon?"

"Is this about David? Because they already asked me about this last night. Some detective called me at the hospital last night and asked if David was here yesterday."

"That was me," said Trey.

"I know. But I wanted to go over a few things myself, if you don't mind." Joan did not want to step on the toes of the younger detective, but she had not been present when David Webster was brought in, and she was not entirely satisfied with his alibi. It seemed too convenient. But she had been called away on a development in a case in Newark, and by the time she learned of Webster's apprehension, his lawyer had already managed to demand and achieve his release. "Mrs. Theobald, were you here with Mrs. Webster all afternoon yesterday?"

"Oh yes," said Birdie. "I never left her."

"What about her son? David Webster?"

Birdie nodded as if trying to put events together in a sequence in her mind. "Yes, I told this fellow here. I called David because I couldn't wake her up. Her breathing was really shallow. He came over and helped me get her here to the hospital."

"What time was that?" Joan asked.

"Oh, it was around three-thirty. Maybe four at the latest."

"And did Mr. Webster stay here at the hospital after that?"

"Oh yes," said Birdie, nodding. "He was here. Until . . . it must have been nine o'clock."

"That whole time. He was right here in this room."

For the first time, Birdie looked at Joan suspiciously. "Yes. He was here."

"And you were awake that whole time?" Joan asked.

Birdie sat up indignantly. "Awake? Of course I was awake. Why wouldn't I be awake?"

"Well, hospital days can be very stressful," said Joan. "Especially when you're a little . . . tired."

"I wasn't tired," said Birdie.

"Maybe you take . . . medications that make you drowsy."

"Not me," Birdie insisted.

"Mrs. Theobald, you were asleep when we walked in just now," Joan pointed out. "And I have to say that there's a strong smell of alcohol in this room."

Birdie stuck out her chin defiantly and clutched her pocketbook protectively to her chest with a guilty look in her eyes. "I may have nodded off for a minute. But if I did, it was just for a minute or two."

Joan looked at her intently. "Could you have been asleep here yesterday?"

"Not asleep," Birdie corrected her indignantly. Then her bravado wilted. "I might have just . . . napped. Catnapped."

Joan raised her eyebrows. Trey Marbery sighed as if acknowledging what he might have missed.

"So," said Joan, "you can't say for sure that Mr. Webster was here from three-thirty to nine o'clock yesterday. He may have left the hospital while you were sleeping."

"I didn't say that. As far as I know, he was here. Why don't you people leave him alone?" said Birdie. "He's never been in trouble. He's a good boy."

* * *

Burke unlocked the door to his silver Lexus and tossed his mail onto a pile of files and papers on the front seat. "Just shove those papers onto the floor," he said.

Emma looked into Burke's luxury car in disbelief. He was so orderly in his office and in the house. It was as if he reserved all the disorder in his life for his car. She could see at a glance that there were unopened bank statements, bills, and correspondence. "You look like you're getting a little bit behind on things, Burke," she said.

Burke sighed. "It's true. I've had a hard time concentrating. Lately."

Emma picked up the pile of papers and started to place them on the backseat, but it was too painful to twist her torso. "I'll just hold them," she said. She settled herself on the front seat, the pile of files and unopened mail on her lap.

"I must be crazy to do this," said Burke as he pulled out of the center's parking lot and onto the main street.

"You're not crazy. You're just not the typical administrator."

Burke shook his head. "I could lose my job for this." Then he glanced at Emma. "Don't worry. I'm not changing my mind. It's too important."

Emma nodded and settled back in the seat. "Do you know where we're going?" she asked.

Burke nodded. "It's not too far."

Emma shifted her weight, uncomfortable under even the stack of envelopes, files, and papers she was holding. That realization reinforced the sense of frailty she was trying so hard to resist. It also made recovery seem a faraway prospect. She thought about putting the papers on the floor of the passenger side, as Burke had suggested. She glanced down at the manila envelope on the top of the pile and lifted her eyebrows at the return address on the envelope.

"The coroner's office?" she said.

Burke glanced over at the envelope. "Oh, did that come?"

Emma lifted it from the stack. "Yeah. Who died?"

"Natalie," he said grimly.

Emma felt chastened. Embarrassed. "I thought it might be about a patient."

Burke shook his head. "I wanted to see the final autopsy report. I've wondered if maybe . . ."

"What?" she asked.

"Well, in light of what happened to you . . . if it might not have been suicide."

Emma frowned at him. "You think she might have been . . . killed?"

Burke shrugged. "It didn't seem possible, but after what's happened to you . . . I don't know. I guess I'm just not sure of . . . anything anymore."

"Burke, what about the suicide note? It wasn't cryptic. It was handwritten, and she was pretty clear about her intentions." The contents of Natalie's note had been obtained by an enterprising reporter and published, to Burke's anguish, in the newspaper, under a photo of the beautiful Natalie.

"That's true," he said. "But I keep thinking that . . . maybe there was something I . . . overlooked. The change in her was so abrupt. Usually, the descent from one of those highs was more gradual. And there was often some kind of trigger. She'd been on such a high over the Solomon Medal, I keep wondering if I missed something . . ."

"Oh, Burke, don't do this to yourself," said Emma. "No one could have tried harder than you. And you know that she'd made other attempts. There is very little you can do when a person is truly committed to the idea of suicide."

Burke did not reply. "There it is," he said pointing to a white cottage nestled in a grove of leafless trees with a fish scale-shingled roof and arched windows. Emma felt her heart start to pound. They knew from Stephanie that Alida had drama club this afternoon, so this was the perfect opportunity to speak to Alida's mother without the girl—or her father—knowing about it. There was one car in the driveway—a minivan. Devlin drove a sports car, which meant he was probably at the university. "Okay," said Emma. "This looks good."

Burke got out of his car and came around to Emma's side. Once she was on the sidewalk, he locked the car, and together they walked toward the front door. Emma hoped someone was home. Despite the minivan being in the driveway, the shades were all drawn, giving the house a gloomy, deserted look. Emma knocked and waited. From inside the house, she could hear the television blaring. Emma knocked again, harder this time, and called out, "Hello?" When Risa Devlin did not come to the door, Emma tried to bend down and peer into the space between the lowered, scallop-bottomed shade and the sill. But she gasped at the pain in her side.

"Let me," said Burke. He crouched down and peered in.

"What do you see?" Emma asked.

"The light from the television," he said, "but there's no one in the room."

"Maybe she's in the yard," Emma said, "and she can't hear us."

"Let's walk around back," Burke said.

Emma descended the front steps and scuffed through the leaves around the side of the house. The yard was empty. At the back of the house, a glassed-in solarium had been added that looked out of proportion and out of place on the historic cottage. Emma could see large plants and a piano in the glass room, the piano topped with tottering piles of sheet music. She could see that there was no one inside, though the inner door to the back of the house was wide open. Emma turned the outside doorknob to the solarium without thinking, and the door swung in. "Oops," she said.

"That's all right. Open it," Burke said. "It's obviously not locked."

"I'll just call out to her from that inner door," she said. Emma and Burke picked their way gingerly across the cluttered floor of the solarium. As Emma passed a pair of closed casement windows, she looked in. The windows gave on to the kitchen, and Emma was startled to see a large, blond-haired woman, barefoot, wearing faded jeans and a satiny, low-cut blouse, seated at the kitchen table. The table was littered with dirty dishes, cutlery, and wadded-up napkins. There was an open half-gallon container of ice cream on the table in front of her, and the woman was slowly spooning the ice cream into her mouth, staring all the while into the glass of a makeup mirror, which sat on the table directly in front of her. She gazed at her own reflection intently, but without expression. She seemed to be studying herself putting the ice cream into her mouth as if she needed reassurance that she was really there.

Emma tapped on the window, and the woman jumped and turned to look, her eyes wide with alarm. Emma waved a hand and grimaced apologetically. The woman yelped and shoved her spoon into the open carton of ice cream. She did not seem angry, although, Emma admitted to herself, she had every right to be. Risa Devlin rose from the table and came to the window, struggling to crank the window open. Emma thought what a pretty face the woman had, even though it was somewhat swollen, and there were dark circles under her large, cornflower blue eyes.

"Mrs. Devlin, I'm so sorry to startle you. I tried knocking at the front door but no one answered."

Risa Devlin blinked and glanced behind her, looking vaguely in the direction of the front of the house. "I didn't hear you," she said. "The TV, I guess. Sorry. What are you doing here?" she said, almost as an afterthought.

"Dr. Heisler and I were wondering if we could talk to you for a minute?"

Anxiety rose instantly to the woman's glassy eyes. "If my husband comes back . . ."

"It's just for a minute. Can we come in? Alida's teacher came to see us."

"Alida!" the woman cried. "Is Alida all right?"

Emma hesitated. She knew what the woman was asking. Had there been an accident? Was her child injured? In that sense, the answer was obvious. "No, no," said Emma. "Alida is okay."

The woman was trembling. "Are you sure?" she asked. "You're not going to tell me something awful, are you?"

"No. Nothing . . . has happened to Alida."

Risa Devlin slumped against the windowsill and clutched her crevice of décolletage with relief, breathing hard. "You scared me," she said.

"I'm sorry," said Emma, knowing that Alida's mother now thought that Alida was in no danger. She had no idea that they were here to suggest injury of another, more profound, kind.

"Come on in," Risa said, pointing to the open door to the solarium.

Emma and Burke entered the house through the solarium's door and followed the barefoot woman down the hall, assuming they were heading to the living room. Instead, Risa Devlin led them to a bedroom that was, unmistakably, the lair of a teenaged girl. The walls were papered with posters of rappers, athletes, and handsome young movie actors. There was a single bed, which was covered with a brightly colored flowered quilt, a desk with a swivel chair, and a white bureau. Risa indicated the swivel chair, and Emma sat down. Burke stood behind her. Risa lay down on the single bed, on her side, and gazed at them. "I hope you don't mind," she said, her voice slightly slurred. "I'm very tired."

"No. It's all right," said Emma. She looked around the room, wondering which girl the room belonged to. Ivy or Alida.

"This was Ivy's room," said Risa as if reading her thoughts. "I spend a lot of time in here. I find it comforting."

"I'm sure it's a comfort," said Emma, although she could tell that this woman was anything but comforted. She was clearly trying to medicate her problems away and had lost sight of what was appropriate—like receiving visitors in the bedroom of her deceased child.

"Why are you here?" Risa asked. "Did something happen at school? Why didn't the teacher come?"

Emma looked up at Burke. "Mrs. Devlin," he said. "I want to thank you for talking to us. I realize that we put you in an awkward position when Ivy was at the center. I wouldn't blame you for refusing to see us. I know your husband is still very angry."

Tears rose to the woman's large blue eyes. "You were trying to help Ivy. I know that. Even if you were wrong about what you thought. We had to be sure."

We? Who's "we"? Emma thought. She had been impressed at the time of their treatment of Ivy with Risa Devlin's bravery in the face of her husband's outrage. She was further impressed that this woman, who must have suffered mightily from Lyle Devlin's righteous indignation, still clung to the belief that she had done the right thing. "Alida's teacher was talking to her at school today," she began.

"Her grades are good," said Risa.

Emma nodded. "She hasn't done anything wrong. It's just . . . after what happened to Ivy, her teacher was thinking that this was a difficult time for her . . ."

Risa's large blue eyes glistened, but the expression on her puffy face did not change. "Of course it is. She lost her sister."

"Her teacher has noticed . . . changes in Alida," Emma continued carefully. "She seems . . . old for her age. She suggested that Alida might want to go to counseling, but Alida indicated that her father wouldn't approve of that. Because of your experience with Ivy."

Risa stared impassively at Emma, her head resting on Ivy's pillow. Emma wondered if she was going to put her thumb in her mouth. She appeared to be drifting away, pulled down by whatever medication she was taking. Emma tried to hold her gaze. "Anyway, Miss Piper came to us to see if there was any way we could straighten out the problem."

"What is the problem?" said Risa.

Emma looked up at Burke. He frowned at Risa Devlin. "Mrs. Devlin, we came to you once before to ask for your help, and you were ready to move heaven and earth for your daughter's sake."

Tears began to trickle down Risa Devlin's face. She shook her head. "It didn't work," she said. "Nothing worked."

Burke held up Alida's notebook, which he had brought with him. "While she was talking to Miss Piper, your daughter, Alida, was drawing something. But after she left, when Miss Piper collected the composition books, she saw Alida's drawing. We thought you might want to see it."

Risa struggled up to a sitting position, her gaze wary, and reached out for the notebook that Burke was holding. Burke handed it to her and watched for the woman's reaction. Risa's eyes traveled over the drawing as if Burke had handed her the photo of the corpse of a loved one, long missing. In her eyes was a combination of horror, sorrow, and recognition.

"Obviously she has been doing her best to hide her . . . distress. I thought you ought to know," Emma said. "'HELP ME.' Can you think why she would write that?"

Risa began to shake her head, her hands trembling as she held the drawing.

"Mrs. Devlin?"

Risa Devlin's face had changed. She looked up and lifted the notebook in her trembling hands. "I can't do this again," Risa said. "I won't." Her sweet voice had an edge, and her fuzzy blue gaze had begun to clear.

CHAPTER 23

Burke poured a glass of mineral water and handed it to Emma, who was sunk into the comfort of a deep-cushioned oatmeal-colored sofa in Burke's living room. "I couldn't believe the way she reacted," Emma said.

Burke nodded and sat down in a buttery leather club chair. "I know. I didn't know what to expect. Risa Devlin seems so . . ."

"Passive," said Emma. "I know. But she's not. It seems she's actually got quite a stiff spine. Although she's nearly broken by Ivy's death."

"I almost hated to lay this on her. With all that she's been through. But I think it was the right decision."

"I do too," said Emma. "She had to know. But I wish she had let us stay with her to confront him. Or called the police. I'm worried about leaving her alone to face him. If it was Lyle Devlin who attacked me, he is a horribly dangerous man."

"I agree with you," said Burke. "But you saw how adamant she was. I didn't want to step in and start telling her what to do. She's had enough of that from her husband. But I plan to call her at regular intervals tonight. If I sense that she's in any danger I'm going to call the police."

"Good," said Emma. All of a sudden, Emma straightened up. "Burke, do you hear someone. Footsteps?"

Burke frowned and then gestured toward the back deck. Emma nodded. Burke got up and walked over to the glass sliders, throwing on the outdoor floodlights.

David was standing on the deck, staring through the floor-to-ceiling sliders.

"David," said Burke. He opened one of the glass doors.

"Honey, what are you doing out there?" Emma asked.

"I thought I'd have a look," said David. "Wondered what I'd see."

"What does that mean?" Burke asked.

David ignored the question and stepped into the living room. He spoke to his wife, who was curled up in a corner of the sofa, her camel-colored skirt tucked beneath her, her discarded boots lying on the carpet. "Well, you look comfortable. I should know by now where to find you," he said. "I went over to the center to pick you up. No one knew where you were. Didn't you realize that I'd be worried? You knew I was going to come and get you after work."

"Oh, David, I'm so sorry," said Emma setting down her glass of water. "I forgot to call you. We were—"

"Who's 'we'?"

"Burke and I," she said. "We went to see Lyle Devlin's wife."

"What for?" David demanded. "You should be staying as far away from that guy as you can." David turned on his friend. "Why in the world would you take her there?"

Burke grimaced. "It was some unfinished business, David. You're right. I should have let you know. But it was a really worthwhile trip. I think you'll agree when we tell you about it. Can I get you something? A glass of wine?"

"I don't want any wine. I want to take my wife home," he said.

"This is my fault, David. I should have realized you'd think something terrible had happened," said Emma. "That was stupid of me."

"No, it was stupid of Burke. You of all people should have realized," David said, turning to Burke.

Burke's gaze was cold.

"David!" Emma's tone reproached him.

"Well, it's true," David insisted.

Emma struggled to her feet and set her glass down on the burl wood cocktail table. "I'm sorry, Burke. This was my mistake. I got so involved in what we were doing. David, it was an important meeting. I promise you that. I just feel bad about not letting you know." Emma stuck her stockinged feet into the boots and straightened out the toffee-colored outfit she was wearing.

"Let's go," said David.

"Okay," said Emma. "I'll tell you all about it on the way to the storage unit."

"The storage unit?" he cried. "It's almost dark."

"You said you'd take me there after work. It won't take long. I need to do this, David." Emma patted her own head gently, to be sure her French braid was still in place.

David shook his head.

"Please. You know I can't drive there myself."

"Is there anything I can do?" Burke asked.

"Stay out of it," said David. Then he turned to Emma. "Do you have the key?"

"Right here in my purse."

"All right. Let's get this over with."

Emma reached up and kissed him. "Thanks," she said. "Burke, I'll see you at work tomorrow."

"I'll walk out with you," said Burke. "I want to get that envelope from the medical examiner out of my car."

David did not speak to Burke. He led the way out the sliding doors and across the back deck, clattering down the steps to the driveway.

* * *

The U-Kan-Keep-It Storage Facility was located in an industrial area of Clarenceville where there were warehouses and a recycling center and the offices of the water company. All were busy during the day but were deserted, now that the workday was over. The facility was comprised of row upon row of locked garage-size units surrounded by a chain-link fence. It had been built in the shadow of a highway bridge alongside the Smoking River. There was a trailer, which served as an office during business hours, and a parking lot beside it.

By the time Emma and David arrived, the office was closed, and the halogen lights in the parking lot and around the units were illuminated. "How do you open that gate to drive inside?" David said.

"I don't know if you can drive in after business hours," she said. "I think they have to open it from inside the office."

"Well, that's stupid," he said irritably. "You can't get into your space after business hours?"

Emma held up her key. "You can get in, you just can't take your car in. You have to park in the lot after business hours."

"That's ridiculous. What if you need to move something?" he said.

"I guess you have to come back during business hours," she said. "But luckily all I have to move is one little pistol. Drop me off and I'll wait for you right here under this light while you park the car."

"Oh no," he said. "Nothing doing. I'm not leaving you alone. Not for a minute."

"Do I have to walk back from the parking lot?" she said, grimacing.

"No. I'm not going to park in the lot. I'm going to leave the car right here."

"But the sign says you can't," she said, pointing.

David straightened out the wheel and turned off the engine. "Well, I have a wife who doesn't need to be walking all the way from that lot. And I'm not leaving you here alone. So if they don't like it, they can give me a ticket."

"They might tow you," she said, although she felt secretly pleased that he was willing to break the rules to accommodate her.

"They're not going to tow me," he said, getting out on his side and coming around to hers. He opened the door and helped her out. "If the cops come, I'll hear them. And I'll explain it to them. Besides, we're only going to be in there for a minute, right?"

Emma nodded as she took his hand and got out of the front seat. Everything hurt, every which way, but the thought of having that gun safely in her possession spurred her on. "Right," she said. "Let's go get it."

At the end of each row of units a letter was clearly painted. Emma and David walked past the rows of units until they came to row G. Thanks to the well-spaced halogen lights, Emma could see all the way down to the end of the row, and there was not another soul around. That didn't stop her from feeling apprehensive as she limped, with David right beside her, down the row to unit 14.

"This is the one," she said, stopping in front of a corrugated metal door. She stuck the key in the lock for number 14 and turned it. The door rolled up on a track, but it was not automatic, and she had forgotten that the door had to be lifted to get it started. For a minute she hesitated, thinking about her stitches. Then she remembered her determination from the night before. She had to prove to him that she was not succumbing to this "victim" mentality. She was fighting back on her own behalf. If she could use a gun, she could open this damn door.

She took a deep breath, bent over, and grabbed the handle.

"Wait a minute, hold it a minute," he said. "What do you think you're doing? Let me do that."

"I can do it," she said.

"Honey, I'm here," he said. "You don't have to do it." He gently displaced her and took over the handle. The door rolled all the way up, clanking as it rose. Emma flipped the switch beside the open door, and a weak bulb illuminated the contents of the storage area. For a moment her heart sank. It was worse than she had remembered. Why did I save all this stuff? she thought.

214

At the time of her mother's remarriage, it had seemed sensible—necessary even—to hang on to the things of her childhood that Kay seemed willing to discard. But now, looking at all the boxes bursting with toys, a broken rocking horse, odd dishes, moldy camping equipment, and childhood videos, she wondered if maybe she too was ready to get rid of the past and start her new life as a wife and a mother without all this baggage.

"God, look at all this junk," he said.

"It's not junk," she said, bristling.

"Did I say junk?" he asked teasingly. "I meant treasures. Look at all these treasures."

"That's better," she said, smiling.

"How are you going to find anything in this?"

"I know where everything is," she said. "Just stay out of my way." With a sigh, she entered the unit and began her search. She peered at all the labels, climbing over rolled-up rugs and tennis rackets until she reached the back of the unit. She had to shift a couple of boxes, even then, to find the one she was seeking. She started to lift a carton marked Linens.

"Don't you pick that up. You'll break your stitches." He began toward her through the accumulation. "Give it to me. I'll move the stuff so we can get out of here."

Standing among the shabby-looking collection of mementos, she felt crowded by his impatience. "David, stop. I want to do this at my own speed. Look, I won't lift anything heavy. I promise. Just . . . let me do this."

He looked at her skeptically, but she was clearly determined.

"All right, I'll wait by the door. But if you come to a heavy box, just let me know and I'll move it for you."

"Fine," she said. "Now go on."

She began to move one box at a time, being sure to test their weights and lift only those that were light as David picked his way back toward the open door. She found the box she was looking for at the bottom of a pile.

"Dad," Emma read aloud from the label she had marked herself on the top of the box. She placed the box on top of a short tower of boxes so that she could look through its contents without bending over. She opened the top and smelled a lingering trace of the aftershave he always wore. She began to lift out the familiar, long-forgotten effects. His old wristwatch was in there, although it no longer ran. There was a canvas fishing hat and a book of essays by H. L. Mencken with slips of notepaper still marking favorite pages. There was a small, retractable telescope, which they always took camping. On a clear night, they would prop themselves up along a lakeshore or a riverbank and search the sky above them for constellations. There was a framed photo of the two of them, holding up a string of fish. She studied the photo, their jubilant, innocent smiles.

She heard David let out a groan and an expletive. "What's the matter?" she said.

"Stubbed my toe on one of these valuable andirons you have hidden in here," he grumbled.

Emma smiled. "Sorry," she said. "Is it bad?" she asked.

"Bad enough. Now we'll both be limping," he said.

"Well, if it makes you feel any better, those andirons are valuable," she said.

"Oh, I do feel better. Let me kick it with the other foot and see if I can break that toe too," he said.

Emma laughed. "You're a baby. Go and lean against the wall, or sit down," she said. "I found the box. It won't take me long."

Get busy, she thought. Don't be dawdling over this stuff. Save the trip down memory lane for another day. She pushed aside the remaining contents of the box, and there on the bottom, snapped into a moldy, suede shoulder holster and belt, was her father's old Smith & Wesson double-action revolver. She smiled, thinking how she used to love to see her dad strap the holster on, because he reminded her of the sheriffs in the old cowboy shows they would watch together on the Western channel. She knew that he liked it for exactly the same reason. Beside the holster, in an equally moldy pouch, were the bullets. She was sure the gun would not be loaded. Mitchell Hollis was religious about unloading the gun after each time they used it. But he had taught her how to reload, and now his many demonstrations came back to her.

From outside the unit, she heard David groan again and then there was a thud, as if he had flopped down on the concrete outside. I hope he didn't really break that toe, she thought. Emma opened the stained pouch and shook some bullets out. Then she lifted the gun and holster carefully from its resting place and, holding the barrel pointed down, unsnapped the holster and pulled the gun out. She moved the cylinder latch and then shook the cylinder open, as her father had taught her. Sure enough, the chambers were empty. One by one, she fed the cartridges into the chambers and then carefully closed the cylinder with both hands. She felt as if Mitchell Hollis was right beside her in that dusty storage room, telling it all to her again.

"David," she cried triumphantly. "I'm all set."

Scooping up the holster and the pouch, Emma tossed everything else back into the box and turned around.

Standing at the open port door, staring at her, was Lyle Devlin.

Emma let out a cry.

The halogen lights glinted off his wire-rimmed glasses and haloed his bristly graying hair. His fists bulged in the pockets of his jacket.

"Mr. Devlin. What are you doing here? Where's my husband," she said. She tried to sound calm and collected, but she could hear the panic in her own voice.

"I thought I told you to stay out of my business," he said.

"I have nothing to say to you," she said. Her heart was pounding. She kept the gun pointed down, hidden from his view, her palm sweaty on the stock where she clutched it.

"First, you sic the police on me. They come around asking me to account for my whereabouts when this happened to you," he said. "Suggesting that I was to blame. I told them that I held no grudge against you. Even though it wasn't true, I told them it was my fault that Ivy died."

Emma met his glaring gaze but remained silent, her stomach churning. Where was David?

"But that wasn't enough for you, was it?" he asked. "You had to prove it was my fault. When you didn't get your way with the cops, you decided to take care of it yourself. Today you came to my home to see my wife. Based on some drawing in my daughter's notebook, you accuse me of being a monster, not a father."

Emma's heart was thudding. "Get away from me. David!" she called out.

Devlin ignored her cry. "You persecute me. You hound me. And then you ask me why I'm here?"

"I didn't—" Emma started to protest.

Devlin suddenly pulled his fists from his coat pockets, raised them up, and grasped the unit's door handle above his head.

"What are you . . . what?" She heard the clank of the door as it began to roll down, descending.

"No, stop that!" Emma cried. She began to stumble across boxes and objects that blocked her path to the door.

Devlin was jerking the door down. It was at his waist. In a moment it would slam shut, trapping her inside.

Could he lock her in here? "Stop it!" she cried.

"Enjoy your stay, bitch."

Emma could see only the lower half of his legs now. She pulled her father's gun to eye level, grasped it with both hands, and squinted down the barrel, pointing it at his shins. Her arms were trembling. She tried to hold them steady. She prayed the old gun still worked, and fired.

There was a horrible scream, and she saw Devlin crumble, grasping his shattered shin and shrieking in pain.

Emma clambered across the space and jammed her wooden rocking horse beneath the sinking door.

"You bitch," Devlin was screaming.

Emma pocketed the gun, grabbed the door handle with a cry of pain, and began to lift. The door rolled back up and Emma staggered out. Devlin was rolling on the asphalt walkway. She fought the temptation to put another bullet into him.

She heard another groan, turned, and saw David sprawled on the cement.

"David!" She fell to her knees and tried to lift him into her arms.

He struggled to a sitting position, gripping his head.

"You're bleeding."

He looked at his own hand. "What happened?" he said.

"Devlin. He was trying to lock me in the storage room."

"Jesus, I never saw him coming. I was leaning against the door, watching you rummage around in there. And then I got sucker punched." He reached up and gingerly patted tiny bits of gravel in his head wound. "I must have hit my head when I went down." Then he looked searchingly at Emma. "Are you all right? Did he hurt you?"

She shook her head. "I shot him," she cried.

"You did?" He grabbed her, squeezing her upper arms. His eyes were wide.

"He's over there. I shot him in the knee."

David looked at the figure on the ground, writhing in pain, and hollering. His expression changed from horror to glee. He pulled her close. "That's my girl. Serves the bastard right," he said. "Way to go."

CHAPTER 24

The Devlin house was dark, except for one light behind a shaded window. A blue minivan was parked in the driveway. Joan Atkins rapped loudly on the door. "Mrs. Devlin," she called out. "It's Lieutenant Atkins and Detective Marbery."

There was silence from inside the house, and she rapped again. "Are you in there, Mrs. Devlin? Are you all right? Please open the door."

After a few more moments of silence, Risa Devlin opened the door.

Joan could hardly believe it was the same woman who she had met during her earlier visit. She was wearing a dark jacket that was buttoned up and belted around her ample waist. Her blond tendrils still waved beguilingly around her face, but her eyes were flinty and her pudgy face was pale. "What do you want?" she said.

"We need to talk to you. Your husband's been shot. He is at the hospital. In police custody."

Risa's eyes widened. "He was shot?"

Joan noticed that she did not inquire as to who shot him, how badly he was injured, or if he was going to be all right. The customary questions. She provided the answers for her anyway. "It's not a life-threatening injury. He was shot in the knee. Could we come in and talk to you for a moment?"

Risa looked vaguely disappointed. "He's going to be all right, then?"

Joan nodded. "He's in surgery right now, having the bullet removed and the knee patched up."

Risa shrugged. "You can come in. But I'm busy packing. And I have to get back to it. We need to get to the airport." Without another word she turned away, leaving the door ajar. Joan and Trey Marbery followed her into the house. Sure enough, right in the front hallway were three suitcases, sitting side by side.

"Where are you going?" Joan asked.

"Back to my family in Wisconsin. My father and my brothers live there. We'll be safe there. Once I tell them . . ." Her voice trailed off. She walked to the foot of the staircase and shouted up the stairs. "Alida? Are you ready?"

The girl's voice was muffled and sounded tearful. "Almost. I'm coming."

"You and your husband had an argument?" Joan asked.

Risa turned and frowned at her. "How did you know?"

"Your husband was shot by Dr. Webster. He was very angry about her coming to see you today. He accosted her, and she shot him," Joan said flatly.

Risa stared at her. "Did he hurt Dr. Webster?"

Joan shook her head and watched Risa's face. "No. Luckily. He injured her husband slightly. But as soon as he's able to answer questions, we want to talk to him about the other attempts on Dr. Webster's life."

Risa's blue eyes widened in horror, and she groped for the banister as her knees seemed to give way. She sat down on the stairs with a thud. "You think he's the one who tried to kill her?"

"We don't know. Dr. Webster pointed out to us just this evening that your husband works in the building across from the station where someone tried to push her onto the tracks, and so far, we have not been able to locate the student whom he claimed he was tutoring at the time. As for the first attempt, you're the one who gave him an alibi for that night. You agreed that he was here watching some Italian movie. Was that true?"

Risa Devlin sighed. "I remember vaguely watching the movie. I couldn't swear to you it was that night."

"Where do you rent your movies?" Trey interjected.

Risa Devlin frowned at him. "Blockbuster. The one on Shelby," she said.

"They'll have a record of when you rented it," said Trey.

"Although that won't tell us when they watched it," Joan said.

"It will if they brought it back the next day," said Trey.

Joan nodded. "Can you check it out?"

"Sure," said Trey. "Right now?"

"When we're done here," said Joan. "Mrs. Devlin, why did Dr. Webster come and see you earlier? Can you remember that?"

Risa nodded, her gaze wandering, as if she was trying to reconstruct something in her mind. "It was about . . ." Risa looked anxiously up the stairs. "Don't you tell Alida. She's been through enough today."

"We need to know what it was that you talked about with Dr. Webster."

Risa looked at her warily. "Didn't she tell you?"

"Not without your permission," she said. "Privileged."

Risa seemed to consider it, and then she shook her head. "I'm not saying anything else. My daughter doesn't need to have this all over the newspapers. No. We're getting away from here. Alida," she cried. "Come down. We have to go."

"Mrs. Devlin. You can't run away from this. If you know why your husband went after Dr. Webster, you're going to have to tell us. You're going to have to testify in court, in fact."

"What did Daddy do?" cried a soft voice from the staircase.

They all looked up. Alida, in a baggy sweatshirt, her eyes red-rimmed, was standing stock-still on the stairs, wearing a backpack and dangling a duffel bag.

"Come on, honey," said Risa. "Never mind about it. We have to go."

Alida did not budge. "What happened?"

"Your dad is in the hospital," said Risa. "He's been shot."

Alida blanched. "Is this because of me?"

"No, baby, of course not," her mother insisted.

"Why would you think that, Alida?" Joan asked.

Alida shook her head. "My parents had a huge fight about me after those two doctors left. My father was screaming at my mom."

"All right, that's enough," said Risa. "Don't say anything else."

The girl looked at her mother with disappointment in her eyes. "You said not to be ashamed. You said it wasn't my fault. Or Ivy's," said Alida.

"What wasn't your fault?" Joan asked.

The girl looked at her mother for permission, for support.

Risa took a deep breath. "No, baby, it wasn't your fault."

"What happened, Alida?" Joan asked gently.

Alida, halfway down the staircase, looked like a scruffy blond angel, the light from the top of the stairs making a halo around her head. Her small voice trembled but was clear. "My dad did stuff. To me. He said he wanted me to know what to do when I had a real boyfriend."

Joan Atkins recoiled inwardly from the revelation, the utter believability of that fatuous excuse for depravity. God, there are a lot of worthless men in this world, Joan thought. So many men who would do anything to get what they wanted, and they didn't give a damn who suffered. Then again, what about the wife? Why couldn't she see what was happening under her nose and do something about it?

As if in response to Joan's thoughts, Risa Devlin's shoulders slumped, and she sank down on the bottom step. "Both my babies. He did it to both my babies. My Ivy was starving herself. Trying to . . . disappear. That's what Dr. Webster said. Disappear. Ivy was trying to . . . escape from him. When

I took Ivy to the center, Dr. Webster tried to tell me what it meant, but I wouldn't believe it."

Risa shook her head hopelessly. "Tonight he walked in with that superior look on his face, talking down to me. But I'd seen the picture from school. They showed it to me. And it dawned on me. I finally understood. He'd moved on. To Alida. How could I have been so blind?" She began to sob.

Alida rushed down the stairs, her bag bumping behind her. She put her arms around her mother's shoulders and buried her face in the dark jacket. "Don't cry, Mom. Let's go to Grandpa's, Mom, like you said. Come on. Let's go before he gets back."

Risa held her daughter close and looked pleadingly at Joan. "Let me get her away from here. Please."

"I need you here for my investigation."

"I'll come back. You can call me. But I need to take my daughter somewhere safe. I can't stay in this house. He must be completely crazy to have done this. To both his daughters. And then . . . that poor woman." Risa shuddered.

Joan looked at her thoughtfully. "I need a statement from you. Written and signed. It won't take long. Then you can go."

Risa nodded. "Okay."

"This is not the end of it, you understand. I'll need to talk to you again."

"I understand," Risa said solemnly.

"All right. We'll knock out your statement as quickly as possible and then I'll have an officer take you to the airport. Do you mind if my officers search your house and your computers?"

Risa looked around at the home she had tried to make. She was leaving this house and hoping never to return. "It's all yours," she said.

* * *

Reporters called so persistently that David ended up turning off the ringer on the phone. It was all anyone could talk about on television. On the radio. Lambert University professor Lyle Devlin had been shot and was in surgery. Police were waiting to question him in connection with the attack in the Pine Barrens on honeymooner Emma Webster and the murder of hunter Claude Mathis, as well as to question him about accusations of sexual abuse of his own daughters. Emma stared at the TV screen, curious at first, and then mesmerized until David switched it off.

"How could he?" she asked, shaking her head.

"He's sick," said David. "But you know that. You're the shrink."

"I just can't understand that mind-set. I mean, I try, but . . . To prey on your own children when they're helpless to resist," she said. "To use them like that. To destroy them. It's almost worse than murder. One expert in the field calls it 'soul murder.' I think that's a good description."

"You tried to warn them. The guy is evil," David said.

"Because you can never really get over something like that," Emma continued. "I mean, the whole idea of trust becomes . . . laughable. If your own parent would do something so selfish and cruel to you . . ."

"I agree. It's . . . awful. But you put a stop to it with your Smith & Wesson. That's something to be grateful for, anyway," he said.

She reached up and touched the bandage on his head. "You're right. How are you feeling?" she asked.

"Well, on the one hand, I've got one hell of a headache," he admitted. "But," he said, smiling, "on the other hand, I forgot all about my toe."

She lifted his hand to her face and kissed it. They sat together on the sofa in their bathrobes, the remains of the pizza they had ordered in a box on the table.

"How 'bout you? Feel better?" he asked.

"Starting to."

A pounding on the front door made Emma shrink into a corner of the sofa, holding the neck of her robe together. David stood up. "They never quit. I'll get rid of them," he said wearily. He got up and walked to the door, opening it a few inches.

Emma heard voices, and then David opened the door wider. Lieutenant Atkins stepped into the foyer, wearing a gray, microfiber trench coat over her suit. She looked into the living room and saw Emma. "Emma," she said. "How are you feeling now?"

"Better, thanks."

"I'm sure you've heard the news. Devlin is having surgery on his knee even as we speak. His wife and daughter are on their way to the airport, heading to the mother's family out in the Midwest. We'll be placing Devlin under arrest once he's out of recovery. Sometime late tonight, I suspect."

"What if he denies everything?" Emma asked.

"We have enough evidence to hold him. His computers are revealing that he had numerous contacts with underage girls. And his daughter signed a sworn statement on the sexual assault charge. Her mother is backing her up all the way."

"What about the attacks on Emma?" David demanded.

"Well, we're going to question him, of course," said Joan carefully.

"Do you have any doubt?" David asked.

Joan gazed at him thoughtfully. She knew that he had good reason to be angry at Devlin. The bandage on his head, and the attempt to lock his wife in the storage unit, were reasons enough. But Joan found his eagerness to blame Devlin to be a bit . . . convenient. "Technically," she said, "Devlin didn't lay a hand on your wife tonight."

"I don't believe this," said David. "He tried to lock her away. And he certainly whacked me," said David, gingerly touching the bandage on his head.

"I know. But so far we haven't tied him to the other attacks," said Joan.

"I told you about the music building being right across from the train station," Emma reminded her.

"I haven't forgotten," Joan said.

"What about the anonymous letters I got? Is there any link to Devlin?"

"No, we don't know who wrote those letters," said Joan. "We're still investigating. It's possible that Devlin will become our prime suspect."

"Instead of me," said David ruefully.

Joan took a deep breath. "As far as why I'm here . . ."

Emma looked up at her.

"Regardless of how much Professor Devlin may have deserved it, Emma, you assaulted him with a deadly weapon. An illegal firearm to boot," she said.

"A deadly weapon . . . !" David cried. "After what she's been through?"

"You did not have a valid license to carry that hand-gun."

Emma blanched. "What are you saying? Are you . . . arresting me?"

Joan smiled and shook her head. "No. I doubt there will be any felony charges filed. I think this can safely be classified as a case of self-defense."

"At least the system isn't completely mad," said David.

"Although you will have to appear in court on a misdemeanor charge and probably pay a fine at some point," the lieutenant warned. "Right now I'm here to confiscate the weapon."

"But I need that gun," Emma protested.

"You're not licensed to use it," Joan reminded her.

"It was my father's. I don't want to part with it," Emma said.

"You'll get it back eventually."

Emma looked up at David as if appealing to him to intervene. Then she remembered that she was trying not to do that. Not to lay it all on him. Emma sighed. "All right, Lieutenant," she said. She got up from the sofa and went to the Stickley-style cabinet in the dining room. She pulled out the gun, which she had unloaded when they got home. She put the holster back into the cabinet and handed the gun over.

"Thank you," Joan said. "Now, try and get some rest. I believe this gun has served its purpose."

Emma walked the lieutenant to the door, closed the door on her retreating figure, and turned around. David was cleaning up the pizza crusts and folding paper plates into the box. "It's not fair," she said.

"No kidding," he said. "But I'm relieved in a way. I wasn't comfortable with the idea of you carrying that gun. Although I admit, you did a great job with it tonight."

"Thanks," she said, smiling. She joined him in the cleanup, wadding up the napkins and picking up their glasses. "Here, why don't you let me finish this?" she said. "You've got a headache."

"I'm okay," he said. "Although I do think I'm about ready to turn in." Together they carried the remains of their take-out dinner into the kitchen and tossed it into the trash. "I'm going to have a shower. And you"—he said, pointing a finger at her—"no more news on TV."

Emma followed him through to the living room and flicked on the TV with the remote. "No news," she promised. "I'm watching the Discovery channel." She sat back down and stared at the TV as sharks glided across the screen and the announcer began to intone interesting facts about the Great Barrier Reef. "Don't get your bandage wet," she called after David.

David winked at her, then he started down the hall to the bathroom. In a few moments Emma could hear the water running. She hesitated, and then got up and went over to the phone. She dialed Burke's number and waited for six rings, but Burke did not answer. His machine picked up. Emma waited through the instructions. Then she said, "Burke, it's Emma. Call . . . call us when you get back. They've arrested Devlin."

She pushed up the volume on the ringer before she hung up the phone and returned to the sofa and the program she had been watching. Even the brightest of tropical fish looked dull on the TV screen. And the sharks seemed to be imprisoned by the small blue screen as if they were trapped in a ghoulish aquarium. She switched the TV off and began to think about making the long trek up the stairs to their bedroom. She had made it down the steps this morning, although it had taken her a while. And she really preferred being back in her own room, but the steps were still a little bit daunting.

Go ahead, she thought. Try it. Don't wait for him to carry you. Give it a try.

She took a deep breath and began the climb. She was on the fourth step when the phone began to ring. She could hear David's shower still running. She couldn't very well call out to him to answer it. But she didn't want to go back to the foot of the steps either. Maybe it's Burke, she thought. And then she realized it was far more likely to be another reporter. If it's Burke, I'll hobble down and pick up when I hear his voice on the machine, she thought. She waited for the several rings and then heard a man's voice recording his message.

"David, this is Bob Cheatham. Look, I feel terrible about missing our interview the other day. There were some postproduction problems on the film I've been doing and they needed me back in California right away. But I owe you one, and I'll make good on it the next time I'm in town. Thanks for understanding."

Then he hung up.

Emma stood on the stairs, staring at the phone. Then, slowly, she started back down.

In a short while David reappeared in the living room gingerly blotting his hair with a towel. "I am beat," he said to Emma, who was sitting on the couch with the TV off. "Hey, I thought you were going to bed. Are we sleeping up or down tonight? 'Cause if you want to sleep upstairs, I'll be glad to carry you again."

Emma did not reply or meet his gaze.

"Honey, what's the matter?" he said. He frowned at her. "What is it? You look . . . sick."

Emma looked up at his freshly shaven face, ruddy from the shower, his hair damp and uncombed. He looked guileless and innocent. Looks could be deceiving, she thought. "We got a phone call while you were in the shower," she said.

"You shouldn't answer the phone. That's why I turned down the ringer volume before. These people just won't let up on us."

"It was Bob Cheatham," she said.

David's face fell. He pressed his lips together and sat down in a chair opposite the sofa. "Oh."

"He said how sorry he was that he had to cancel your interview the other day."

David sighed.

"Where were you," she said coldly, "if you didn't go to New York?"

He opened his hands in a gesture of innocence. "I did go to New York. I didn't know he was going to cancel. I found out when I got to the restaurant."

She thought about how frightened she had been when she had returned home from Kellerman's. When the wind was howling, and the nurse was gone. So frightened that she ended up calling the police over an open window and a slamming door. "So you did what? Stayed for lunch?" she asked sourly.

"No. No, of course not. Nevin called the restaurant. Told me that Cheatham had canceled and asked me to pick up another interview instead. The guy was a French novelist, very elusive, who was leaving the country the next day, and Nevin needed me to grab him. I had to jump in a cab and go meet him in the Village."

Emma just stared at him.

"Em, I was right there in the city. I couldn't turn him down. I had to take the job. Nevin needed me to cover it for him."

Emma stood up and pulled her bathrobe tie tighter around the waist. "I'm going to bed," she said.

"Emma."

She turned on him. "Why didn't you just tell me that? Why lie about it?"

"Because I knew you would react like this. I knew you would take it the wrong way. You didn't want me to go in the first place. If I told you I accepted another assignment instead of rushing home . . ."

She did not reply. She made her way slowly to the downstairs bedroom, where she took off her robe, laid it on the end of the twin bed, and carefully got under the covers. She could hear David as he moved around the first floor, double-checking the locks and turning off the lights.

In a few minutes he came into the room and took off his robe as well. He turned off the light and sat down carefully on the bed beside her. She turned on her side with her back to him. Their breathing was audible in the dark.

"I should have told you," he said.

"Yes, you should have," she said.

He placed a hand lightly on her shoulder, but she shook it off. "Emma, listen, I know this sounds stupid, but I thought I was sparing your feelings."

"You were lying, David. Please get off my bed. It hurts when your weight pulls it down."

David sighed and stood up. He looked at her for a moment. Then he went around to the cot. "Emma, I intended to tell you the truth when I got home. I figured you were safe with the nurse, and I would just explain how the plans had changed. I knew you would understand that. You're not the kind of woman who goes crazy over a change in plans. I wouldn't have married you if that was the kind of person you were. So, yes, I intended to tell you."

Emma said nothing.

"But then, when I got back and found out you were at Burke's and that the nurse had walked out, I felt guilty. Knowing you were here all alone. And frightened. I didn't want to make it worse by telling you that I took another assignment."

"Excuses."

David flopped down on his back on the cot and stared up at the ceiling.

After a few silent minutes, Emma turned over and looked at him. "What?" she demanded. "What are you thinking about?"

"I'm thinking that you're right. That is what I do. I make excuses. Anything but tell the truth. I'm afraid that that's who I am, Emma," he said, his voice hollow. "I tried to tell you it was a mistake for you to marry me. I knew you would regret it."

Emma lay down again with her back to him. "I didn't say I regretted marrying you," she said.

They lay tensely, side by side, in their separate beds, and then, after a few moments, he propped himself up on one elbow, put his hand out, and tentatively touched her arm. She did not shake it off. "You don't know how much I need you," he whispered. "More than you can imagine. I'm going to try to be the husband you hoped for. No guarantees, but I will try. And at least tonight," he said, "the most important thing is resolved. They've arrested the man who tried to . . . hurt you."

"Lieutenant Atkins didn't say that," she said.

"It is Devlin. It has to be," he said. "And now I know you are safe."

"Maybe," she said.

"You are," he said. "It's over now. You'll see."

She did not reply. In a few moments he lay down again on his cot. A few minutes later, he was breathing evenly. As if all was well in their world. His complacency made her angry. His lies forgotten, he slept peacefully. But why shouldn't he? He was right. The police had Lyle Devlin. There was nothing more to fear. Still, she lay beside her sleeping husband, wide awake.

CHAPTER 25

The next morning, Joan Atkins arrived at the Clarenceville police station around ten o'clock and stopped at the coffee machine to pour herself a mug as she looked around the busy squad room.

Trey was seated at his desk. Perched on the chair beside him was a girl with a heart-shaped face wearing cat's-eye glasses and a turquoise blue Orlon cardigan that she probably thought of as vintage—meaning she bought it at a thrift shop.

"Morning, Lieutenant," said a passing patrolman.

"Morning," said Joan.

Hearing her voice, Trey looked up. Then he rose from his seat and walked over to the coffee machine, holding a sheet of paper.

"Morning, ma'am. You better look at this."

"What is it, Detective?" Joan asked, sipping her coffee.

Trey stolidly held out the sheet of paper. Joan frowned and took it.

"It says Lyle Devlin rented the video of that Italian flick the night of the attack on Emma Webster," said Trey. "He returned it the next day."

"Okay," said Joan slowly, feeling a pinprick of apprehension.

"Plus, you see that girl over there sitting by my desk? That's Olive Provo."

Joan recognized the name. "Devlin's tutorial student."

"You better talk to her," said Trey.

Joan set down her coffee cup and walked over to the girl seated beside Marbery's desk. "Miss Provo? I'm Lieutenant Atkins of the state police. We have been trying to track you down. Where have you been?"

"I didn't know you were looking for me," the girl said.

"We checked with your roommate, your advisor. Nobody knew where you were."

Olive rolled her eyes. "Am I going to get in trouble?" she said.

"I don't know. What did you do?" said Joan.

"I spent the night with a guy, okay?"

"That's your business. I don't care about that," said Joan.

"Well, he's a married guy. He's a violinist with the Portland Symphony. I met him when I did an internship there this summer. And he was in town . . ."

Joan held up a hand to stop the girl in midrecitation of her dangerous liaison. "It's not important," she said.

Olive looked crestfallen, enjoying her self-portrayal as a scarlet lady. It was not a role one would select for her on appearance alone. "Oh," she said. "Well, anyway, I didn't tell anybody because it was a secret."

"We just need you to answer a simple question. Where were you Tuesday afternoon between the hours of four-thirty and six-thirty?"

The girl grinned, showing dimples, which sweetened her face. "Wow. How cool. Am I a suspect for something?"

"This isn't a joke, Miss Provo," said Joan.

The dimples faded away. "Okay. Let me see. I was . . . at my tutorial in the music building with Professor Devlin. I heard he's in trouble . . ."

"And during this tutorial, did Professor Devlin leave the room at any time?"

Olive considered this, and Joan knew, with an unpleasant certainty, that this young woman was about to exonerate Lyle Devlin. "The answer to that would be no," said Olive. "Not at all. I am working on a solo piece for the winter concert. I play the cello . . . and he was giving me an extremely hard time about my piece because I kept screwing up on the eighth notes . . ."

Joan nodded. "Would you be willing to sign a sworn statement to that effect? That you were with Professor Devlin the whole time?"

Olive's little comma-shaped eyebrows rose above her glasses. "Yeah. Sure."

Joan turned to Trey Marbery. "Can you oversee the preparation of that statement for me, Detective?"

"Yes, ma'am." Trey took a step closer and spoke into Joan Devlin's ear. "Sorry, ma'am. I guess Devlin's not our guy."

"Apparently not."

"There's something else," said Trey.

"Great," said Joan. "What?"

"The desk sergeant got a call on Tuesday from an agency that sends out private duty nurses. They said one of their nurses had walked off the job without any explanation. She hasn't responded to phone messages they left for her, so they went to her apartment, and she didn't answer the door. The sergeant on duty told them we can't start searching for an adult until forty-eight hours had passed. So they called back this morning, because they still haven't heard from her."

"Marbery," said Joan impatiently, "you know this is a local matter. I'm only here to deal with the case involving Mrs. Webster, because the case involves two jurisdictions. Some missing nurse—"

"Hear me out," said Trey. "According to the agency the client's name was McLean."

"So?" Joan asked irritably.

"Rory McLean was paying for the nurse, but she was sent to take care of his stepdaughter, Emma Webster. That's where she disappeared from. The Websters'. The sergeant didn't recognize the name of McLean when they first called. But I figure there may be something suspicious about this nurse's disappearance. I mean, the last place she was seen was Emma Webster's house."

"Shit," said Joan.

"That's what I thought," said Trey.

* * *

Emma had not fallen asleep until dawn, and she was not ready to be awakened when the phone rang. When she opened her eyes she saw David, in the dim light of the office bedroom, sitting on the edge of his cot, murmuring into the phone. Then he hung up and turned to look at her. "Did that wake you up? I'm sorry."

"It's all right. Who was it?" she asked.

"Birdie, calling from the hospital. They're letting my mother go this afternoon around one, and she needs my help to take her home."

"Can I come with you?" she said.

David frowned at her. "I don't know if that's a good idea," he said gently. "I'm going to have my hands full with her and the oxygen tank and all that."

"You're saying I'd be in the way."

"No," he said patiently. "I'm just saying that you aren't a hundred percent yourself. You don't need to be trooping up and down the hospital corridors."

"Whatever you think," she said, feeling a little insulted.

"I know you'd like to visit with her and help her get settled, but it might be better for you to visit once she's back in her own house, in her own bed. Is that okay?"

"Sure," she said, mollified.

"But you can't stay here alone," he said. "Not even for an hour or two."

"I'll be all right. They've got Devlin now," she said.

"No. Until we know for sure, I don't want you here by yourself. I did look into getting a bodyguard for you

236

yesterday. I talked to a guy who used to play in the NFL who does this for a living. He lives about twenty minutes away from here. He said all I needed to do was call him and he'd come over. He gave me a few references, and I checked them out. He's got a good rep."

"You did all that?" she asked.

"Sure. I said I would."

"Thanks." Emma gazed at him. In the morning light she wondered why she had been so angry at him last night. His lie about the interview might have been . . . unnecessary, but it wasn't some sort of unforgivable deception.

"So, why don't I give him a call?" David said. "Tell him we need him here by one o'clock this afternoon. Then I can go pick up my mother and get her situated without having to worry."

"Actually, you know what," Emma said. "Don't bother calling this guy. I think maybe I'll go into work today. I have my group this afternoon, and I'd like to meet with them. By the time my group's over, you'll probably be done taking Helen home, and you can come and get me. I'll go see your mom when she's settled back in her own house."

"You have to have the security guard at work with you," he said. "Just in case."

"All right. Just in case."

* * *

Joan Atkins stood on the front porch of the brick-front duplex where Lizette Slocum lived and pounded on the door for the tenth time. Lizette's mailbox, which was attached to the wall beside the door, was stuffed full of mail. A short, pleasant-looking woman wearing a johnny-collared sweatshirt embroidered with hummingbirds stepped out onto the adjacent porch. "There hasn't been a peep over there in the last few days," the woman offered.

"Do you know Miss Slocum?" Joan asked.

The woman shook her head. "She only moved in a few months ago. My husband and I say hello when we see her, but that's about it."

"When was the last time you saw her?" Joan asked.

The woman frowned. "I saw her on Monday morning, leaving here."

"Do you normally see her every day?" Joan asked.

"No, not every day," said the woman. "But you do hear a person, coming and going."

"Who's the landlord here?" Joan asked.

"His name is Jarvis. I'll get his number. I've got it inside," said the woman. She disappeared into her own house just as Trey Marbery came hurrying up the sidewalk to the foot of the porch steps.

"What is it?" said Joan.

"I heard it on the two-way radio. A couple of our officers just located her car. It's parked at the bus station."

Joan stepped away from Lizette's front door and leaned against the porch. "The bus station? So maybe that's why we can't find her. Maybe Miss Slocum took a bus trip. We better see if anyone there can remember selling her a ticket."

The woman in the hummingbird sweatshirt emerged from her house with a slip of paper. "This is the landlord's number," she said.

"Thanks," said Joan, taking the piece of paper. "He may have to come over here and let us in. Does he live far away?"

"He lives the next town over," said the woman.

"When you saw Miss Slocum on Monday, did she mention she might be leaving town?"

The woman shook her head. "She didn't mention anything. We just waved."

"She didn't ask you to take in her mail for her or anything?"

"No. Do you think she went away on a trip?"

"I hope so," said Joan.

* * *

Emma was seated in the circle of chairs for her group session when Sarita Ruiz led in a new patient named Rachel, who was missing both her eyebrows and her eyelashes. Emma greeted the girl kindly and told her to take a seat. She felt her energy for work coming back to her, her desire to root out the psychic pain that caused a pretty girl to look in the mirror and pluck every hair and eyelash from her face.

The group consisted of six that day—four boys and two girls. One of the boys was Kieran, who slumped in his chair and refused to meet her gaze. She began the group by deflecting questions about her injuries and turned the talk firmly back to their lives. "I'd like to hear about the future that each of you imagines for yourself. The dreams you have that you tell yourself will never come true. But still, you secretly hope for them. Finish this thought. In five years I'd like to be . . ."

The group members avoided one another's gaze, all too timid to put their dreams out where they could be publicly trashed. "What about you, Kieran?" Emma asked. "For example, I know that you are a songwriter and a guitar player of considerable skill. When you watch MTV, do you ever imagine a music video of yourself?"

Kieran did not look up or reply.

Emma leaned forward and spoke to them earnestly. "I'm not trying to set anybody up here for ridicule. I think you all know that's not what this group is about. Each and every one of you has shown, in some very tangible way, that you feel hopeless about the future. I'm asking you to imagine yourself in a future that excites you."

"I'll be dead," said Kieran dully.

Emma turned to Kieran. God, that tattoo is revolting, Emma thought, trying not to stare at the third eye. "That's what you imagine?" she said. "What about your music? No one will ever hear it," Emma said.

"Yes, they will," Kieran insisted. "They'll play my music everywhere and they'll say, 'Love kills. Sex kills. He was trying to tell us.'"

One of the boys snickered, and the other kids in the group stared at Kieran as if he had landed in their midst in a flying saucer.

"Why do you say that, Kieran?" Emma asked.

Kieran looked at her as if she were dense. "Sex is the ultimate drug," he said. "Everybody knows it, but nobody wants to talk about it."

Emma looked around the group. "Anyone want to comment on that?" she asked.

Then the eyelash-less Rachel meekly raised her hand.

"Rachel?" Emma said.

"Sometimes I think about becoming an aromatherapist."

The boys all started sniffing the air. And we're off, Emma thought.

* * *

Once the session was over Emma turned down the corridor to Burke's office. Geraldine was not at her desk, and the door to Burke's office was open. "Burke," Emma called out.

There was no answer. Emma went up to the door and looked inside, hoping to see him there, lost in thought, or listening to someone on the telephone, but the room was empty. The bare branches of a silver birch snapped against the long panes of the bay window behind his desk. There was no overcoat on the coatrack. The banker's lamp on his desk was not lit. Burke, where are you? she thought. For a moment she had a terrible thought. Burke had been with her at Lyle Devlin's house. There was no answer at Burke's house last night. He hadn't called them back. What if Devlin attacked Burke before he came after Emma, and she shot him in the knee? What if Burke was lying injured somewhere, or worse?

She saw Geraldine Clemens carrying a coffee mug into the reception area.

"Geraldine," she said, coming out of Burke's office.

"Oh my Lord, you startled me."

"Is Burke here today?"

"No. He called this morning and said he wouldn't be in. Said he was involved in some kind of urgent business."

"Oh, I see. Good," said Emma, relieved. "As long as you talked to him."

"Any message for him?" Geraldine asked.

Emma shook her head and walked out into the hall. Kieran was clomping by, chains and buckles jangling, his car keys jingling in his hand.

"Glad you came today, Kieran," she said.

Kieran stopped and looked at Emma, tongue-tied again. "Uh, yeah," he said.

Emma fell into step with him on the way to the front door.

"You leaving, Dr. Webster?" he asked.

"Yeah," said Emma. "I'm still taking it a little bit easy."

"You need a lift?" he asked, reddening slightly.

"You drove?" she asked, surprised. Most of the kids at the center had lost their licenses due to drug or alcohol problems.

"Oh yeah," he said. "I got my own car."

"Well thanks, Kieran, but my husband's coming for me."

Kieran shrugged. "Okay."

"Don't speed," she said.

"Can't. The cops pull me over every time they see me as it is."

Emma glanced at the magenta hair and the third eye. I'll bet they do, she thought.

"Have a good weekend, Kieran." Stay safe, she thought.

CHAPTER 26

Audie Osmund gazed in disgust from the plastic Baggies full of illegal prescription drugs on his desk to the clean-cut, neatly dressed, handcuffed young man seated in front of Audie's beat-up, army green metal desk.

"Farley, you should be ashamed of yourself. You, a teacher. Selling this poison to your own students." Audie shook his head.

"I wasn't—" Bob Farley began to protest.

"Don't bother," Audie said. "Just don't bother. We caught you red-handed, my friend. That little girl you sold these pills to at the school dance, where you were supposed to be a chaperone, is my sergeant's niece. We've had our eye on you for months. We've just been biding our time, waiting for you to approach her."

"It's entrapment. When my lawyer gets here—" Farley announced.

"It's not entrapment when you approached her," said Audie. "You are going away for this, and the parents around here will breathe a lot easier because of it."

"Those kids'll find another source," Farley said.

Audie shook his head. "It must be sad to have so little self-respect. Gene," Audie bellowed to his sergeant. "Come get this scum. I can't stand to look at him."

Tall, muscular Gene Revere, neat in his khaki uniform, came into Audie's office and nudged Farley to his feet. "Come on, you . . ."

As Farley stood up, Gene said to Audie, "That woman's here to see you. The one who saw the husband out at the Zamskys' cabin?"

Audie sat up straighter. "Mrs. Tuttle?"

"That's the one."

"Send her in."

Gene dragged the drug pusher to his feet and began to haul him out of Audie's office. "Go on in, miss," he said.

Donna Tuttle, her black hair spiky, wearing a brown Henley shirt, which showed off her very fine figure, beneath a camouflage jacket, edged past the scowling, preppy-looking teacher and into the chief's tiny office. "Chief Osmund, my son gave me your message. I was going to call you, but then I figured I would just come on in and see you when I got back," she explained.

"Mrs. Tuttle. So good of you to come in. You sit right down there. I want to show you this picture. How's your memory today?"

"Sharp as a tack," she said, nodding her head.

"Be right back," Audie muttered. He went out into the main room of the tiny station house and rummaged on Gene Revere's desk for the manila folder they had prepared for Donna Tuttle's visit. He found it without much difficulty. The file held six photos. One of them was a photo of David Webster. The others were mug shots of men somewhat similar in appearance. None of them was as square-jawed, or generally good-looking, as David Webster, but they all had longish dark hair and no glasses or facial hair. That was the best Audie could do.

Audie carried the folder back into his office and leaned over his desk on the side where Mrs. Tuttle was seated. He blocked her view as he removed the six photos from the folder and set them out in two rows of three on his desk, facing her. Then he stepped back so she could see them. "Now," he said.

"I want you to look at these photos and tell me which one of them was the man you spoke to at the Zamskys' cabin that day. The day you told me about."

Donna Tuttle nodded solemnly, a citizen ready to do her part for truth and justice. She stood up and leaned over the desk, frowning as she picked up each of the photos and muttering to herself. Audie saw her pick up the photo of David Webster and stare at it. Audie tried not to give away any inkling of his own feelings.

Donna tilted the photo back and forth, and then looked at Audie. "He's a looker, isn't he?" she said. "Looks like a movie star."

Audie leaned forward. "Is that the man you saw at the house that day?" he asked.

Donna sighed and chuckled. "Oh yeah. You don't forget a face like that." She set the photo back down, glanced once again at the rogues gallery, and then shook her head. "And by the way, you know what? I was thinking about it. You asked me if he was alone out there and I said I didn't see anybody."

"Yeah?"

"Well, for some reason it bothered me. Like I hadn't exactly told the truth about it. But then I remembered. I didn't see another person. But I did see a bra and a pair of women's panties on the porch railing. Like they'd been washed out and hung out there to dry."

Audie exhaled and sat back heavily in his chair.

"Did I do something wrong?" Mrs. Tuttle asked.

"No," said Audie. "You did fine."

"If there's any other way I can help, Chief, I'd be happy to—"

"Chief," called out Gene Revere.

Audie stood up. "What is it, Sergeant?"

"Some kind of attack out on Chapel Hill Road. We better get out there pronto."

"Mrs. Tuttle, I have to go," said Audie.

Donna Tuttle tried to reply, but before she could, Audie had grabbed his jacket and cap and was out the door.

* * *

David led Emma out of the front steps of the Wrightsman Youth Center and closed the door behind them.

He reached out a hand to help her down the steps.

Emma stopped short and watched as Kieran Foster roared off in his late-model PT Cruiser, thinking about what he had said at the group. That he planned to be dead in five years. How did his life get to be so hopeless? Of course, it could just be teenaged gothic romanticism. For these kids, sex, love, and death made for a potent brew. Still, among her patients, any talk of death had to be taken seriously.

"What's the matter?" David said.

Emma shook her head. "One of my kids."

David frowned. "Come on. Let's get in the car," he said. He took her by the arm and led her toward the car. "The only kid I'm worried about is the one you're carrying in your belly there." He helped her into the passenger seat and then went around and got into the driver's side.

"How did it go with your mother?" she asked as he pulled out into the road.

David shrugged. "I got her home," he said. "She thinks I'm my brother, Phil."

"Really?" Emma asked. "A little confused?"

"More than a little. Birdie was already pouring rum into her coffee when I left."

"Into your mother's coffee?" Emma exclaimed.

"No, her own. Although it might not hurt. My mother's heart needs a jump start."

"What did the doctor say?"

"He said this is a temporary respite."

"Oh, honey, I'm sorry."

David shrugged. "Maybe a heart will come along."

Emma glanced at him as he drove. She knew it had to bother him that his mother mistook him for his brother, even as he was trying to care for her. And he had to be worried about her failing health, even though he rarely talked about it. In one way, she admired his stoic attitude. But Helen was the only parent he had ever really known. The prospect of her imminent death had to be frightening. Emma presumed that he was afraid, and that he kept his fears hidden. But now, she wondered. Was it more deception on his part? He admitted last night that he had trouble with the truth. Would she ever really know how he felt?

He glanced over at her. "What?" he asked.

Emma shook her head. "Shall we go over there now so I can visit her?"

"You know what?" he said. "She was sleeping when I left. It would be better if we went later. And I am starving. How about we go out for a late lunch? I read about this little inn a few miles out of town that serves all afternoon. Let's give ourselves a break. Try to enjoy the afternoon. What do you say?"

Suddenly, Emma realized that she too was ravenous. "That sounds good."

* * *

It had not been difficult to locate and interview the ticket sellers who were on duty at the Clarenceville bus station on Monday afternoon. It was exactly the same crew that was working on this Thursday afternoon. Earlier, Trey and Joan had entered Lizette Slocum's apartment with the aid of Jarvis, the landlord, who arrived after a half an hour's wait, and ascertained that Lizette had not written anything about a trip in her daybook or on her wall calendar. Because the nurses' agency did not have a photo of Lizette, they were looking for one in her apartment. They picked up a photo off Lizette's desk of a smiling Lizette and an older woman whom she resembled. The woman with the hummingbird

246

sweatshirt told them that the photo looked recent. They took it with them to the bus station.

As one clerk after another asserted that they did not remember selling a bus ticket to Lizette Slocum, Joan got on the phone and asked the manager of the Toyota dealership to come down to the bus station and bring his skeleton keys for the year and model of Lizette's car. Eager to cooperate with the police, the manager said he would be there shortly. Now Joan stood looking out at the brown Toyota in the parking lot as she waited for the results of Trey's last interview. He was meeting with the bus station supervisor, who had retrieved the week's worth of surveillance tapes and was going through the tapes of Monday afternoon to see if Lizette Slocum appeared anywhere on them. The side door to the bus station opened, and a dark-haired man with a mustache came in wearing a tie and sports jacket. "I'm looking for Lieutenant Atkins?" he said.

Joan walked over to him. "Are you Mr. Vetri?"

"I am," he said.

"I'm Lieutenant Atkins." She shook hands with the salesman. "You brought the keys?"

"Got 'em right here," said Vetri cheerfully, patting his jacket pocket.

Just then, Trey Marbery emerged from the supervisor's office. Joan looked at him questioningly.

Trey shook his head.

Joan took a deep breath. "All right," she said. "Let's open the car up."

The three of them walked across the parking lot to the brown Toyota. The early twilight of November was beginning to descend on them. The manager tried several keys, and then they heard the locks click. They opened the driver's door and looked inside. The car was not new, but it was extremely clean inside. No empty paper coffee cups, no loose change on the floor, no empty plastic soda bottles under the seat. Lizette Slocum was a person of tidy habits. Joan straightened up from inspecting the backseat and looked across the roof at Trey, who had been searching the passenger side.

"Trunk?" she said.

Trey nodded.

"Mr. Vetri, can you pop the trunk for us?"

"Sure thing," said the manager cheerfully. He found the key and put it into the lock. Then he pressed the lever and pulled it open. His eyes widened and a look of anguish came over his face. "Oh no," he cried as if he'd been deceived. "She's in there. Did you know she was in here?"

Joan and Trey looked into the trunk. Lizette Slocum was curled up, her backpack thrown on top of her. Her eyes were open, and her skin was a splotchy gray.

Joan Atkins sighed. "I was afraid she might be," she said.

* * *

It was nearly five and the sky was charcoal gray when David and Emma returned to their cul-de-sac after their long, leisurely lunch and headed down the street toward their house. Emma let out a groan of dismay as she recognized the unmarked police car parked in front of her home.

Lieutenant Atkins and Detective Marbery got out of the car, slamming the doors. David sighed, pulled in the driveway, and came around to help Emma out of the front seat.

"We need to talk to you both," said Joan Atkins without preamble. "Let's go inside."

"Of course," said Emma.

David said nothing but led the way up the walk and opened the door. Emma offered them a seat in the living room. Joan refused for both of them.

"I hope you don't mind," said Emma as she took a seat. Joan shook her head.

"What is it now, Detective?" said David.

"Several things. Number one, Mr. Devlin's alibi checked out. He is no longer a suspect either for the attack on your wife in the Pine Barrens nor the attack at the train station," said Joan bluntly.

"What?" David cried. "You let him go? You saw what he did to me. What he tried to do to Emma."

"He's still under arrest for the sexual assault of his daughter. But he is no longer a suspect in the attack on you, Dr. Webster."

"Is there any question about his alibi . . . ?" Emma asked.

"None at all," said Joan. "It wasn't Devlin."

Emma looked up at David from where she sat. David was raking his hand through his hair.

"That's not everything. Acting on a missing persons report filed by her place of employment, we began a search for Lizette Slocum, the nurse whom your stepfather—"

"I know," said Emma. "Have you found her?"

"Yes, we found her," said Joan grimly. "We found her dead, stuffed in the trunk of her car, which was left at the bus station."

"Oh my God," Emma said as she felt her stomach start to churn.

"Jesus," said David. He came and sat down close to Emma, absently kneading her hand.

"We're not yet sure how she died. We're waiting for the coroner's report. But we do know that Lizette Slocum was last seen alive right here in this house, taking care of you, Dr. Webster. We are theorizing now that the person who tried to kill you came here to attack you and found Lizette instead. I'd like to know where you were at the time she disappeared."

"I went downtown," Emma said. "When I came back, she was gone . . . I thought she left because I . . . kind of . . . sneaked out without telling her." Emma suddenly remembered the Do Not Disturb sign that had been ripped off her door. It wasn't the nurse who tore it from the door, she thought. It was someone who had come to the door, expecting to find her asleep in there, and was furious to find her gone. "Yes," she said slowly. "I think someone else was here." She explained about the sign.

"I should have realized there was something wrong when she left so abruptly and didn't let anyone know."

"Yes," said Joan Atkins. "You should have. We wasted precious time because we didn't know that her disappearance was linked to you."

"It's not my wife's fault," David protested.

"And what about you, Mr. Webster? Where were you on the day that Lizette Slocum disappeared?" Joan asked.

"I was in New York. Doing an interview," David said.

"We'll need to get in touch with that person," said Trey, holding his pen poised over his pad.

"Well, I don't have a number for him. He's . . . in Europe."

"How inconvenient," said Joan Atkins.

"You can call my editor. He'll tell you. I was with a French author named Bernard Weber."

"Where did you meet him?"

"A restaurant. In the Village."

"I need names. I need dates, times, and places," Joan said loudly, "and I need them right now."

"If you talk to me in that tone of voice," David said, "I'm going to call my attorney and you can talk to him."

"Stop, David. Forget the attorney," Emma cried. "Just give her the information. That poor woman is dead." She could see the fury on his face, but she didn't care. "Right is right," she said. "Do it. You know you were in the city. Why make this difficult?"

David got up from the couch and went into his office. Emma did not look at the detectives. In a few minutes, David came back into the room and handed them a sheet of paper. "Here. Talk to everybody. Knock yourself out."

Joan pocketed the paper. "This investigation into the attacks on your wife is ongoing, Mr. Webster. Do not leave the state under any circumstances. Mrs. Webster, your life is still in danger. I would recommend that you hire someone to protect you. Round the clock. If you like, we can recommend someone."

"That's all right," said Emma. "My husband found a bodyguard for me. We will call him."

Joan Atkins looked at Emma with narrowed eyes. "I'm not sure that's the wisest course of action. Why don't you let the local police advise you on who would be competent to protect you? You need someone who is experienced with this kind of situation."

"We don't need your advice, okay?" said David.

Joan turned and glared at him. "I was talking to your wife. Call the station and ask to speak to the desk sergeant. He can help you. He's expecting your call."

Before David could reply, Joan nodded to the younger detective, and the two of them headed for the door.

David sat back down on the sofa and clapped his head in his hands.

"I can't win," he said. "I'm back to being the prime suspect. They're determined to make a case against me."

Emma sat back against the sofa cushions, stunned by these latest developments. "That poor woman," she said, shaking her head. "She came here to take care of me and ended up dead. It's unbelievable. Who would want to kill me that badly? Do you ever think about that?"

"Of course. I've thought about little else since last Saturday," he said. "I figured it was Devlin. Or maybe, I don't know . . . whoever sent you those notes. I don't know. I just wish the cops would try to figure it out instead of insisting on blaming it on me . . . I have a sinking feeling that they're not going to believe Nevin, or even Weber, if they manage to get a hold of him."

Emma frowned at him. "Now you're sounding paranoid, David. Your alibi is solid as far as Ms. Slocum's death is concerned. Once they talk to Nevin, or track down the author, they'll realize it. Besides, they don't even know how she died yet. They may find traces of DNA on her body that will lead them to another suspect. That's who's really to blame."

"You're right," said David.

"So, try not to worry."

"Try not to worry," he scoffed. "The police think I tried to kill you. They're busy trying to work up a case against me while your life is still in danger."

"I know. But I still feel safe as long as I'm with you."

David sighed and shook his head. "Well, we have to hire a bodyguard. That's all there is to it. And what was all that crap about their bodyguards being able to protect you better than someone I could call? What do they think? That I'm going to hire a killer instead of a bodyguard? It's like Kafka! It's a nightmare."

"Dammit, David," she cried, "we can't worry about what they think. Let them think what they want."

All of a sudden, the phone rang, and they both jumped. David hurried across the room and picked it up. He frowned. "Chief Osmund, yeah," he said in a surly tone. "What do you want? You want to talk to my wife?"

He was listening intently. Then he looked at Emma, his eyes wide with astonishment. "Really? My God. Excuse me. Really? Tonight. Yes, we'll come. Where should we meet you? Okay. Yes, we'll be there. Okay."

Emma sat up, staring at him as he hung up the phone. "What happened?"

David put down the phone and stared at her. "That was Chief Osmund. God, I almost hung up on him."

"What did he want? Tell me."

David sat down beside her on the sofa.

"You're trembling," she said, clutching his forearm. "Tell me."

David raked his hand through his dark hair. "He said there's been another attack in the Pine Barrens. Same everything. Ski mask. The works."

Emma gasped and covered her mouth. "Oh my God."

David nodded and started to grin. "But this time, they think they've got him."

CHAPTER 27

"Can't it wait? We're almost there, honey," David said.

"Obviously, you have never been pregnant," she said.

"All right. All right. There's a gas station up ahead. They'll have a restroom. I'll get us some gas," he said.

"Thanks, honey. Oh, David, I feel . . . hopeful. If this is the guy, then this nightmare will finally be over."

"I'd like to believe that," David said, frowning. "But we know that you were a specific target. You haven't forgotten the attack at the train station."

Emma shuddered "Hardly. But at least there's a chance."

"We're going to be all right," David said. He flashed her his sad-eyed smile, which always made her heart turn over.

"God, I can't wait until we have our lives back," she said.

"Me neither," he said. "Here. We'll pull in here."

Evening had come to the Pine Barrens, and Emma hoped it would be the last evening she would ever spend here. The call from Chief Osmund had given her a renewed hope that all would be resolved, that the danger was past.

The chief wanted her to view their suspect in a hooded lineup to see if she could pick him out by his size and body language. They also wanted to question her again, given what they had learned from the latest victim. This man could be

253

Claude Mathis's killer. Emma understood all too well how important this was to Chief Osmund. It was even more important to her. She looked around as David pulled off the highway and into the service station. The jagged outlines of the pines, which surrounded them, loomed black against the moonlit sky.

There was a missing persons poster with a picture of a pretty girl on the pump as well as a sign that read The Attendant Carries No Money. Please Pay Inside.

The man who came to the car window had hooded eyes and was lacking several teeth. "What can I do for you?" he asked.

"Fill it," said David.

Emma leaned across the seat. "Excuse me. Do you need a key for the restroom?"

The man breathed through his mouth and studied her with a faintly hungry look. "No, ma'am," he said. "Help yourself."

Emma forced herself to smile. "Thanks."

The attendant began to jockey the lid off their gas tank and insert the nozzle of the pump.

Emma grabbed her purse and climbed out of the passenger's side of the Jeep.

"Do you want me to go with you?" David asked.

"You don't have to," she said.

"Come on," he said. "I better. I'll stand guard."

Emma smiled, relieved. "Okay. That would be good. It's so creepy around here."

Together they walked over to the side of the service station, and Emma turned the knob on the door marked Ladies. She steeled herself for whatever unpleasant conditions she might find there, but when she turned on the bright overhead light, she was relieved to see that the restroom was neat and clean. She poked her head out.

"Civilized," she said to her husband.

David smiled and jammed his hands into his pockets. His hair shone in the halogen lamplight, and Emma felt her love for him well up in her heart as he waited for her like a sentry, guarding her safety. Emma closed the door and locked it. On the wall in front of her was the same missing persons poster that she had seen on the pumps outside. This time she was close enough to read it. The edges of the poster were curling, and a section that had ripped was held together with yellowing tape. The poster announced the disappearance of Shannon O'Brien, who had gone missing from this very service station several months ago, after finishing her shift. No wonder they have these posters everywhere, Emma thought. There was a blurry photo of the auburn-haired, freckle-faced girl, as well as statistics of her age, height, weight, etc. At the bottom of the poster it said, *Anyone with any information contact Chief Audie Osmund.* Below that was the address of the police station and the phone number.

Emma glanced at her watch. It had taken them a while to get going. She knew she should be dreading this evening, but the truth was that she was almost dizzy with excitement. This evening could mean the end of her fears, of the ugly suspicions, of her interrupted life. She was so grateful to Chief Osmund for letting her be a part of the resolution of this crime. Grateful that he wanted her to come right away and not leave it till tomorrow.

Seeing the chief's number right there on the poster gave her an idea. I'll call him, she thought. And tell him we're almost there. We'll be arriving soon. She quickly relieved herself, washed her hands, and then fished in her pocketbook for her phone. She turned around and gazing at the missing persons poster, punched in the number for Sheriff Osmund at the bottom of the poster, which she was able to read in the bright light of the restroom.

"Police," said a female voice.

"Yes, I want to talk to Chief Osmund. This is Emma Webster."

"Can someone else help you?" the woman asked. "Chief Osmund isn't here."

Emma frowned. "Oh, there must be some mistake," said Emma. "We're meeting him there tonight. I just . . . I just wanted to let him know that we would be arriving very soon."

The woman at the other end was silent. "I don't know what to tell you."

"Would you just check in his office? I'm sure he's not usually there at this hour but—"

"I'm telling you. He's not here," the woman said. "And he's not coming back. His grandson had an awards dinner tonight and Audie and his wife went to it. He was talking about it all afternoon."

Emma was silent.

"Is there someone else who can help you?" the woman asked.

"I was supposed to view a lineup tonight," said Emma.

"A lineup? Oh. Well, maybe Gene is in charge of that. Let me get Gene Revere for you. Hang on a minute." Emma's heart was pounding. Just a misunderstanding, she told herself. That's all. Emma heard the phone muffled, and the woman speaking in a loud voice. Then she got back on the line.

"Honey, Gene says there's no lineup tonight. He don't know what you're talking about."

Emma's face was burning. "Look. Chief Osmund called me. This is Emma Webster. I was the one . . . I was attacked the night Claude Mathis was killed."

"Oh," said the woman, her voice suddenly sounding interested. "How are you doing now, honey?"

"I'm doing fine," said Emma, relieved to finally be recognized, acknowledged. "Chief Osmund called and told my husband about the latest attack. He said they were holding the guy. That's what he said. There was going to be a lineup."

"No," said the woman. "We didn't have no attack. Unless . . . Was he talking about the rottweiler that bit the guy out on Chapel Hill Road this morning?"

"Rottweiler?" Emma said weakly.

"That's the only attack we've had around here in the last couple of days. But we don't do dog lineups. I'm pretty sure of that," she said, chuckling.

Emma was silent.

"Look, I'm sorry, Mrs. Webster. I don't know what to tell ya. There's been some kind of mistake. Believe me, if there was another attack on a person, I'd know about it. But that dog biting the woman on her bicycle was the only thing that's happened around here in the last day or so."

Emma punched the off button on her phone and stood staring, unseeing, at the poster on the wall.

The bathroom doorknob rattled, and Emma let out a cry.

"Emma, are you okay in there?" David asked. "What's taking you so long?"

CHAPTER 28

Emma stared at the rattling knob as if it were a hissing snake.

"Are you okay in there?" David called out. "Emma, answer me."

Emma's mouth was dry. She did her best to moisten her lips. "I'm okay," she managed to say.

"Hurry up, honey. Chief Osmund's waiting for us. Let's get going."

Emma's heart was thudding and her knees felt like they were about to give way. She groped for the sink and turned on the faucets. "Right there," she managed to croak.

She tried to collect her thoughts. To make sense of what she had just heard on the telephone. Chief Osmund was not waiting for her. No one was waiting for her. It was all a lie. That phone call was not from Chief Osmund. David had said it was, but it wasn't.

"Who were you talking to in there?" David asked. "I heard your voice."

"Nothing," she said. "I'll be right out."

She didn't know whether to cry or scream. The conclusion was obvious. Inescapable. Her husband was waiting for her on the other side of that door. Waiting to betray her. Or worse. Kill her. Her and their baby. David? Could it be

David? The David she loved and had promised her life to? Why? Why would he do such a thing? It couldn't be. Weren't they happy? Hadn't he told her so a million times? But a swirl of stern, familiar faces and warning voices warred for dominance in her head. Oh God, no, she thought. He wouldn't do that to me. He loves me. He couldn't. She leaned against the sink, clutching her stomach. NO.

And then, in the midst of her terror and abject misery, she suddenly found another way to explain it. There was another possibility. Remote, but possible. Maybe David was a victim of this hoax, just as she was. Maybe someone was pulling a scam on him too. Maybe whoever wanted to kill her had lured them both down here with a fake call. After all, how many times had David talked to Chief Osmund? How well did he know his voice?

Yes, that had to be it. Hope rose in her heart, shaky as a newborn colt. She was not alone, not betrayed, not her husband's intended victim, not the stupidest woman who had ever lived. For a moment, her heart sailed. And then it plummeted.

That's right, she thought. Be stupid all over again. Be trusting. Insist that you know better than the police because you are in love and because you are willing to believe in your husband no matter what.

The doorknob twisted again. "Emma. What's going on? Is it the baby?" he asked.

Emma put her hand on her stomach and looked down at that hand. Inadvertently, he had given her the answer. Yes, she thought. It is. It is the baby. The only one who is completely and utterly innocent in all this. And in mortal danger. That's the whole point. Whoever made that phone call wants to kill us. Both of us. Whether or not David is cooperating, or being duped, the person on the other end of the line was a killer. There was no wiggle room for the wrong guess. I have to protect you, Aloysius, she thought. Your life depends on me. I can't trust anyone but myself.

Somehow, that thought, however horrifying, was also calming.

Call for help, she thought. Obviously not Chief Osmund, she thought. Lieutenant Atkins. She fumbled in her purse, found the lieutenant's card, and punched in the number with trembling fingers. After two rings, the voice mail answered. Oh shit, she thought. "Lieutenant, it's . . . Emma Webster. I'm in the Pine Barrens. I'm in trouble," she whispered, hoping to be heard over the sound of the running water.

Emma punched off the lieutenant's number and called 911. When the operator answered she whispered, "Help. I think my husband wants to kill me."

"Where are you, ma'am?" the operator asked.

"At a gas station."

"Where is the gas station?"

"I don't know," Emma cried.

"I can't hear you, ma'am . . . and I'm not getting any address. You're on a cell phone?"

"Yes, he's right outside," whispered Emma.

"We need an address—even a route number would be helpful."

I don't even know where I am, Emma thought.

"Emma, I don't believe you're all right," David shouted. "I'm gonna force this door open."

Emma pushed the off button, dropped her phone back in her bag and tried to calm the mad beating of her heart. "Everything's fine," she said, turning off the faucets. "Here I come."

She unlocked the door and opened it. David was standing just outside on the blacktop, peering at her.

"Are you okay? You look sick."

She stared into David's eyes, which were now, perhaps had always been, the eyes of a stranger. She had thought she knew that face, knew those eyes. Hadn't those hazel eyes mirrored her deepest feelings, shared them, sworn undying love and loyalty? It was so tempting to lean on him, to tell him all she knew and trust him to help her work it out. She wavered in her heart, but her gut reminded her of all that was at stake. Only trust yourself. "I'm fine," she said. "Just my nerves."

"Well, I have to pay for the gas inside the minimart, and then we'll be on our way."

"Okay," she said. He had to pay for the gas. He probably left the keys in the ignition. While he was inside the minimart, she would get behind the wheel, lock the doors, and leave him there. Drive away. She could drive, whether she was supposed to or not. A few popped stitches were nothing. This was a matter of life or death.

She wouldn't drive farther into the Pine Barrens. She would turn around and go back the way they had come. Back toward Clarenceville.

David slipped his hand beneath her arm, and Emma jumped. "Are you sure you're okay?" he asked.

"Fine," she said irritably, steeling herself to allow him to hold her arm.

"Come with me," he said. "I don't want you out here by yourself."

"I'm just going to go to the car," she said. "I'll be fine."

"Did you see that creep who was pumping the gas? You come with me."

"No," she protested. "I need to sit. I feel a little woozy."

"Probably the smell of the gas from the pumps," he said. "Here, come inside with me and get away from that smell. No arguments. You know you hate the smell of gas, especially now that you're pregnant." He knows me, she thought. He knows I like milk, no sugar, in my coffee, and he knows that I sleep on my side and that I love lily of the valley and hate the smell of gasoline. How could you know, and indulge, and chuckle over a person's every little habit and tic, and all the time be planning to kill them? How could it be? You can't answer that question right now, she reminded herself. You just have to get away from him.

He was steering her toward the lighted door of the minimart, even though she was dragging her feet like lead weights as her hope for escape slipped away. She could yell at him or try to run. But who would help her? That gas-pumping cretin who had leered at her? He'd probably laugh at her or join in the chase. Inside the minimart she could see a woman at the cash register. Maybe the woman would help her, she thought.

"Come on," he said. "What's the problem, Emma?"

"Nothing," she said. "No problem."

His hand firmly gripping her elbow, he led her up to the counter. The woman behind the cash register, a cold-looking blonde with bleached hair, was shouldering a phone to her ear, muttering into the receiver, and did not even look up as she checked the price of David's gas. Emma's heart sank. She was not going to be able to explain her predicament. She couldn't. The woman wouldn't even meet her pleading gaze. Emma looked around the little store and suddenly noticed a lighted Exit sign in the back of the store.

She withdrew her arm from David's hand. "I'm hungry. I'm going to get something to eat and maybe a . . . a soda to settle my stomach."

"I'll get it for you," he said.

"Is this going to be credit or cash," the woman with the phone snapped.

David turned to look at the cashier.

"I'll go grab something. I'll be right back," said Emma.

Before he could reply, she started down the aisle, passing bags of chips, cookies, Kitty Litter, and Kleenex. She headed toward the refrigerated cases at the back and opened one of the doors, pretending to look inside. Instead, she looked down the aisle toward the Exit sign. A hand-lettered sign was posted at the entrance to the corridor beneath the sign. Employees Only, it read. Do Not Enter.

Emma closed the door to the cold case. She took a deep breath. You have to do this, she thought. No time left to decide. She bolted down the aisle across the back of the store and ducked into the forbidden corridor. There was a washroom on the left, which also had an Employees Only sign on it. On the right were stacks of boxes. Emma hurried past them and saw the door leading to the outside.

Don't be locked, she thought. Please God. Don't let it be locked. She pressed on the waist-level bar, and the door opened with a loud clank. The gas station attendant came out of the washroom and saw her.

"Hey, you're not allowed back here," he said indignantly.

Emma did not bother to reply. She pushed the door open and stumbled out into the weed-choked lot behind the station and the blackness of the night.

CHAPTER 29

Brambles caught on the blue-green cape as Emma plunged through the dry grass and weeds. She stubbed her toe on a rock that looked like a clod of earth in the moonlight and stumbled over the empty plastic bottles and crushed soda cans littering the overgrown lot behind the minimart. The nearest bank of trees was to her right. She headed in that direction, grateful for the visibility the moon provided.

She knew she had only a few moments to get away, a few moments before her husband noticed that she had not come back or realized that the attendant's protest had been directed at his wife. A few moments before he came after her, searching for her, trying to capture her. Why, David? her soul cried out, but immediately she stopped herself. No time for that now. Make a plan. Okay, okay, she thought. Go into those trees. Once you're hidden, try to call the police again. Call for help.

For a moment she wondered, who else can I call? Her first thought was Burke, and then she remembered. Burke was gone. Off on some personal business.

Who else? If Lieutenant Atkins was still unavailable, she could try the Clarenceville police. They knew her whole story. And they would believe her right away. They would be able to dispatch troopers to her rescue.

I can do that, she thought, panting as she reached the copse of fir trees. After, I can try Lieutenant Atkins again. Her breathing was ragged from fear and the unaccustomed effort of running. She could feel the pull of the stitches in her side, on her legs. Her skin felt fiery. She kept going, hiding herself in the cover of the trees.

From the direction of the service station, she heard an inchoate shout. It was her name. She knew it was her name. David had discovered she was gone. He was after her. Don't panic, she thought. Stop and call. He can't hear you from where he is. You can barely make out what he is shouting. Although she knew. He was coming after her.

With trembling fingers, she punched in the numbers on her cell phone and held it to her ear, praying that Atkins would answer this time. She's still not there, still has her phone turned off, there's no one to help you, she thought, panic rising.

"Hello."

Emma's heart leapt. "Lieutenant Atkins?" she whispered.

"Speak up. I can't hear you. Who is this?"

She spoke aloud, in the quietest possible voice. "It's Emma Webster. I'm . . . in danger."

"I got your message. Where are you?" Joan demanded.

"I'm hiding in a grove of trees. I'm in the Pine Barrens."

"The Pine Barrens. What the hell are you doing there?"

"I thought. There was a call . . ." She didn't know how to explain.

"Never mind," Joan barked. "Where in the Pine Barrens are you?"

She wished she had paid more attention to the signs as they drove. She had figured that David knew the way. "I'm not sure. There's a service station right nearby."

"Emma, the Pine Barrens are a million acres. You could be anywhere. What exit did you get off at? What kind of service station?"

Emma craned her neck, but she could not see the sign in front of the minimart. "I don't know. I thought we were going to the same place as before, but now I don't know. You have to help me. I'm hiding but I don't know how long—"

She gasped. Now she could see David. He had walked around to the back of the minimart and was calling her name.

"Ask them for help in the service station," Joan said in an agitated tone. "Go in and tell them you're in danger."

"I can't," she said. "He's there."

"Who is it, Emma?" Joan demanded. Then there was a silence. "It's your husband, isn't it? That shit."

Emma was silent.

"As a matter of fact, Chief Osmund left me a message too. His witness picked your husband's photo out of a lineup. The witness said he was there in that cabin of Zamsky's several months ago. With a woman. Wasn't you, was it?"

Emma had to force back tears. "No," she whispered. As she clutched the phone, quivering, she watched David begin to pick his way across the littered lot behind the minimart. Why did you do this to me? she thought.

"Emma, listen to me. You have to give us some idea of where to find you," Joan Atkins said.

"I can't," she croaked. And then, suddenly, she remembered.

"Lieutenant," she said. "There's a poster. A missing persons poster. A girl used to work at this service station and she disappeared. Shannon O'Brien was her name. Isn't there a missing persons register? Maybe if you look her up, you can find out what service station it is. The location, you know?"

"Right," Joan exclaimed. "That's great, Emma. That's using your head. We can find the place from that. It'll take a few minutes on the computer, but we can find it. Once we do, I'll have men on the way. You just sit tight and stay on the line. We're coming to get you."

"Thank you," Emma whispered. She was listening to Joan Atkins's voice, but her gaze was fixed on David, who had stopped, looked up, and then looked toward the trees where she was hiding. He was gazing right at her across the dark field. He can't see you, she told herself. It's impossible.

All he can see is darkness. But it was no use. He was starting to walk her way, his eyes fixed on her location.

Emma dropped the phone in her bag and fled, crashing through the low branches, tripping over roots and beginning to bleed from her broken sutures. She had no idea where she was running. She zigzagged through the trees, turning one way and then another, looking back for a second but seeing no one behind her, only darkness, all around. She wasn't on a trail. She was just pinballing from tree to tree. How would Lieutenant Atkins ever find her, even if she did find the service station?

And then, up ahead of her, flickering through the pine needles on the branches that surrounded her, Emma saw something that made her feel faint with relief. The lights of a house. Someone was there. In their house. Someone she could plead with for help. Beg them to let her in until the police came. She only hoped it was not some drooling, wild-eyed Piney. But then she reminded herself of Claude Mathis. One of those Pineys had given his life to try and save her. Once more, she needed saving. Please, God, she thought. Let me get there before David finds me.

Ignoring the pain that seared her legs and side, Emma pitched herself through the dense tangle of tree branches, using her forearms to clear a pathway, the pine needles slapping and stinging her as she went. The far-off, flickering light urged her on, a beacon of hope in the darkness.

As she made her way toward the light, she noticed that she no longer heard David's voice calling to her. Either he was in silent pursuit, a thought that filled her with dread, or he had given up chasing her. It seemed unlikely that he would give up the chase. But she didn't have the time or the will to try to figure out his plan. She had her plan. That was all she could do. Presumably, the police were already on their way to rescue her. Once she got inside that lit-up house, she would find her phone and speak to Joan Atkins, tell her exactly where she was cached. Wait for rescue. The lights were closer, ever closer. She called on all her strength and thought of her baby.

Her face raw from the whipping of the pine branches, Emma finally emerged at the edge of the clearing where the lit house sat. The sight of the house up close, however, was not reassuring. Even in the moonlight, the house appeared dingy, covered with asbestos shingles, a stack of empty, cracked flowerpots by the front door. A clutch of chewed-up Indian corn hung on the peeling front door. The lights from inside the house were diffused by the grime on the windows.

Emma hesitated. Suddenly, from a dark, tin-roof shed at the end of the clearing, she heard a faint whinny. A horse. Something about the idea of a horse was reassuring, comforting. Animals were gentle and could not betray you. Rather than knock at the door, not knowing what she would find, maybe she should hide in the makeshift barn.

You're just being paranoid, she chided herself, because of all that's happened to you. So the people in this house aren't rich or particularly house proud. That doesn't mean that they won't help you. Besides, they have a horse. They're animal lovers. That's usually a good sign. She had just about changed her mind, decided to knock at the door, when she suddenly heard the sound of wheels on gravel slowly coming up the drive. She saw the flash of headlights, and her mind was made up. She bolted across the clearing to the tin-roofed shed and dove inside, hiding herself behind a bale of hay.

The horse tied up in the shed looked at her with its large, gentle eyes and made a snorting sound. "Shhh . . ." Emma said.

She began to rummage in her purse for the phone and held it to her ear. "Lieutenant Atkins?" she whispered.

There was no sound on the line. It was as if it had died somewhere along the way. Emma pushed every button and then shook the phone in frustration, but there was the same dead air on the line. All of a sudden she heard the sound of a car approaching. She looked out and realized that she had hidden herself just in time. The car that pulled into the clearing was their Jeep. Emma's heart was hammering as she saw the Jeep stop. David left the car running, jumped out, walked up to the front door of the house, and knocked. He peered all around, as if he suspected her presence. Emma pulled herself back behind the hay bale, pulling a dusty blanket that lay on the earthen floor of the shed up over her. She prayed for the horse not to start kicking up a ruckus and give her away.

In another minute, she heard muffled voices. Two male voices, talking. She lifted herself up just far enough to glimpse David standing on the step, talking to a young guy in a shapeless flannel shirt wearing a baseball cap. He was silhouetted in the doorway by the light behind him, the brim of the cap pulled low on his head. David's voice was animated, urgent as he gestured around the clearing, and Emma abruptly lowered her head and hid, trying to make herself invisible. He's searching the nearest places in the area. He's asking that kid if he's seen me. Her heart was thudding. At least, thanks to Emma's hesitation, the young guy didn't know she was here and couldn't give her away. She heard the kid bawl, "Mom," into the house, but didn't hear if there was any reply.

After a few minutes, the voices ceased, and then she heard the crunch of David's footsteps on pine needles. Did he ask the kid if he could look around? Was he coming to search the makeshift barn? Emma's heart was pounding so hard that she couldn't breathe. All of a sudden, she heard the car door slam, and the engine roar. He turned the Jeep around in the clearing and began to roll back down the driveway through the woods, toward the road.

Oh thank God, Emma thought. Her heart was still hammering, but now it was pounding with relief and hope. He's gone. We're safe. She placed her hand on her belly and blessed her baby. Now we know there's a woman in the house, thanks to the kid yelling for his mother. We'll go up there and ask for her help. Find out the exact location and call the police. They probably had a landline, even if her cell wouldn't work. Thank you, God, Emma thought. Thank you.

Throwing off the dusty horse blanket, Emma straightened up. She patted the horse on his long, soft nose and then crept toward the door of the barn. She was still afraid to walk out into the moonlight. Staying in the shadows, she edged her way around the clearing and then rushed up to the front door and knocked. Looking anxiously around her, she rubbed her hands together as she waited for the door to open.

When she heard the lock snap back and the doorknob turn, she drew in a deep breath, ready to try and explain her problem as coherently as possible.

Donna Tuttle opened the door.

"Oh, thank God," Emma said. "I'm sorry to bother you but I'm desperate. I need your help," she implored the woman in the doorway. And then, looking closely at her, Emma froze.

The woman smiled with her lips, but her eyes were glacial. "What a surprise," she said.

Emma stared and shook her head as if she did not trust what her eyes registered. She clutched the doorframe to keep herself from sinking to the ground. "You're alive?"

CHAPTER 30

"I Must be dreaming," Emma said. Tears sprang to her eyes. "Natalie, is it you? Oh my God." Emma tried to take it in. It was Natalie, but not Natalie. Her red hair was dyed black, and she wore a shapeless plaid shirt. But it was her, and she was alive. Emma reached out to hug her friend. Natalie was wooden in her embrace, and Emma quickly released her.

Emma shook her head. "I can't believe my eyes. And to find you here, in this . . . godforsaken place. The one door I knock at. It seems . . . absurd, but here you are."

Natalie did not smile. "It's not a coincidence. David's uncle's place is in the next clearing up the road. I assume that's where you were going."

It crossed Emma's mind to wonder how Natalie knew where David's uncle lived, but it seemed unimportant. If it was the nearest house, why wouldn't she know? Emma brushed her questions aside and stared at her friend, enjoying for a moment the longed-for but unimaginable pleasure of seeing a loved one return from beyond the grave. "Do you realize that everyone thinks you're dead, Nat?" Emma asked.

A defiant look flickered across Natalie's beautiful face. "I know," she said.

"What happened? Did you survive the fall? Did you change your mind? What happened?"

Natalie looked anxiously around the clearing and then took her arm. "Come inside," she said. She pulled Emma in and slammed the door shut.

Emma went willingly, studying her old friend as Natalie locked the door. Emma could discern the lithe, strong body hidden by the baggy clothes. And even under that mop of dyed black hair, there was no mistaking Natalie's fine features and translucent skin, which glowed pearly even in the yellowy shaded lights of the dingy, unkempt house.

Emma shook her head. "Nat, I don't understand. I feel like I'm hallucinating. What are you doing here? Why are you hiding out like this?" Even as she asked, an explanation came to her. It was entirely possible that Natalie might be unable to face the embarrassment of admitting that she had not really taken her own life. "Look, you shouldn't feel . . . ashamed if you changed your mind about the suicide. No one will be angry. It's wonderful. It's a miracle that you're still alive. Come home. Burke has been in mourning for you. We all have."

"Oh, Emma," said Natalie, shaking her head. "I'd forgotten what you were like. Always the steady one. The rock. No problem is too great for Emma."

At first Emma had thought her friend was saying something kind about her, but then she felt the sting of Natalie's sarcasm. She looked around the ramshackle, unkempt house. "Well, you need to face up to what you've done." But then her compassion for her friend welled up again. "Look, let me take you home. I'll help you."

"You've got your own problems," said Natalie.

Emma froze. Her heart constricted at the truth of those words. "What do you know about that?"

"Well, that attack on the night of your wedding happened just beyond those trees," Natalie said. "It's not exactly a secret around here."

Emma realized that it was true. Anyone who lived around here would know about the attack. For one moment, the shock of seeing Natalie had made Emma forget all about David, and the fact that her life was in danger. "It's true," she said. "David was just here. Did you see him? If you did, he must not have recognized you. He's . . . trying to find me."

"Are you hiding from him?" Natalie asked.

"Yes. Because . . . I think he's the one. The one who's been trying to kill me."

Natalie raised her eyebrows. "Really?"

"I'm afraid so. Oh God, it's a long story," said Emma. "A nightmare really. Who was it that answered the door to him, anyway?"

"A friend," said Natalie.

"He called you 'Mom,'" said Emma.

"I'm not his mother," Natalie said.

"So, why . . . ?"

"It's just easier this way," Natalie snapped. "But tell me more, Emma. What are you going to do now? Why do you think that your husband is trying to kill you?"

"It's a long story," said Emma, suddenly overcome with weariness.

"If you need to escape from him, you could disappear," said Natalie. "Like I did."

"Why should I disappear?" Emma cried. "No way. I'm going to see that he pays for what he's done. I'm not going to live on the run and hide from him. Unlike him, I've done nothing to be ashamed of. The police will get him for what he's done to me."

Natalie gazed back at her impassively.

"What?" Emma said.

"You're like a little policeman yourself," Natalie mused. "Trying to maintain law and order."

This time there was no mistaking the insult. It was very like the way that David had insulted her, telling her that she reminded him of a cop. And it made her equally angry. "At least I know right from wrong," said Emma. "What you're doing here is wrong. Letting Burke suffer, thinking you are dead while you indulge your hurt feelings . . ." Then, suddenly, another disquieting thought occurred to Emma. "Wait a minute. Burke identified your body."

"The great psychologist," Natalie scoffed. "He believed exactly what he was supposed to believe. He read my handwritten note, saw my car by the bridge. When they found a decomposed body in the water with red hair, wearing my clothes, my jewelry, he made a positive I.D. Declared me dead," she exulted.

"Well, if it wasn't you in that river, who was it?" Emma demanded.

"What does it matter? You don't know her," Natalie said irritably. "She worked in a gas station around here."

Emma thought of the poster she had seen at the service station. The pale-skinned, redheaded girl who had disappeared after her shift. "Shannon O'Brien?" Emma cried.

Natalie looked at her warily. "Well, very good, Emma. Very clever."

Emma shook her head. "I don't understand. How could she be wearing your clothes? Your jewelry."

"My wedding ring, even. I thought that was a nice touch."

Emma pressed on her own chest to keep herself from retching. "You mean . . . you . . . put her there? In the river."

Natalie nodded. "After I dressed her in my things."

"Oh my God. Did you find her body somewhere? Oh Natalie, you didn't . . ." Her voice trailed away.

Natalie's gaze was cool and blank. "She was a drug addict. She was nodded out, lying by the side of the road in waist-high weeds when we . . . I found her. Not dead, admittedly, but it was only a matter of time."

"You could have called for help. For an ambulance."

"She just would have done it again. Now she's buried in my grave. There's nothing more to be done."

Emma shook her head. "Why? Why would you do that?"

"Actually, when I found her, it gave me the idea. If everyone believed I was dead, it would be better," Natalie said. "After all, the life of Natalie White, the poet, was over.

274

I was ruined. My life was ruined. I figured that at least suicide would make my work more interesting. Might even make me a cult figure, like Sylvia Plath."

"Over? Ruined? What are you talking about? You were riding high. You just won the Solomon Medal."

Natalie shook her head impatiently. "They would have taken it away from me. My reputation would have been destroyed. I had to die. I certainly wasn't about to go to jail. There was no other choice."

"You're not making any sense," said Emma warily.

"Oh, forgive me," said Natalie sarcastically. "I thought your husband might have told you."

"Told me what?" Emma asked.

Natalie snorted. "How all that wonderful publicity about the Solomon Medal backfired on me. You see, there was an accident last spring. An old man got run over. Some retired professor from the college."

"Oh yes. I remember that vaguely. It was a hit-and-run, wasn't it?"

Natalie shrugged. "There was a witness. Some guy who was videotaping his girlfriend's comings and goings on that block. He videotaped the accident, but he never told the cops because he was married and he didn't want his wife to find out about the girlfriend. Anyway, he saw me on TV and he recognized me from the videotape. He was threatening to ruin me. He was blackmailing me."

Emma stared at her. "It was you? You were the driver?"

"He was old," Natalie protested as if the victim's age made her crime negligible.

"Oh my God."

"Spare me the self-righteousness," said Natale, disgusted.

"Excuse me for being . . . shocked. You killed that man. And what about Shannon? Her family doesn't even know where she is," Emma cried.

Natalie shrugged. "I can't help that."

Emma shook her head. "God, you are so selfish. It really doesn't matter to you, does it? None of it."

Natalie glared at her. "I'm selfish? You can say that? You, the girl with the perfect family and the perfect life. You don't know what I suffered in my life . . ."

"Oh, sure I do, Nat," said Emma in disgust. "Your terrible childhood. Everybody knew what you suffered. I listened to it a million times. I comforted you a million times. Not know what you suffered? You never would let anyone forget."

"Emma, you bitch!" Natalie cried. She reached out and pushed Emma over with all her might. Too stunned to react or stop her fall, Emma fell to the grimy floor, landing with a thud on her knees. Gasping, she extended her arms to steady herself.

Natalie reached up under her flannel shirt and into a leather sheath concealed there. She pulled out a hunting knife, holding it aloft. Before Emma could rise, Natalie kicked her in the side with the toe of her heavy work boot. Emma felt the stitches split and the sticky sensation of blood spreading beneath the arm of her loose, stretchy shirt.

"Now get up," Natalie commanded.

Gasping for breath, Emma grabbed her throbbing side, astonished at the turn this bizarre reunion had taken. She thought of resisting, but the look in Natalie's eyes was terrible. It was a good bet that Natalie would use that knife on her at any moment. She had to cooperate. Had to hope that maybe she could reason with her. For a minute she thought of the other person, the man she had seen at the door in the ball cap. Who was he, and where had he gone? Was he still here? Maybe she could appeal to him, whoever he was, to help her.

"Get up," Natalie shrieked, poking Emma in the shoulder with the knife. Emma scrambled to her feet. Natalie pressed the knife's tip to Emma's throat. "Go," she said. And Emma went where she was prodded. They passed from the filthy, garbage-littered kitchen, to a small bedroom with nothing in it but a rumpled, unmade bed that smelled of sex and sweat, and a straight-backed chair, as well as a pile of clothes and a plastic bag full of toiletries lying on a bureau.

"Sit," Natalie commanded, banging the chair down in the middle of the room. Emma knew she was too weak to fight, that she would have to acquiesce. Especially because she felt the point of the knife sticking into the back of her neck. Emma sat down on the chair, and Natalie opened a nearby drawer and grabbed a length of rope that was coiled there. She looped it around Emma and began to make knots in it as she went.

Emma took a deep breath and tried to keep her arms as far from her torso as possible as the rope went around her. Natalie looped it and wove it until Emma was trussed to the chair.

"Why are you doing this to me, Natalie?" Emma demanded. "I never hurt you. I've been your friend through all of it, all these years. Even on my wedding day, I was wishing you were there with me. Despite all the bad times, I still wished I could share it with you."

Natalie's eyes blazed. "Oh, yeah. I really hated to miss that. Your wedding."

Emma looked at Natalie and suddenly felt a new fear, blooming like a black rose in the middle of her chest. "Wait a minute. You said earlier you thought David might have told me about you. About the hit-and-run."

"But he didn't, did he?" said Natalie.

"How could he have known about that?"

A sly grin spread across Natalie's face. "You really don't know, do you? He kept our secret."

"What secret?"

"Well, think about it, Emma. Who do you think I would call for help if some bastard came along trying to blackmail me?"

"Your husband," Emma said. "Burke."

Natalie rolled her eyes. "Burke. Oh sure. He'd be a lot of help. He'd be all sympathy. Can't you just imagine it? Mr. Pure-as-the-driven-snow. He'd be giving me a lecture on my role in the breakdown of society's mores."

"Burke adored you."

"His wife, the poet. I was a prop in his perfect little universe. The brilliant, beautiful wife who required just a minor little bit of psychological fine-tuning. No. I don't think so. Burke couldn't have coped with the thought of his precious bride as a killer. He was better off believing I was dead. No, I did not tell Burke."

Emma looked at her with wide eyes. "A friend?" she said.

"A friend." Natalie began to smile. "I suppose you could say that. A friend. A special friend. A friend who I used to meet for afternoon delights at your little honeymoon cabin over the rise there."

"You and David."

"Oh yes," said Natalie.

"He wouldn't have kept that from me," Emma protested weakly.

"But he did. Didn't he?"

"Yes," she whispered.

"Sorry," said Natalie.

Emma felt as if she couldn't breathe, couldn't catch her breath. Even though she had expanded her chest to keep the bonds from holding her too tightly, it was as if no air would enter her body. She pictured David there, with Natalie, in that hideaway where he'd brought Emma for their honeymoon. David and Natalie, adulterous lovers trysting in the very cabin where he had carried Emma over the threshold to their new life. The cabin where she'd been slashed by an ax. The place where he had tried to kill her.

The cruel thought pierced her, and she let out a moan. She knew what it was to wish to die.

CHAPTER 31

Natalie's eyes were alight. "You really didn't know, did you? He kept our secret. You didn't know that he was mine. That he loved me."

The door to the bedroom banged back and a young man in a sweatshirt stood framed there, his eyes black with rage. He had taken off his Eagles cap. Emma saw the shock of magenta, the third eye. "Stop it," he cried. "Stop talking about him like that. He's not yours. He's gone. He's nothing to you anymore. You have me. I'm the one who loves you. What about me?"

"Kieran." Emma stared at him.

"Get out of here," Natalie said.

"You're mine. You said so. You said you were mine. Why do you have to keep talking about him all the time? He's not here to help you. I'm the one who's here."

"Calm down. Let's talk out there," Natalie said.

Kieran's eyes were frantic. "What do I have to do? I've done everything you wanted me to do. I've done everything. Why do you have to torture me? I thought we were going to end all this and get away from here. You said so. You promised me. Why did you let her in? Why did you have to tell her?"

"She needs to know. She thinks I'm lying. Tell her, Kieran. Tell her how you saw us together at my house. You saw what a real man does. You must have enjoyed it. You stayed to watch, even when I didn't know you were there."

Kieran clapped his hands over his eyes and shook his head. "I don't want to remember," he said, wailing like a wounded child. "You said you were through talking about him. I'm not helping you anymore." He flung himself into the other room.

"Kieran," Natalie cried, rushing after him. "Baby, don't."

Emma could hear the sound of their voices rising and falling from the living room. She strained to make out the words. "Of course I do, baby," Natalie crooned. Their voices grew quiet, and Emma did her best to decipher what they were saying. Strained to hear David's name. To punish herself by catching every reference to him, to imagine him in bed with Natalie, betraying her.

"Ah shit," Kieran wailed. "I've had enough. I can't stand it anymore. When will it be over?"

Suddenly, it was quiet in the other room. What's going on? she thought. When will what be over? And Kieran? That misguided, messed-up kid. Had he known all along that Natalie was alive? And kept her secret? Now that she thought about it, she remembered his tortured lyrics, his loneliness. She remembered that he used to show his lyrics to Natalie.

How had they gotten from there to here? From cookies and gentle criticism to this godforsaken hovel in the woods? Emma remembered him saying that he planned to die for love. Now she understood that it was for the love of Natalie, a woman pretending to be dead. Emma's head was reeling from the unexpected, but one thing she knew for sure. This situation was volatile and dangerous. They were keeping her tied up. They saw her as a threat, and obviously the two were living in some kind of alternate reality where faking one's death was all right. It was a reality Emma did not dare remain in. The first order of business was to get away from them. As far away as she could.

Use your head. There was no way to get to the phone. It was in her purse, in the other room where it had fallen when Natalie pushed her over. Besides, when she'd tried to use her phone outside, there had been no reception. So calling for help would not be an option. She tried not to allow herself to dwell on that grim possibility. She looked around the room, trying to figure out a means of escape. There was one grimy, multipaned window, which looked as if it had not been opened in years. Otherwise, there was the door into the other room, and that was not a possibility.

First things first, she thought. You have to get out of these ropes. She took a deep breath and she thought of her baby, not yet born, who needed to live. I will not let them kill us, Aloysius. I will not let you die at their hands. She tried to concentrate on the ropes. Just as she had pulled them apart when Natalie was tying them, she now contracted every muscle and pulled her arms close together. She could feel them loosen, but not by much. She did the same thing with her legs, trying to find room between her legs and the chair. How long will this take? she thought. How long do I have?

She began to work the bonds as best she could, expanding and contracting her muscles to create wiggle room. It was slow and painful, and she kept one ear on the murmurs and shouts that were coming from the other room. She thought of shouting herself, but it seemed futile. The nearest house was the Zamskys' and there was no one there. So she worked her bonds and she prayed. And all of a sudden, she had an idea. Maybe if she looped the rope on her wrists around one of the dingy brass knobs on the low bedposts, she could use the knob to pry loose the ropes. It was worth a try. It meant that she had to move the chair to the bed and do it quietly. Hunching her shoulders, she leaned forward and lifted her butt until the legs of the chair came off the floor. Balancing the chair on her back she scuffled over to the bed, trying her best to minimize the number of times a chair leg struck the floor with a thwack. Finally, she reached the bed and was able to lean back and set the chair down.

She glanced at the door, but there was no sign that any-one had heard her. She could hear the murmur of voices again from the other room. Now, she thought. She turned her back to the bedpost and raised herself up, chair and all, from the floor, at the same time lifting her tethered hands to swing them over and around the brass knob, so she could work the ropes loose, riding them against the knob. That was her plan, but because she could not see behind her, when she lifted her arms to bring them down around the knob and leaned forward, she missed and toppled over, chair and all, to the floor. She lay there on her side, still tethered to the chair, wanting to cry out, every muscle in her body aching from the pain of her fall.

The voices in the other room stopped momentarily as she came crashing down. She could hear the bedroom door open, though she could not see it.

"She fell over," she heard Kieran say.

"Leave her like that," said Natalie.

Emma felt tears spring to her eyes, both from the pain and from the hopelessness of her situation. Clumps of dust from under the bed tickled her face and seemed to suffocate her. She stared, unseeing, at a mound of dark clothing that had been stuffed or kicked under the bed. A fleece hood, pant legs, and sleeves were visible sticking out of the dark jumble, and so was something else. It took Emma a moment of staring to recognize it. It was a knitted ski mask. Black. With red rims around the eyeholes.

Emma jerked back and stifled her own scream.

The clothes of her attacker. The same attacker both here, in the Pinelands, and at the train station.

I did everything you asked me to do, Kieran had said.

What did you do, Kieran? Was it you who tried to kill me? Or Natalie? What about David? she thought, confused. One of them wore those clothes and came at me with an ax, and, when that failed, tried to push me in front of a train.

She thought of the two people conspiring in the other room. One she had called a patient, the other, a friend. Emma felt weak and sick to her stomach at the thought of that much hatred aimed at her from the people she had cared for.

You did nothing to deserve that hatred, she reminded herself. Don't let them defeat you. Think of your baby.

Using her feet, she pushed herself away from the bed, scuttling backward across the floor, like a crab turned sideways. When her chair hit the wall, she was jarred from head to toe. She began to rock backward carefully until the chair felt anchored, and then slowly, painstakingly, she shifted her weight and worked the chair upright again. It was painful and difficult, and when at last she was seated, still tied, in the corner of the room, she was gasping for breath, her heart pounding.

From outside of the house, she heard a faint, familiar sound. A whinny. Not once. But several times. Was the horse just making noise, or could he possibly be alert to someone else in the area? Could the police have somehow found their way to her? Or was she just grabbing at straws, trying not to see the hopelessness of her own situation? Hoping against hope, she turned her head and looked over her shoulder, knowing that all she would see was the black night outside the window.

She almost screamed. A man looked back at her, his face pressed to the grimy pane, his sad, hazel eyes filled with horror at the sight of her.

* * *

"Stop," Joan Atkins cried. "What the hell is that?"

Audie Osmund, summoned by his dispatcher from the awards dinner for his grandson, had joined in the search. Gathering up half a dozen men, he had met up with Joan Atkins and Trey Marbery at the service station that Emma had described. When they had entered the minimart to make inquiries, the bleached blonde behind the counter said with a disinterested shrug, "Maybe the lady had a reason for wanting to ditch the husband."

"She sure was in a hurry," the attendant had added, pointing out the back door to them. And so they had begun to hunt for Emma.

Audie ordered his men to fan out from the back door of the minimart, feeling sure she must have left a trail. How far could she get in her condition—an injured, pregnant woman on foot?

"She's probably wearing that woolly cape," Joan had offered. "Surely it will get caught on branches and bushes. Use that to track her." Several officers started out on foot, but Audie, who knew the dirt roads around here, offered to drive. Now Joan sat tensely beside him in the front seat of his truck while Trey had folded himself into the narrow space behind the front seat. With the headlights on bright, they began to drive through the woods, Joan still fretting aloud that they might have been better off on foot. Every ten seconds, she would try again to get through to Emma's cell phone, but to no avail.

And then, all at once, Joan saw something. "Over there," she cried.

Audie frowned. "That's the road to the uncle's place," he said.

"Don't you see something up there?" Joan insisted.

Audie peered up the road toward the Zamskys'. Through the darkness of the trees, he did think he saw something. "A light?" he said.

"Is that from the house?" Joan asked.

Audie shook his head. "Too faint for that."

"You're right," said Joan. It was even fainter than the glow of a flashlight in the night. And unlike a flashlight, it was fixed. It had about the intensity of a single, weak bulb. "Let's go see about it," she said. "It will only take a minute to check it."

Pulling the truck off the road, Audie hopped out and retrieved his own flashlight from the trunk while Joan and Trey jumped out of the cab and began to walk up the rutted dirt path toward the faint light.

"Emma!" Joan cried out. "Can you hear us?"

284

Audie caught up with them, gripping his brightly lit, long-handled flashlight like a weapon. The light source was just past a curve in the dirt drive. They rounded the curve, and then they saw it.

A car was stopped in a clump of pines, along the edge of the road, tipped nearly on its side off the sloping dirt shoulder. The front door on the passenger's side hung open, branches hanging over and around it, and the open door had caused the inside car light to come on. There was no passenger or driver visible. The car looked empty.

Joan approached the car cautiously, drawing her gun. There was definitely something ominous about this abandoned car with an open door. Who would leave it there? Why would anyone be on this road anyway? All of a sudden, from the direction of the empty car, she heard a faint sound. A human voice, groaning.

Emma, she thought.

Wielding his flashlight, Audie began to run toward the car.

"Who's there?" Trey cried. "Who is it? Mrs. Webster, is that you?"

The car was a gray, late-model Lexus. In the back window was a parking sticker for the Wrightsman Youth Crisis Center. As they approached the car, Trey suddenly exclaimed, "I think I know that car. It belongs to Dr. Heisler. The director of the Wrightsman Center." As they reached the vehicle they realized that the car door was being propped open by a human body that had fallen halfway out, and was wedged between the open door and the low-lying branches of the pines that crowded the edge of the road.

Ignoring the potential damage to her well-tailored pantsuit, Joan pushed away the branches and climbed in, lifting the man's upper body out of the tangle of branches. Burke Heisler's face was barely recognizable for the blood, and his half-closed eyes had a milky gleam.

"Dr. Heisler," Joan cried. "What happened to you?" If Joan hadn't heard the groan, she would have presumed the man was dead. It looked as if he had been beaten savagely and propped up in the driver's seat. Judging from the dried blood everywhere, he had been in the car for some time, and the weight of his slumped body must have finally pushed open the door. Or he had somehow managed to open it himself in an effort to escape.

Audie unhooked his radio from his belt and began to call for help.

"Help is coming, Dr. Heisler. Hang in there. They're on their way," said Joan.

There was no response, and Joan wondered if the psychiatrist was unconscious. His breathing was extremely shallow. "What happened to you?" she said softly, not really expecting an answer.

Burke's eyelids fluttered, and Joan saw the glazed stupor in his eyes. "Natalie," he whispered.

"That's his wife," said Trey, who was on the other side of Burke, helping Joan keep Burke propped up until the ambulance arrived. "The one who killed herself."

Joan shook her head. "Poor guy," she said.

"Alive," Burke whispered.

"No, sir," said Trey gently. "Your wife died. Do you remember?"

"Alive," Burke whispered again. "In these woods. Help her. Help Emma."

CHAPTER 32

Emma swallowed the cry that rose to her throat. David, she thought. He brought a finger to his lips, warning her to be silent. She pleaded with him with her eyes, and he nodded slightly. He had come back. Why? What could have made him come back? She nodded back to him, and then turned her head quickly, looking to the bedroom door, which had begun to scrape against the floor.

Her heart hammered as she saw them enter.

"What are you doing? How did you get over there?" said Natalie with a frown.

Emma glared at this woman whom she had loved and then mourned. "I looked under the bed. I saw the clothes," said Emma. "The ski mask and the hoody."

Natalie did not try to pretend that she did not understand. "I should really throw them away. I won't need them again."

"Burn them," said Kieran.

"It was you," Emma said. "You're the one who tried to kill me."

Natalie did not bother to deny it.

"Why?" Emma said.

"So that you would die, and he would have to go to jail for it. Call it my parting shot. For the traitors."

287

"You and David were the traitors. You betrayed me. And Burke," Emma said.

Natalie shrugged. "You weren't satisfied with being a little rich girl. You had to try and take what was mine. David was mine."

"Don't say that," Kieran muttered.

Emma gazed at Natalie in disbelief. "And Claude Mathis who tried to save me. And the nurse who was taking care of me. Why did you have to kill her?" Emma cried.

"Kieran killed the nurse," Natalie said.

"Don't tell her," Kieran cried.

"Why not? She won't tell. She won't be alive to tell. Kieran was supposed to kidnap you and bring you to me. But the nurse answered the door instead. He panicked and hit her. And then he found out you weren't even there. Not very smooth, but . . ."

"You were glad I did it," he protested.

"Kieran, why do this to me?" Emma pleaded. "We've talked so many times at the center. In the group."

Natalie laughed. "He killed Burke too. He does whatever I tell him."

"Burke!" Emma felt as if her heart was being shredded. "Not Burke!"

"Somehow Burke began to suspect I wasn't dead. I don't know how."

Immediately, Emma thought of the autopsy report lying on the front seat of Burke's car. Somehow he *had* come to suspect . . .

"Burke was poking around up at the Zamsky house when I stumbled across him. Imagine my surprise. Luckily Kieran was there to help."

"You don't care what happens, do you, Natalie?" Emma asked.

"She cares. She cares about me. She and I are going away together," Kieran said. "And never be apart."

Emma looked at him sadly. "Oh, Kieran, you don't believe that, do you? She's just using you and then she'll throw you away."

He was holding the knife in his right hand, and Natalie was edging in behind him, an excited smile in her eyes and on her lips. He turned and looked at Natalie. His young eyes were full of pain. "That's not true," he said.

"She's just stalling," Natalie observed. "She knows she's going to die."

"It's not too late for you, Kieran. Don't do what she says," Emma pleaded.

"I have to. She's everything to me," he said.

"The police are coming. You won't get out of this."

He did not meet her gaze, but she saw his eyes. There was a flicker of fear there. Just a flicker, but it gave her a moment's hope.

"She doesn't love you, Kieran. She doesn't love anyone," Emma insisted.

"She does love me. From the first time I showed her my songs, she realized I was a genius."

Emma looked into Kieran's eyes, and instantly she saw what she had to do. It was cruel, but she had no other choice. No other weapon. Divide and conquer. "Kieran, I hate to tell you this, but she made fun of your songs. She said they were simple and pathetic," Emma said reluctantly.

Kieran's eyes widened, and when he turned them on Natalie, his face seemed ragged with doubt. "You told me I was a genius."

"She's making it up. Don't listen to her," Natalie said. "We know the truth."

Kieran turned and slapped Emma's face. Emma's head jerked back.

"You're a liar," he said.

Emma's face burned where he had slapped her. "I'm not lying," Emma insisted.

"What are you waiting for?" Natalie cried. "Don't listen to her."

"Did you say that? Did you say my songs were pathetic?"

Natalie snatched the hunting knife from his hand, jabbing it in the air, threatening both Kieran and Emma.

"Natalie, for God's sake," Kieran said. "Give that to me."

"If you can't do it, I will. You can't do it, can you?" Natalie cried. "You can't kill her."

"I can and I will," Kieran said. "Give me the knife."

Natalie raised the knife with both hands. "Are you too weak, Kieran?"

"Of course not," he said, trying to reach for her, to embrace her.

Natalie held him off, jabbing the air around him with the knife. Kieran ignored the blows she was trying to inflict on him and grabbed at her wrists. "Of course not. I love you," he cried. "I have no life without you, Natalie. Of course I'll kill her for you."

Natalie lowered the knife warily. His back to the door, Kieran reached for her and pulled her close. Natalie allowed him the embrace, encircling his ungainly body with her own arms, the knife still in her hand. Kieran pressed his defaced forehead into her shoulder.

Eyes wide open, Natalie looked past him to the doorway. "David," she exclaimed.

Kieran stepped back, eyes blazing, and threw off her embrace. The knife fell from her hand and clattered to the floor. Kieran grabbed her by the neck with both his hands and began to throttle. "No," he cried. "Stop it. Stop wishing I was him."

David sprang across the room, wielding a tire iron, and whacked it across Kieran's back. The boy's grip on Natalie loosened. He staggered and cried out.

David did not hesitate. He struck a blow at Kieran's shoulder that then glanced off the side of his head. Kieran crumpled to the floor.

Natalie was staring at David.

David crouched down and pushed the boy over, picking up the knife. Kieran was unconscious, a bruise blackening the side of his face. David stood up. Emma watched him, her heart in her throat. He looked at Natalie. Then he turned and cut the bonds that tied Emma to the chair and handed the knife to her. In that instant, Natalie understood. She threw herself at him, clawing at his face, pummeling him with her fists. Screaming.

Ignoring her rage, David lifted the tire iron and held it up.

"Natalie," he shouted, making himself heard over her cries. "Don't make me kill you. I promise you, if I hit you with this thing, I will kill you."

Natalie stopped for a moment and stepped back, eyes wide. Emma raised the knife, ready and willing to plunge it into Natalie if she came one step closer, but Natalie did not notice. She was gazing at Emma's husband.

"How did you know I was here?" Natalie asked.

David returned her gaze coldly. "I was searching for Emma. When I came to the door, I knew there was something familiar about the boy. I was driving away and I kept thinking I had seen his face. Trying to place him. It was the hat that threw me off. Hiding the pink hair and that ugly-assed eye on his forehead. Mentally, I tried to remove the hat. And then I remembered. The boy with the three eyes. From the Wrightsman Center. Emma's patient. She was so kind to that kid. What did you do to him?"

Natalie ignored his question. "I told Emma about us, David. She didn't know."

David's face reddened. "There's nothing to tell," he said dully.

"Really?" Natalie asked. "Nothing to tell?"

Emma saw the guilt in David's eyes and she knew that it was true. He and Natalie were lovers. It was not some figment of Natalie's fevered imagination.

"There was no reason to tell her. It was a meaningless affair. Especially, when I thought you were dead . . ."

"Meaningless? You loved me," she cried.

"I never loved you," David said.

"You did," Natalie cried. "You did and you know it. Don't bother to deny it for her sake." Natalie looked at Emma with loathing. "He couldn't get enough of me."

"I don't want to know," Emma said dully.

"Don't talk to my wife," said David. "Spare her your venom."

Natalie glared at David. "Did you mourn for me?" Natalie cried. "Did you weep over my grave?"

David shook his head. "Weep for you? Hardly. I thought it was justice, although you took the coward's way out. You ran over that old man. You got out of the car to make sure he was dead and then kept on going."

"Were you with her when it happened?" Emma cried, horrified.

David shook his head. "No. I didn't even know about it until the guy with the videotape contacted her. I had already met you and broken it off with her, but she called me and pleaded with me. Said she had a horrible problem and only I could help."

"So you went to her again."

David was staring at Natalie. "I went to her. She told me everything and begged me to help her."

Natalie glared back at him.

"And you helped her?" Emma asked.

"I told her to turn herself in," he said. "Or I would."

"You didn't give a damn about helping me," Natalie said.

"You killed a man, Natalie," said David.

Natalie shook her head. "You make it sound so right-eous. Tell the truth, David. You wanted me out of the way so you could marry this heiress for her money. But I wasn't going to give you the satisfaction. Did you think I would just go away quietly and let you get away with that? Did you think you wouldn't have to pay for your crimes? I asked you for help and you betrayed me. Whose crimes are worse?"

Outside the house, cars were roaring into the clearing and doors were slamming. Emma looked toward the window. She could hear Chief Osmund on a bullhorn, yelling for his men to shoot to kill if necessary. And Joan Atkins was urging caution in a cool but insistent tone. Emma knew she should feel elated, but all she could feel was numb.

"The police are here," Emma said.

David looked sadly at Emma, who turned away from his gaze. Then he looked back at Natalie. "Your crimes are worse. But tell that to my wife, who will not look at me. And to my best friend whom I did betray . . ."

"Burke is dead," Emma said dully. "They killed him."

"NO," David protested.

"That's what they said," said Emma.

David blanched and seemed to sway slightly. "He was never anything but good to you, Natalie. He did everything in his power to help you."

"He kept me a prisoner in his little well-ordered world. With his theories and his medications and his 'Kiss The Cook' aprons. I was dying slowly living there with him. I told you that the first time we were together. Remember?"

"David," Emma said, recoiling. "My God."

"I remember," said David. "I remember thinking at that moment that my friend Burke was too good for you. That I should walk away from you and never look back."

"But you didn't," she cried triumphantly. "Did you?"

Emma held her breath for a moment. Wishing he would deny it. Say it wasn't so.

David shook his head. "No, I didn't."

There was a pounding on the door. "Police," yelled Audie Osmund.

"Come in," Emma cried, gripping the knife tighter and holding it high, ready to strike if she had to. "We're in here."

"Save me," Natalie whispered to David, stepping over Kieran's limp body on the floor. Her cheeks were flushed, her alabaster skin beaded in sweat.

Emma looked at him, wondering what he felt, wondering how she could have known him so little. His face was expressionless.

"Never," David said. "Not even if I could."

CHAPTER 33

It was after midnight when they were finished, for the time being, with the police, the hospital, and the press. Natalie was in jail, held without bail. Kieran was treated at the hospital and then he too was arrested and held in jail. Burke was in critical care, but conscious. The doctors were optimistic about his prognosis. He told the police that he began to suspect that Natalie was not dead when Emma received the shell dish as a wedding present. The autopsy results confirmed to him that he had identified the wrong body. And he had gone in search of his wife. With dire results.

David and Emma had given their statements, advised by Mr. Yunger, who had shown up in a tuxedo, called away from a New Jersey Bar Association dinner, to shepherd them through the process. They had run the gauntlet of reporters, Yunger insisting that they would not compromise their testimony by speaking to the press. Now, finally, they were home. David unlocked their front door and held it open as Emma slowly and painfully made her way inside. She unfastened the toggle clasp on her cape. David lifted the ripped and stained garment off her shoulders and hung it on a hook inside the closet door. "We should throw this thing away," he said.

"NO," said Emma sharply. "No. I want to keep it."

Emma walked to the door of the living room and leaned against the doorframe as David went around switching on the standing lamp and the various amber glass table lamps. Emma looked around the room. It was relatively tidy, thanks to the late Lizette, who had cleaned it up for them before she met her death at Kieran's hand. Some trace of the efficient, doomed nurse seemed to linger, a sorrowful note in the room. Once Emma and David had imagined themselves on cold nights like this, cuddled in front of their fireplace, the room illuminated by candles and the color of the glass lamps. But now, even in the warm, amber glow, the room did not beckon her.

"Come and sit down," David said.

Emma felt too numb and exhausted to protest. She went over to the leather sofa and sat down in the corner, against a large, tapestry pillow.

"Can I get you anything?" he asked.

Emma shook her head. "I feel like we've been gone for years," she said.

"I know," he said.

She studied him for a moment. "Did you ever suspect?" she asked.

"Never," he said. "I'm ashamed to admit this, but I had really begun to think that it might be Burke."

"Burke?" she cried.

"I didn't know what to think. The notes at your job. He could have been responsible. I thought he might have found out about my affair with his wife. I was becoming pretty paranoid."

"Poor Burke," Emma said.

"I know. But they think he'll be okay."

Emma shook her head. "How is he supposed to ever recover from this? The shock. The betrayal . . ."

They were silent for a moment. "I don't know," David said. "We all have to recover."

"Somehow," she said.

"Tomorrow we'll start over again. Start fresh."

"I've been thinking," she said.

"What?"

"I think I'll go out to Chicago tomorrow. And stay with my mother and Rory for a while."

He was silent. She waited for a response, but there was none. Finally, she looked at him.

"Why?" he said, staring straight ahead.

"Because I feel like I need to . . . get away."

"From me," he said.

"Just get away."

"From us," he said accusingly.

"David, I don't want to argue. I'm too tired."

"From our marriage."

"What marriage?" she snapped.

For one second she looked at him balefully, directly in the eye. She saw that she had wounded him. In a way, she was glad. In a hollow way. She looked down at her hands, flexing them in her lap. "Look, don't get me wrong. I am grateful to you for finding me. For coming after me. And I don't want you to misunderstand. I don't blame you for what Natalie tried to do to me. She's mentally ill and she's cruel. It's a terrible combination. I owe you my life, David. I'll never forget that."

"Well, that's really touching," he said bitterly. "Considering that you assumed I was trying to kill you."

Emma straightened up. "What would you have thought, if you were me?" she demanded, refusing to be ashamed. "I had to assume that. I am carrying a baby. I couldn't take a chance with my baby's life. If you're insulted, well, I'm sorry. I didn't see myself as having a lot of choices."

"I know," he said.

They sat tensely, side by side, not touching. Emma was aware of her heart aching. A little part of her wanted simply to say so. Admit to her pain, because it was true. But he might interpret that to mean that it was all right. That everything was all right. And it wasn't.

"Tell me what you're thinking," David said at last.

Emma did not reply. She knew that nothing David had done would ever compare to Natalie's crimes. But betrayal was not really a crime with levels.

"We're not going to make it if you don't tell me," he pleaded. "Just tell me."

"So you can say it isn't true."

She saw a flicker of anger in his eyes. Before he could respond she said, "I can't understand how you justified it to yourself."

David flinched but did not look away.

"How you took the wife of your closest friend for a lover."

"I wanted to," he said.

Tears sprang to her eyes, and she almost wondered why. "That's great, David," she said.

"I know it."

"Have you no loyalty? How could you do that to Burke?"

David drew in a deep breath. "I could say she seduced me, but I'm not a teenager. I wanted her, and I thought . . . I don't know." He exhaled. "I wish I could tell you how I agonized over it. But in the end, I did it. Even if I did agonize over it, that wouldn't change what I did."

"He was your dearest friend."

"He was more like a brother to me," said David. "Complete with rivalry. As a kid, I always envied him. That's not an excuse, by the way."

Emma was silent.

"What else are you thinking?" he asked.

"Isn't that enough?" she cried.

"Yeah," he said. "But it's not all."

She didn't want to say it out loud because deep in her heart, she suspected that Natalie must have been lying. But even a lie can fester inside you. He was looking at her. Waiting.

"She said you still loved her. Even though you married me."

David stared at her, silently insisting that she meet his gaze. Finally, she acquiesced.

"Do you believe that?" he asked.

Emma said nothing.

"Look. I'm not going to tell you all about my affair with Natalie, Emma. Neither one of us is a masochist. But I will tell you this. When I went to see her, after the blackmailer called, I asked her to tell me about the accident. The old man's death. She told me everything. She was exhilarated, she was speeding, singing along to a CD, and then bam. She hit him. She never saw him walking by the side of the road. She got out to look, and the old man was dying. She looked all around and didn't see anyone. And it occurred to her that she was lucky. That if she left right away, everything would be fine. Because no one would know." David shook his head. "How can you think I ever loved her?"

"But you wanted her. You wanted her enough to betray your friend."

"I acted like a pig," he said.

"And with me? What was it with me?"

"Emma. You know what it was. What it is. Surely you haven't forgotten us. Emma, I am just not that good an actor. You know?"

Emma knew. She thought of all their days and nights together. The way their bodies met, heart and soul. "I know," she said. "I'm just so mad at you. For not being . . . what I thought you were."

"Honorable?" he asked.

Tears came to her eyes again, and she let them fall.

David sighed. "You know, when you started to get those crazy letters, I actually thought for a moment that they sounded like something Natalie would write. But then I thought, Natalie is dead. I wasn't even capable of imagining what she did."

"Were those her letters in the locked drawer?"

David nodded. "Yes. After I broke it off, she kept sending them to me. They were . . . ravings. It was fascinating. In a repulsive sort of way."

"I can imagine," Emma said glumly.

"Emma, it's over now. You don't need to go to your mother's," he said. He slid right beside her on the couch and carefully put his arm around her. "You need to stay here with me. We need to start our marriage over. Get ready for our baby. We need to prove that Natalie did not destroy our dream."

Emma shook her head helplessly.

"Look, I'm not any good at this," he said. "All my life I despised my father, and I acted just like him. I've always been good at leaving, not staying. But when I made those wedding vows to you, I said them from the heart. They were for you and our baby too. Our children. You're the smart one, Em. Help me figure out how to do this."

His handsome face was near hers, and his sad eyes searched hers. More than anything she wanted to let go and relax against him. She looked away, looked at the blackness outside the windows, and thought of spring, when the baby would be born. How she longed for those endless, pale blue evenings. No more darkness. "She turned to face him directly. "Did you sleep with her again, after we met?"

"No," he said.

Yes. No. What did it really prove? she wondered. How could you ever really know?

"I did not betray you, Emma," he said. "I will never betray you."

"How can I believe you?" She looked at him, wondering.

"I can't tell you that," he said.

"Swear it," she said. "Swear it on our baby's life."

David hesitated. Then he shook his head. "No. I won't," he said. "Leave our baby out of it. This is between you and me."

To her surprise, his words filled her with relief. She realized that she had posed him an impossible condition. After all, it was the nature of lovers to promise to be true. And to mean it, at least for the moment, with all their hearts. But a parent, a father, did not barter his child's life, just to get his way. In denying her request, he had actually convinced her it might be possible to try again. There was no going back to the innocent bliss of her wedding day. She would have to mourn that loss for a while.

Emma sighed. "I think maybe if I just spend some time away from you. Go out to my mother's. It might help," she said. "I need time to think."

"No, Em. Think here. Think with me. I'll give you plenty of room. All the room you want. But this is no time to be apart. Stay here." He picked up her left hand, where her gold band glinted. "For better or for worse. That's what we promised."

She looked down at her hand in his. "That is what we promised," she admitted.

"We're due for some 'better,'" he said.

She took a deep breath and nodded.

"Can we start over?" he asked.

She frowned, wondering if they could. He was not the prince she had imagined him to be. She knew perfectly well that it was foolish to imagine any man a prince. But all the same, she had.

He lifted her fingers to his lips and kissed them. "We can make it, Em," he said. "If you can forgive me and let us try again, we can make it. The three of us. You, me, and our baby."

"The three of us," she said, imagining her baby safely sleeping inside of her. She did want to believe they would be a family. That was why she married him in the first place. He was no prince, but a man, like any other. Their life would not be perfect, but it was the life she wanted. Forgiveness was a good place to start. She hesitated, and then she made her choice. She reached out and ran her fingertips down the side of his face. And in her heart, she prayed for grace.

THE END

ACKNOWLEDGMENTS

Special thanks to Dr. Jacqueline Moyerman for insights, information, and ever-interesting discussions. And thanks, as always, to the team who kept me on the blacktop through this detour-filled trip: Art Bourgeau, Sara Bourgeau, Meg Ruley, Jane Berkey, and Maggie Crawford.

Thanks also to Louise Burke, for the beautiful paperbacks, to Peggy Gordjin for taking me to many foreign ports, and to all at Albin Michel in Paris, especially Tony Cartano, Francis Esminard, Joelle Faure, Danielle Boespflug, Sandrine Labrevois, and Florence Godfernaux for innumerable kindnesses.

Thank you for reading this book.

If you enjoyed it please leave feedback on Amazon or Goodreads, and if there is anything we missed or you have a question about, then please get in touch. We appreciate you choosing our book.

Founded in 2014 in Shoreditch, London, we at Joffe Books pride ourselves on our history of innovative publishing. We've been honoured to be shortlisted for Independent Publisher of the Year at the British Book Awards for the last three years.

www.joffebooks.com

We're very grateful to eagle-eyed readers who take the time to contact us. Please send any errors you find to corrections@joffebooks.com. We'll get them fixed ASAP.

9 781804 056646